# VOL. 2: A WOE THAT IS MADNESS

CREATED BY: JOHN ARCUDI & JAMES HARREN



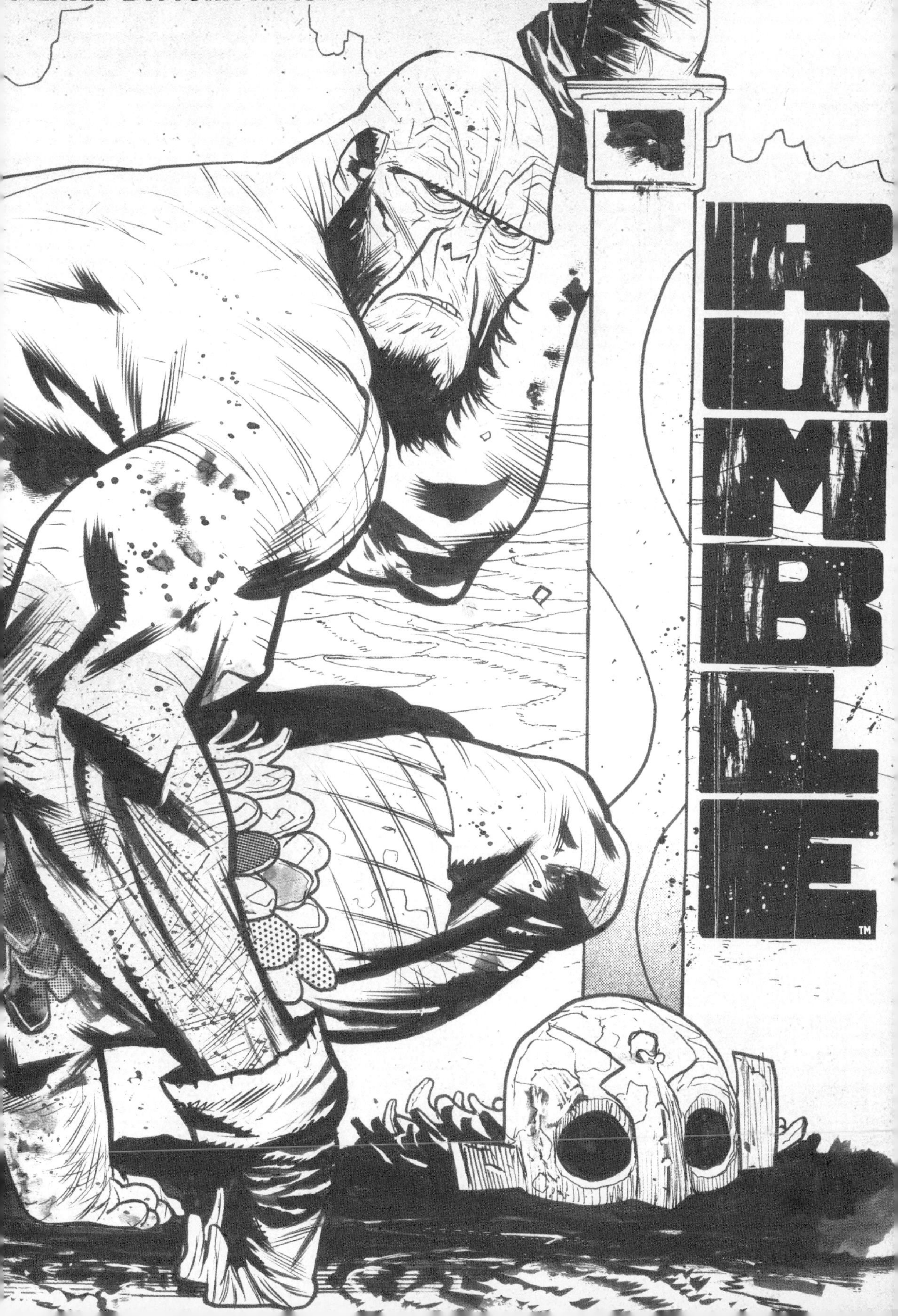

# RUMBLE™

**JOHN ARCUDI**
**JAMES HARREN**
Co-creators

**DAVE STEWART**
Color Art

**CHRIS ELIOPOULOS**
Letters

**VINCENT KUKUA**
Book Design

FOR IMAGE COMICS, INC.

ROBERT KIRKMAN - Chief Operating Officer
ERIK LARSEN - Chief Financial Officer
TODD MCFARLANE - President
MARC SILVESTRI - Chief Executive Officer
JIM VALENTINO - Vice-President

ERIC STEPHENSON - Publisher
COREY MURPHY - Director of Sales
JEFF BOISON - Director of Publishing Planning & Book Trade Sales
JEREMY SULLIVAN - Director of Digital Sales
KAT SALAZAR - Director of PR & Marketing
EMILY MILLER - Director of Operations
BRANWYN BIGGLESTONE - Senior Accounts Manager
SARAH MELLO - Accounts Manager
DREW GILL - Art Director
JONATHAN CHAN - Production Manager
MEREDITH WALLACE - Print Manager
BRIAH SKELLY - Publicity Assistant
SASHA HEAD - Sales & Marketing Production Designer
RANDY OKAMURA - Digital Marketing Designer
DAVID BROTHERS - Branding Manager
ALLY POWER - Content Manager
ADDISON DUKE - Production Artist
TRICIA RAMOS - Production Artist
VINCENT KUKUA - Production Artist
JEFF STANG - Direct Market Sales Representative
EMILIO BAUTISTA - Digital Sales Associate
LEANNA CAUNTER - Accounting Assistant
CHLOE RAMOS-PETERSON - Administrative Assistant

IMAGECOMICS.COM

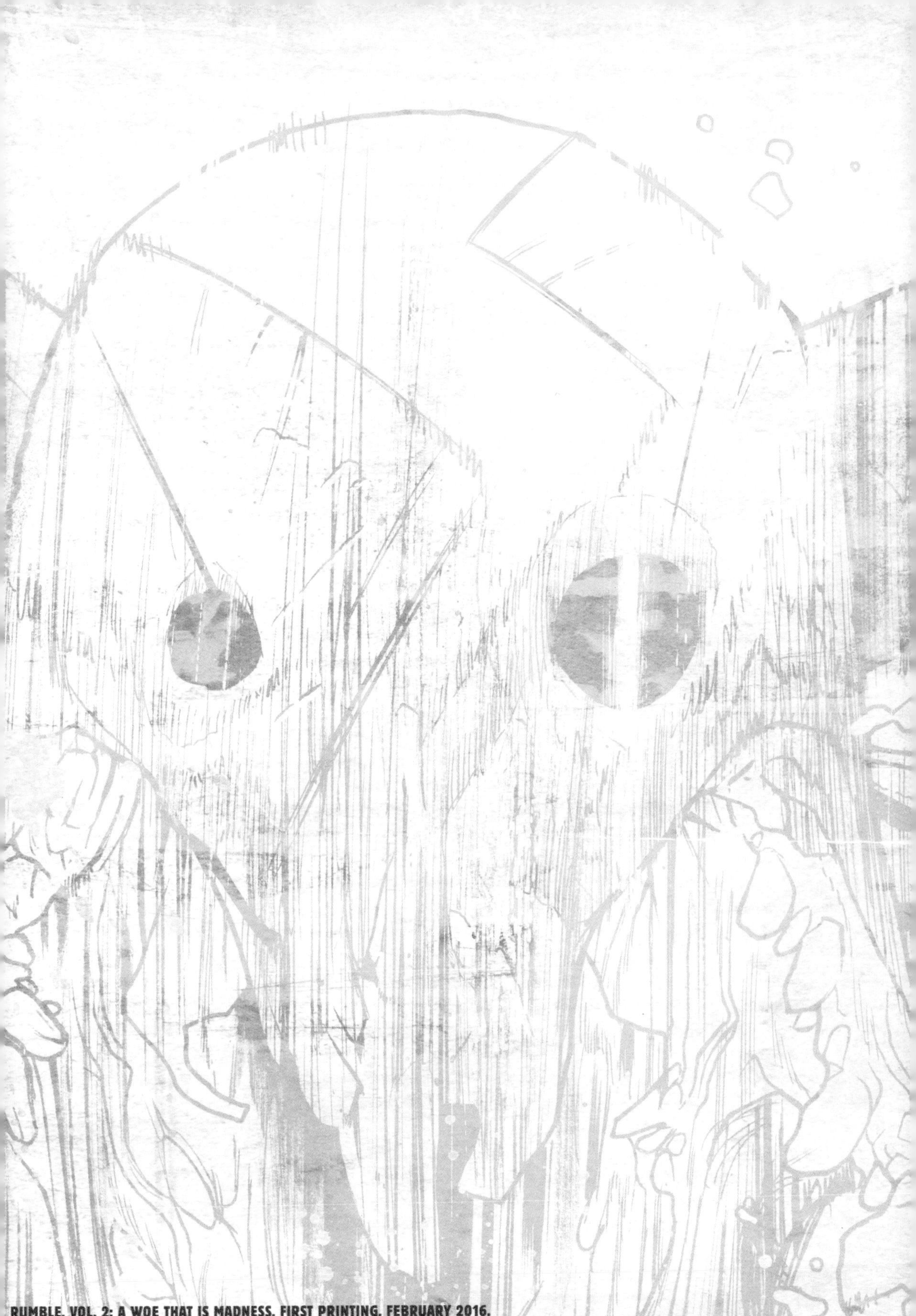

**RUMBLE, VOL. 2: A WOE THAT IS MADNESS. FIRST PRINTING. FEBRUARY 2016.**
**ISBN: 978-1-63215-604-4**

Published by Image Comics, Inc. Office of publication: 2001 Center Street, 6th Floor, Berkeley, CA 94704.  PRINTED IN THE U.S.A. For information regarding the CPSIA on this printed material call: 203-595-3636 and provide reference: RICH–667095.

# CHAPTER ONE

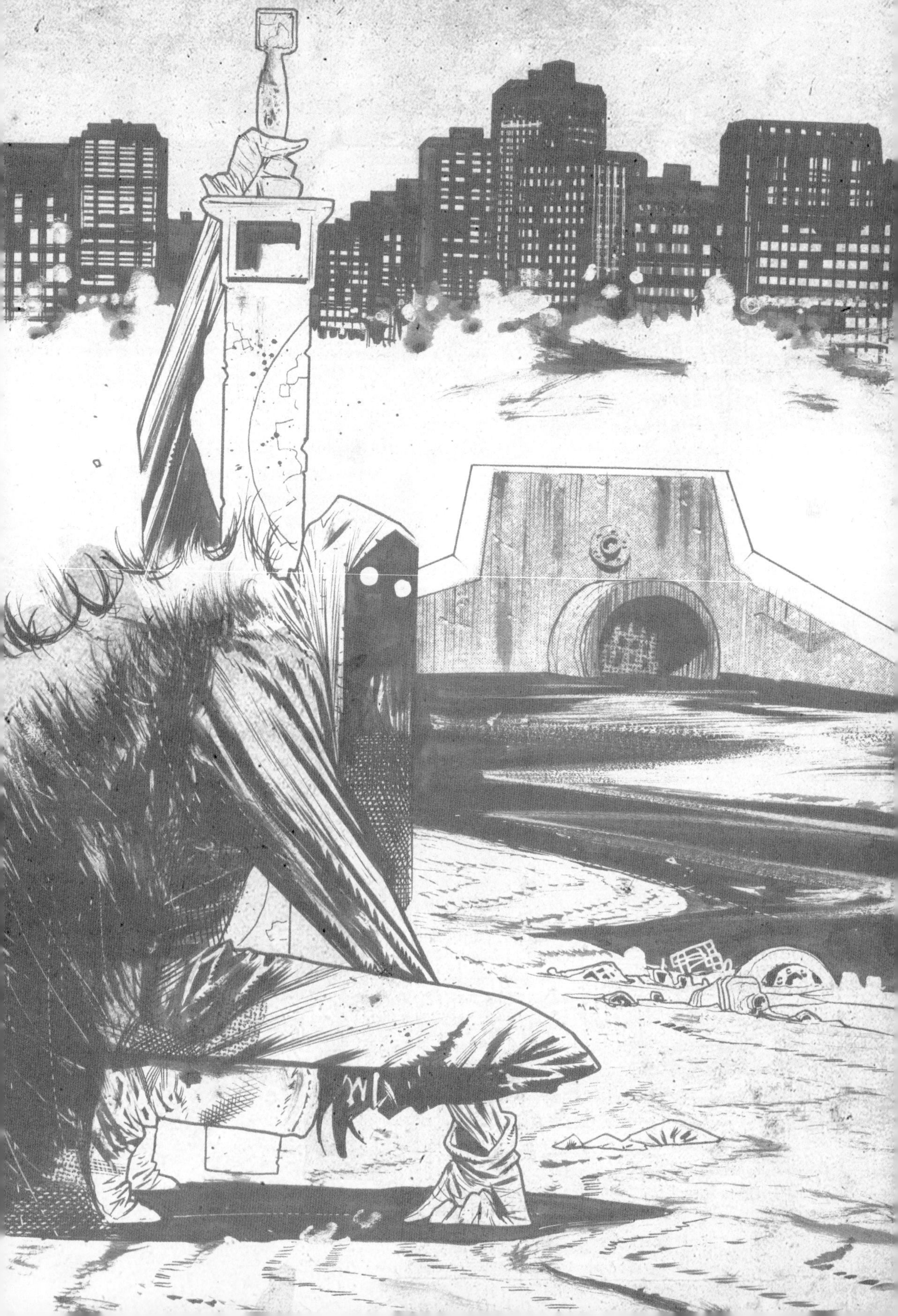

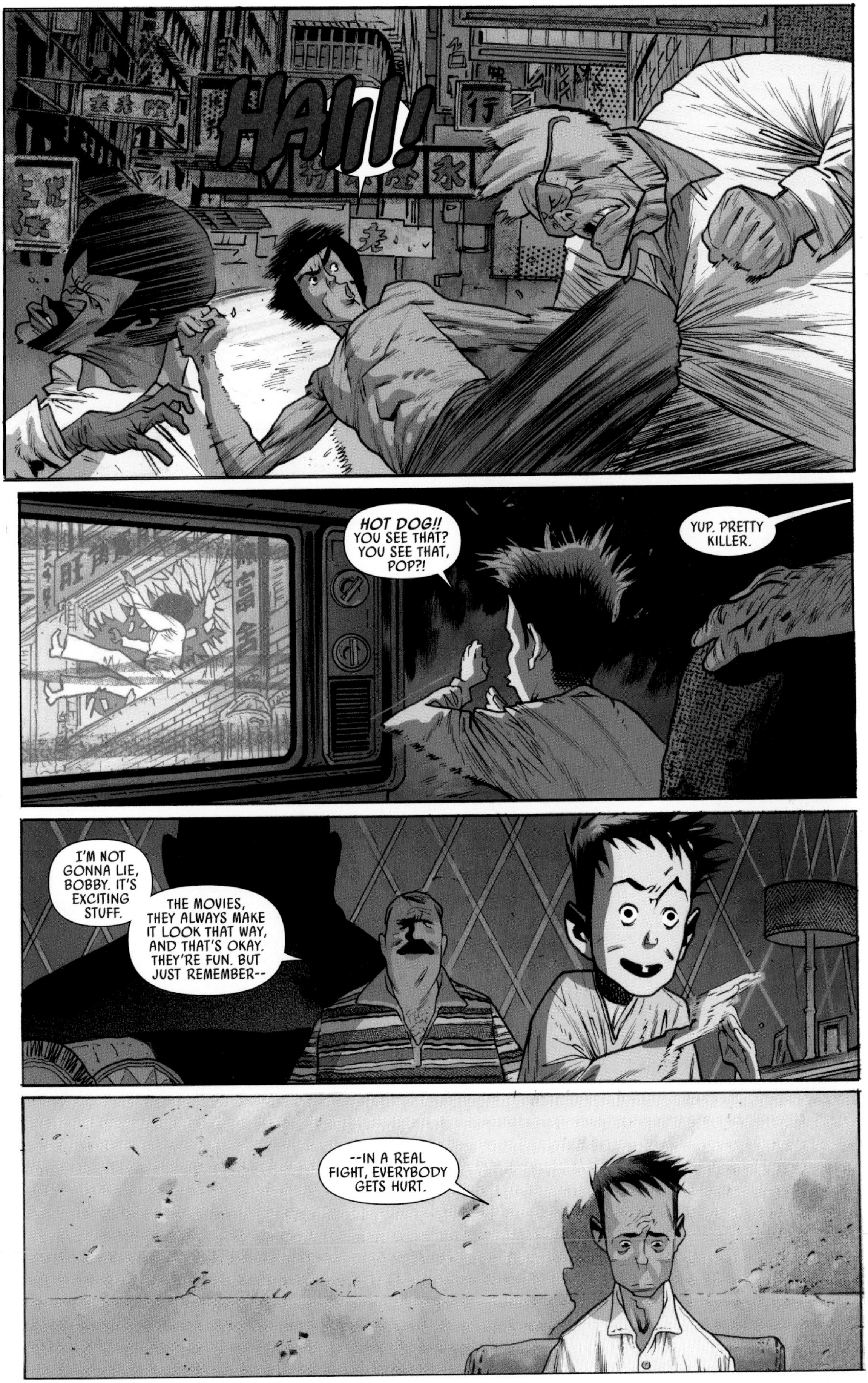
HAII!
HOT DOG!! YOU SEE THAT? YOU SEE THAT, POP?!
YUP. PRETTY KILLER.
I'M NOT GONNA LIE, BOBBY. IT'S EXCITING STUFF.
THE MOVIES, THEY ALWAYS MAKE IT LOOK THAT WAY, AND THAT'S OKAY. THEY'RE FUN. BUT JUST REMEMBER--
--IN A REAL FIGHT, EVERYBODY GETS HURT.

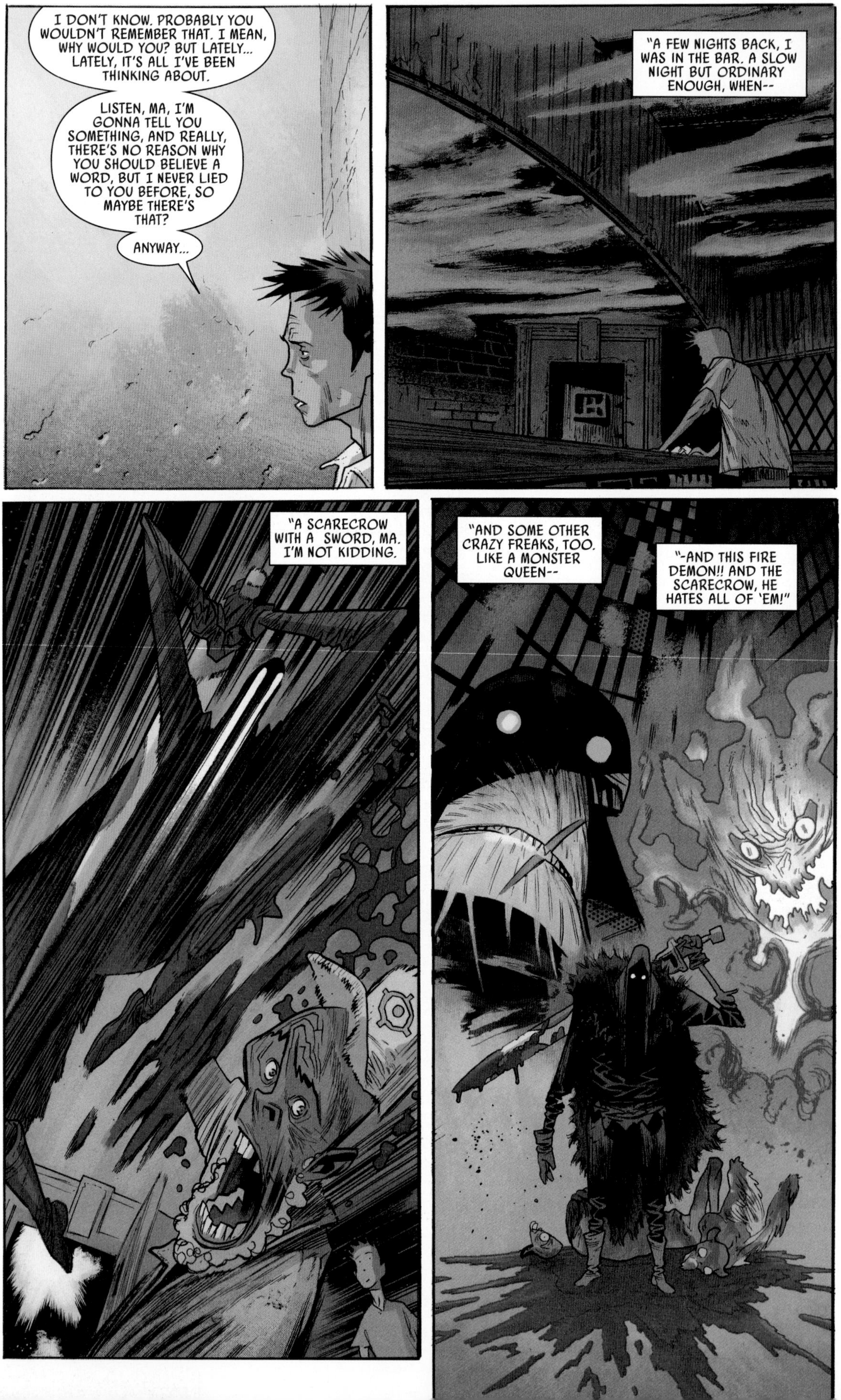
I DON'T KNOW. PROBABLY YOU WOULDN'T REMEMBER THAT. I MEAN, WHY WOULD YOU? BUT LATELY... LATELY, IT'S ALL I'VE BEEN THINKING ABOUT.
LISTEN, MA, I'M GONNA TELL YOU SOMETHING, AND REALLY, THERE'S NO REASON WHY YOU SHOULD BELIEVE A WORD, BUT I NEVER LIED TO YOU BEFORE, SO MAYBE THERE'S THAT?
ANYWAY...
"A FEW NIGHTS BACK, I WAS IN THE BAR. A SLOW NIGHT BUT ORDINARY ENOUGH, WHEN--
"A SCARECROW WITH A SWORD, MA. I'M NOT KIDDING.
"AND SOME OTHER CRAZY FREAKS, TOO. LIKE A MONSTER QUEEN--
"-AND THIS FIRE DEMON!! AND THE SCARECROW, HE HATES ALL OF 'EM!"

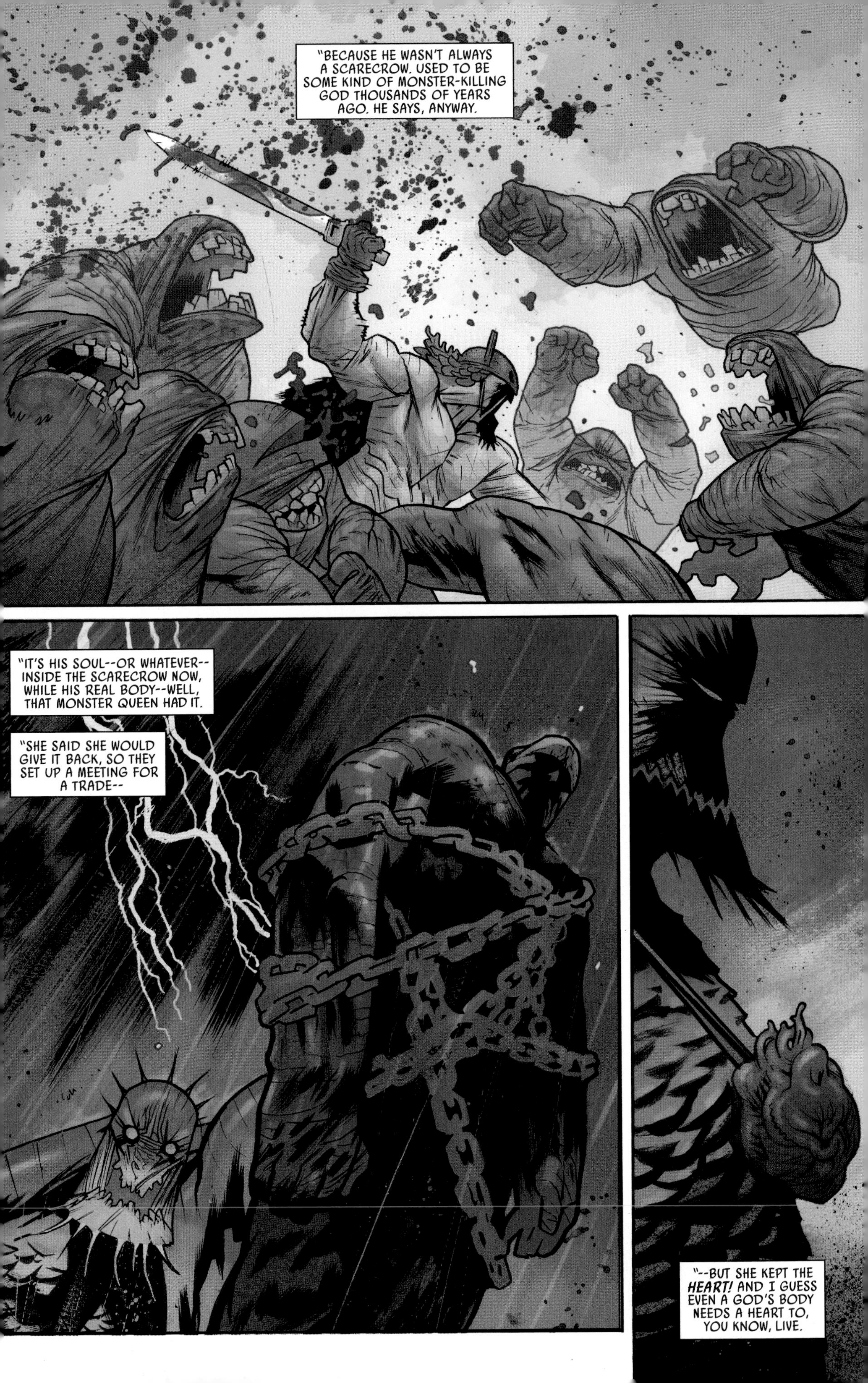
"BECAUSE HE WASN'T ALWAYS A SCARECROW. USED TO BE SOME KIND OF MONSTER-KILLING GOD THOUSANDS OF YEARS AGO. HE SAYS, ANYWAY.
"IT'S HIS SOUL--OR WHATEVER--INSIDE THE SCARECROW NOW, WHILE HIS REAL BODY--WELL, THAT MONSTER QUEEN HAD IT.
"SHE SAID SHE WOULD GIVE IT BACK, SO THEY SET UP A MEETING FOR A TRADE--
"--BUT SHE KEPT THE HEART! AND I GUESS EVEN A GOD'S BODY NEEDS A HEART TO, YOU KNOW, LIVE.

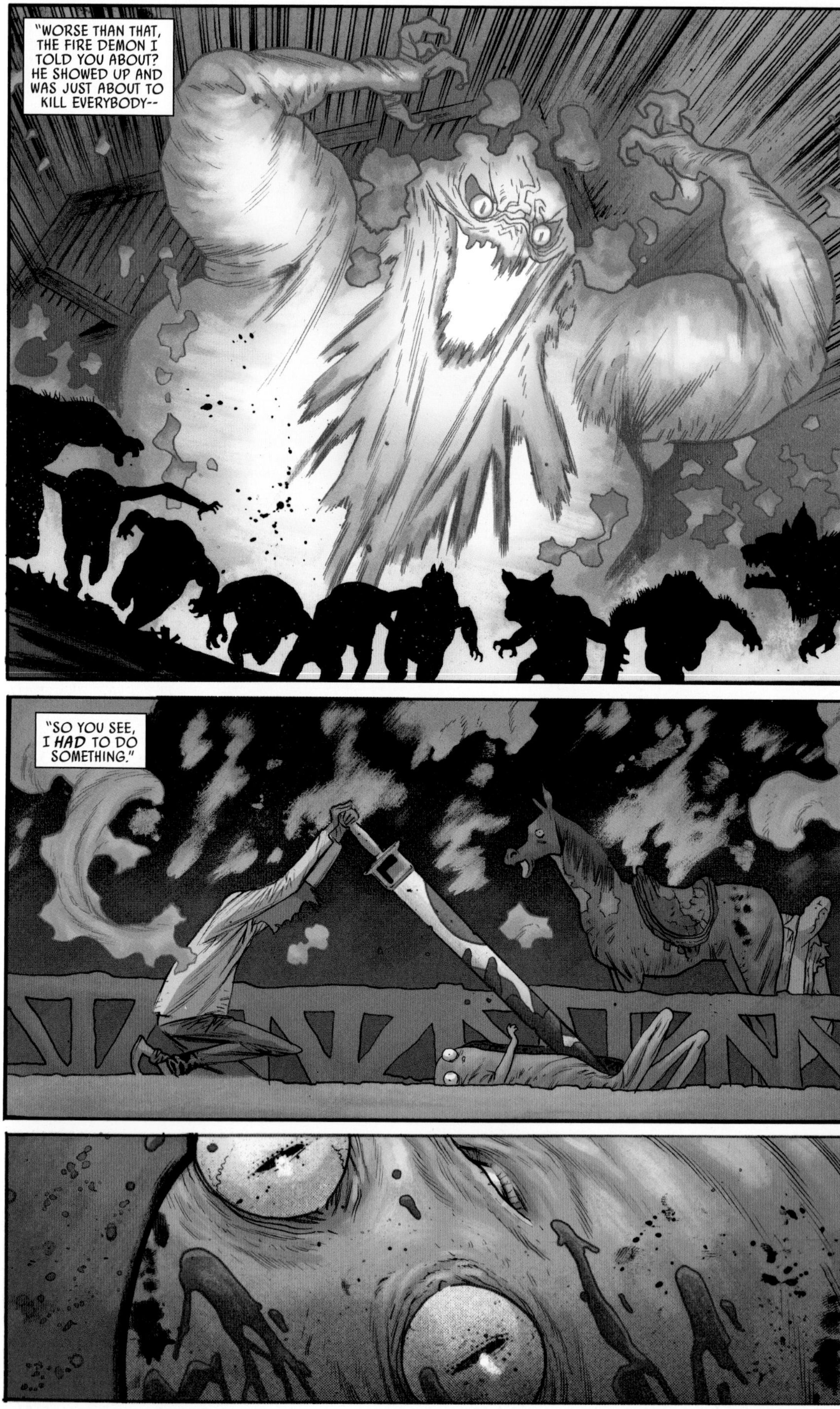
"WORSE THAN THAT, THE FIRE DEMON I TOLD YOU ABOUT? HE SHOWED UP AND WAS JUST ABOUT TO KILL EVERYBODY--
"SO YOU SEE, I *HAD* TO DO SOMETHING."

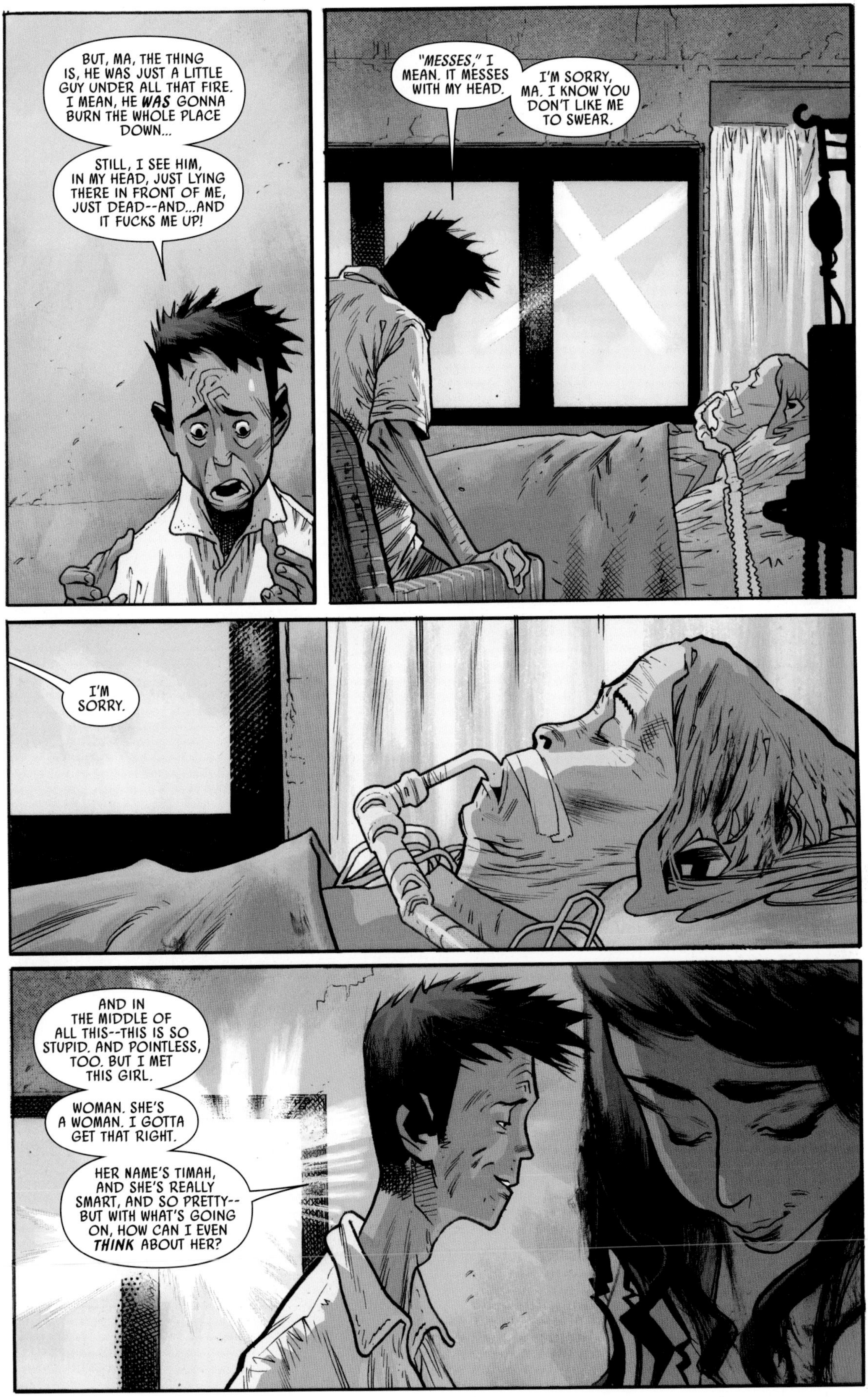
BUT, MA, THE THING IS, HE WAS JUST A LITTLE GUY UNDER ALL THAT FIRE. I MEAN, HE *WAS* GONNA BURN THE WHOLE PLACE DOWN...
STILL, I SEE HIM, IN MY HEAD, JUST LYING THERE IN FRONT OF ME, JUST DEAD--AND...AND IT FUCKS ME UP!
*"MESSES,"* I MEAN. IT MESSES WITH MY HEAD.
I'M SORRY, MA. I KNOW YOU DON'T LIKE ME TO SWEAR.
I'M SORRY.
AND IN THE MIDDLE OF ALL THIS--THIS IS SO STUPID. AND POINTLESS, TOO. BUT I MET THIS GIRL.
WOMAN. SHE'S A WOMAN. I GOTTA GET THAT RIGHT.
HER NAME'S TIMAH, AND SHE'S REALLY SMART, AND SO PRETTY--BUT WITH WHAT'S GOING ON, HOW CAN I EVEN *THINK* ABOUT HER?

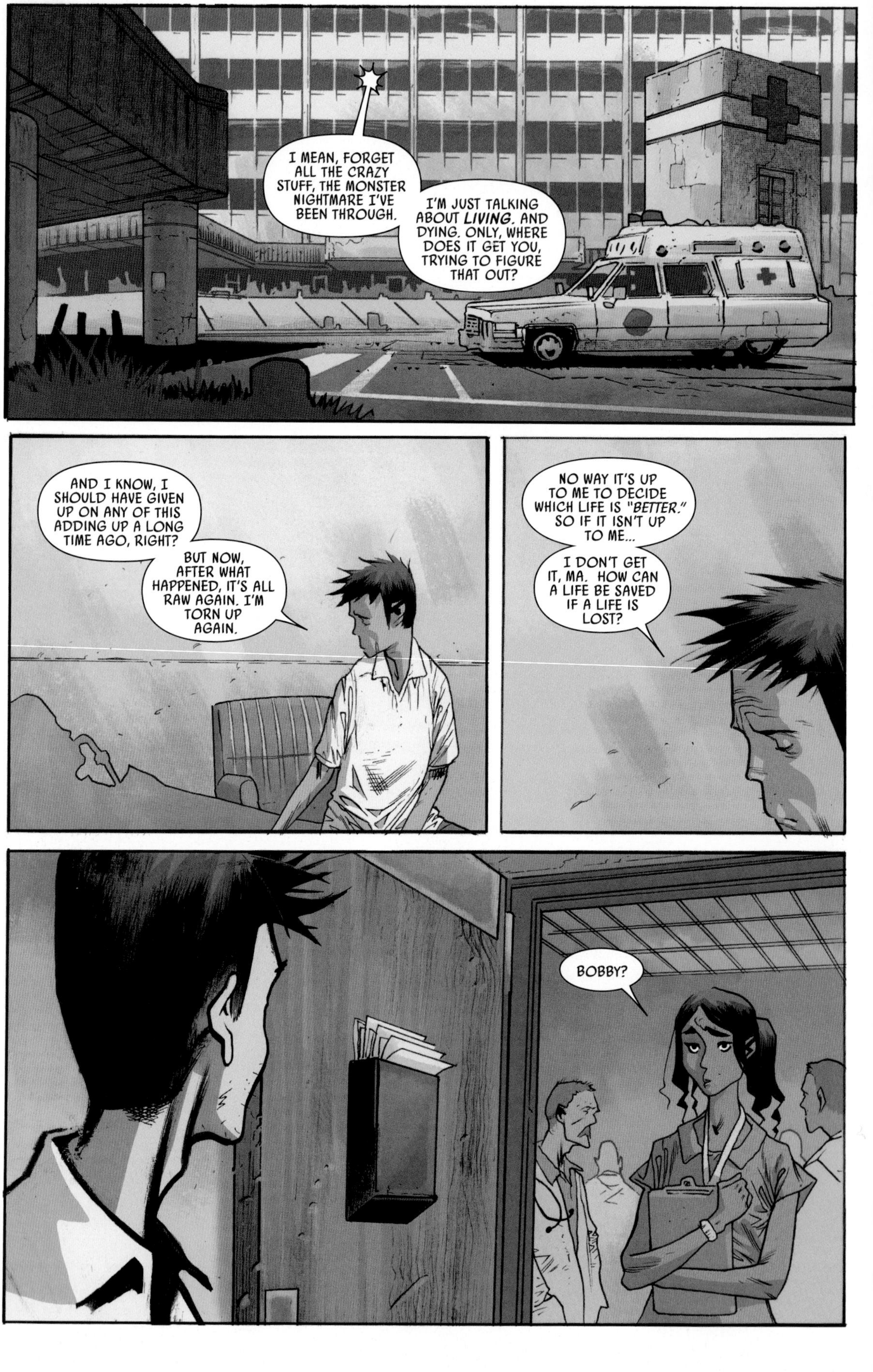

I MEAN, FORGET ALL THE CRAZY STUFF, THE MONSTER NIGHTMARE I'VE BEEN THROUGH.
I'M JUST TALKING ABOUT **LIVING.** AND DYING. ONLY, WHERE DOES IT GET YOU, TRYING TO FIGURE THAT OUT?
AND I KNOW, I SHOULD HAVE GIVEN UP ON ANY OF THIS ADDING UP A LONG TIME AGO, RIGHT?
BUT NOW, AFTER WHAT HAPPENED, IT'S ALL RAW AGAIN. I'M TORN UP AGAIN.
NO WAY IT'S UP TO ME TO DECIDE WHICH LIFE IS "*BETTER.*" SO IF IT ISN'T UP TO ME...
I DON'T GET IT, MA. HOW CAN A LIFE BE SAVED IF A LIFE IS LOST?
BOBBY?

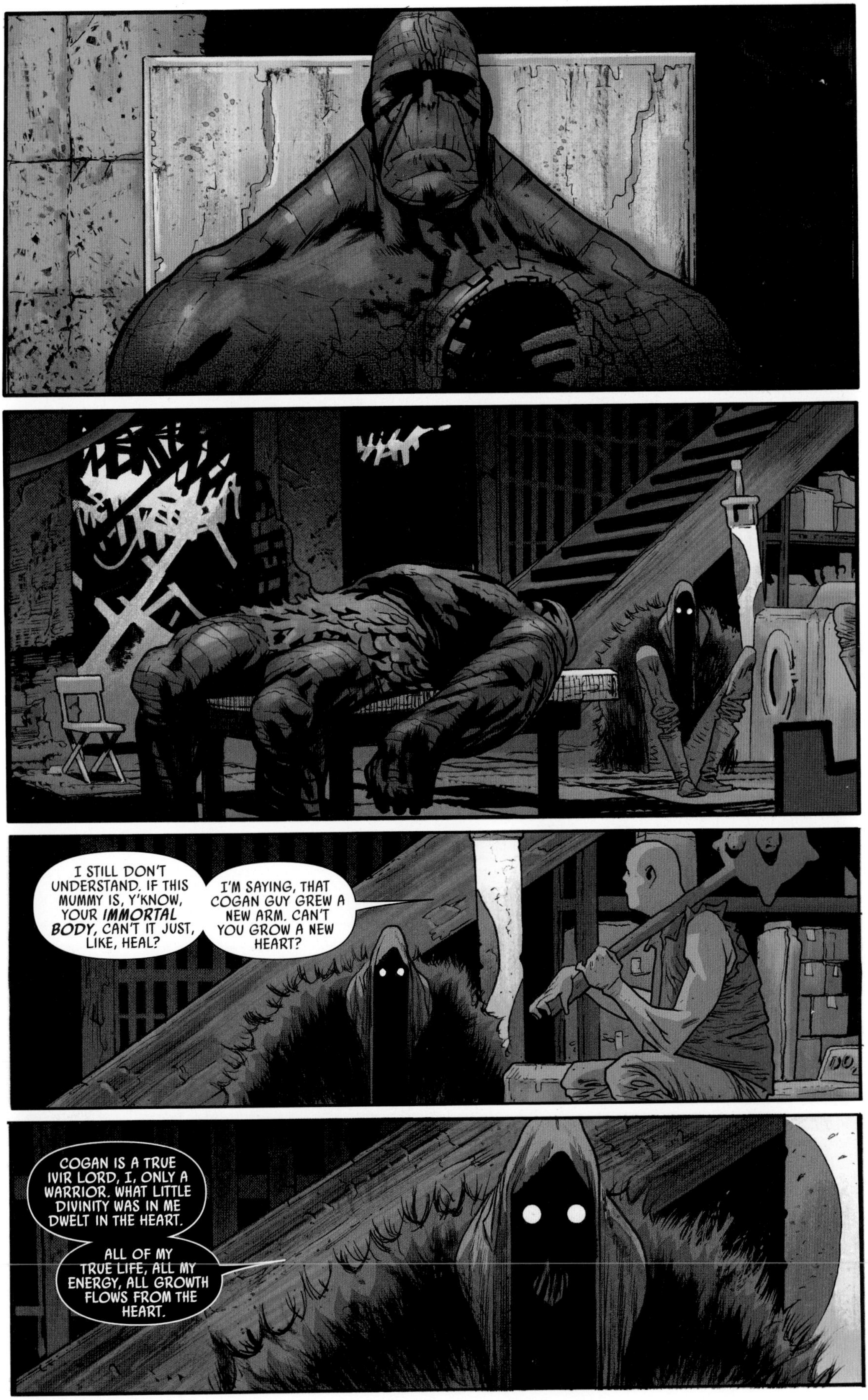
I STILL DON'T UNDERSTAND. IF THIS MUMMY IS, Y'KNOW, YOUR *IMMORTAL BODY*, CAN'T IT JUST, LIKE, HEAL?
I'M SAYING, THAT COGAN GUY GREW A NEW ARM. CAN'T YOU GROW A NEW HEART?
COGAN IS A TRUE IVIR LORD, I, ONLY A WARRIOR. WHAT LITTLE DIVINITY WAS IN ME DWELT IN THE HEART.
ALL OF MY TRUE LIFE, ALL MY ENERGY, ALL GROWTH FLOWS FROM THE HEART.

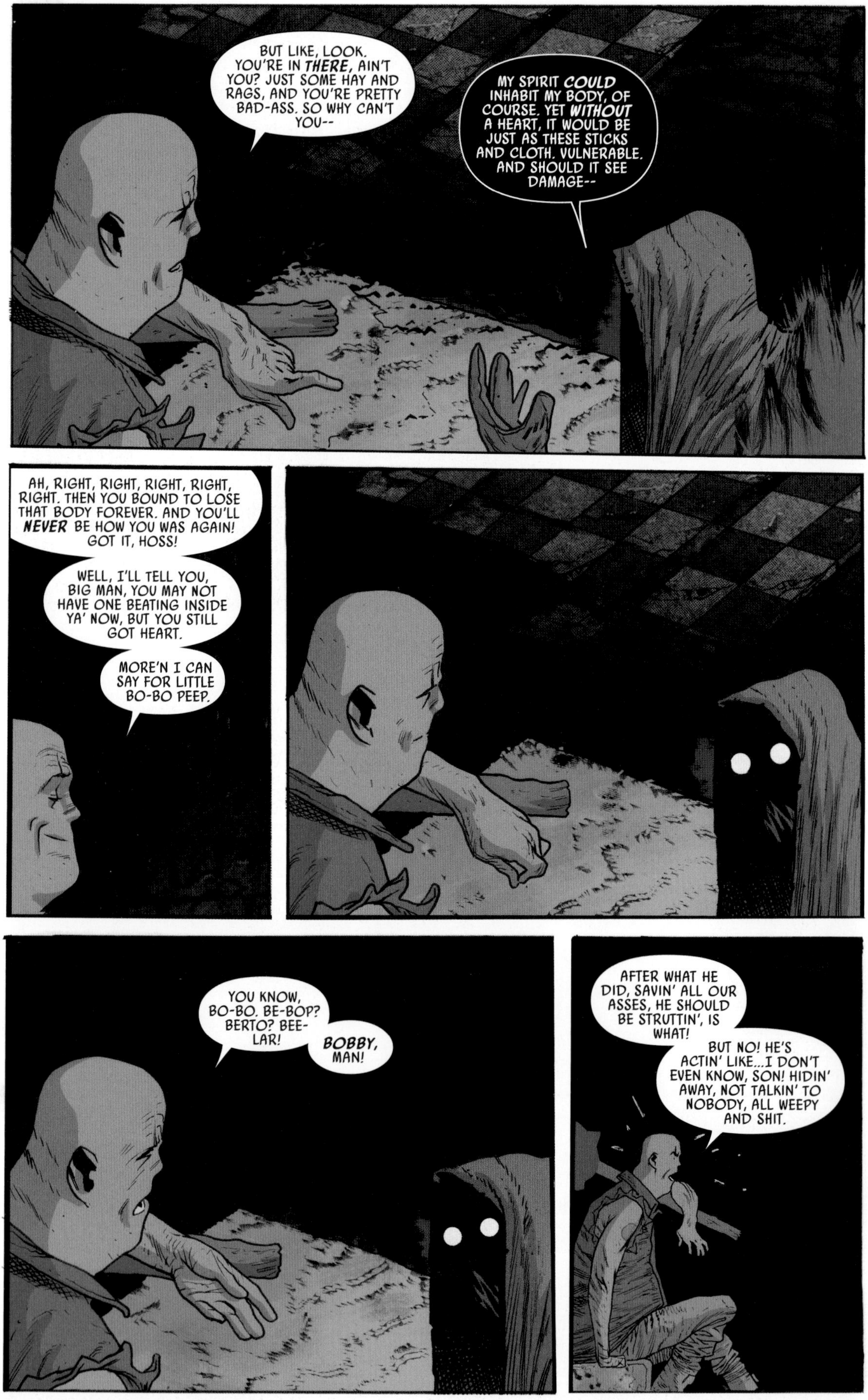
BUT LIKE, LOOK. YOU'RE IN *THERE*, AIN'T YOU? JUST SOME HAY AND RAGS, AND YOU'RE PRETTY BAD-ASS. SO WHY CAN'T YOU--
MY SPIRIT *COULD* INHABIT MY BODY, OF COURSE. YET *WITHOUT* A HEART, IT WOULD BE JUST AS THESE STICKS AND CLOTH. VULNERABLE. AND SHOULD IT SEE DAMAGE--
AH, RIGHT, RIGHT, RIGHT, RIGHT, RIGHT. THEN YOU BOUND TO LOSE THAT BODY FOREVER. AND YOU'LL *NEVER* BE HOW YOU WAS AGAIN! GOT IT, HOSS!
WELL, I'LL TELL YOU, BIG MAN, YOU MAY NOT HAVE ONE BEATING INSIDE YA' NOW, BUT YOU STILL GOT HEART.
MORE'N I CAN SAY FOR LITTLE BO-BO PEEP.
YOU KNOW, BO-BO. BE-BOP? BERTO? BEE-LAR!
*BOBBY*, MAN!
AFTER WHAT HE DID, SAVIN' ALL OUR ASSES, HE SHOULD BE STRUTTIN', IS WHAT!
BUT NO! HE'S ACTIN' LIKE...I DON'T EVEN KNOW, SON! HIDIN' AWAY, NOT TALKIN' TO NOBODY, ALL WEEPY AND SHIT.

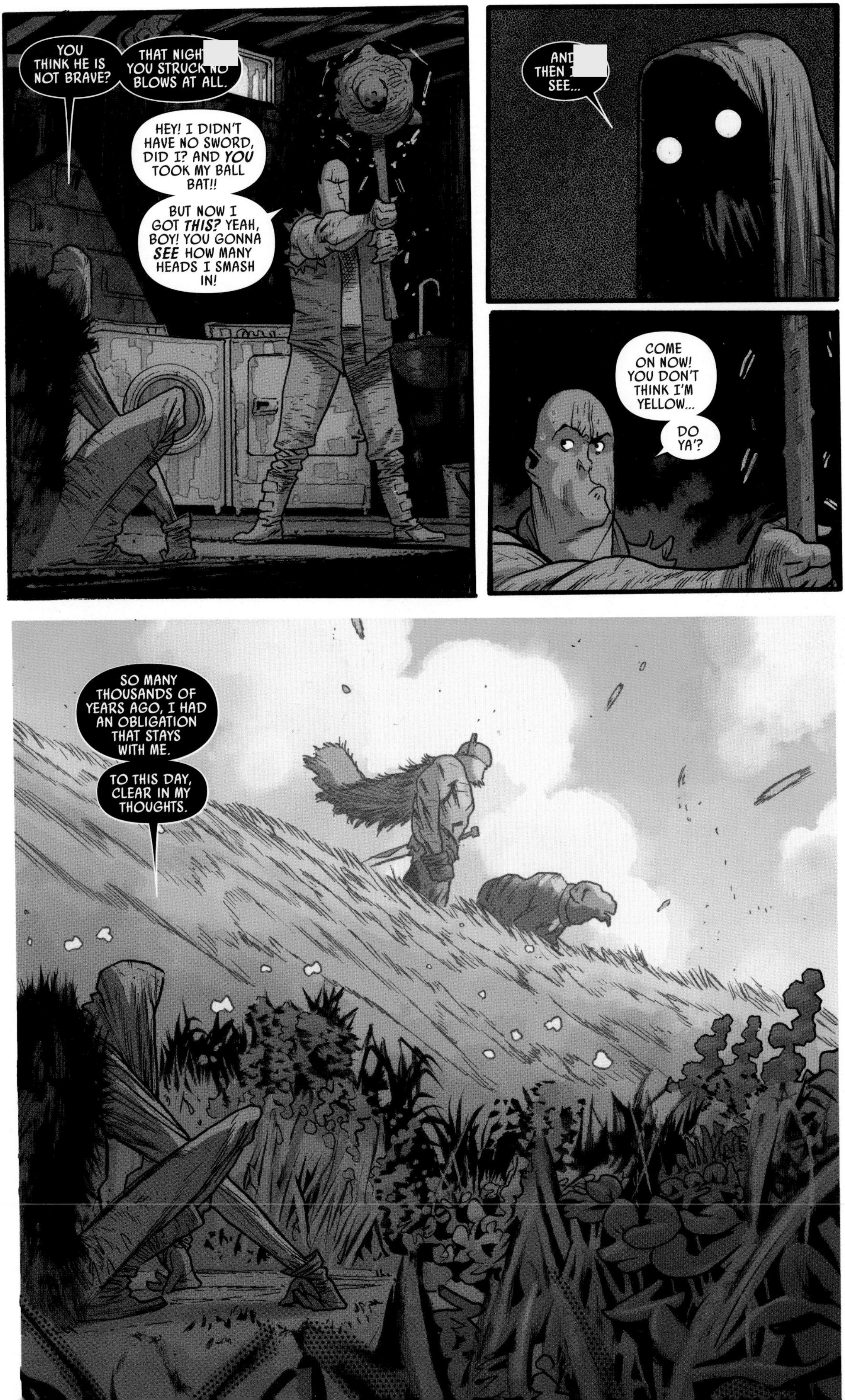
YOU THINK HE IS NOT BRAVE?
THAT NIGHT YOU STRUCK NO BLOWS AT ALL.
HEY! I DIDN'T HAVE NO SWORD, DID I? AND YOU TOOK MY BALL BAT!!
BUT NOW I GOT THIS? YEAH, BOY! YOU GONNA SEE HOW MANY HEADS I SMASH IN!
AND THEN I SEE...
COME ON NOW! YOU DON'T THINK I'M YELLOW...
DO YA'?
SO MANY THOUSANDS OF YEARS AGO, I HAD AN OBLIGATION THAT STAYS WITH ME.
TO THIS DAY, CLEAR IN MY THOUGHTS.

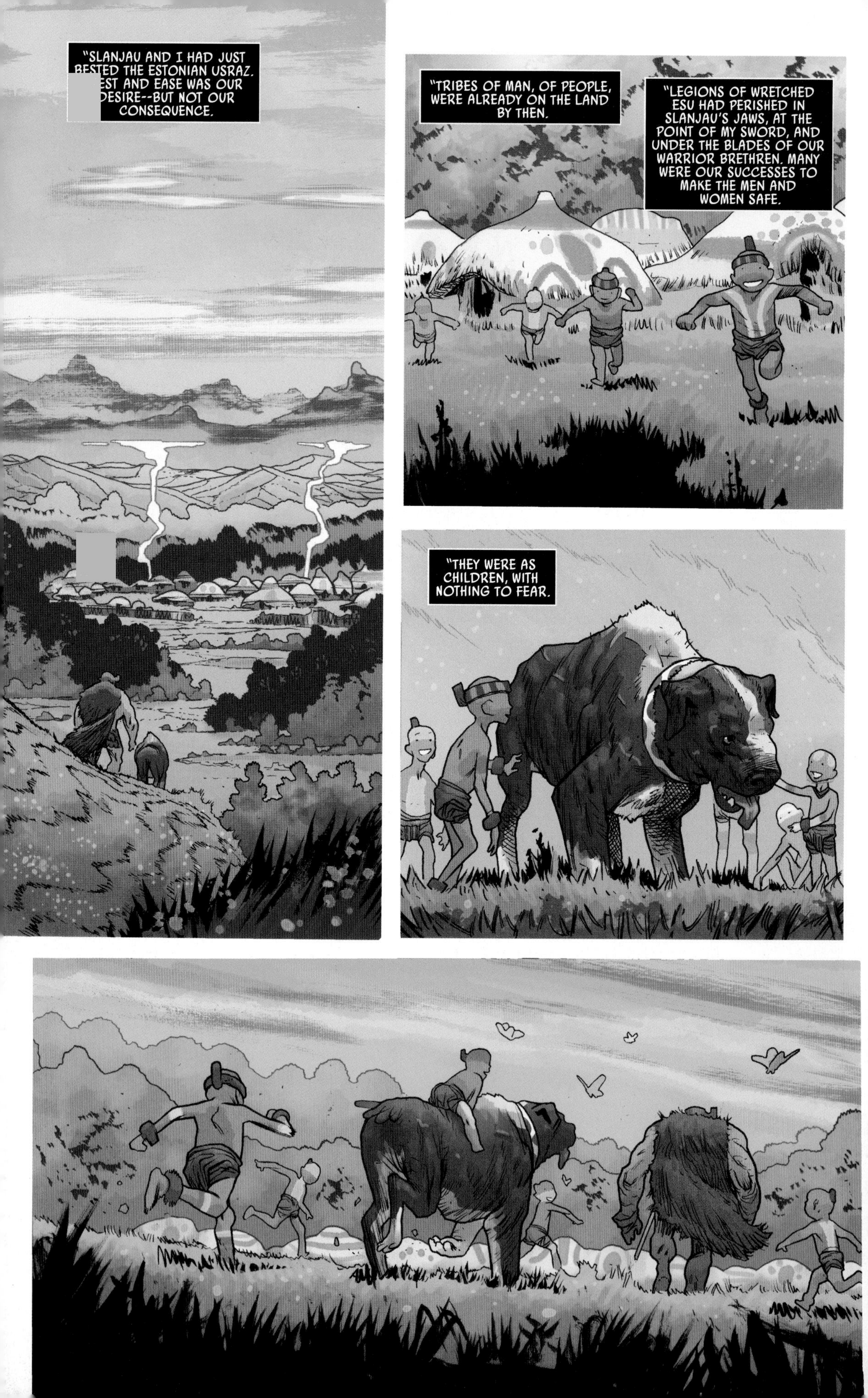
"SLANJAU AND I HAD JUST BESTED THE ESTONIAN USRAZ. EST AND EASE WAS OUR DESIRE--BUT NOT OUR CONSEQUENCE.
"TRIBES OF MAN, OF PEOPLE, WERE ALREADY ON THE LAND BY THEN.
"LEGIONS OF WRETCHED ESU HAD PERISHED IN SLANJAU'S JAWS, AT THE POINT OF MY SWORD, AND UNDER THE BLADES OF OUR WARRIOR BRETHREN. MANY WERE OUR SUCCESSES TO MAKE THE MEN AND WOMEN SAFE.
"THEY WERE AS CHILDREN, WITH NOTHING TO FEAR.

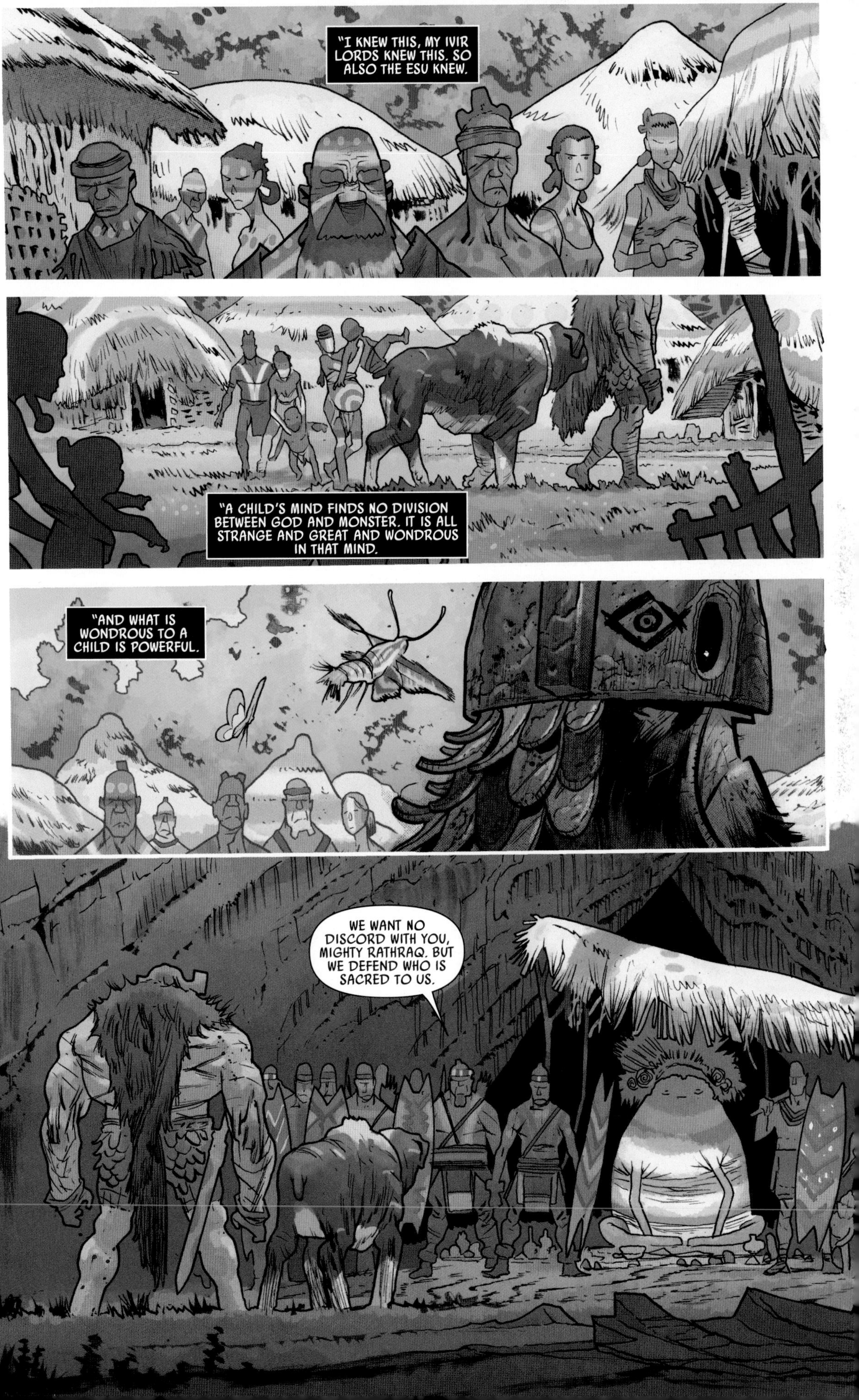
"I KNEW THIS, MY IVIR LORDS KNEW THIS. SO ALSO THE ESU KNEW.
"A CHILD'S MIND FINDS NO DIVISION BETWEEN GOD AND MONSTER. IT IS ALL STRANGE AND GREAT AND WONDROUS IN THAT MIND.
"AND WHAT IS WONDROUS TO A CHILD IS POWERFUL.
WE WANT NO DISCORD WITH YOU, MIGHTY RATHRAQ. BUT WE DEFEND WHO IS SACRED TO US.

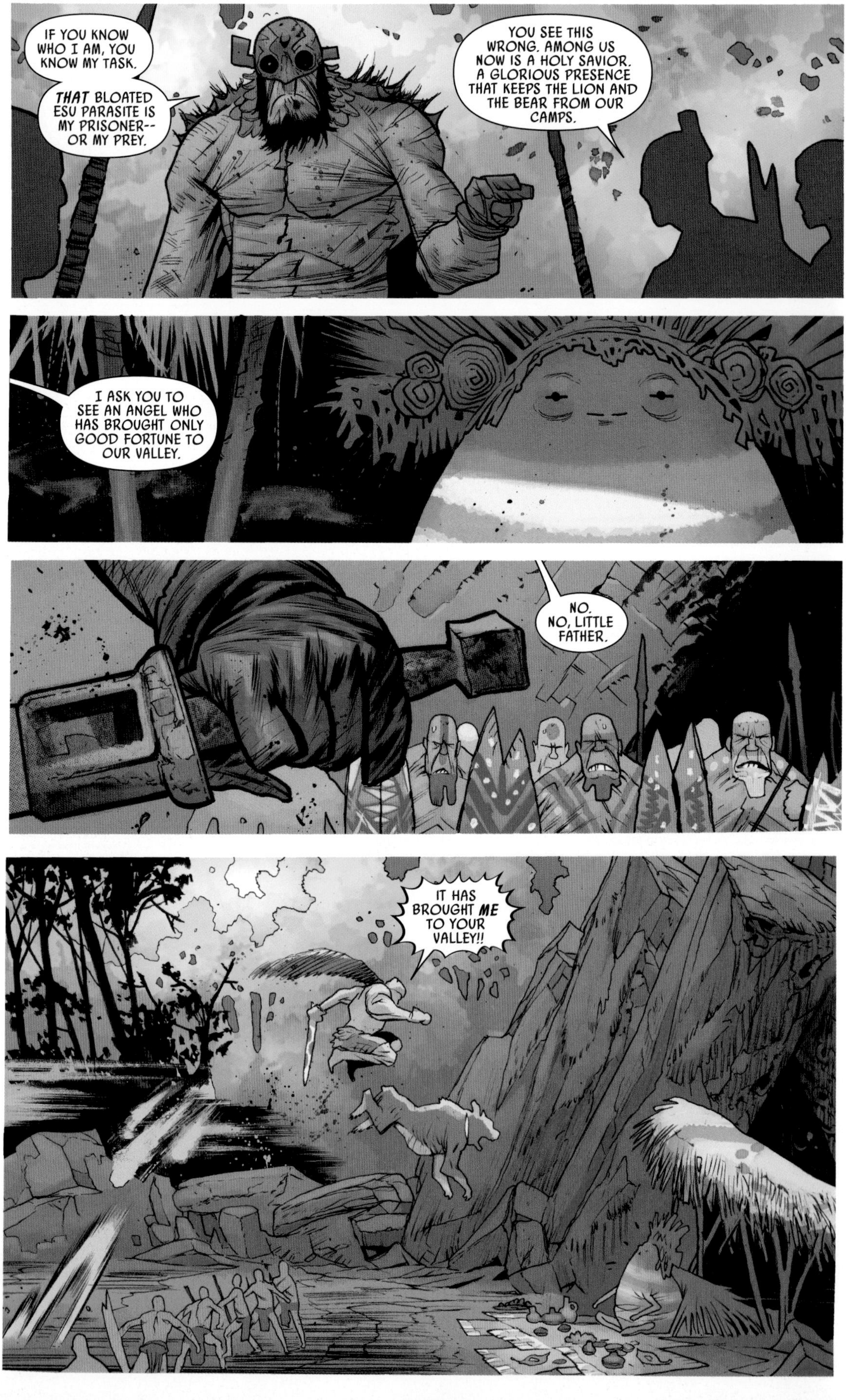
IF YOU KNOW WHO I AM, YOU KNOW MY TASK.
THAT BLOATED ESU PARASITE IS MY PRISONER-- OR MY PREY.
YOU SEE THIS WRONG. AMONG US NOW IS A HOLY SAVIOR. A GLORIOUS PRESENCE THAT KEEPS THE LION AND THE BEAR FROM OUR CAMPS.
I ASK YOU TO SEE AN ANGEL WHO HAS BROUGHT ONLY GOOD FORTUNE TO OUR VALLEY.
NO. NO, LITTLE FATHER.
IT HAS BROUGHT ME TO YOUR VALLEY!!

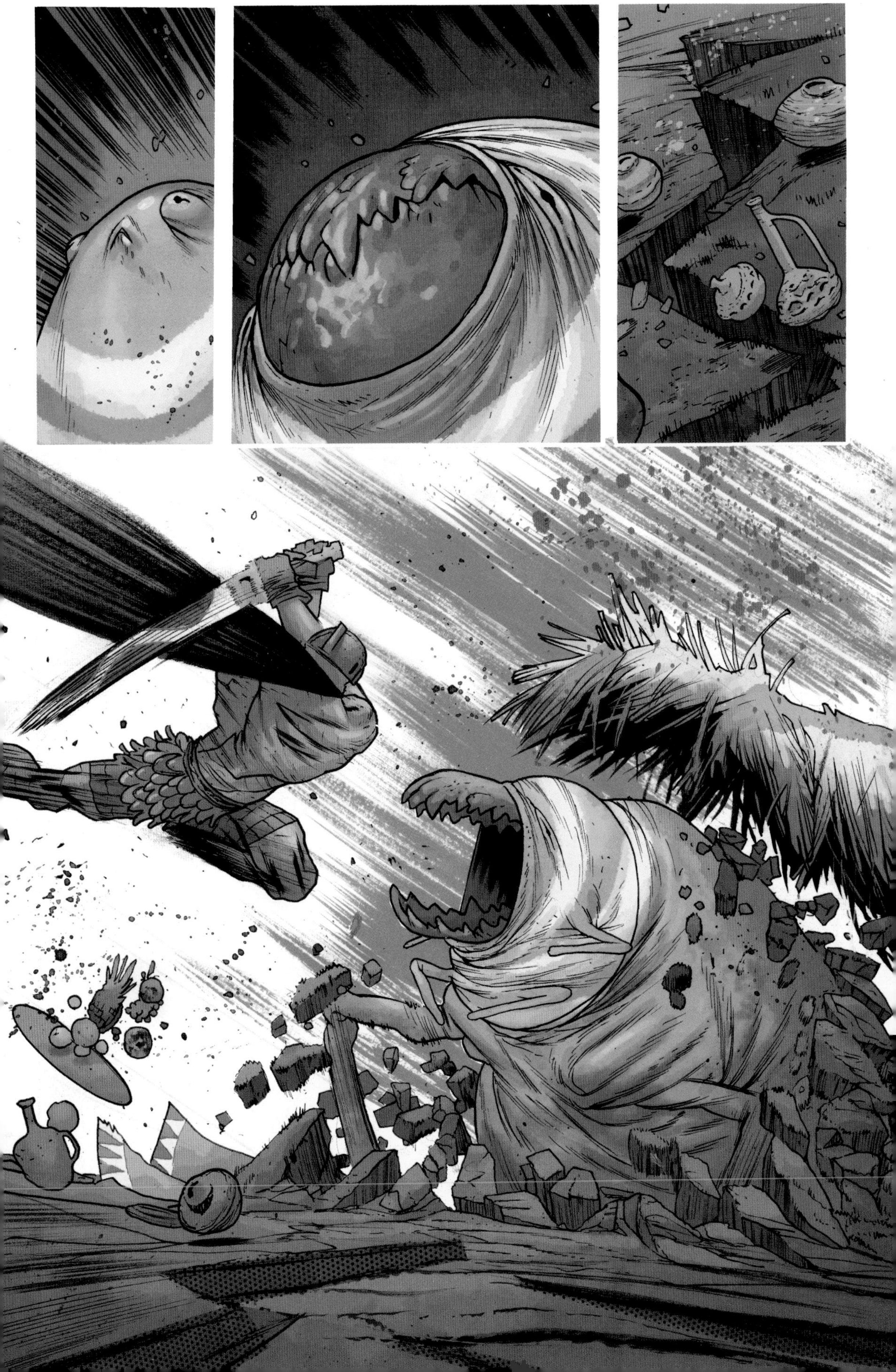

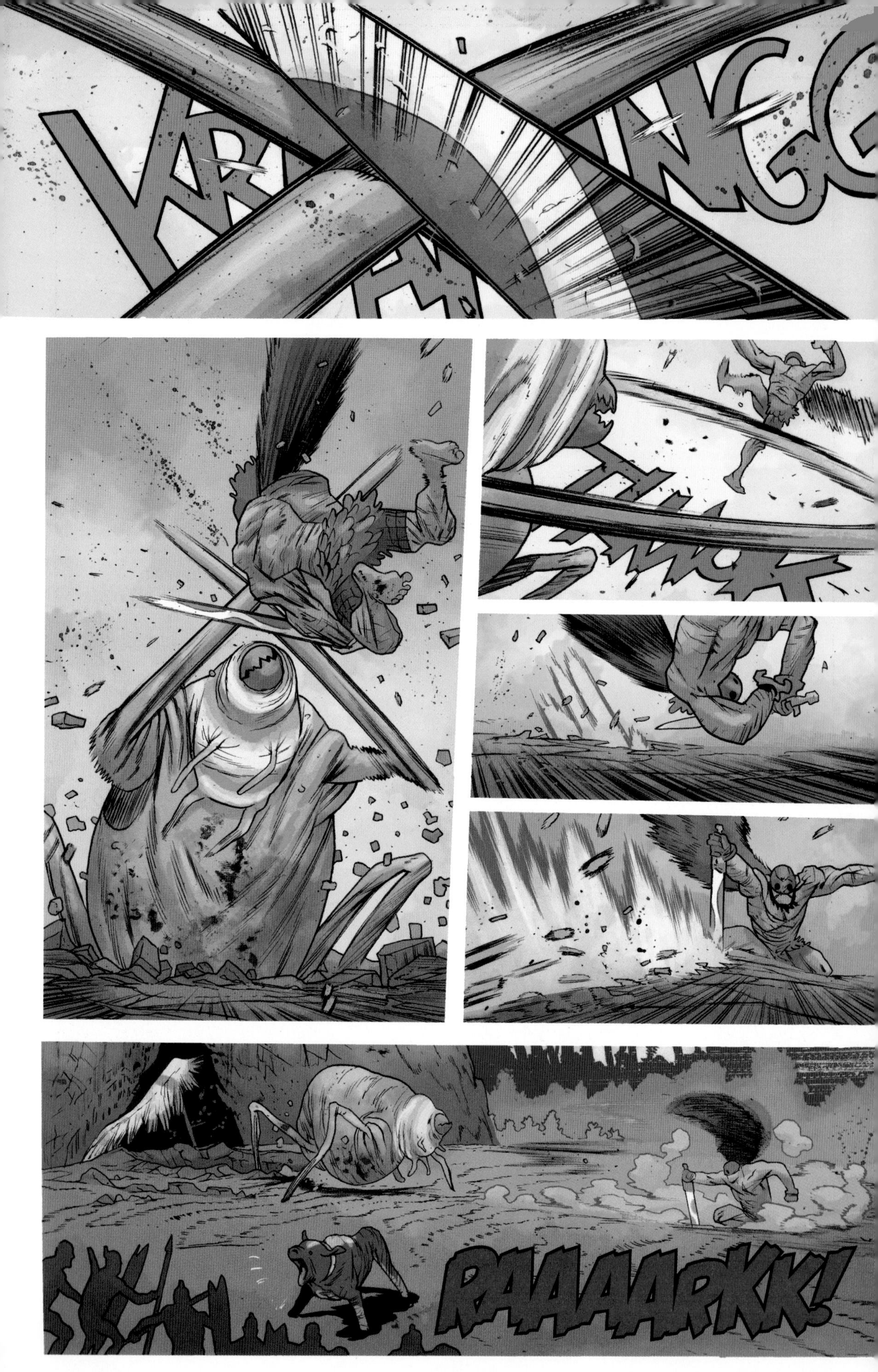
RAAAARKK!

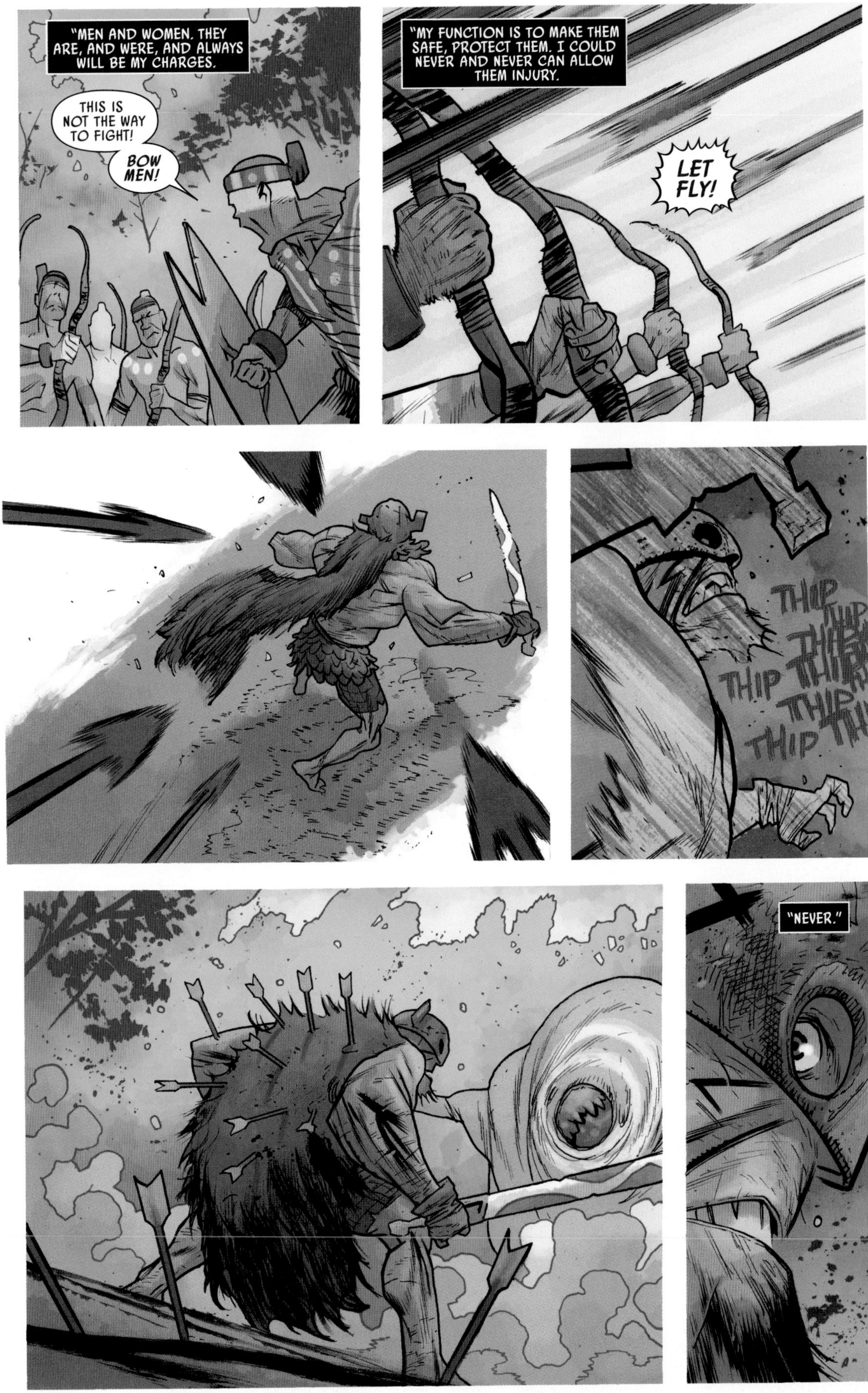
"MEN AND WOMEN. THEY ARE, AND WERE, AND ALWAYS WILL BE MY CHARGES.
THIS IS NOT THE WAY TO FIGHT!
BOW MEN!
"MY FUNCTION IS TO MAKE THEM SAFE, PROTECT THEM. I COULD NEVER AND NEVER CAN ALLOW THEM INJURY.
LET FLY!
THIP
THIP
THIP
THIP
THIP
"NEVER."

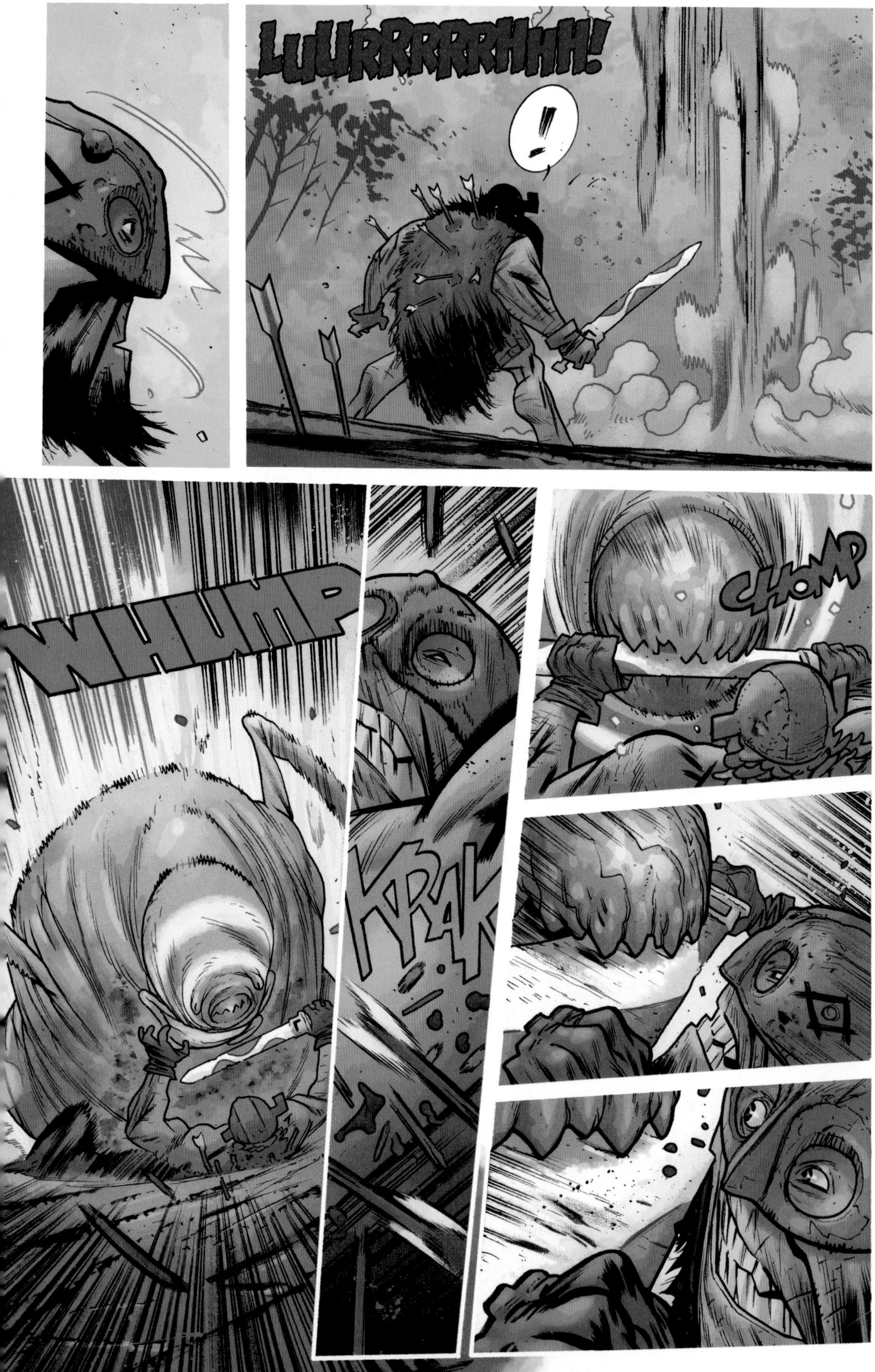
LUURRRRRHHH!
!
WHUMP
KRAK
CHOMP

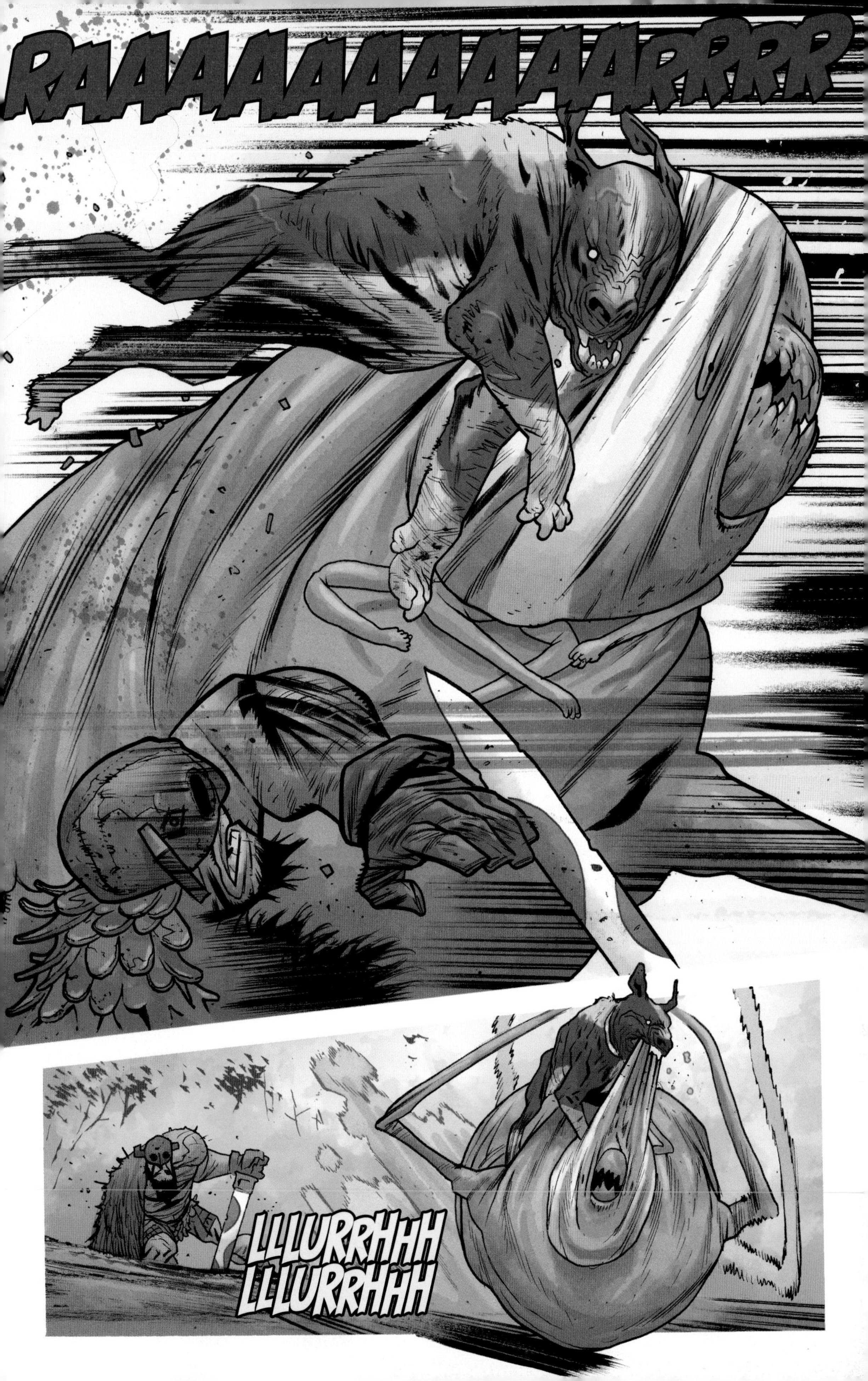
RAAAAAAAAAAARRRRR
LLLURRHHH
LLLURRHHH

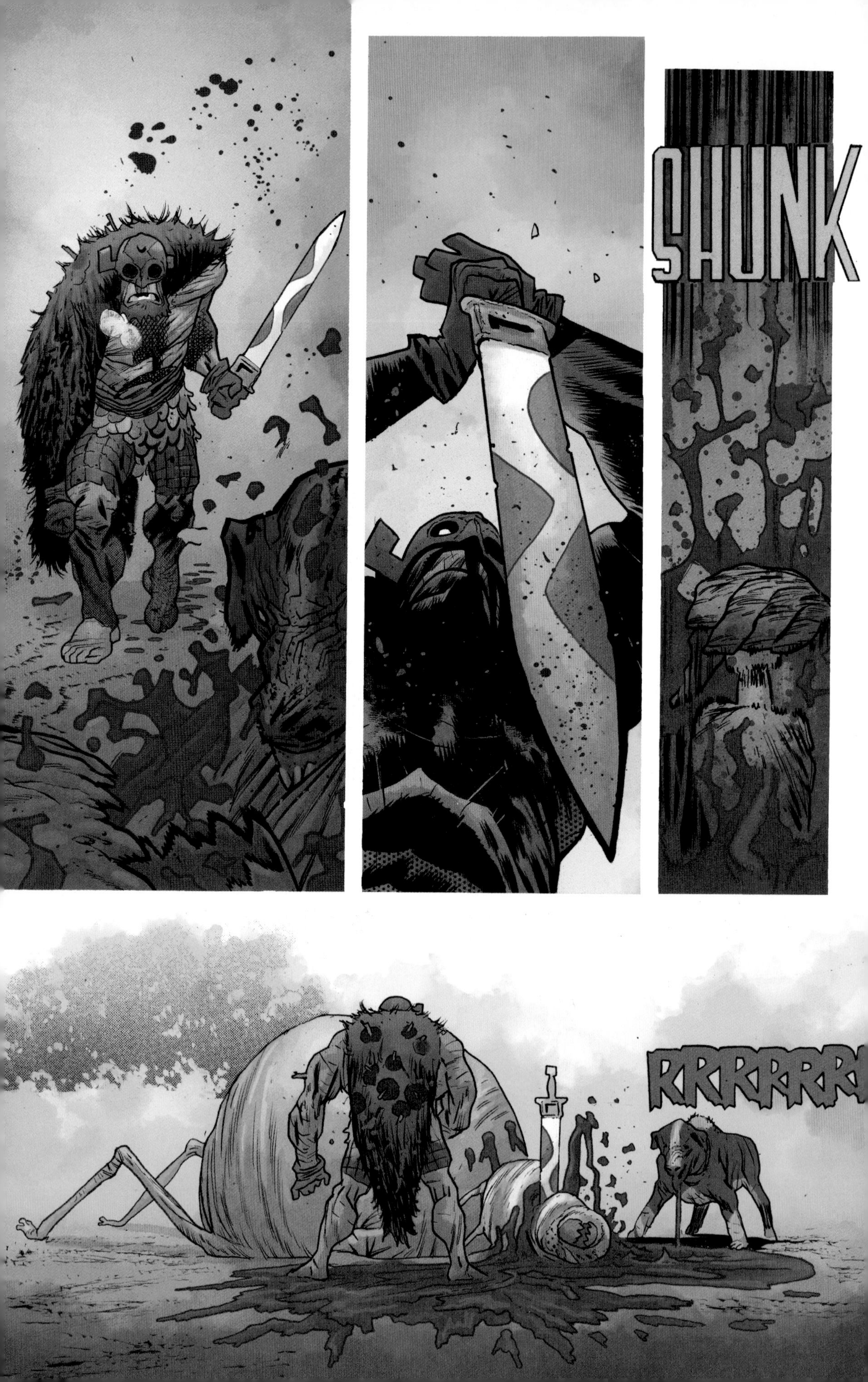
SHUNK
RRRRRRR

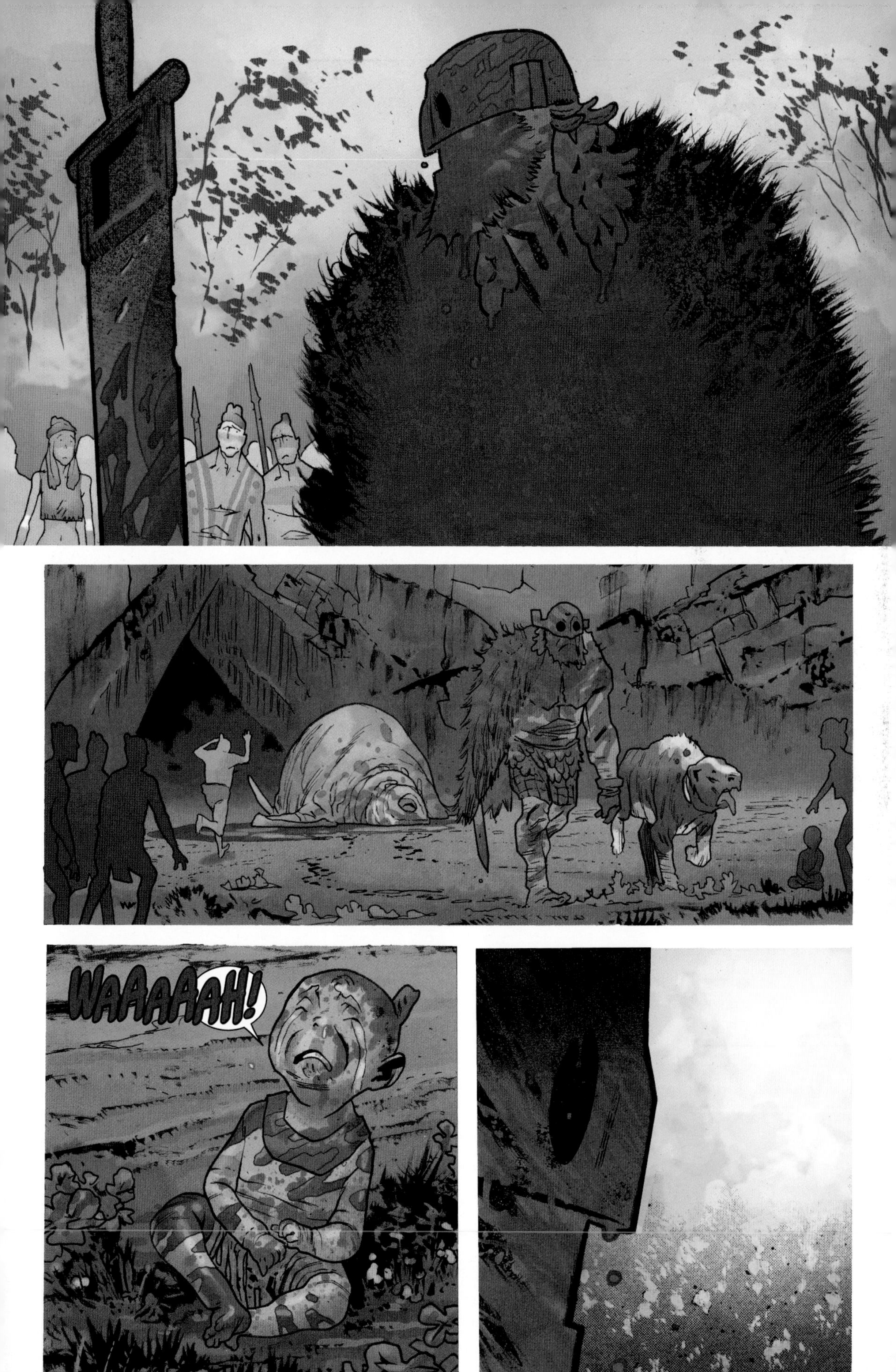
WAAAAAH!

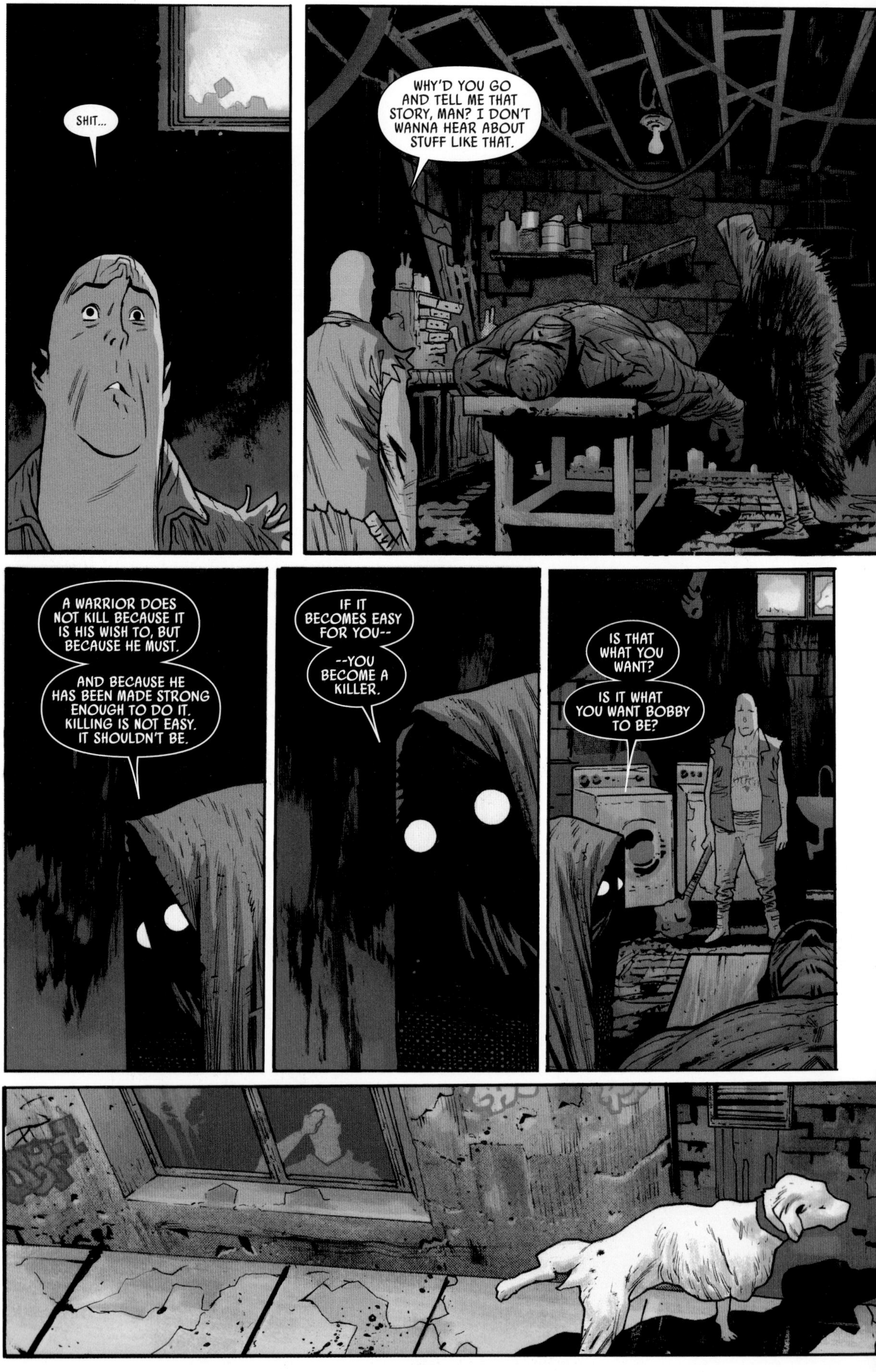
SHIT...
WHY'D YOU GO AND TELL ME THAT STORY, MAN? I DON'T WANNA HEAR ABOUT STUFF LIKE THAT.
A WARRIOR DOES NOT KILL BECAUSE IT IS HIS WISH TO, BUT BECAUSE HE MUST.
AND BECAUSE HE HAS BEEN MADE STRONG ENOUGH TO DO IT. KILLING IS NOT EASY. IT SHOULDN'T BE.
IF IT BECOMES EASY FOR YOU--
--YOU BECOME A KILLER.
IS THAT WHAT YOU WANT?
IS IT WHAT YOU WANT BOBBY TO BE?

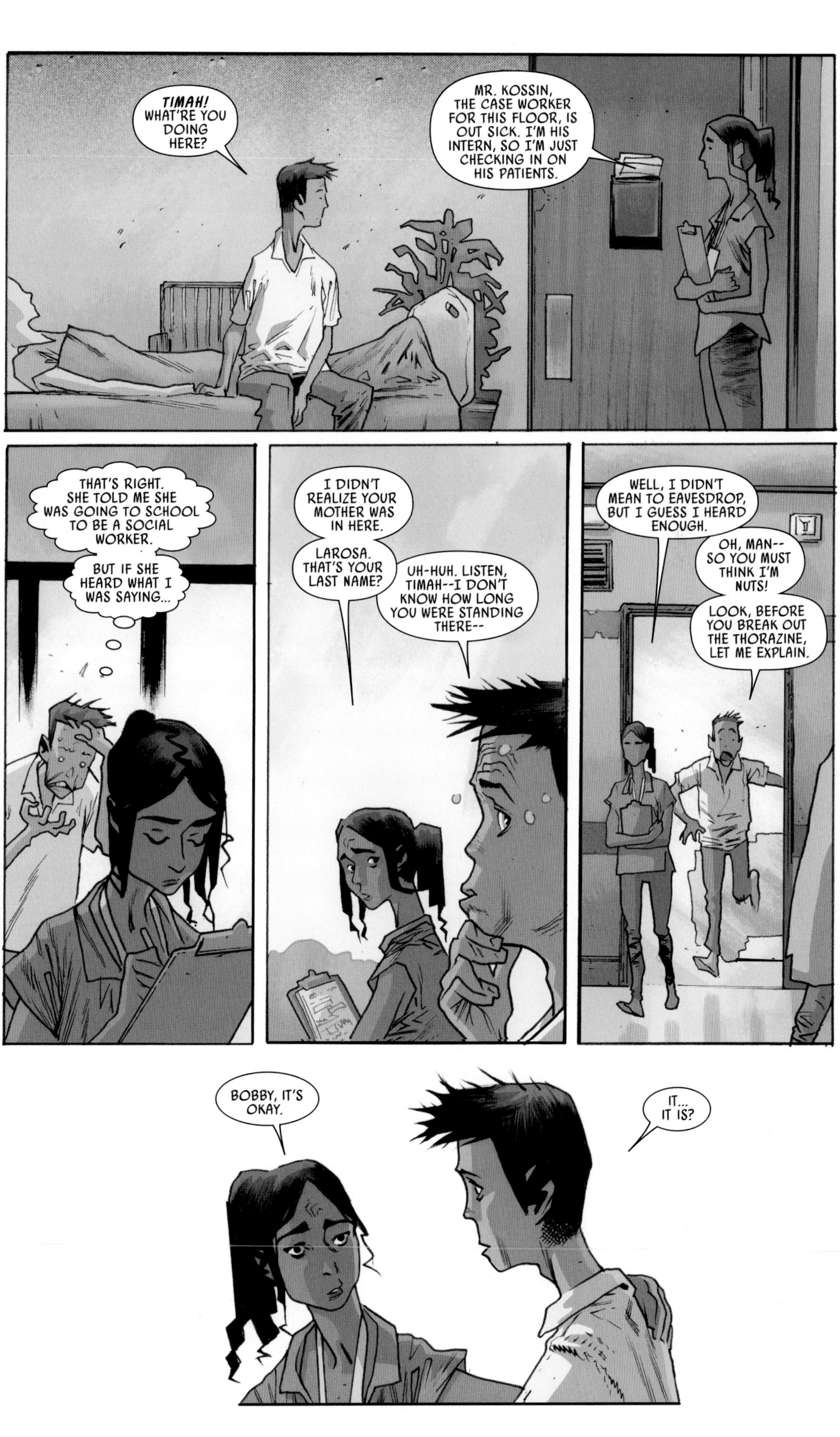
TIMAH! WHAT'RE YOU DOING HERE?
MR. KOSSIN, THE CASE WORKER FOR THIS FLOOR, IS OUT SICK. I'M HIS INTERN, SO I'M JUST CHECKING IN ON HIS PATIENTS.
THAT'S RIGHT. SHE TOLD ME SHE WAS GOING TO SCHOOL TO BE A SOCIAL WORKER.
BUT IF SHE HEARD WHAT I WAS SAYING...
I DIDN'T REALIZE YOUR MOTHER WAS IN HERE.
LAROSA. THAT'S YOUR LAST NAME?
UH-HUH. LISTEN, TIMAH--I DON'T KNOW HOW LONG YOU WERE STANDING THERE--
WELL, I DIDN'T MEAN TO EAVESDROP, BUT I GUESS I HEARD ENOUGH.
OH, MAN--SO YOU MUST THINK I'M NUTS!
LOOK, BEFORE YOU BREAK OUT THE THORAZINE, LET ME EXPLAIN.
BOBBY, IT'S OKAY.
IT... IT IS?

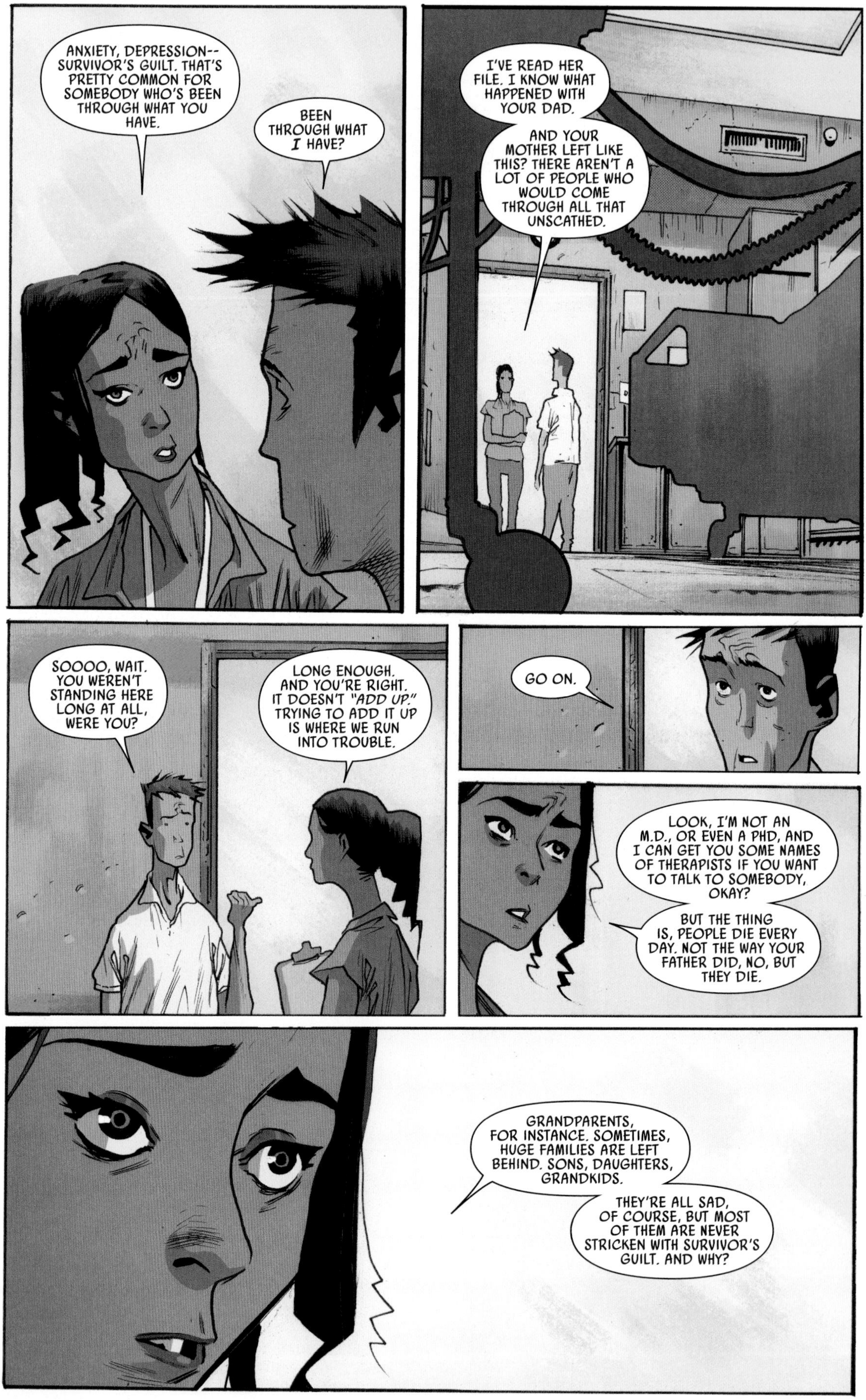
ANXIETY, DEPRESSION-- SURVIVOR'S GUILT. THAT'S PRETTY COMMON FOR SOMEBODY WHO'S BEEN THROUGH WHAT YOU HAVE.
BEEN THROUGH WHAT *I* HAVE?
I'VE READ HER FILE. I KNOW WHAT HAPPENED WITH YOUR DAD.
AND YOUR MOTHER LEFT LIKE THIS? THERE AREN'T A LOT OF PEOPLE WHO WOULD COME THROUGH ALL THAT UNSCATHED.
SOOOO, WAIT. YOU WEREN'T STANDING HERE LONG AT ALL, WERE YOU?
LONG ENOUGH. AND YOU'RE RIGHT. IT DOESN'T "*ADD UP.*" TRYING TO ADD IT UP IS WHERE WE RUN INTO TROUBLE.
GO ON.
LOOK, I'M NOT AN M.D., OR EVEN A PHD, AND I CAN GET YOU SOME NAMES OF THERAPISTS IF YOU WANT TO TALK TO SOMEBODY, OKAY?
BUT THE THING IS, PEOPLE DIE EVERY DAY. NOT THE WAY YOUR FATHER DID, NO, BUT THEY DIE.
GRANDPARENTS, FOR INSTANCE. SOMETIMES, HUGE FAMILIES ARE LEFT BEHIND. SONS, DAUGHTERS, GRANDKIDS.
THEY'RE ALL SAD, OF COURSE, BUT MOST OF THEM ARE NEVER STRICKEN WITH SURVIVOR'S GUILT. AND WHY?

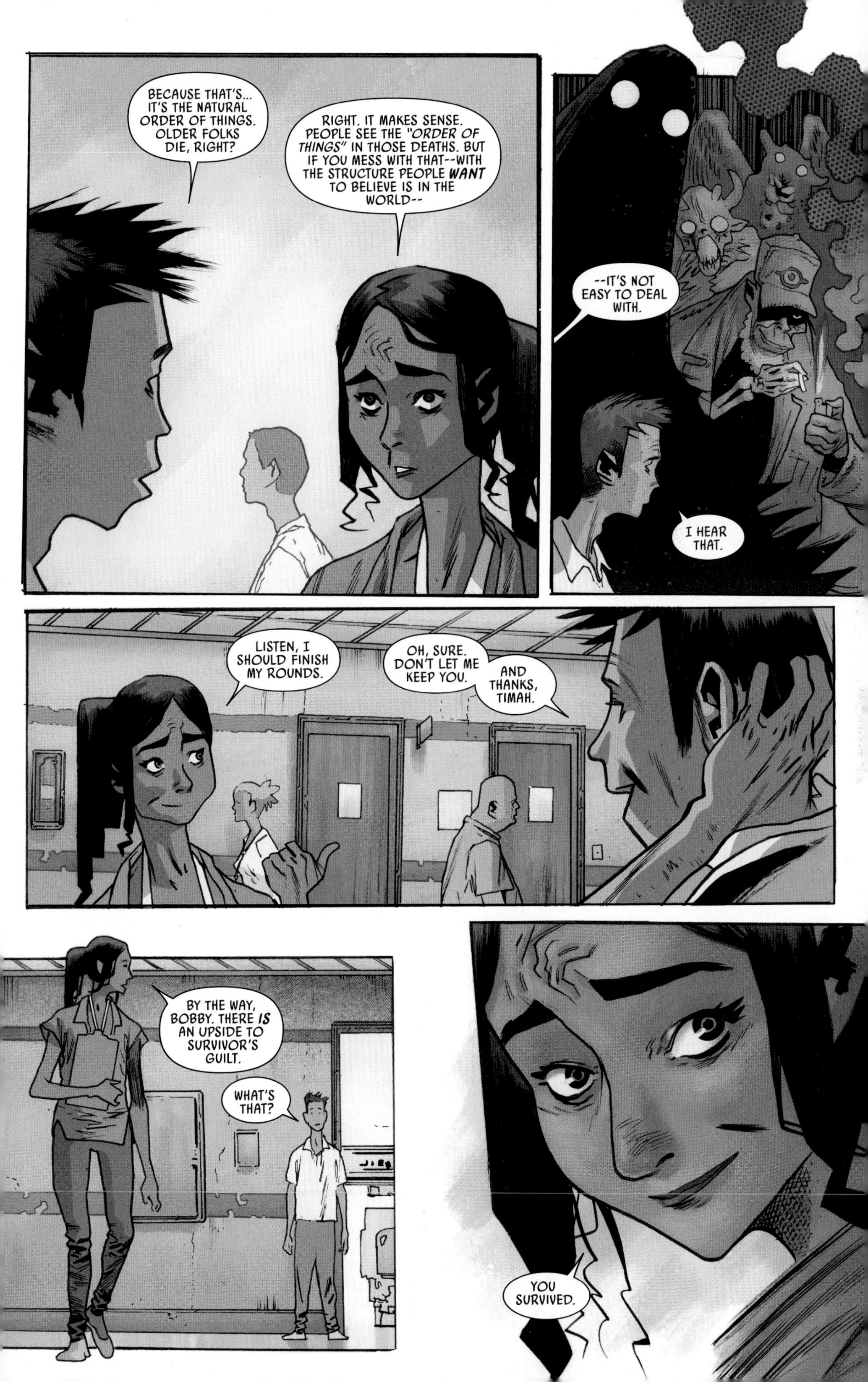
BECAUSE THAT'S... IT'S THE NATURAL ORDER OF THINGS. OLDER FOLKS DIE, RIGHT?
RIGHT. IT MAKES SENSE. PEOPLE SEE THE "*ORDER OF THINGS*" IN THOSE DEATHS. BUT IF YOU MESS WITH THAT--WITH THE STRUCTURE PEOPLE ***WANT*** TO BELIEVE IS IN THE WORLD--
--IT'S NOT EASY TO DEAL WITH.
I HEAR THAT.
LISTEN, I SHOULD FINISH MY ROUNDS.
OH, SURE. DON'T LET ME KEEP YOU.
AND THANKS, TIMAH.
BY THE WAY, BOBBY. THERE ***IS*** AN UPSIDE TO SURVIVOR'S GUILT.
WHAT'S THAT?
YOU SURVIVED.

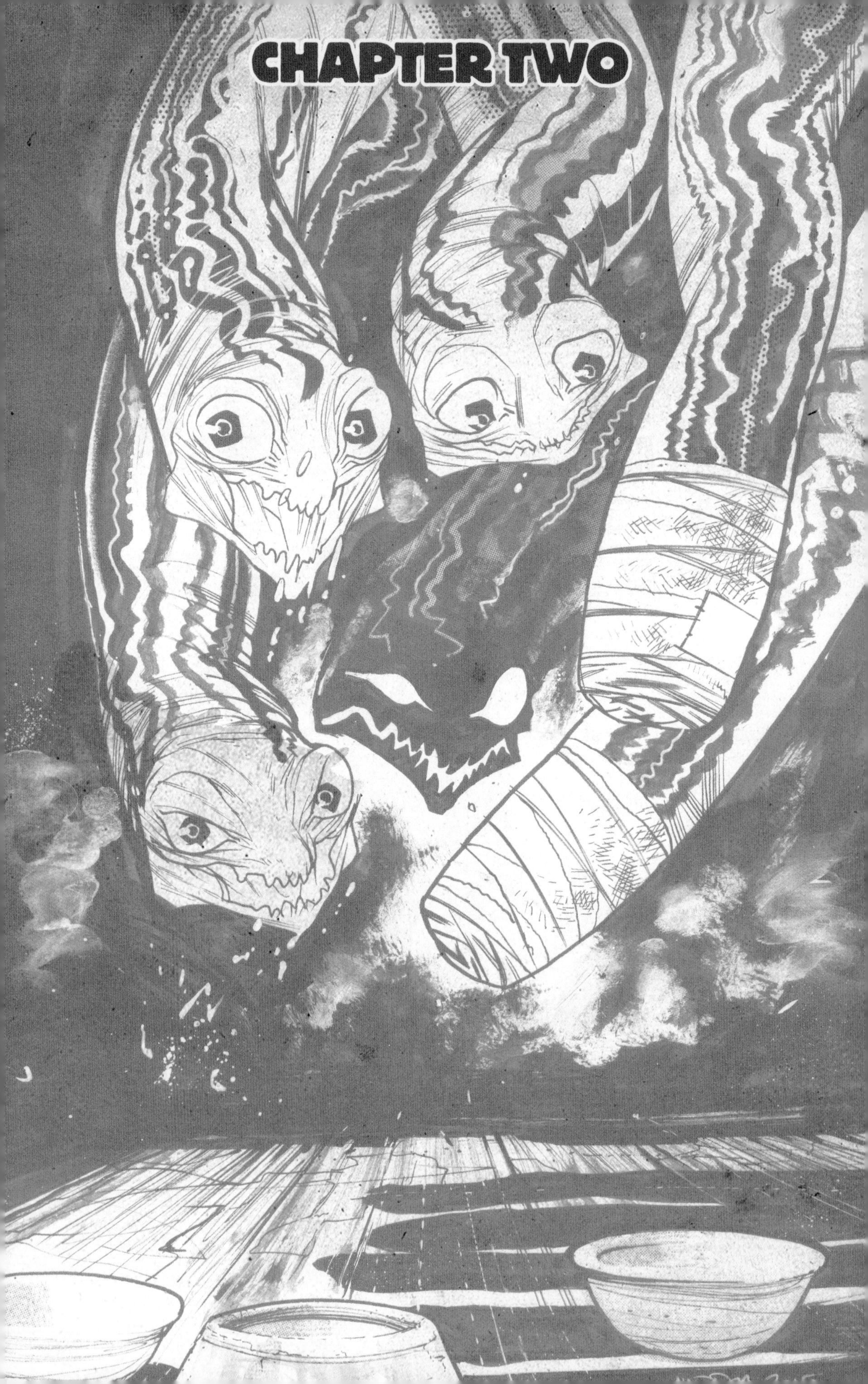
CHAPTER TWO

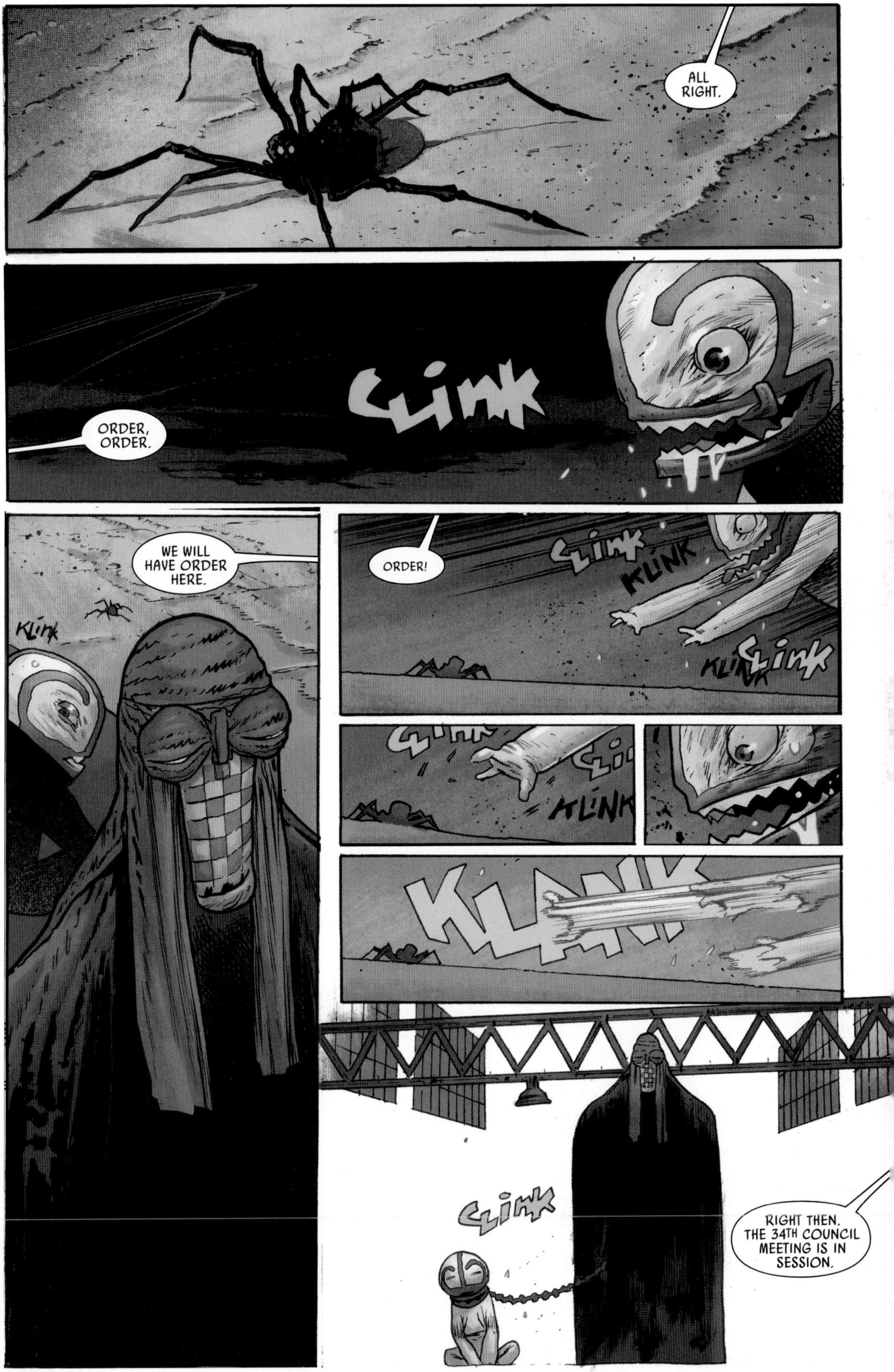
ALL RIGHT.
ORDER, ORDER.
CLINK
WE WILL HAVE ORDER HERE.
KLINK
ORDER!
CLINK
KLINK
KLINK
CLINK
KLINK
KLANK
CLINK
RIGHT THEN. THE 34TH COUNCIL MEETING IS IN SESSION.

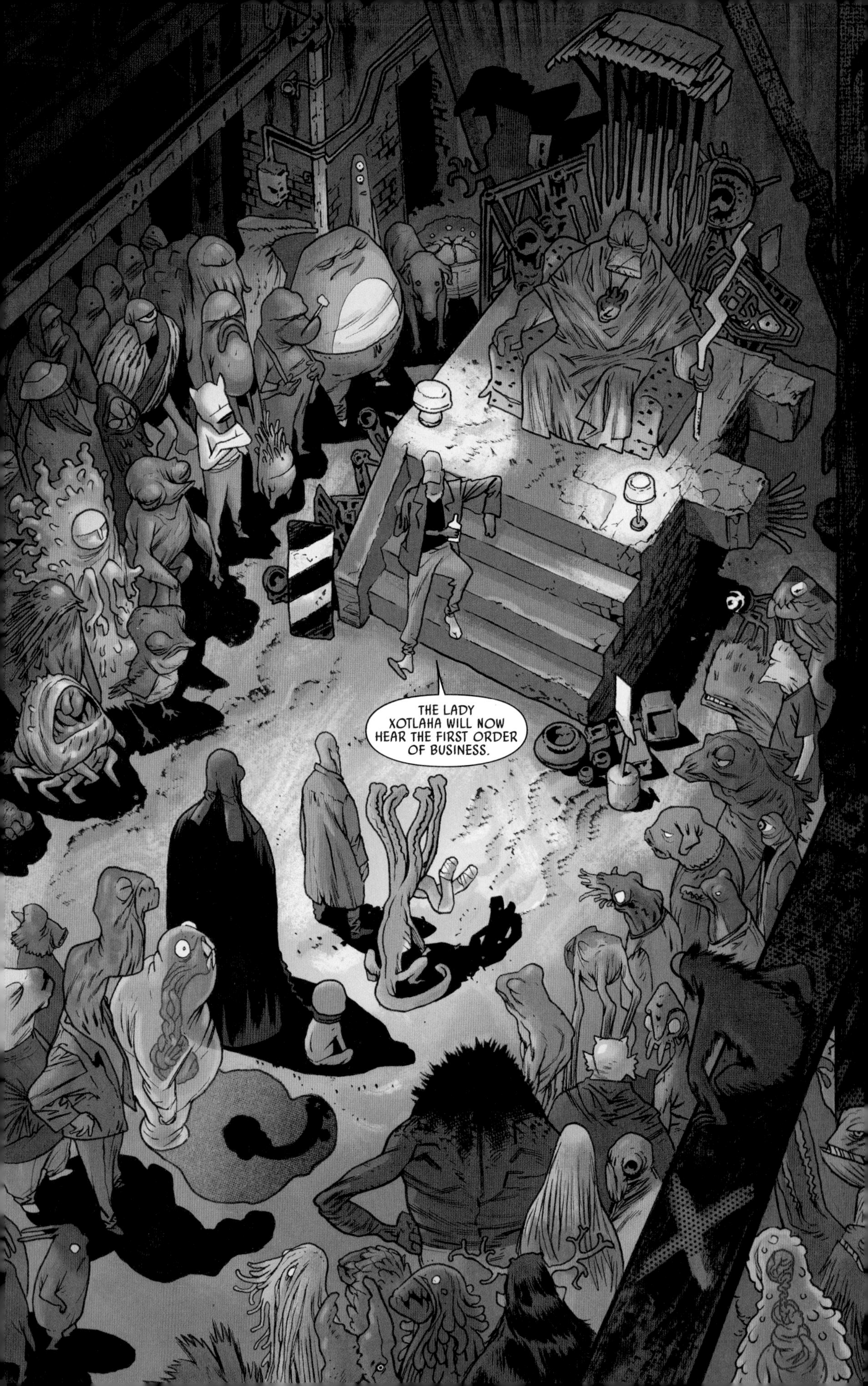
THE LADY XOTLAHA WILL NOW HEAR THE FIRST ORDER OF BUSINESS.

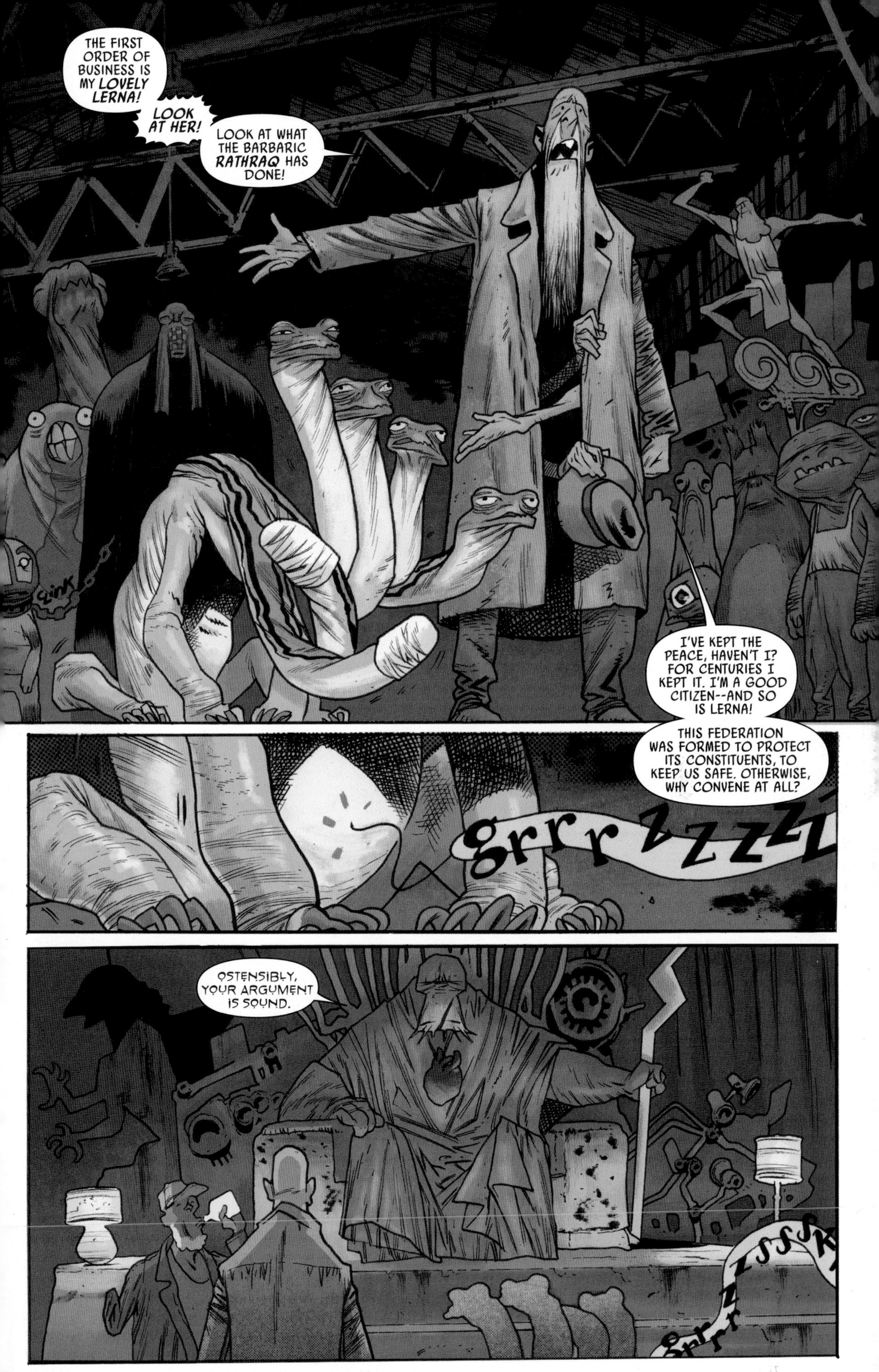
THE FIRST ORDER OF BUSINESS IS MY LOVELY LERNA!
LOOK AT HER!
LOOK AT WHAT THE BARBARIC RATHRAQ HAS DONE!
CLINK
I'VE KEPT THE PEACE, HAVEN'T I? FOR CENTURIES I KEPT IT. I'M A GOOD CITIZEN--AND SO IS LERNA!
THIS FEDERATION WAS FORMED TO PROTECT ITS CONSTITUENTS, TO KEEP US SAFE. OTHERWISE, WHY CONVENE AT ALL?
grrrZZZZZ
OSTENSIBLY, YOUR ARGUMENT IS SOUND.
grrrZZSSSK

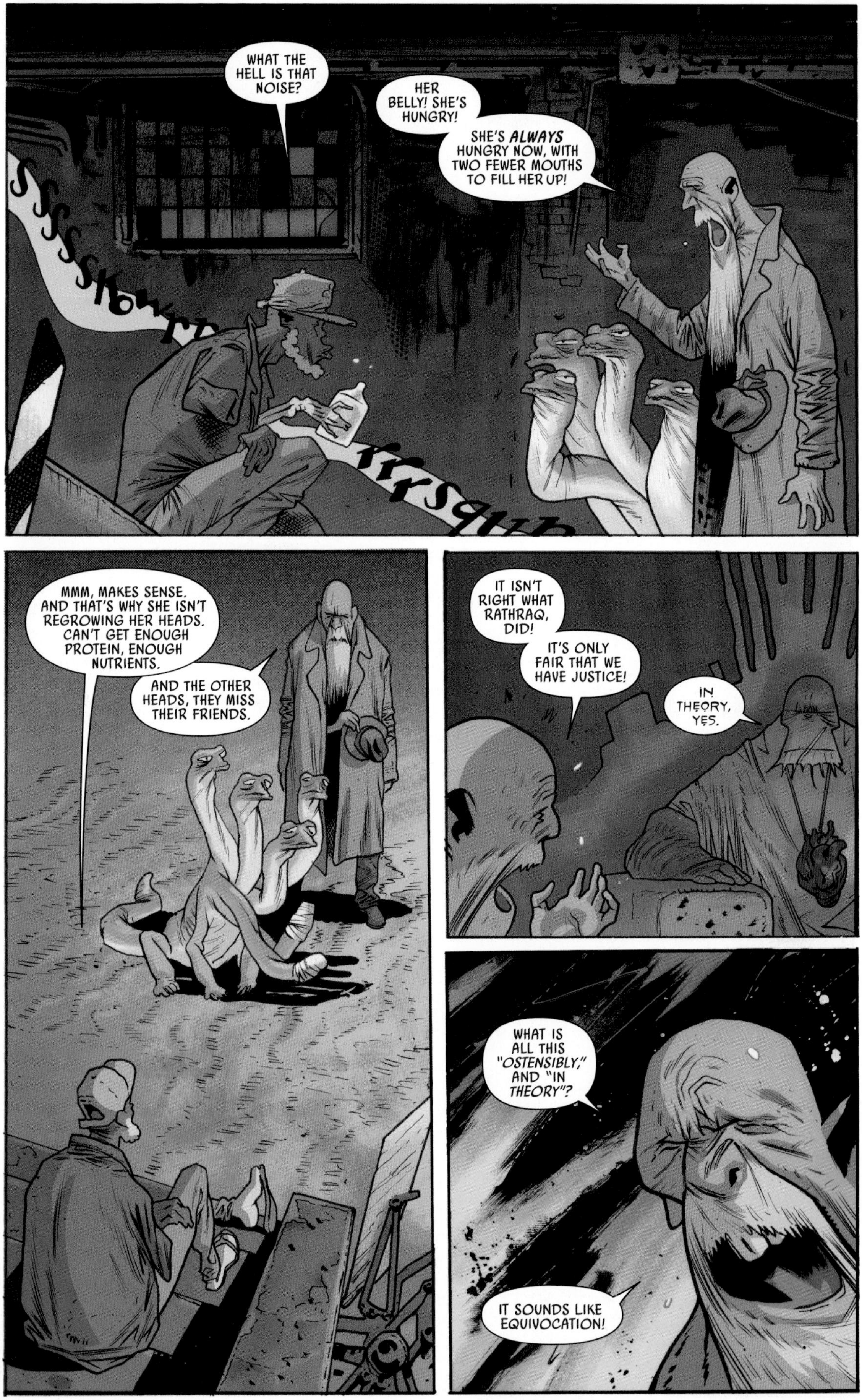
WHAT THE HELL IS THAT NOISE?
HER BELLY! SHE'S HUNGRY!
SHE'S *ALWAYS* HUNGRY NOW, WITH TWO FEWER MOUTHS TO FILL HER UP!
SSSSSKOWRR
RRRSQUB
MMM, MAKES SENSE. AND THAT'S WHY SHE ISN'T REGROWING HER HEADS. CAN'T GET ENOUGH PROTEIN, ENOUGH NUTRIENTS.
AND THE OTHER HEADS, THEY MISS THEIR FRIENDS.
IT ISN'T RIGHT WHAT RATHRAQ, DID!
IT'S ONLY FAIR THAT WE HAVE JUSTICE!
IN THEORY, YES.
WHAT IS ALL THIS *"OSTENSIBLY,"* AND "IN *THEORY*"?
IT SOUNDS LIKE EQUIVOCATION!

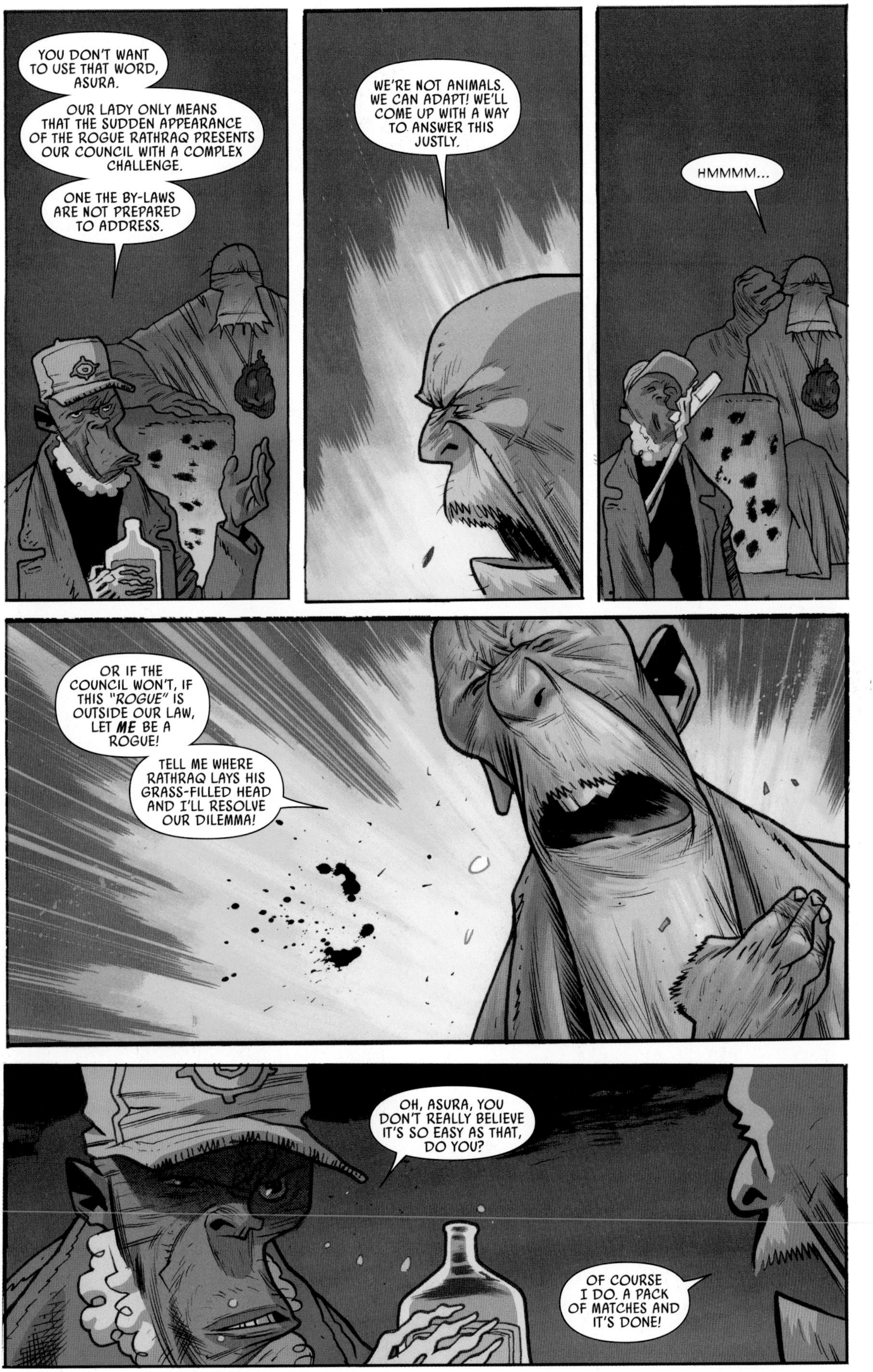
YOU DON'T WANT TO USE THAT WORD, ASURA.
OUR LADY ONLY MEANS THAT THE SUDDEN APPEARANCE OF THE ROGUE RATHRAQ PRESENTS OUR COUNCIL WITH A COMPLEX CHALLENGE.
ONE THE BY-LAWS ARE NOT PREPARED TO ADDRESS.
WE'RE NOT ANIMALS. WE CAN ADAPT! WE'LL COME UP WITH A WAY TO ANSWER THIS JUSTLY.
HMMMM...
OR IF THE COUNCIL WON'T, IF THIS "ROGUE" IS OUTSIDE OUR LAW, LET ME BE A ROGUE!
TELL ME WHERE RATHRAQ LAYS HIS GRASS-FILLED HEAD AND I'LL RESOLVE OUR DILEMMA!
OH, ASURA, YOU DON'T REALLY BELIEVE IT'S SO EASY AS THAT, DO YOU?
OF COURSE I DO. A PACK OF MATCHES AND IT'S DONE!

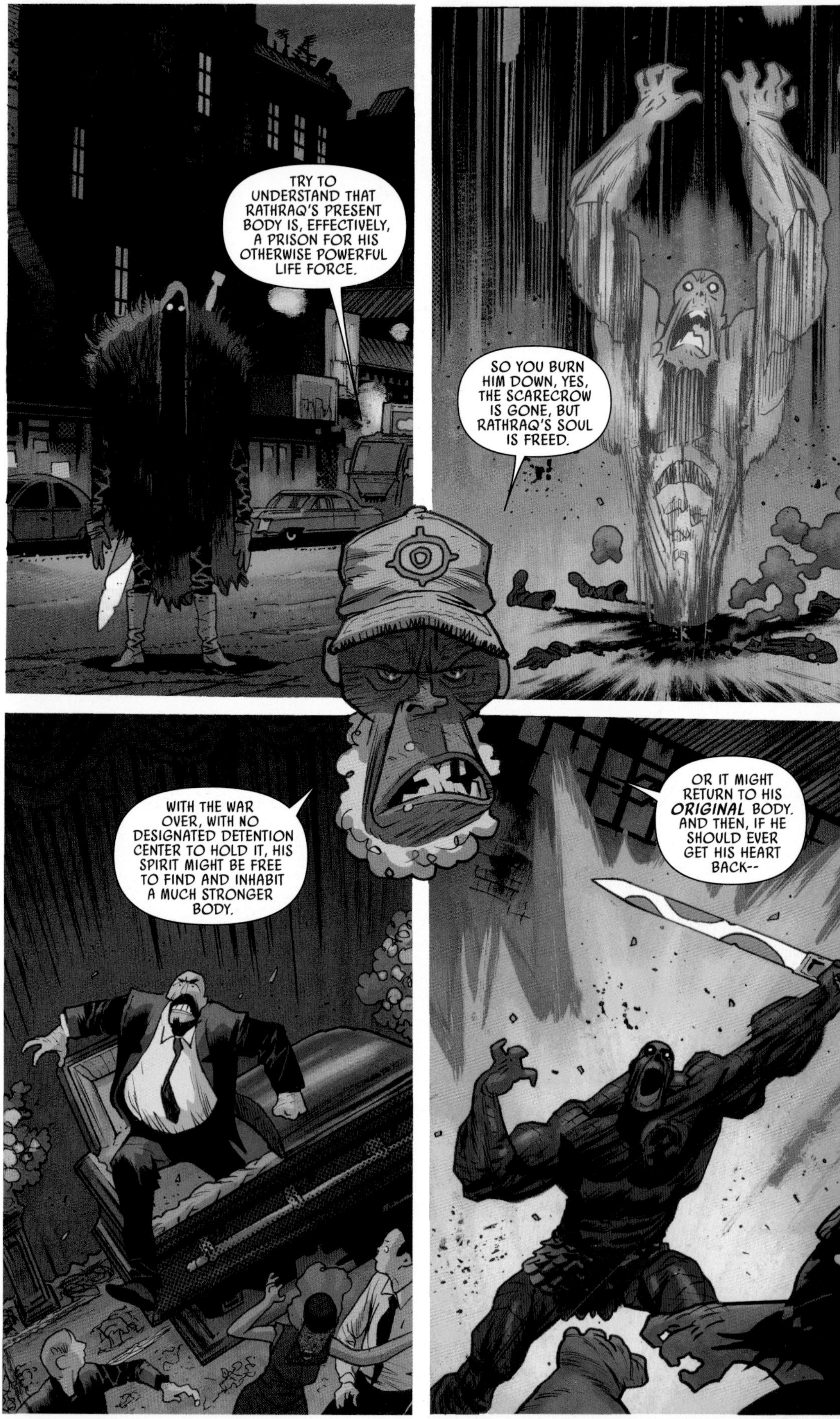
TRY TO UNDERSTAND THAT RATHRAQ'S PRESENT BODY IS, EFFECTIVELY, A PRISON FOR HIS OTHERWISE POWERFUL LIFE FORCE.
SO YOU BURN HIM DOWN, YES, THE SCARECROW IS GONE, BUT RATHRAQ'S SOUL IS FREED.
WITH THE WAR OVER, WITH NO DESIGNATED DETENTION CENTER TO HOLD IT, HIS SPIRIT MIGHT BE FREE TO FIND AND INHABIT A MUCH STRONGER BODY.
OR IT MIGHT RETURN TO HIS ORIGINAL BODY. AND THEN, IF HE SHOULD EVER GET HIS HEART BACK--

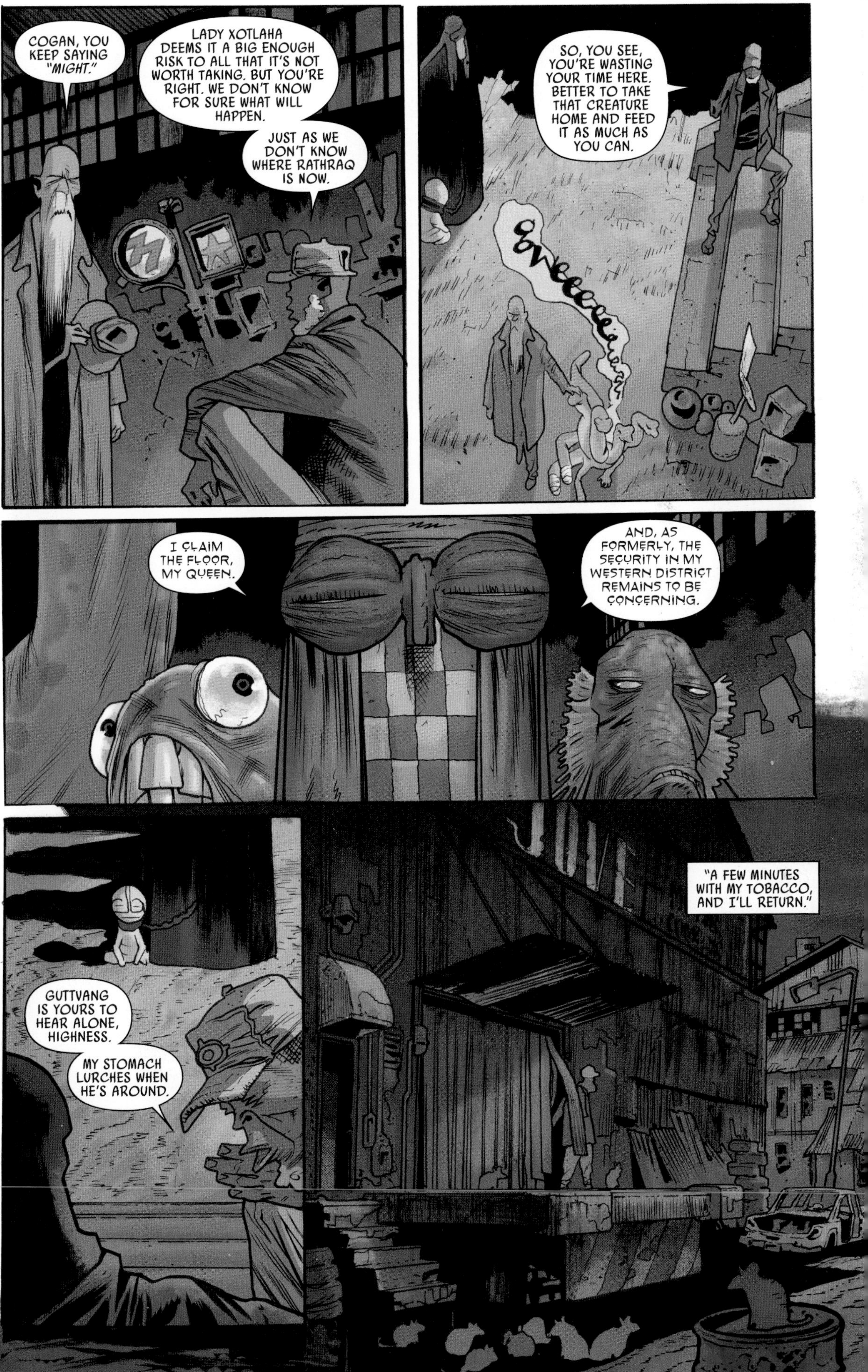
COGAN, YOU KEEP SAYING "MIGHT."
LADY XOTLAHA DEEMS IT A BIG ENOUGH RISK TO ALL THAT IT'S NOT WORTH TAKING. BUT YOU'RE RIGHT. WE DON'T KNOW FOR SURE WHAT WILL HAPPEN.
JUST AS WE DON'T KNOW WHERE RATHRAQ IS NOW.
SO, YOU SEE, YOU'RE WASTING YOUR TIME HERE. BETTER TO TAKE THAT CREATURE HOME AND FEED IT AS MUCH AS YOU CAN.
I CLAIM THE FLOOR, MY QUEEN.
AND, AS FORMERLY, THE SECURITY IN MY WESTERN DISTRICT REMAINS TO BE CONCERNING.
GUTTVANG IS YOURS TO HEAR ALONE, HIGHNESS.
MY STOMACH LURCHES WHEN HE'S AROUND.
"A FEW MINUTES WITH MY TOBACCO, AND I'LL RETURN."

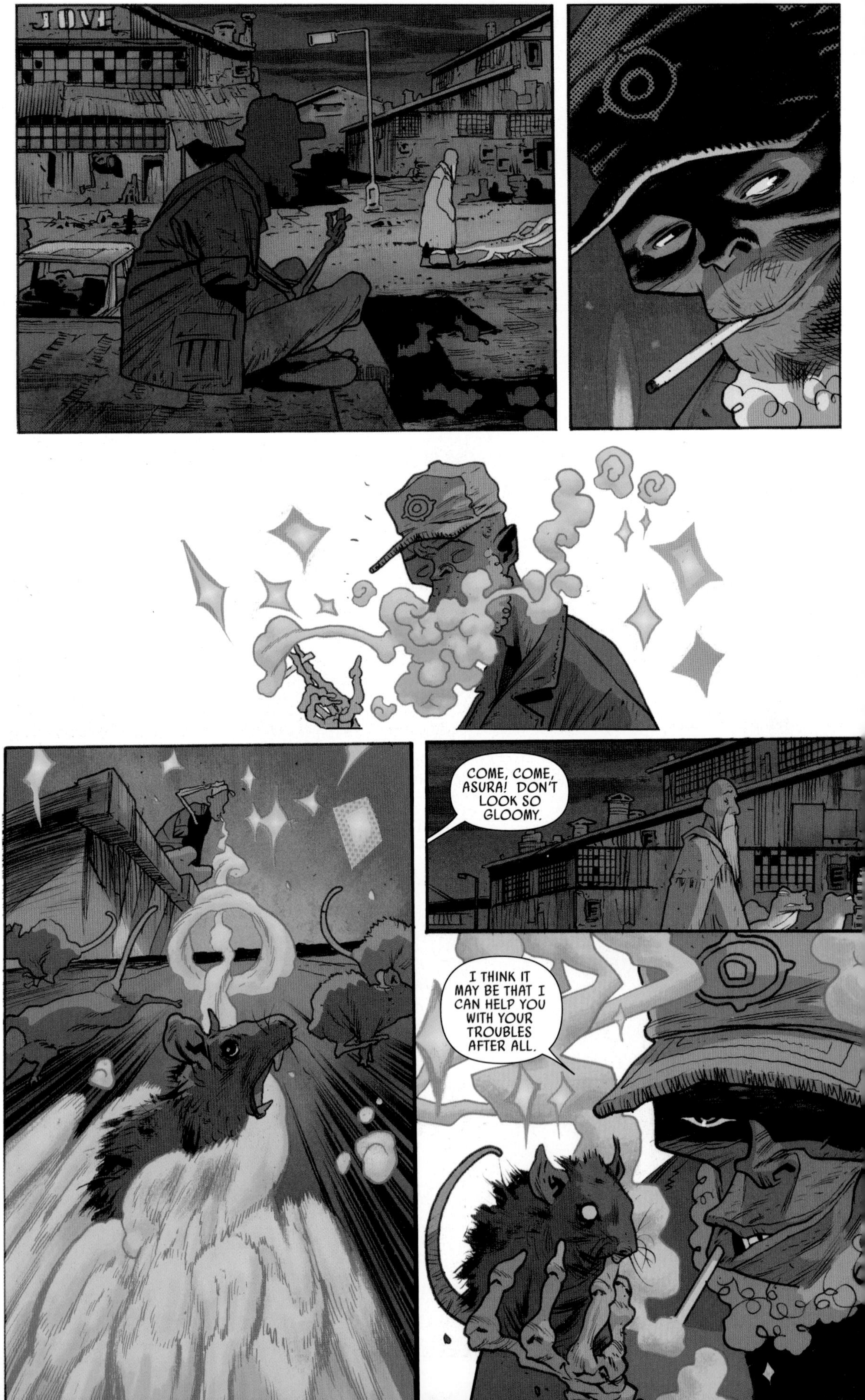
JOVE
COME, COME, ASURA! DON'T LOOK SO GLOOMY.
I THINK IT MAY BE THAT I CAN HELP YOU WITH YOUR TROUBLES AFTER ALL.

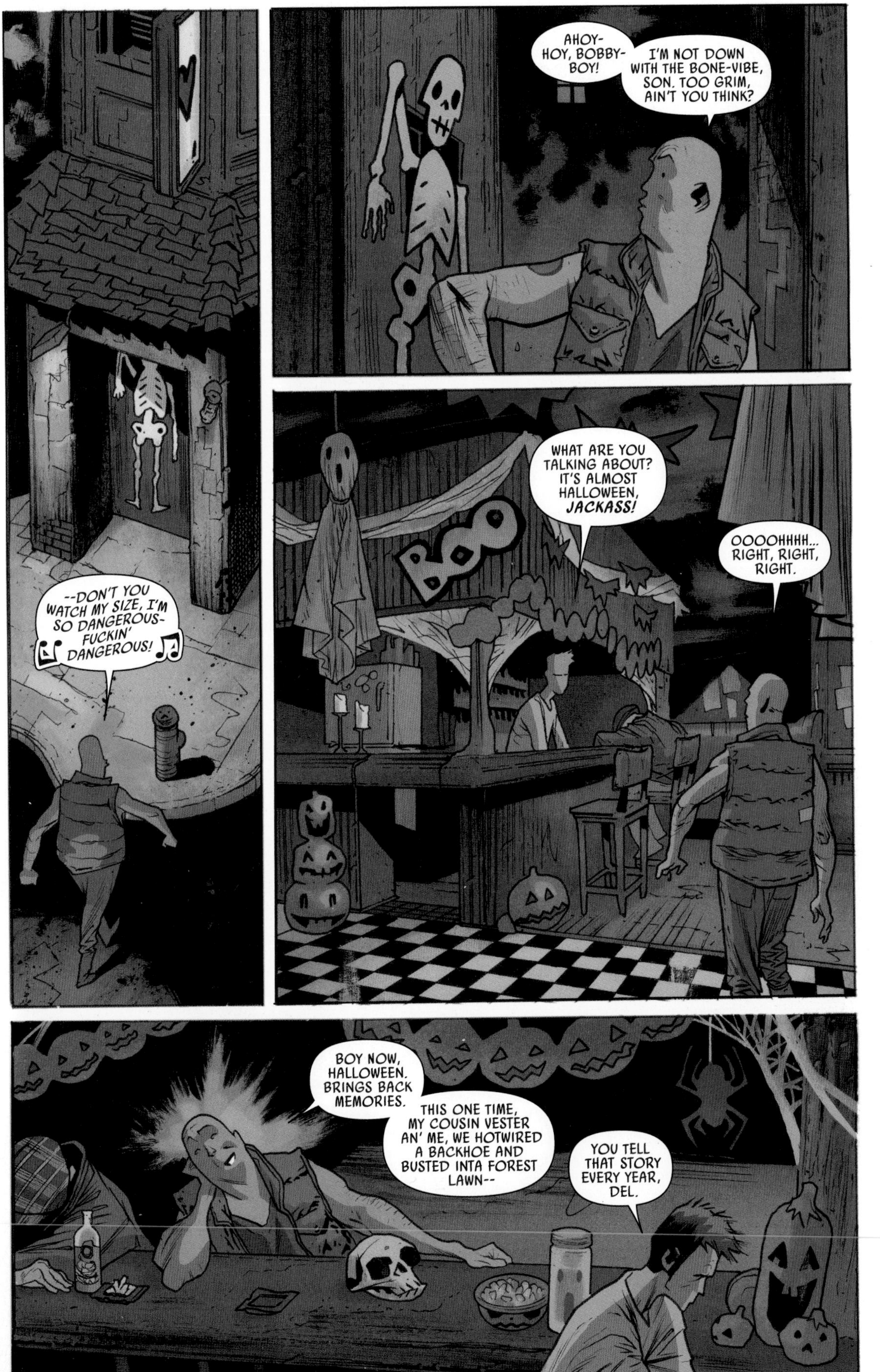

--DON'T YOU WATCH MY SIZE, I'M SO DANGEROUS-FUCKIN' DANGEROUS!
AHOY-HOY, BOBBY-BOY!
I'M NOT DOWN WITH THE BONE-VIBE, SON. TOO GRIM, AIN'T YOU THINK?
BOO
WHAT ARE YOU TALKING ABOUT? IT'S ALMOST HALLOWEEN, JACKASS!
OOOOHHHH... RIGHT, RIGHT, RIGHT.
BOY NOW, HALLOWEEN. BRINGS BACK MEMORIES.
THIS ONE TIME, MY COUSIN VESTER AN' ME, WE HOTWIRED A BACKHOE AND BUSTED INTA FOREST LAWN--
YOU TELL THAT STORY EVERY YEAR, DEL.

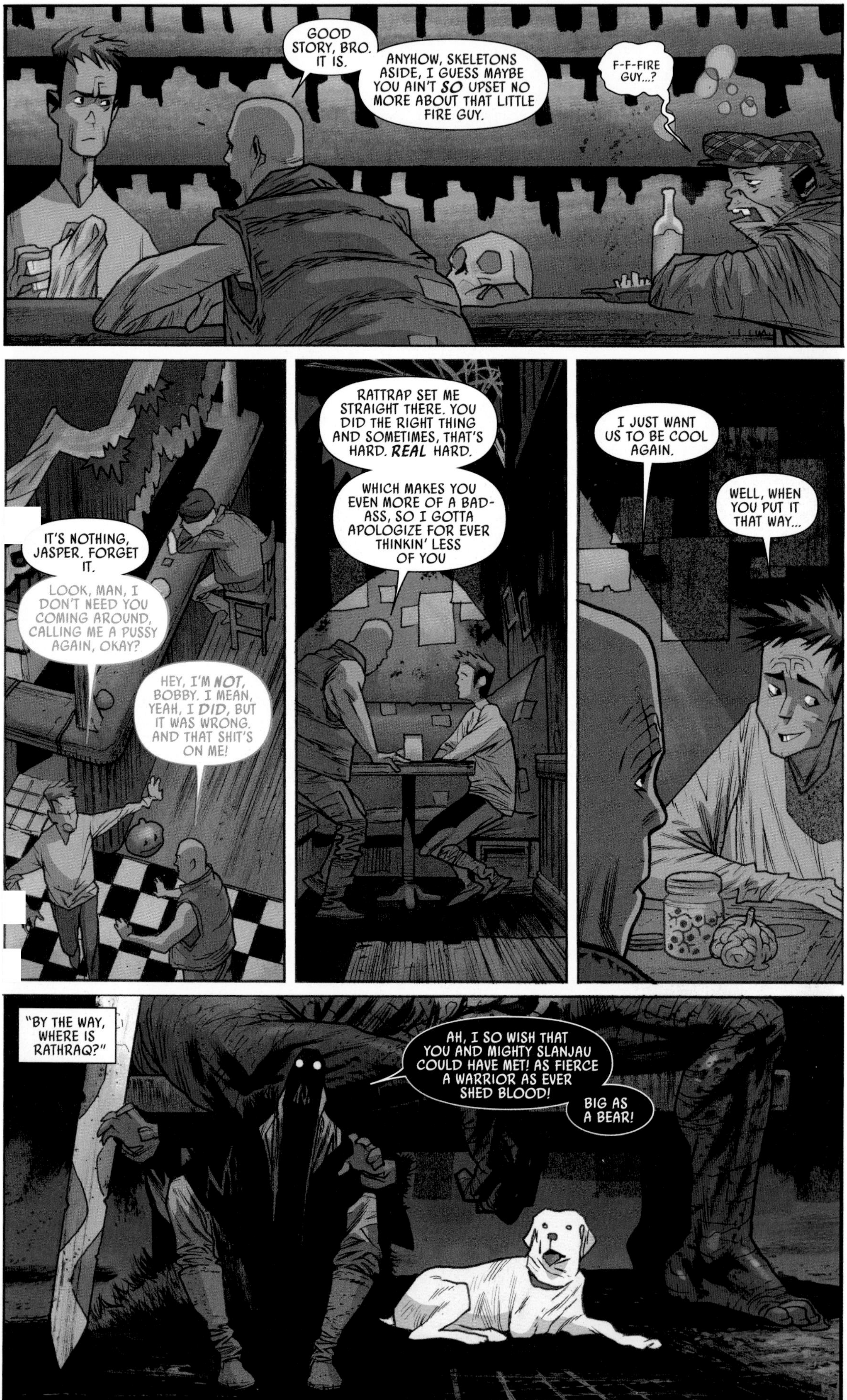
GOOD STORY, BRO. IT IS.
ANYHOW, SKELETONS ASIDE, I GUESS MAYBE YOU AIN'T SO UPSET NO MORE ABOUT THAT LITTLE FIRE GUY.
F-F-FIRE GUY...?
IT'S NOTHING, JASPER. FORGET IT.
LOOK, MAN, I DON'T NEED YOU COMING AROUND, CALLING ME A PUSSY AGAIN, OKAY?
HEY, I'M NOT, BOBBY. I MEAN, YEAH, I DID, BUT IT WAS WRONG. AND THAT SHIT'S ON ME!
RATTRAP SET ME STRAIGHT THERE. YOU DID THE RIGHT THING AND SOMETIMES, THAT'S HARD. REAL HARD.
WHICH MAKES YOU EVEN MORE OF A BAD-ASS, SO I GOTTA APOLOGIZE FOR EVER THINKIN' LESS OF YOU
I JUST WANT US TO BE COOL AGAIN.
WELL, WHEN YOU PUT IT THAT WAY...
"BY THE WAY, WHERE IS RATHRAQ?"
AH, I SO WISH THAT YOU AND MIGHTY SLANJAU COULD HAVE MET! AS FIERCE A WARRIOR AS EVER SHED BLOOD!
BIG AS A BEAR!

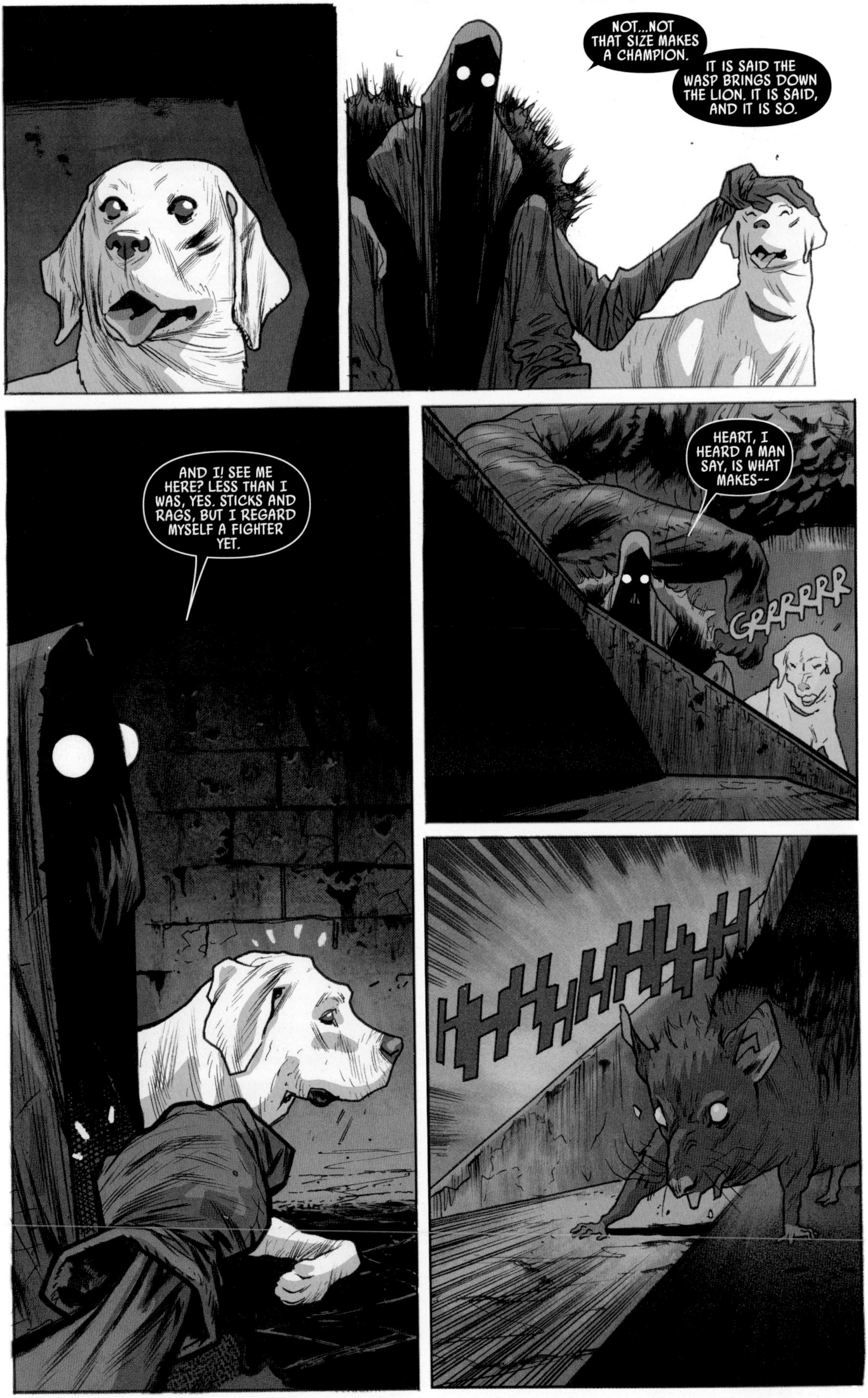
NOT...NOT THAT SIZE MAKES A CHAMPION.
IT IS SAID THE WASP BRINGS DOWN THE LION. IT IS SAID, AND IT IS SO.
AND I! SEE ME HERE? LESS THAN I WAS, YES. STICKS AND RAGS, BUT I REGARD MYSELF A FIGHTER YET.
HEART, I HEARD A MAN SAY, IS WHAT MAKES--
GRRRRRR
HHHHHHHHH

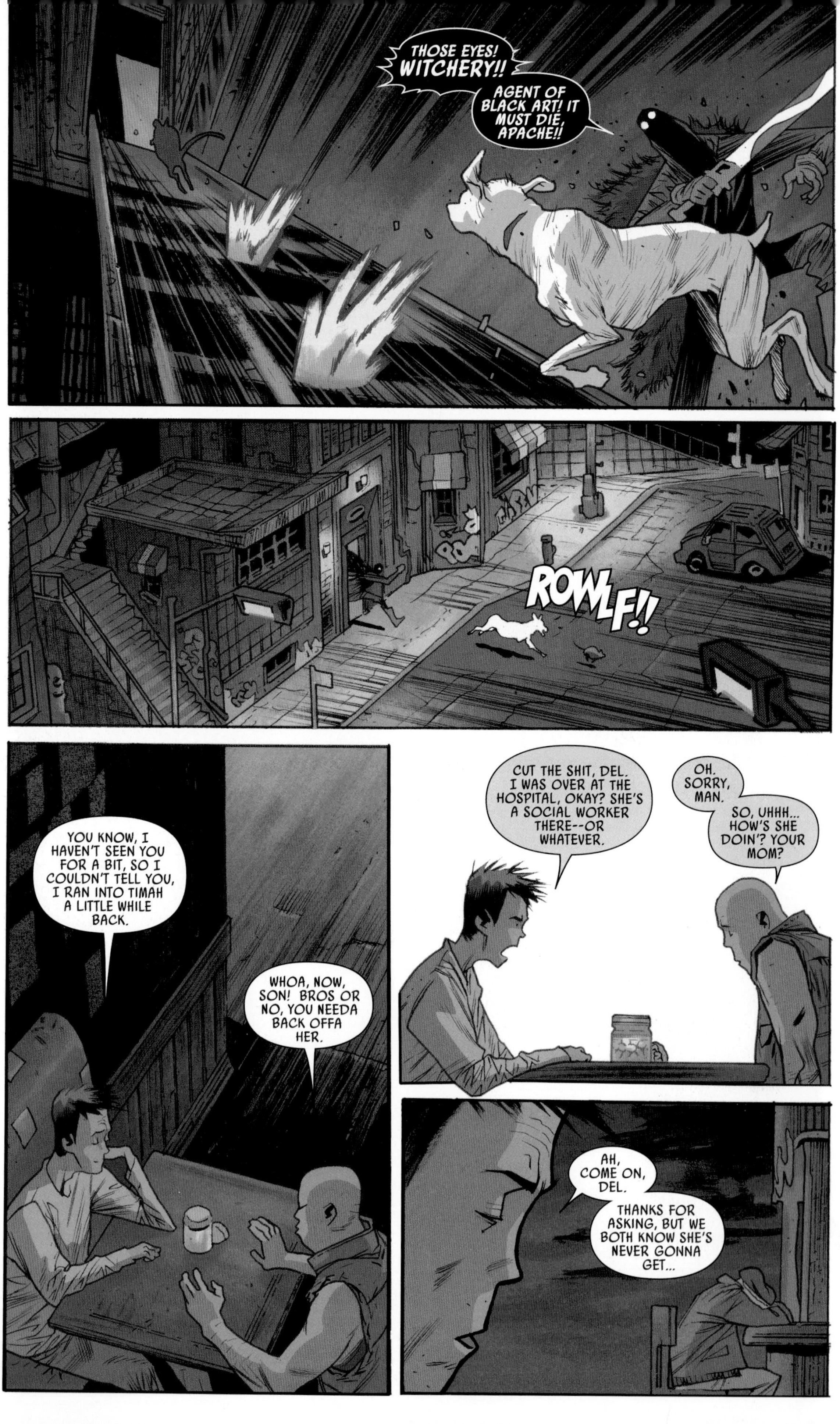
THOSE EYES! WITCHERY!!
AGENT OF BLACK ART! IT MUST DIE, APACHE!!
ROWLF!!
YOU KNOW, I HAVEN'T SEEN YOU FOR A BIT, SO I COULDN'T TELL YOU, I RAN INTO TIMAH A LITTLE WHILE BACK.
WHOA, NOW, SON! BROS OR NO, YOU NEEDA BACK OFFA HER.
CUT THE SHIT, DEL. I WAS OVER AT THE HOSPITAL, OKAY? SHE'S A SOCIAL WORKER THERE--OR WHATEVER.
OH. SORRY, MAN.
SO, UHHH... HOW'S SHE DOIN'? YOUR MOM?
AH, COME ON, DEL.
THANKS FOR ASKING, BUT WE BOTH KNOW SHE'S NEVER GONNA GET...

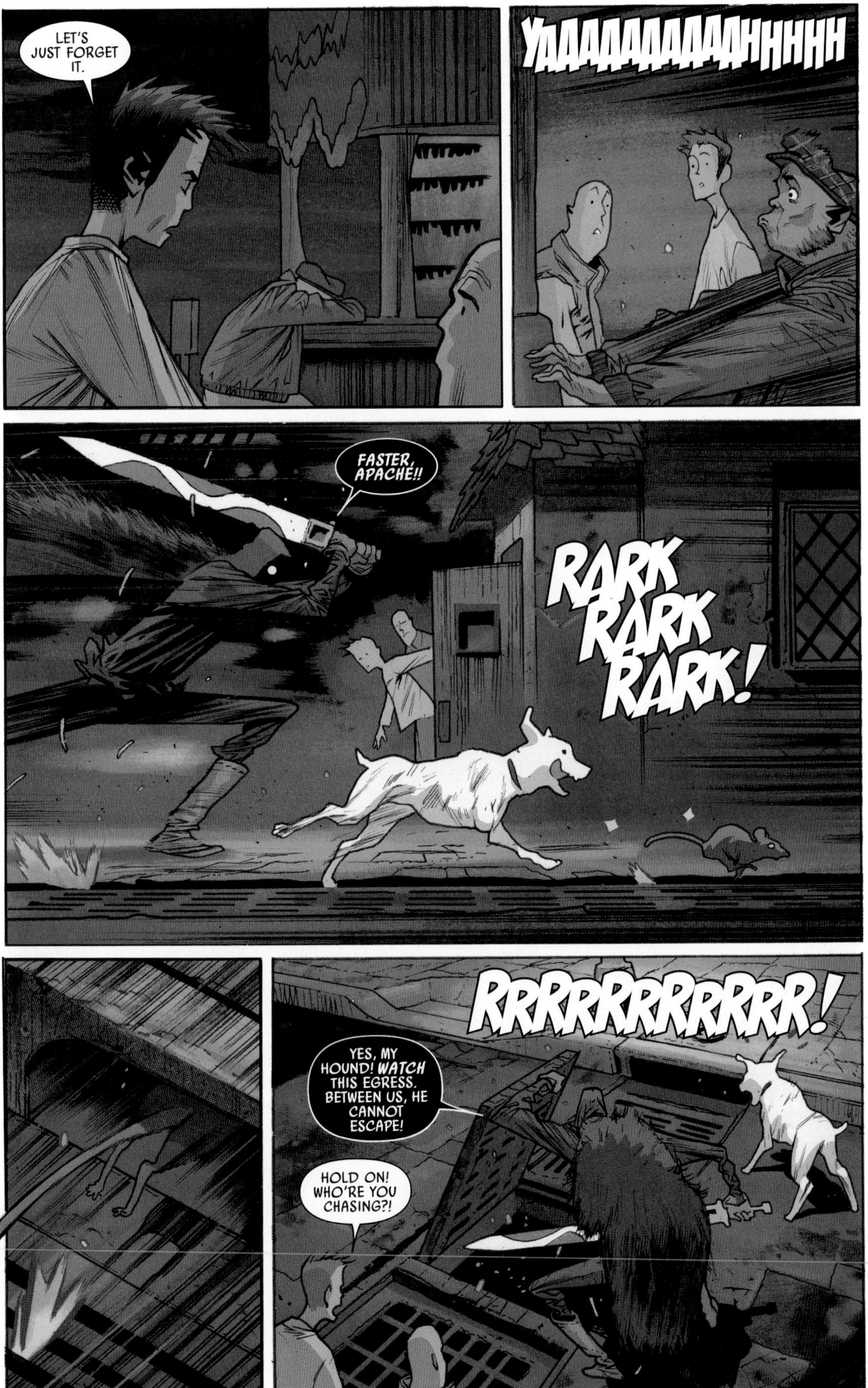
LET'S JUST FORGET IT.
YAAAAAAAAAAHHHHH
FASTER, APACHE!!
RARK RARK RARK!
RRRRRRRRRRR!
YES, MY HOUND! WATCH THIS EGRESS. BETWEEN US, HE CANNOT ESCAPE!
HOLD ON! WHO'RE YOU CHASING?!

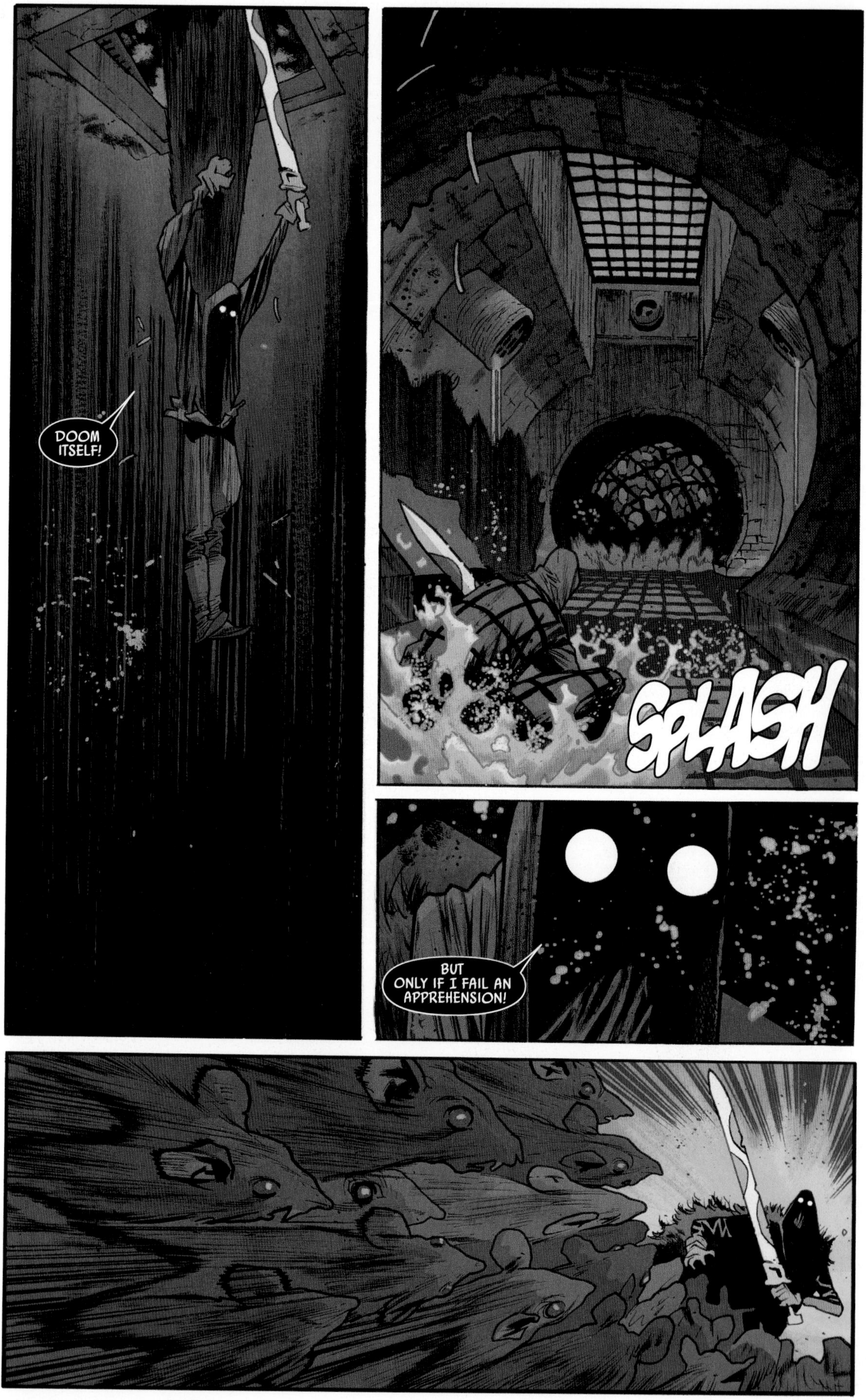
DOOM ITSELF!
SPLASH
BUT ONLY IF I FAIL AN APPREHENSION!

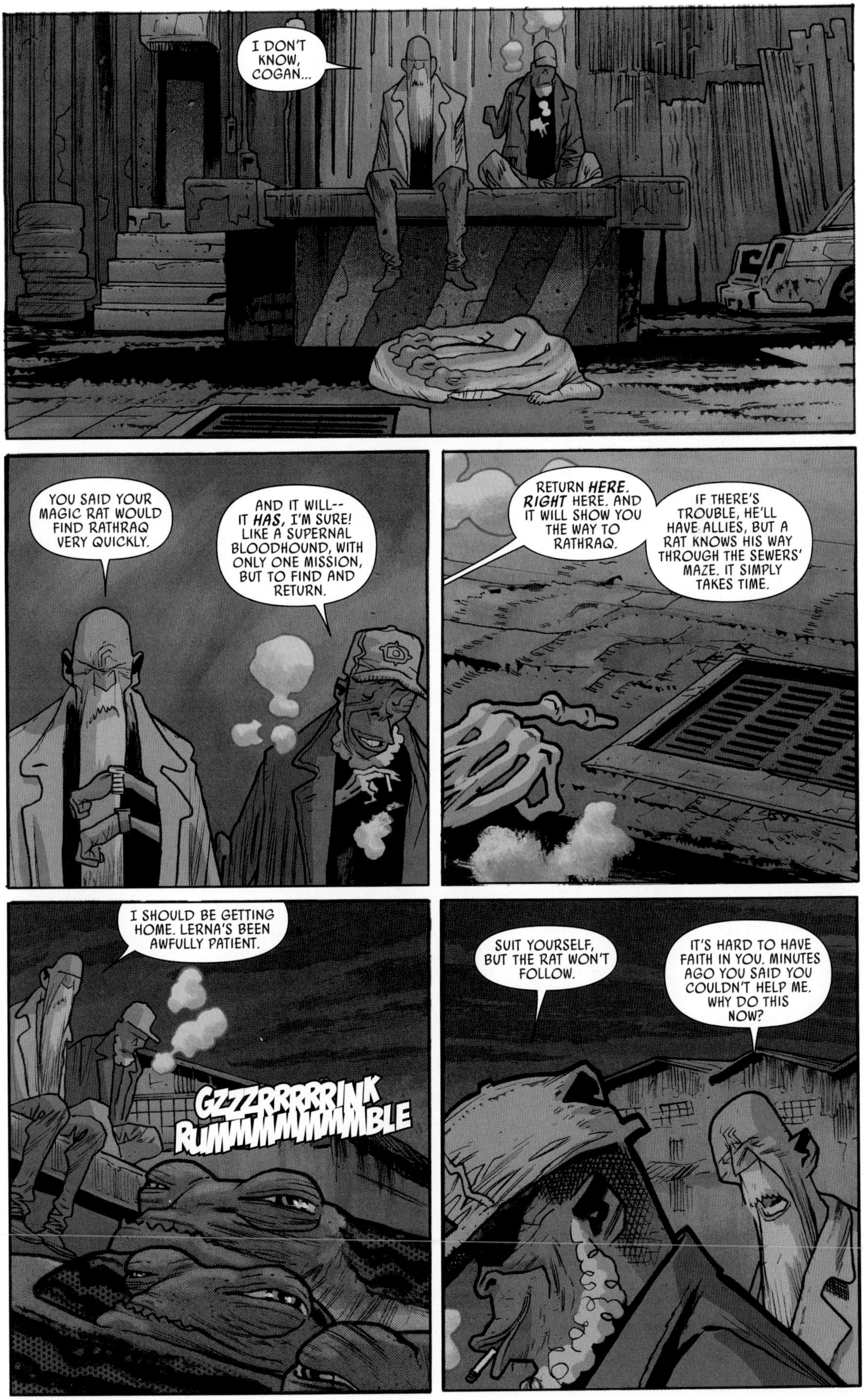
I DON'T KNOW, COGAN...
YOU SAID YOUR MAGIC RAT WOULD FIND RATHRAQ VERY QUICKLY.
AND IT WILL-- IT HAS, I'M SURE! LIKE A SUPERNAL BLOODHOUND, WITH ONLY ONE MISSION, BUT TO FIND AND RETURN.
RETURN HERE. RIGHT HERE. AND IT WILL SHOW YOU THE WAY TO RATHRAQ.
IF THERE'S TROUBLE, HE'LL HAVE ALLIES, BUT A RAT KNOWS HIS WAY THROUGH THE SEWERS' MAZE. IT SIMPLY TAKES TIME.
I SHOULD BE GETTING HOME. LERNA'S BEEN AWFULLY PATIENT.
GZZZRRRRRINK
RUMMMMMMMBLE
SUIT YOURSELF, BUT THE RAT WON'T FOLLOW.
IT'S HARD TO HAVE FAITH IN YOU. MINUTES AGO YOU SAID YOU COULDN'T HELP ME. WHY DO THIS NOW?

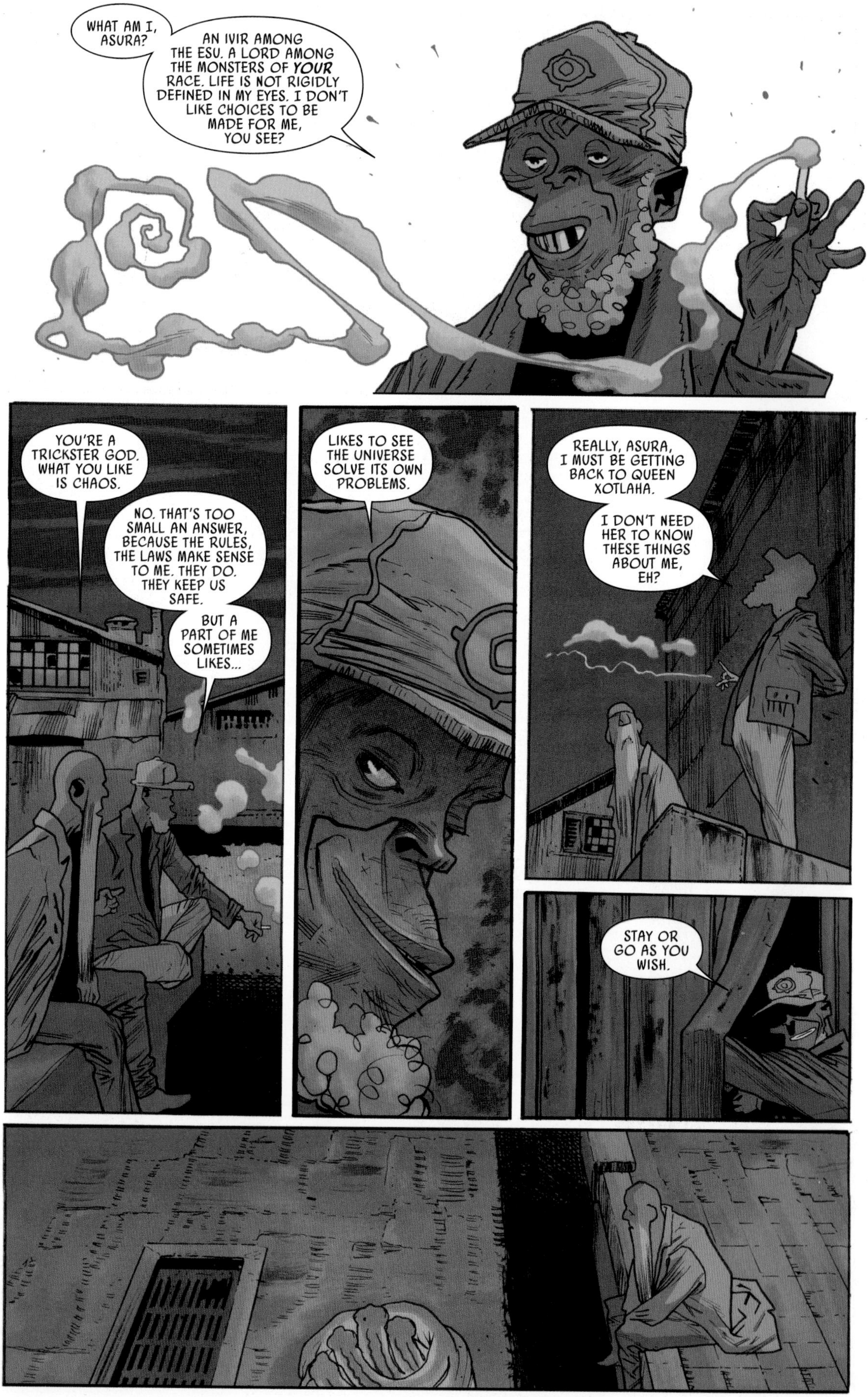
WHAT AM I, ASURA?
AN IVIR AMONG THE ESU. A LORD AMONG THE MONSTERS OF *YOUR* RACE. LIFE IS NOT RIGIDLY DEFINED IN MY EYES. I DON'T LIKE CHOICES TO BE MADE FOR ME, YOU SEE?
YOU'RE A TRICKSTER GOD. WHAT YOU LIKE IS CHAOS.
NO. THAT'S TOO SMALL AN ANSWER, BECAUSE THE RULES, THE LAWS MAKE SENSE TO ME. THEY DO. THEY KEEP US SAFE.
BUT A PART OF ME SOMETIMES LIKES...
LIKES TO SEE THE UNIVERSE SOLVE ITS OWN PROBLEMS.
REALLY, ASURA, I MUST BE GETTING BACK TO QUEEN XOTLAHA.
I DON'T NEED HER TO KNOW THESE THINGS ABOUT ME, EH?
STAY OR GO AS YOU WISH.

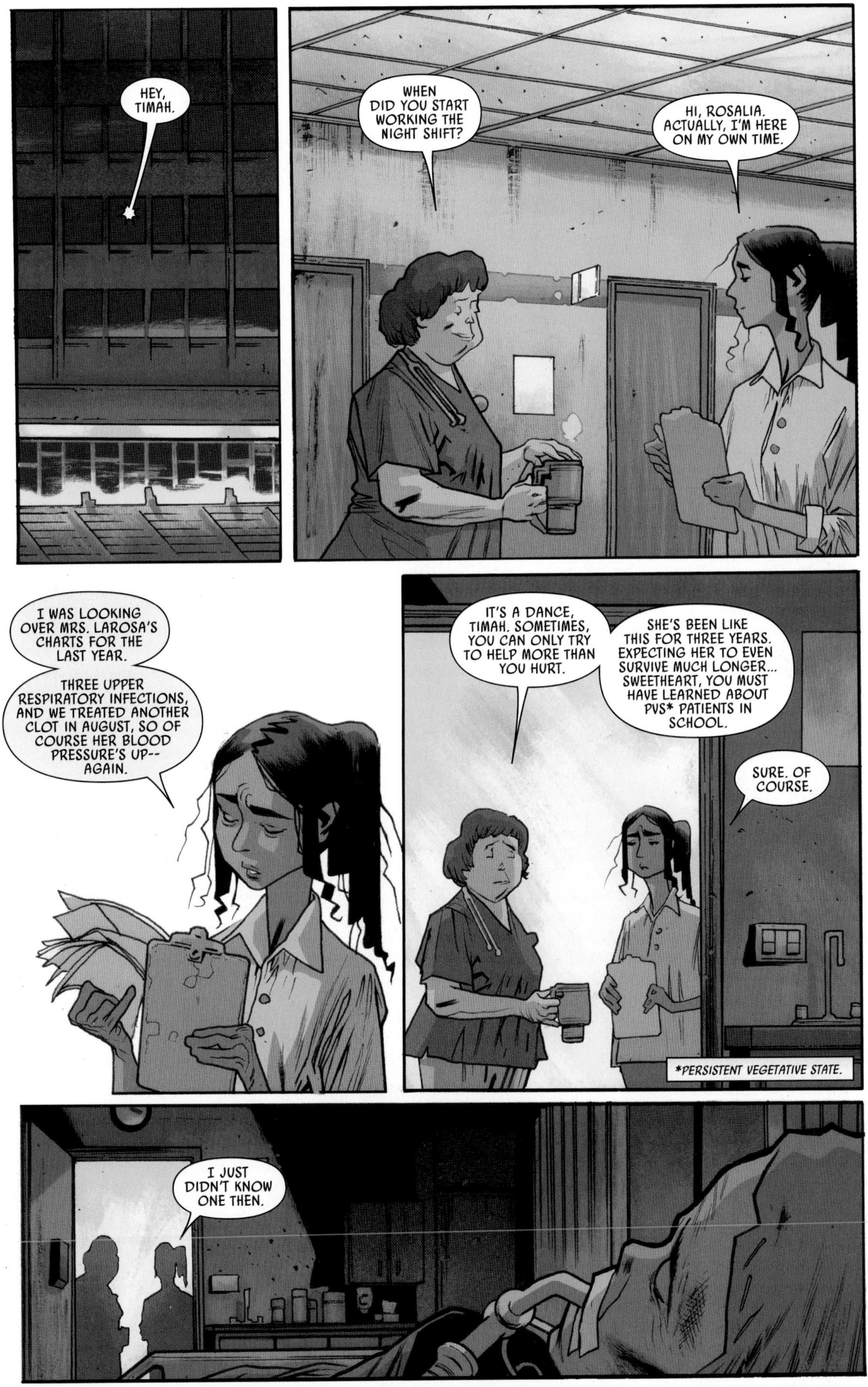
HEY, TIMAH.
WHEN DID YOU START WORKING THE NIGHT SHIFT?
HI, ROSALIA. ACTUALLY, I'M HERE ON MY OWN TIME.
I WAS LOOKING OVER MRS. LAROSA'S CHARTS FOR THE LAST YEAR.
THREE UPPER RESPIRATORY INFECTIONS, AND WE TREATED ANOTHER CLOT IN AUGUST, SO OF COURSE HER BLOOD PRESSURE'S UP-- AGAIN.
IT'S A DANCE, TIMAH. SOMETIMES, YOU CAN ONLY TRY TO HELP MORE THAN YOU HURT.
SHE'S BEEN LIKE THIS FOR THREE YEARS. EXPECTING HER TO EVEN SURVIVE MUCH LONGER... SWEETHEART, YOU MUST HAVE LEARNED ABOUT PVS* PATIENTS IN SCHOOL.
SURE. OF COURSE.
*PERSISTENT VEGETATIVE STATE.
I JUST DIDN'T KNOW ONE THEN.

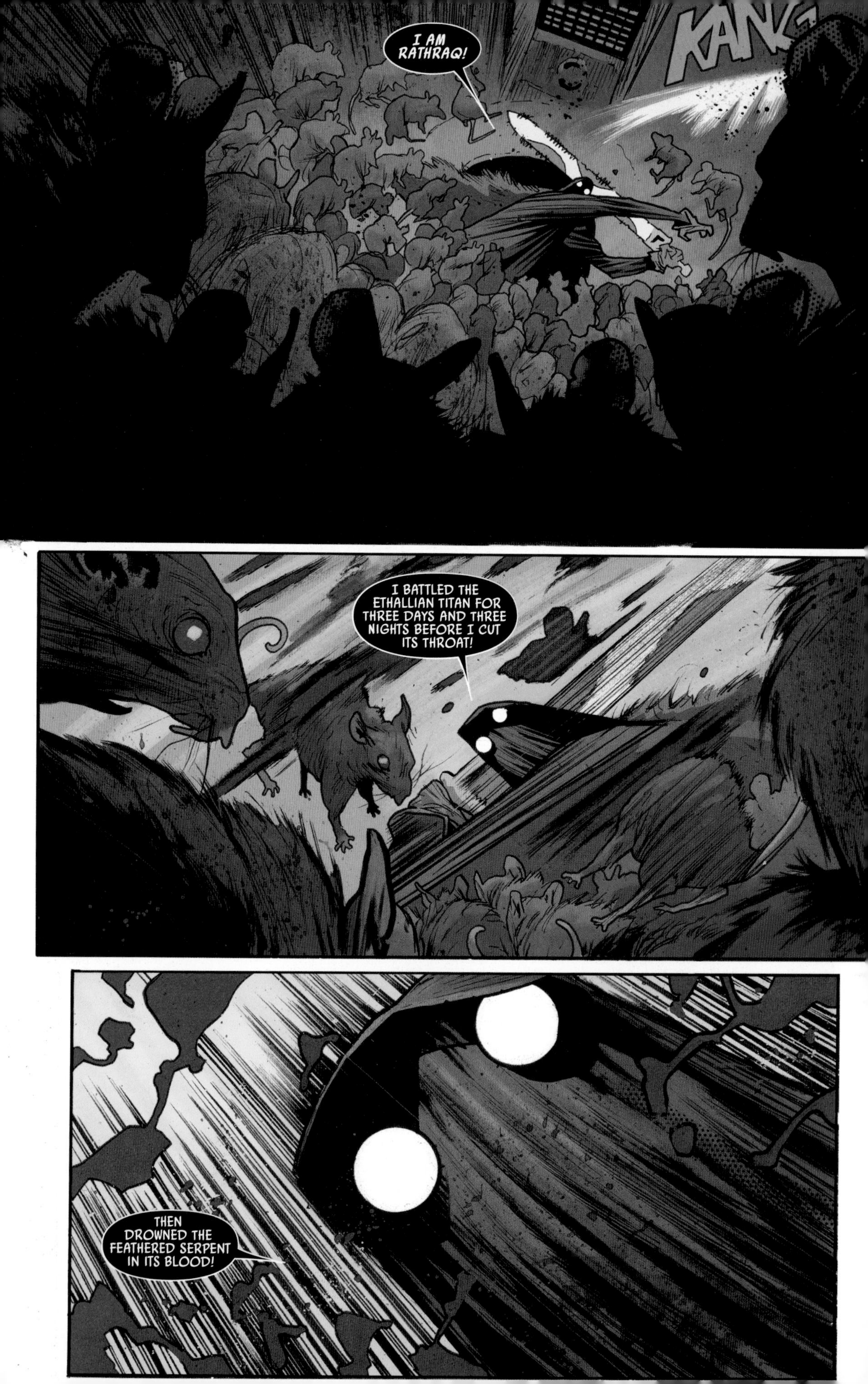
I AM RATHRAQ!
KANG
I BATTLED THE ETHALLIAN TITAN FOR THREE DAYS AND THREE NIGHTS BEFORE I CUT ITS THROAT!
THEN DROWNED THE FEATHERED SERPENT IN ITS BLOOD!

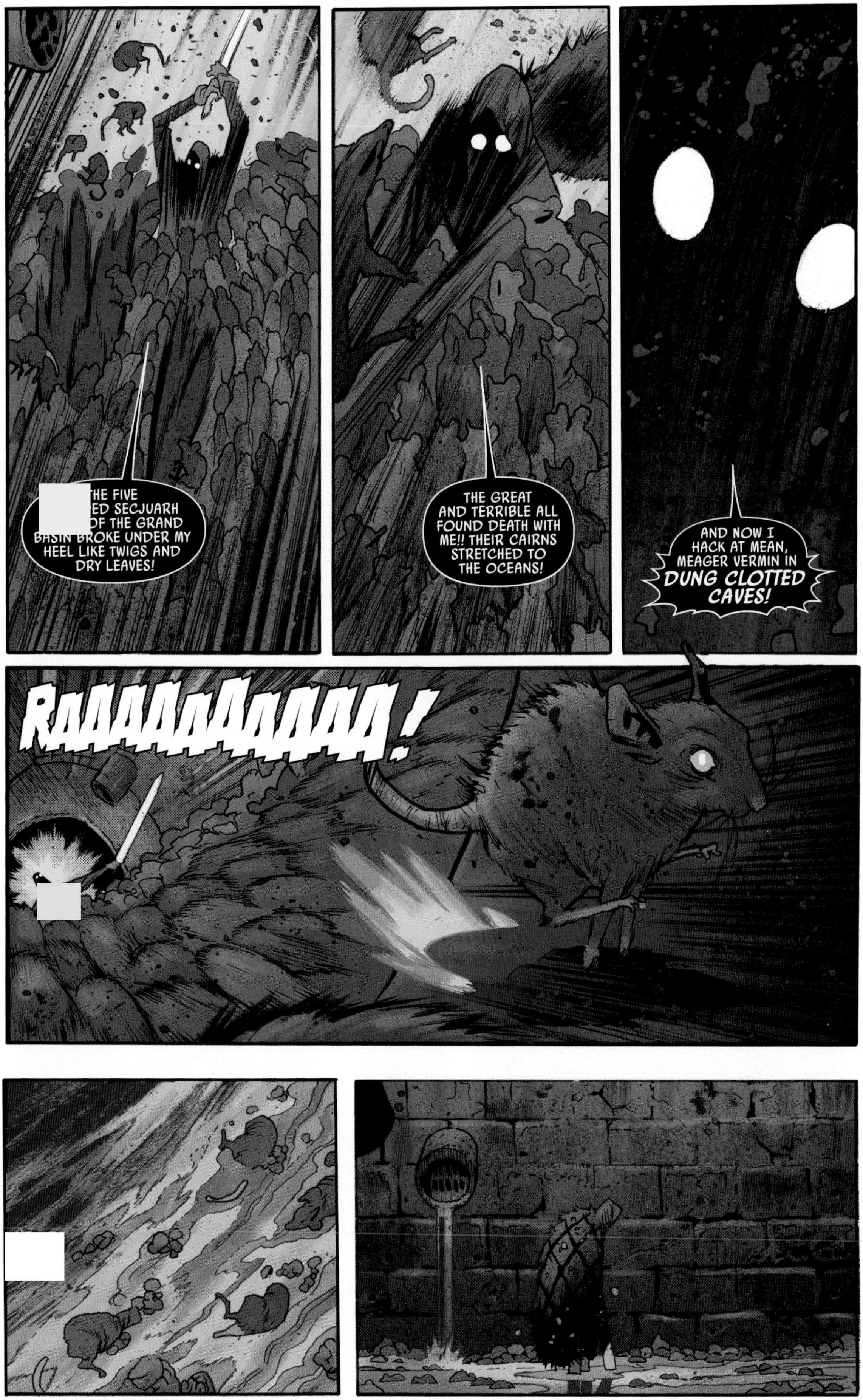
THE FIVE ED SECJUARH OF THE GRAND BASIN BROKE UNDER MY HEEL LIKE TWIGS AND DRY LEAVES!
THE GREAT AND TERRIBLE ALL FOUND DEATH WITH ME!! THEIR CAIRNS STRETCHED TO THE OCEANS!
AND NOW I HACK AT MEAN, MEAGER VERMIN IN DUNG CLOTTED CAVES!
RAAAAAAAAAA!

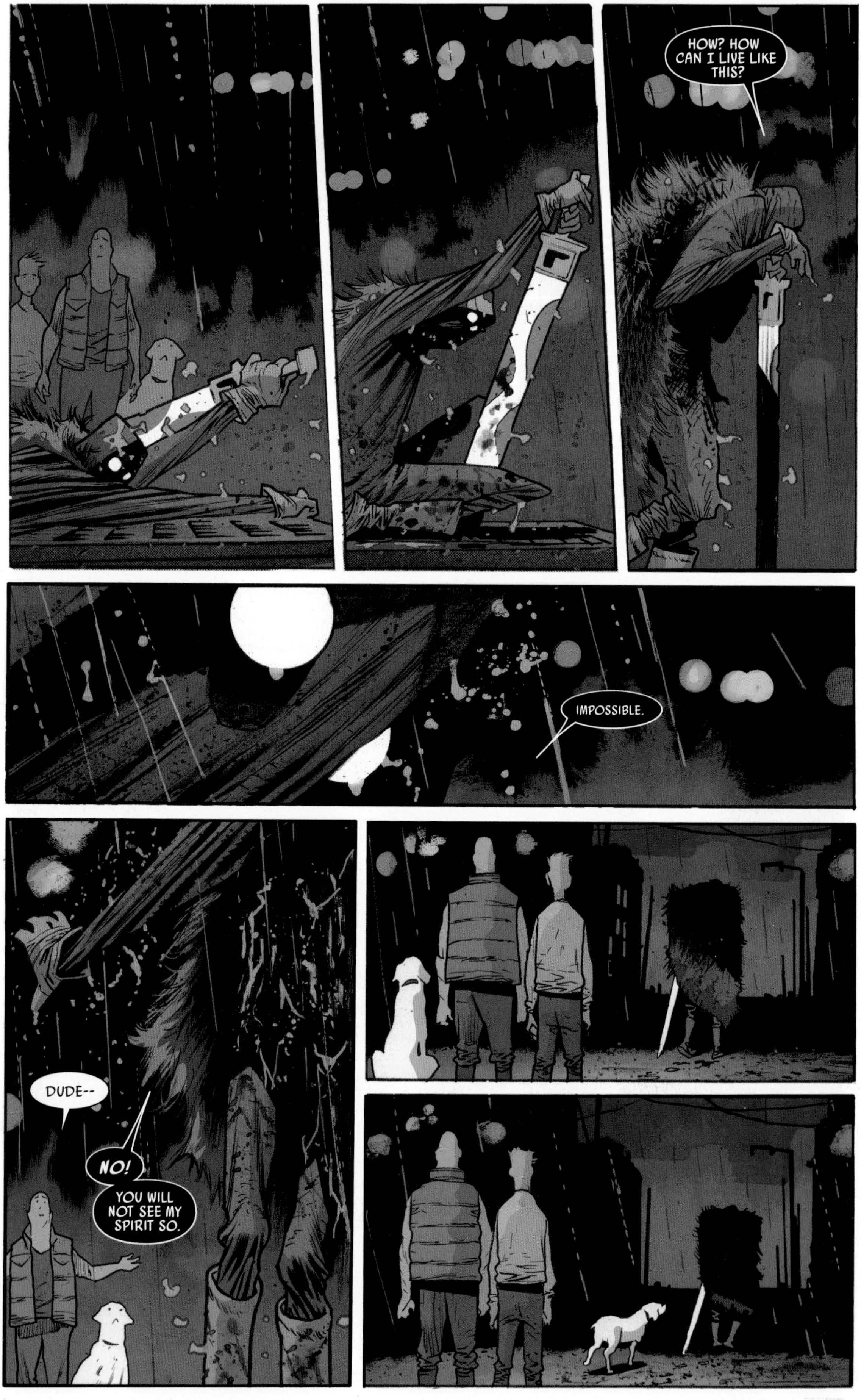
HOW? HOW CAN I LIVE LIKE THIS?
IMPOSSIBLE.
DUDE--
NO!
YOU WILL NOT SEE MY SPIRIT SO.

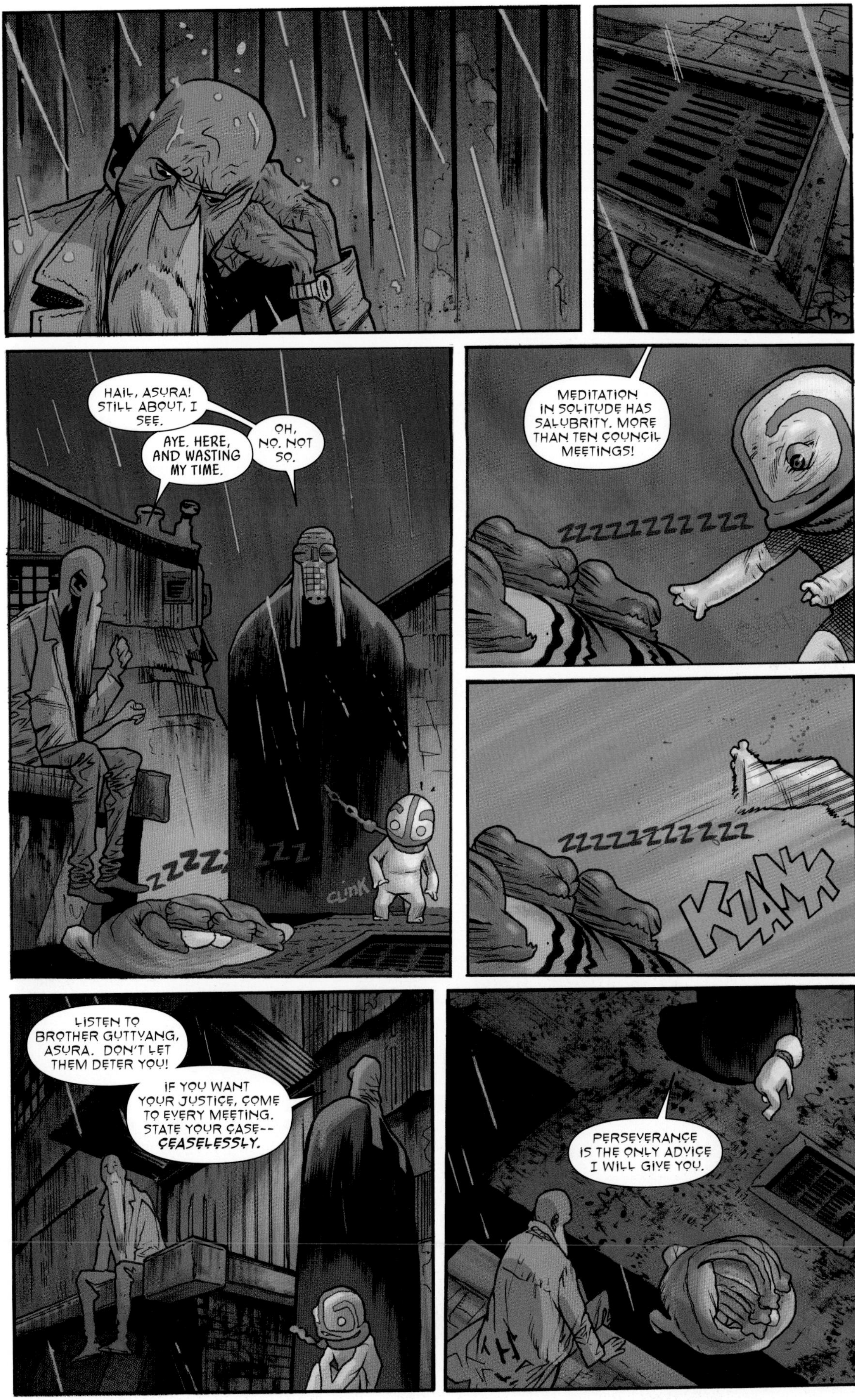

HAIL, ASURA! STILL ABOUT, I SEE.
AYE. HERE, AND WASTING MY TIME.
OH, NO. NOT SO.
ZZZZZ
ZZZ
CLINK
MEDITATION IN SOLITUDE HAS SALUBRITY. MORE THAN TEN COUNCIL MEETINGS!
ZZZZZZZZZZZZ
ZZZZZZZZZZZZ
KLANK
LISTEN TO BROTHER GUTTYANG, ASURA. DON'T LET THEM DETER YOU!
IF YOU WANT YOUR JUSTICE, COME TO EVERY MEETING. STATE YOUR CASE-- CEASELESSLY.
PERSEVERANCE IS THE ONLY ADVICE I WILL GIVE YOU.

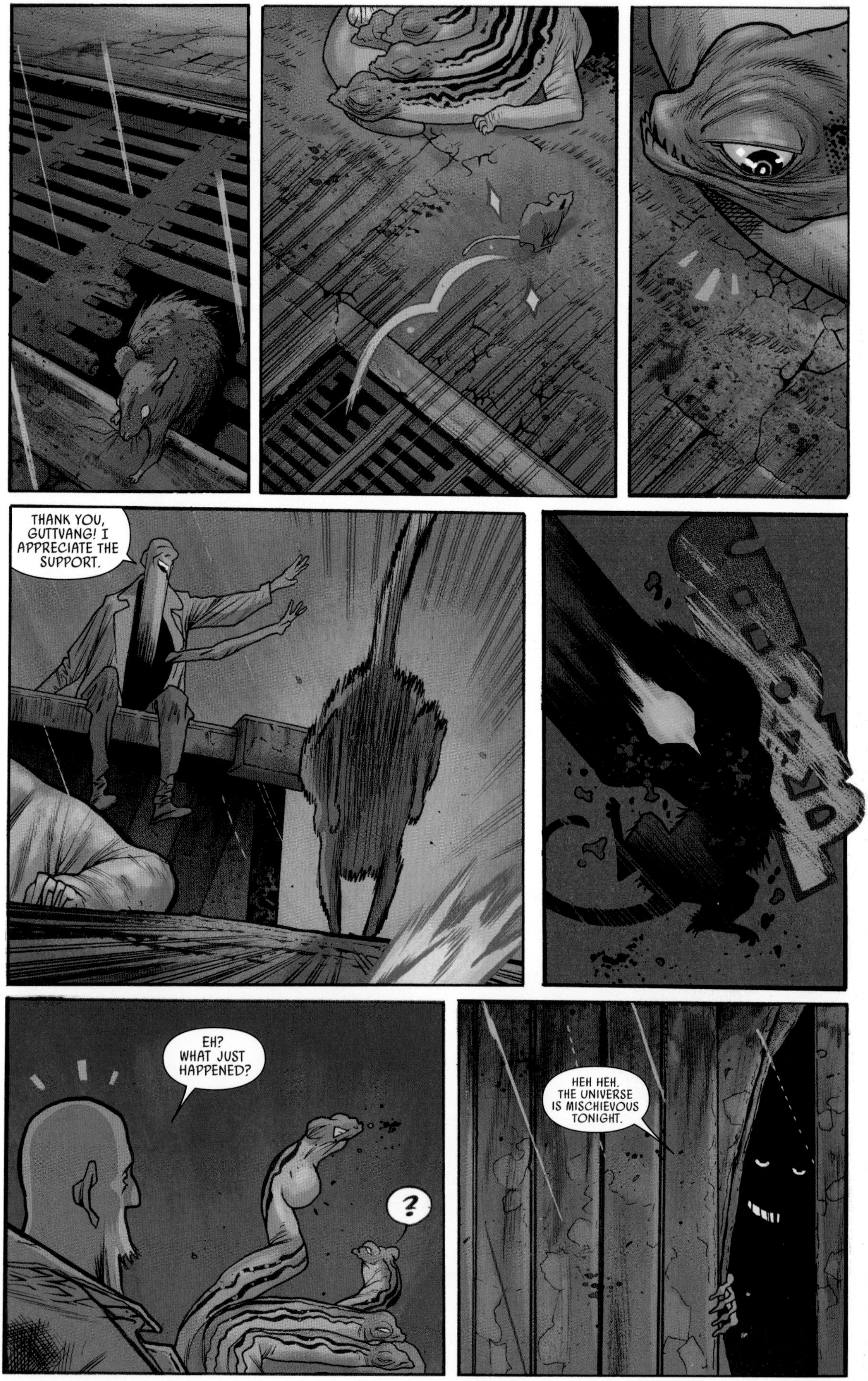
THANK YOU, GUTTVANG! I APPRECIATE THE SUPPORT.
EH? WHAT JUST HAPPENED?
?
HEH HEH. THE UNIVERSE IS MISCHIEVOUS TONIGHT.

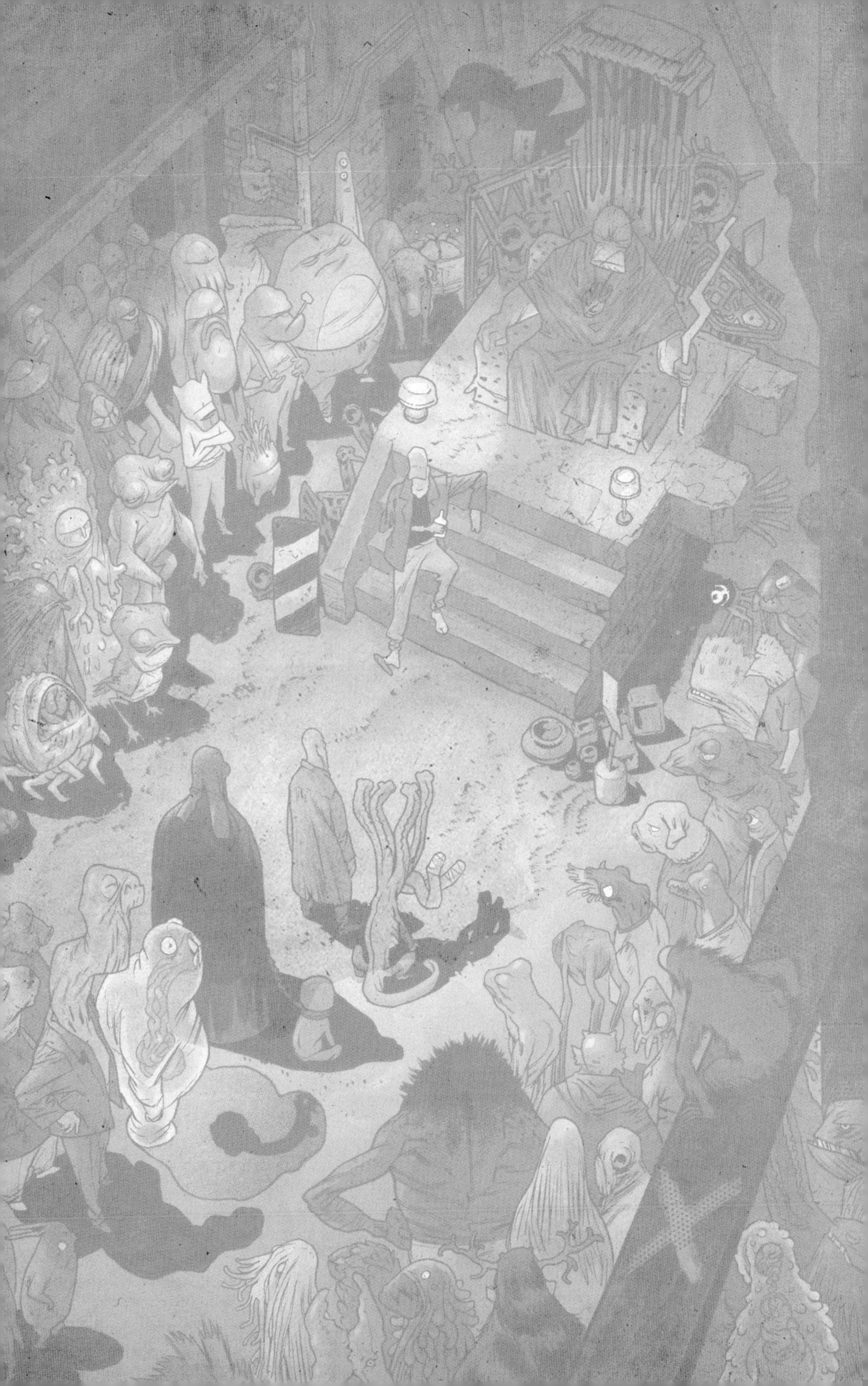

# [redacted]HAPTER THR[redacted]

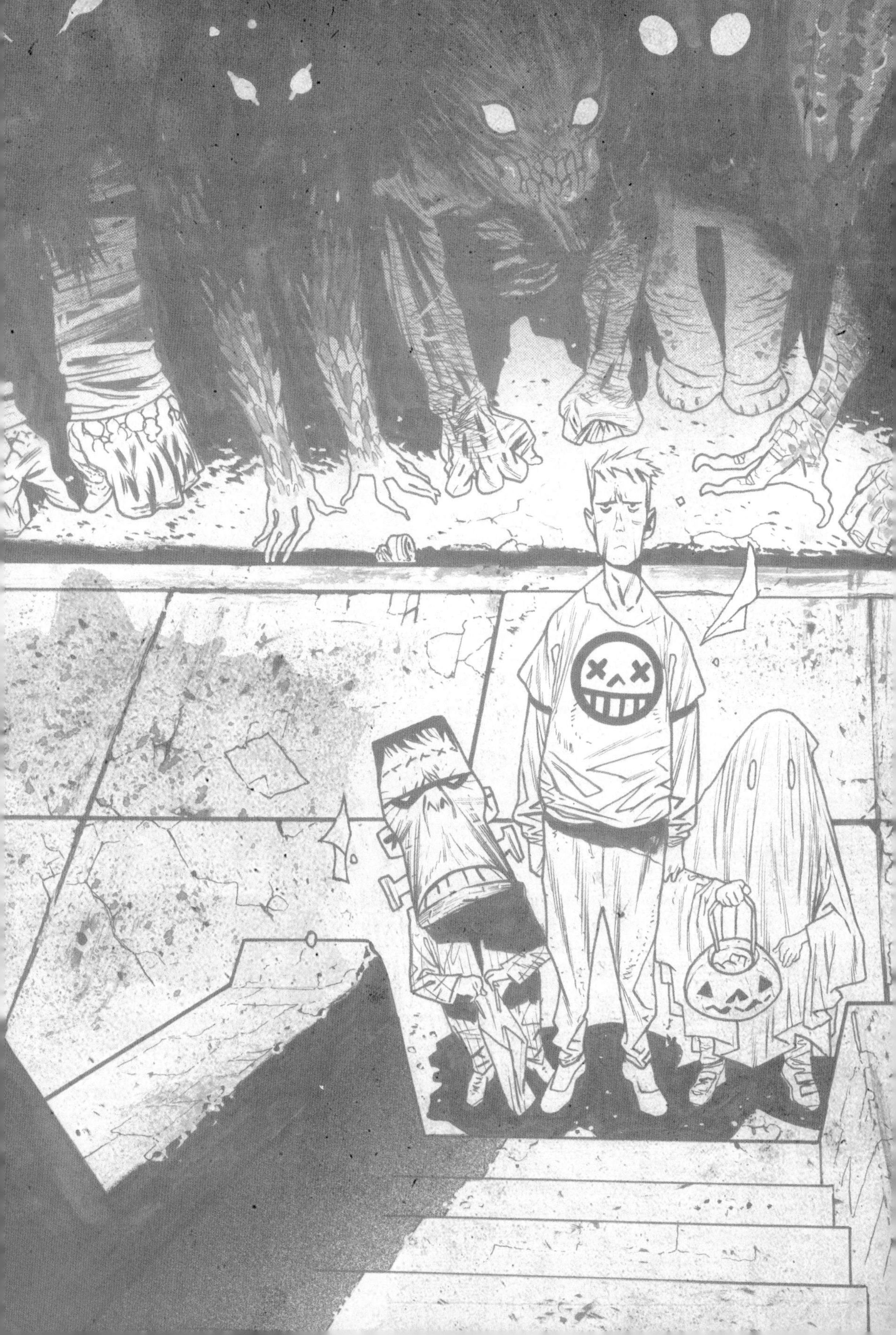

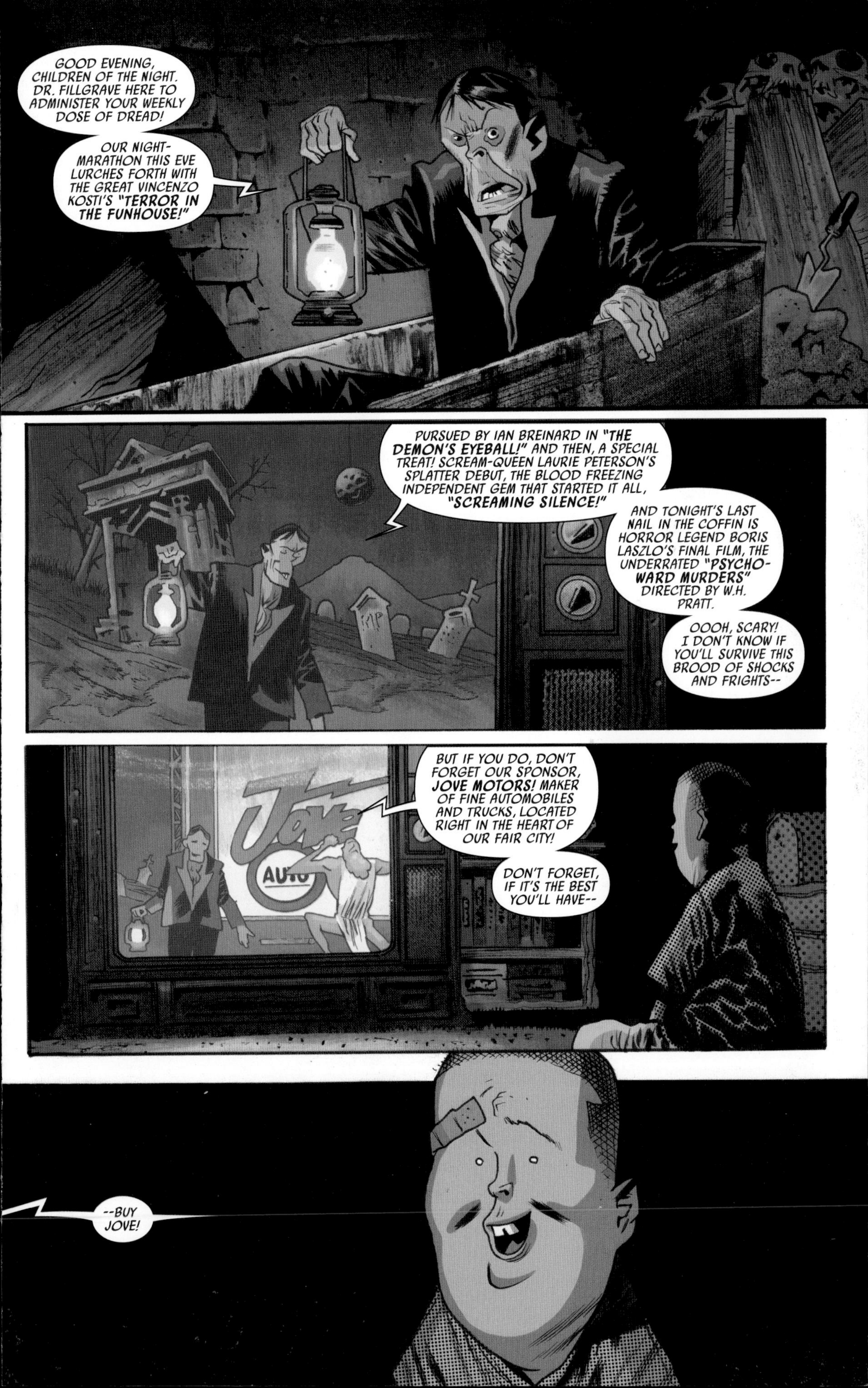
GOOD EVENING, CHILDREN OF THE NIGHT. DR. FILLGRAVE HERE TO ADMINISTER YOUR WEEKLY DOSE OF DREAD!
OUR NIGHT-MARATHON THIS EVE LURCHES FORTH WITH THE GREAT VINCENZO KOSTI'S "TERROR IN THE FUNHOUSE!"
PURSUED BY IAN BREINARD IN "THE DEMON'S EYEBALL!" AND THEN, A SPECIAL TREAT! SCREAM-QUEEN LAURIE PETERSON'S SPLATTER DEBUT, THE BLOOD FREEZING INDEPENDENT GEM THAT STARTED IT ALL, "SCREAMING SILENCE!"
AND TONIGHT'S LAST NAIL IN THE COFFIN IS HORROR LEGEND BORIS LASZLO'S FINAL FILM, THE UNDERRATED "PSYCHO-WARD MURDERS" DIRECTED BY W.H. PRATT.
OOOH, SCARY! I DON'T KNOW IF YOU'LL SURVIVE THIS BROOD OF SHOCKS AND FRIGHTS--
BUT IF YOU DO, DON'T FORGET OUR SPONSOR, JOVE MOTORS! MAKER OF FINE AUTOMOBILES AND TRUCKS, LOCATED RIGHT IN THE HEART OF OUR FAIR CITY!
DON'T FORGET, IF IT'S THE BEST YOU'LL HAVE--
--BUY JOVE!

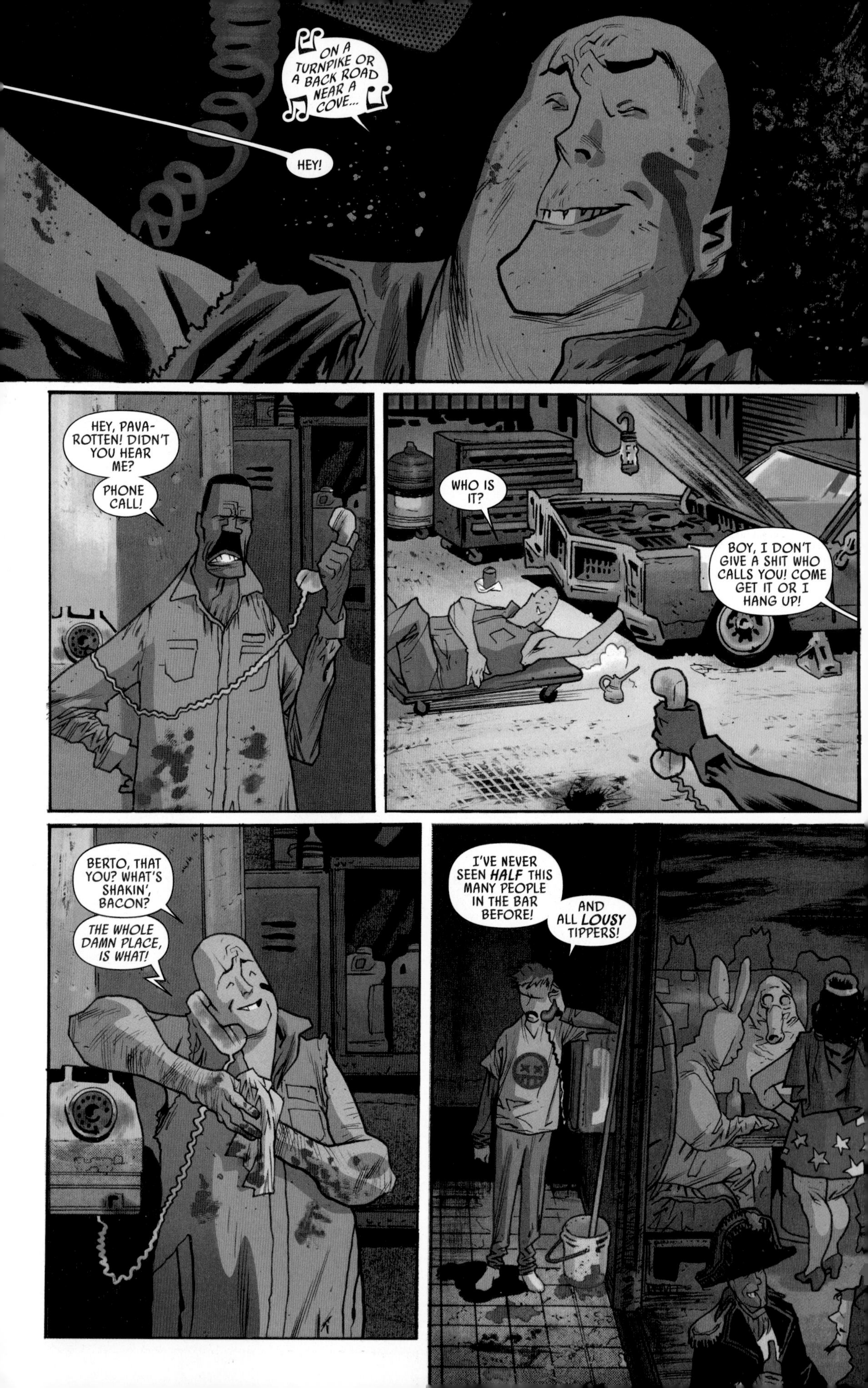
ON A TURNPIKE OR A BACK ROAD NEAR A COVE...
HEY!
HEY, PAVA-ROTTEN! DIDN'T YOU HEAR ME?
PHONE CALL!
WHO IS IT?
BOY, I DON'T GIVE A SHIT WHO CALLS YOU! COME GET IT OR I HANG UP!
BERTO, THAT YOU? WHAT'S SHAKIN', BACON?
THE WHOLE DAMN PLACE, IS WHAT!
I'VE NEVER SEEN HALF THIS MANY PEOPLE IN THE BAR BEFORE!
AND ALL LOUSY TIPPERS!

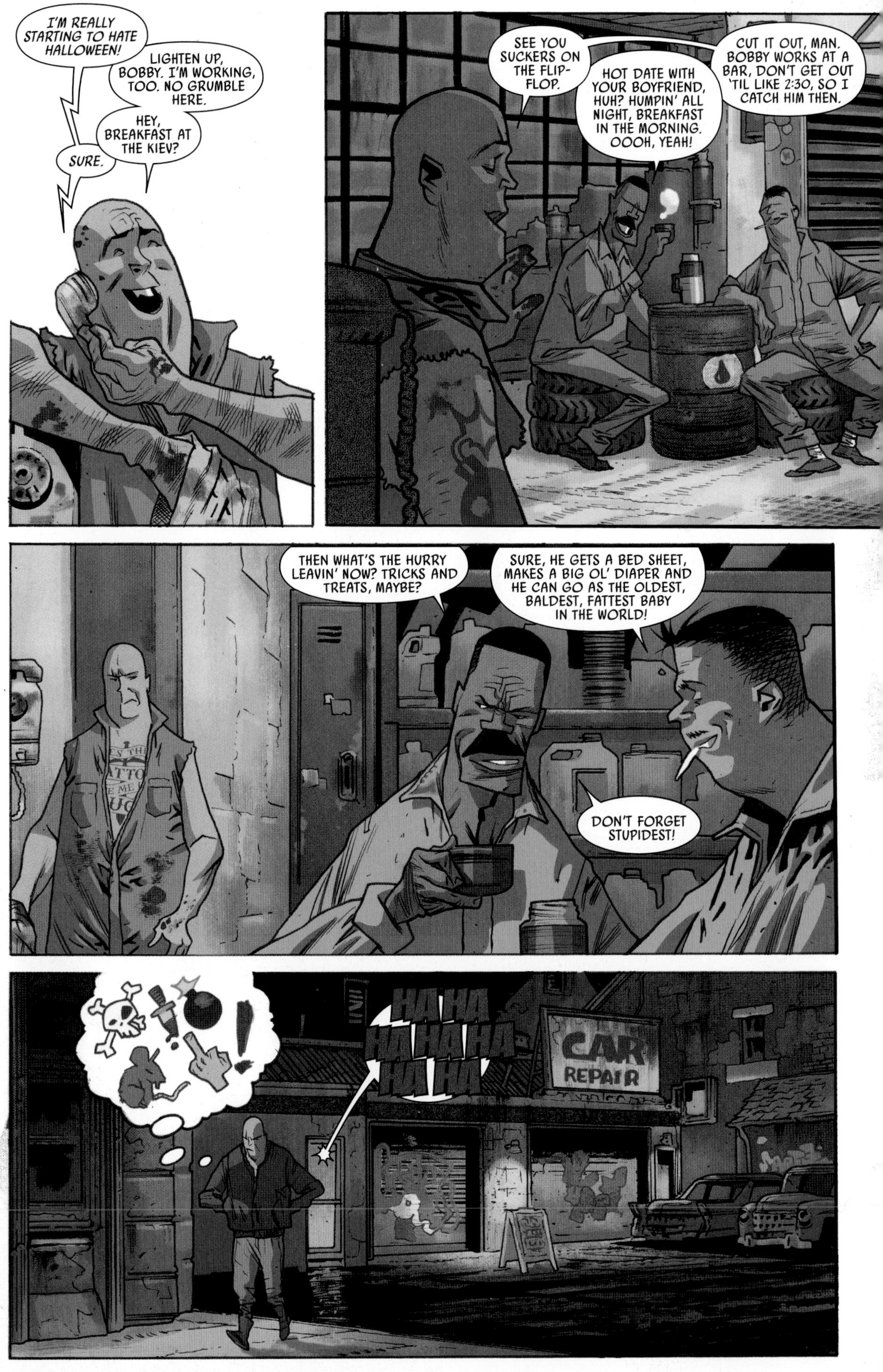
I'M REALLY STARTING TO HATE HALLOWEEN!
LIGHTEN UP, BOBBY. I'M WORKING, TOO. NO GRUMBLE HERE.
HEY, BREAKFAST AT THE KIEV?
SURE.
SEE YOU SUCKERS ON THE FLIP-FLOP.
HOT DATE WITH YOUR BOYFRIEND, HUH? HUMPIN' ALL NIGHT, BREAKFAST IN THE MORNING. OOOH, YEAH!
CUT IT OUT, MAN. BOBBY WORKS AT A BAR, DON'T GET OUT 'TIL LIKE 2:30, SO I CATCH HIM THEN.
THEN WHAT'S THE HURRY LEAVIN' NOW? TRICKS AND TREATS, MAYBE?
SURE, HE GETS A BED SHEET, MAKES A BIG OL' DIAPER AND HE CAN GO AS THE OLDEST, BALDEST, FATTEST BABY IN THE WORLD!
DON'T FORGET STUPIDEST!
HA HA HA HA HA HA HA
CAR REPAIR

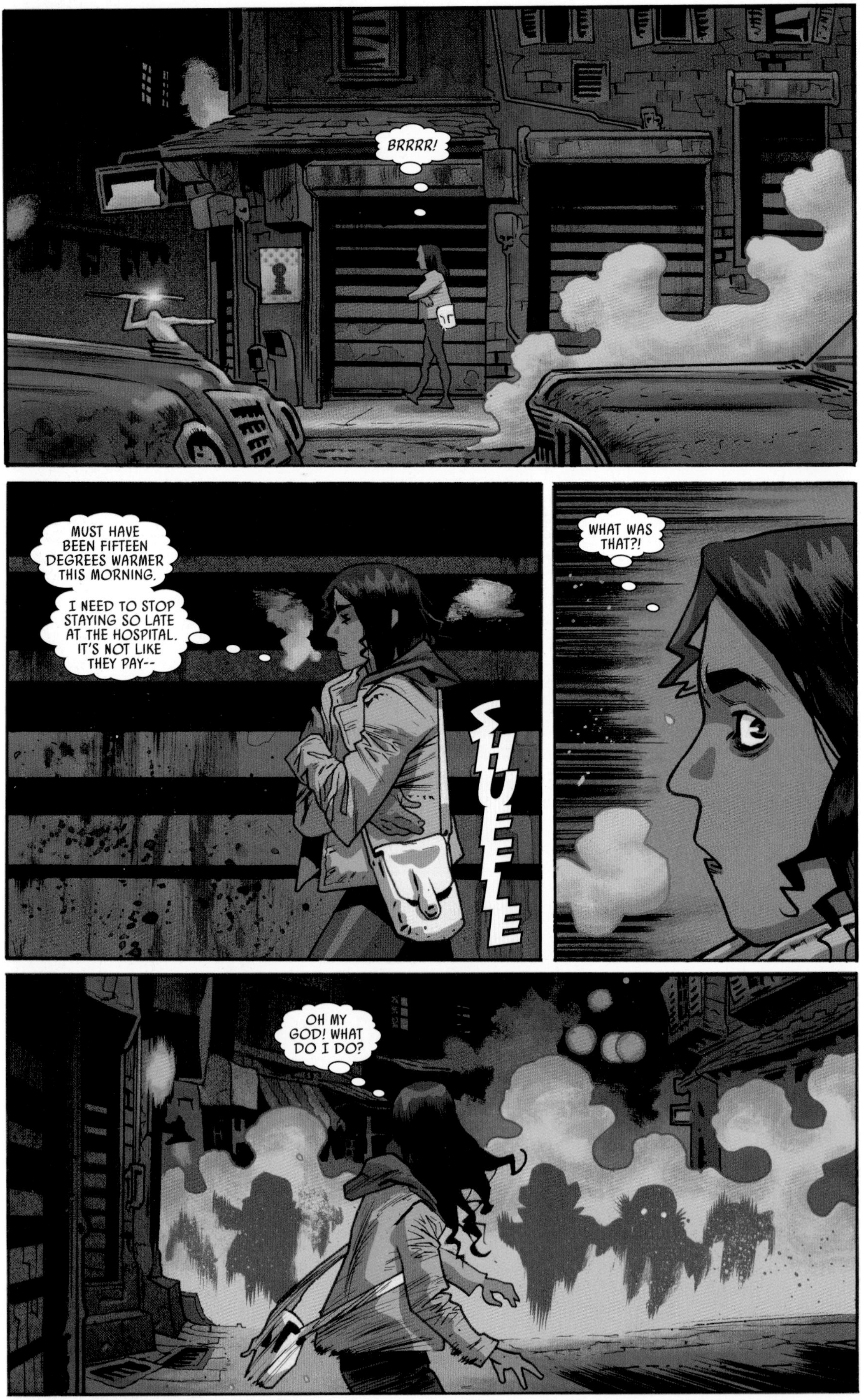
BRRRR!
MUST HAVE BEEN FIFTEEN DEGREES WARMER THIS MORNING.
I NEED TO STOP STAYING SO LATE AT THE HOSPITAL. IT'S NOT LIKE THEY PAY--
SHUFFLE
WHAT WAS THAT?!
OH MY GOD! WHAT DO I DO?

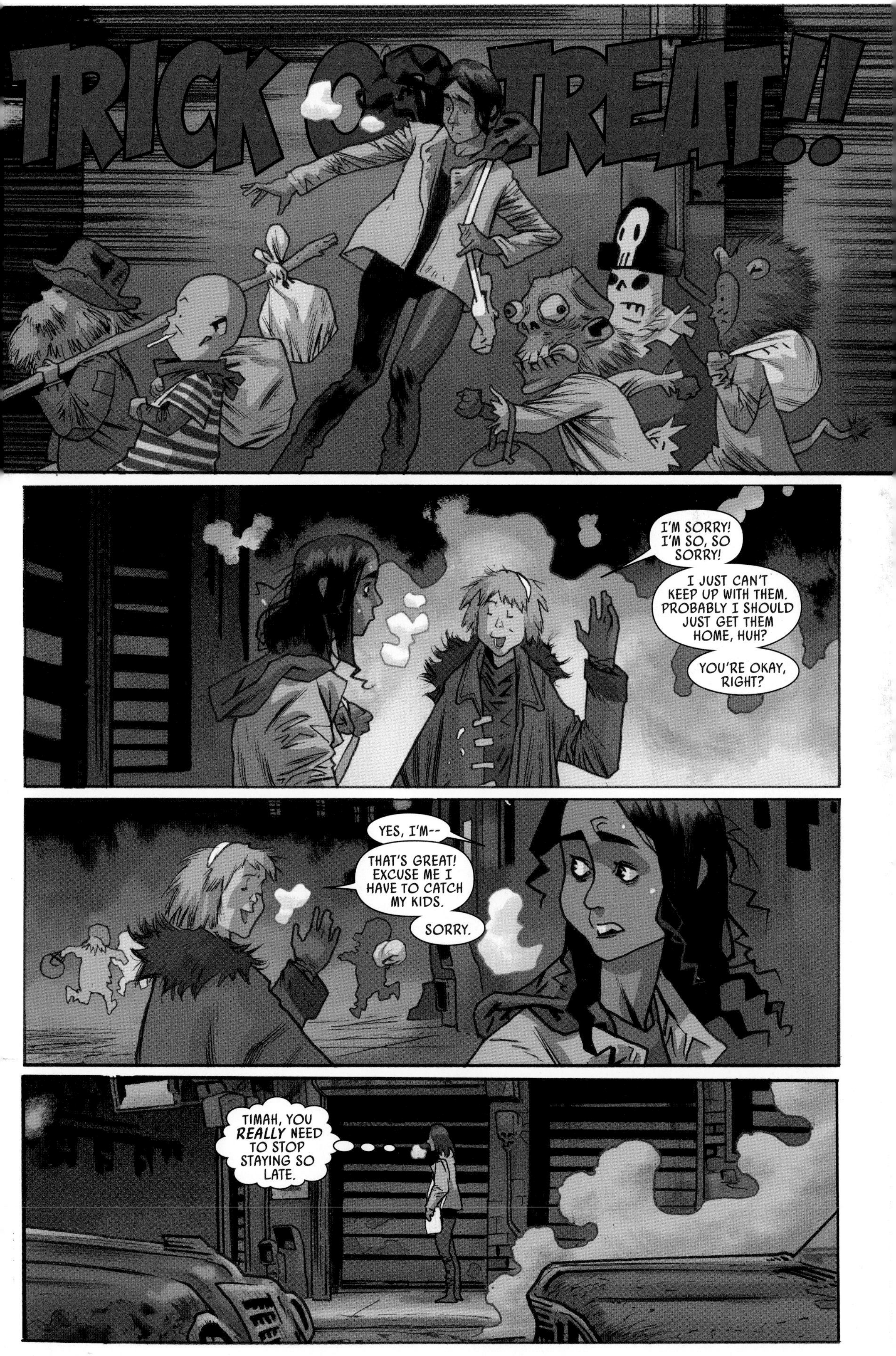
TRICK OR TREAT!!
I'M SORRY! I'M SO, SO SORRY!
I JUST CAN'T KEEP UP WITH THEM. PROBABLY I SHOULD JUST GET THEM HOME, HUH?
YOU'RE OKAY, RIGHT?
YES, I'M--
THAT'S GREAT! EXCUSE ME I HAVE TO CATCH MY KIDS.
SORRY.
TIMAH, YOU *REALLY* NEED TO STOP STAYING SO LATE.

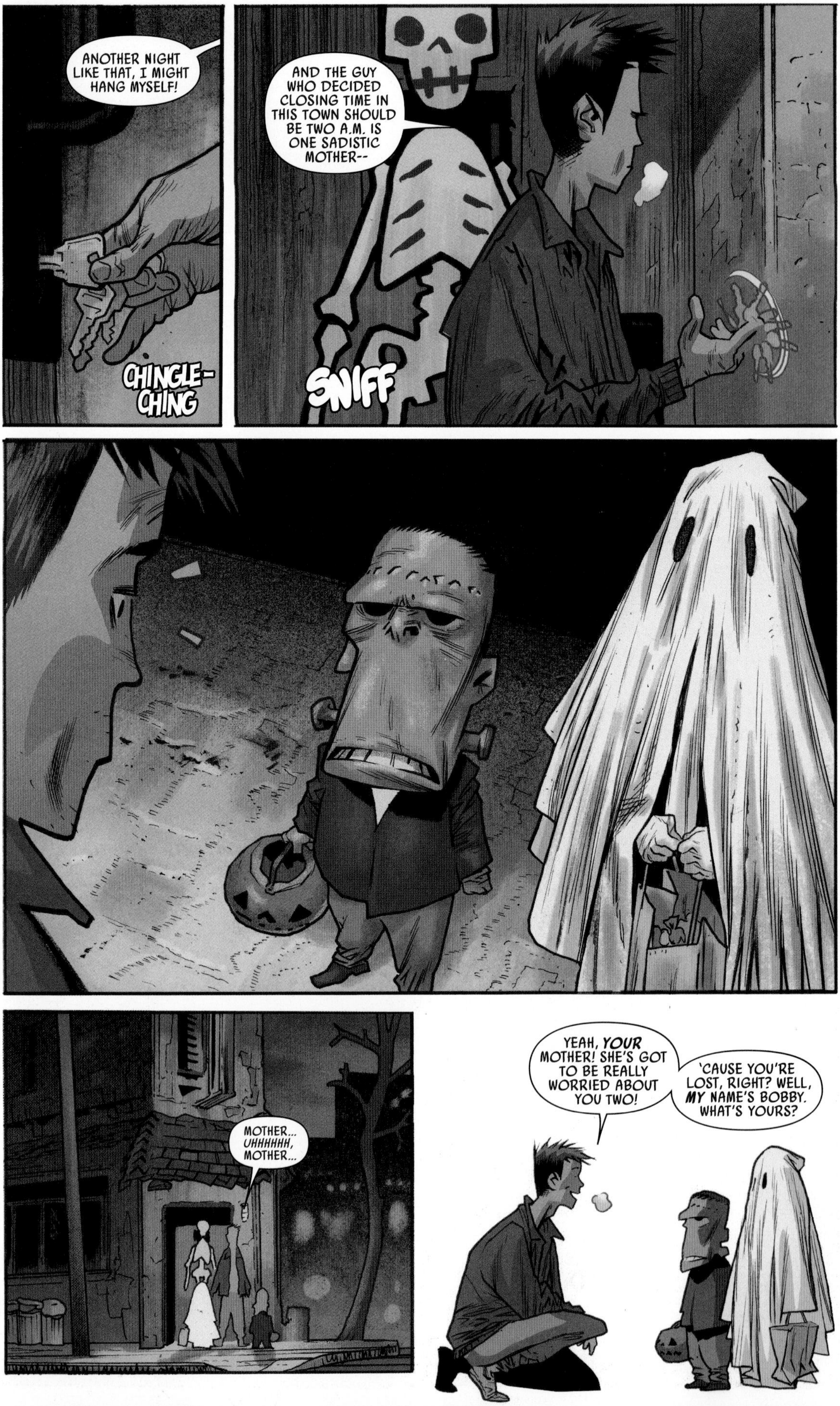
ANOTHER NIGHT LIKE THAT, I MIGHT HANG MYSELF!
CHINGLE-CHING
AND THE GUY WHO DECIDED CLOSING TIME IN THIS TOWN SHOULD BE TWO A.M. IS ONE SADISTIC MOTHER--
SNIFF
MOTHER... UHHHHHH, MOTHER...
YEAH, *YOUR* MOTHER! SHE'S GOT TO BE REALLY WORRIED ABOUT YOU TWO!
'CAUSE YOU'RE LOST, RIGHT? WELL, *MY* NAME'S BOBBY. WHAT'S YOURS?

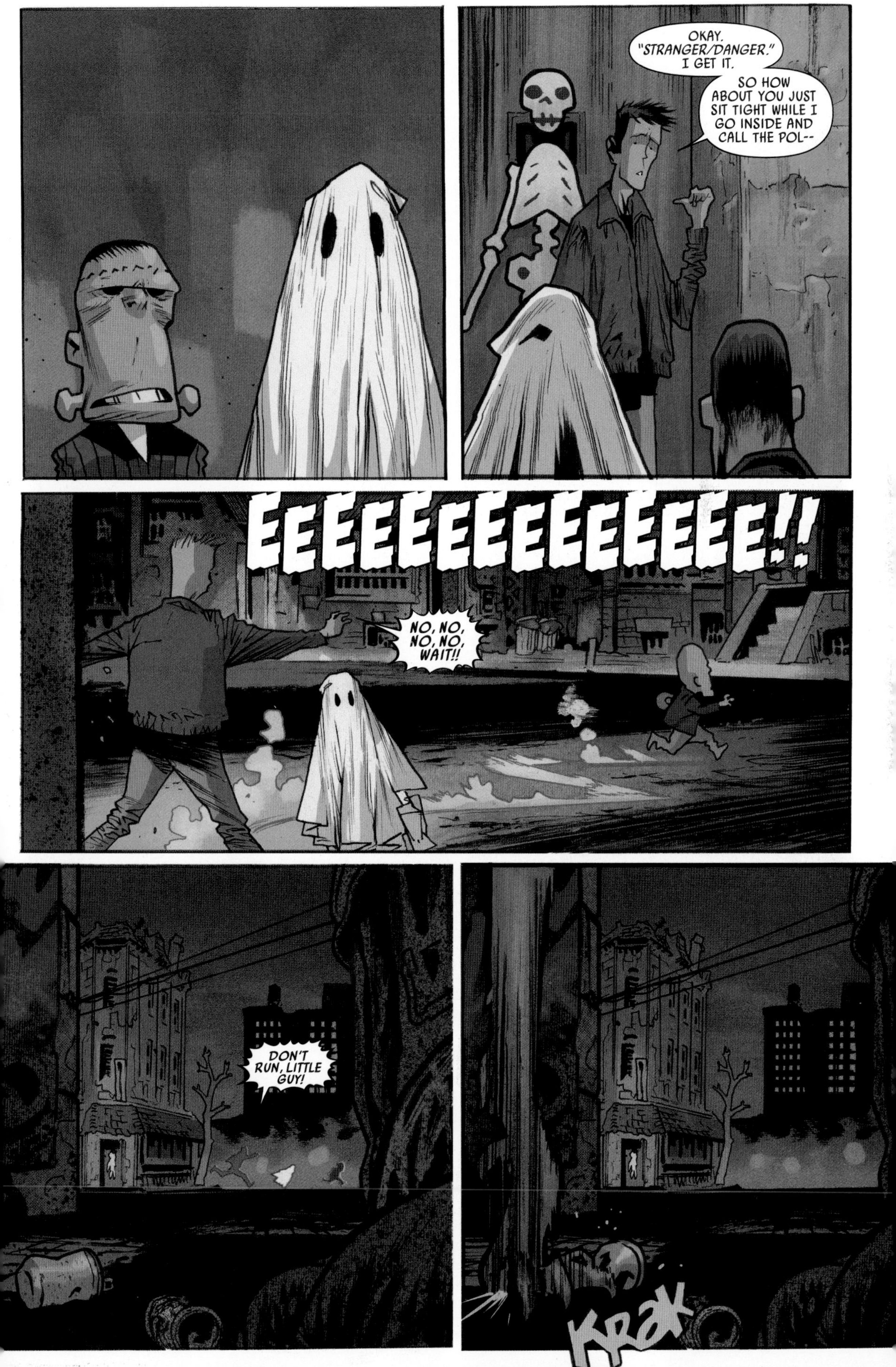
OKAY. "STRANGER/DANGER." I GET IT.
SO HOW ABOUT YOU JUST SIT TIGHT WHILE I GO INSIDE AND CALL THE POL--
EEEEEEEEEEEEEE!!
NO, NO, NO, NO, WAIT!!
DON'T RUN, LITTLE GUY!
KRAK

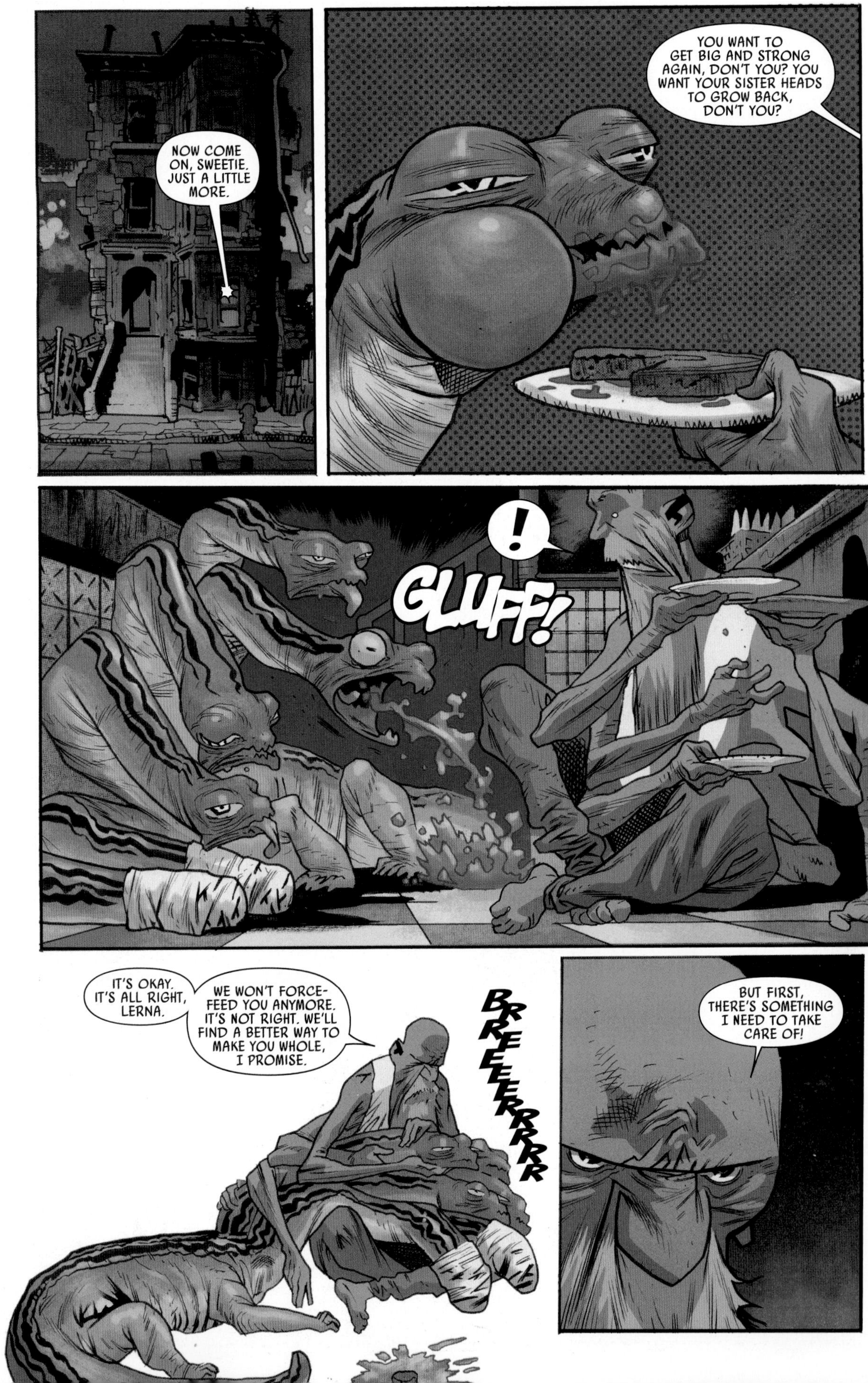
NOW COME ON, SWEETIE. JUST A LITTLE MORE.
YOU WANT TO GET BIG AND STRONG AGAIN, DON'T YOU? YOU WANT YOUR SISTER HEADS TO GROW BACK, DON'T YOU?
!
GLUFF!
IT'S OKAY. IT'S ALL RIGHT, LERNA.
WE WON'T FORCE-FEED YOU ANYMORE. IT'S NOT RIGHT. WE'LL FIND A BETTER WAY TO MAKE YOU WHOLE, I PROMISE.
BRREEEERRRRR
BUT FIRST, THERE'S SOMETHING I NEED TO TAKE CARE OF!

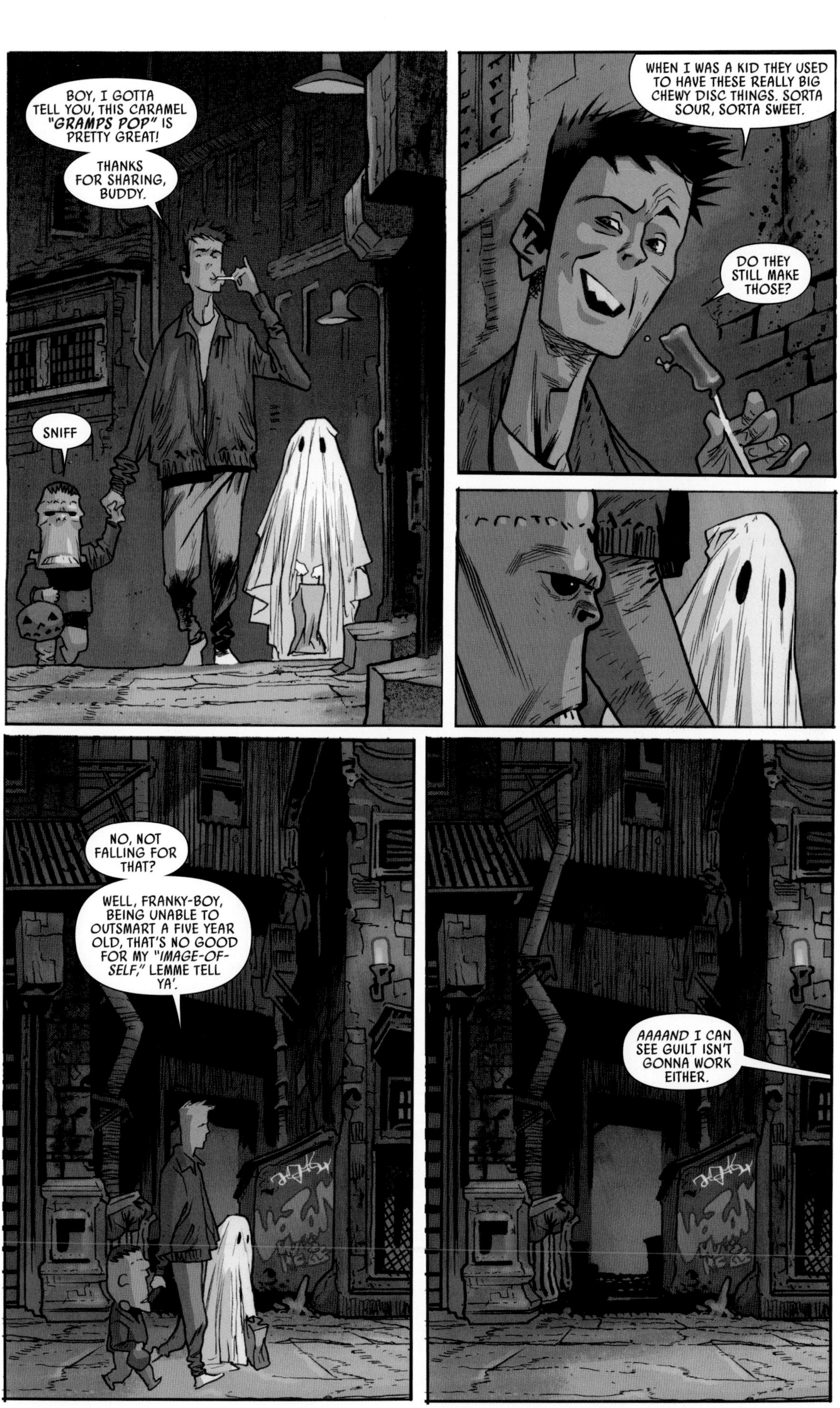
BOY, I GOTTA TELL YOU, THIS CARAMEL "GRAMPS POP" IS PRETTY GREAT!
THANKS FOR SHARING, BUDDY.
SNIFF
WHEN I WAS A KID THEY USED TO HAVE THESE REALLY BIG CHEWY DISC THINGS. SORTA SOUR, SORTA SWEET.
DO THEY STILL MAKE THOSE?
NO, NOT FALLING FOR THAT?
WELL, FRANKY-BOY, BEING UNABLE TO OUTSMART A FIVE YEAR OLD, THAT'S NO GOOD FOR MY "IMAGE-OF-SELF," LEMME TELL YA'.
AAAAND I CAN SEE GUILT ISN'T GONNA WORK EITHER.

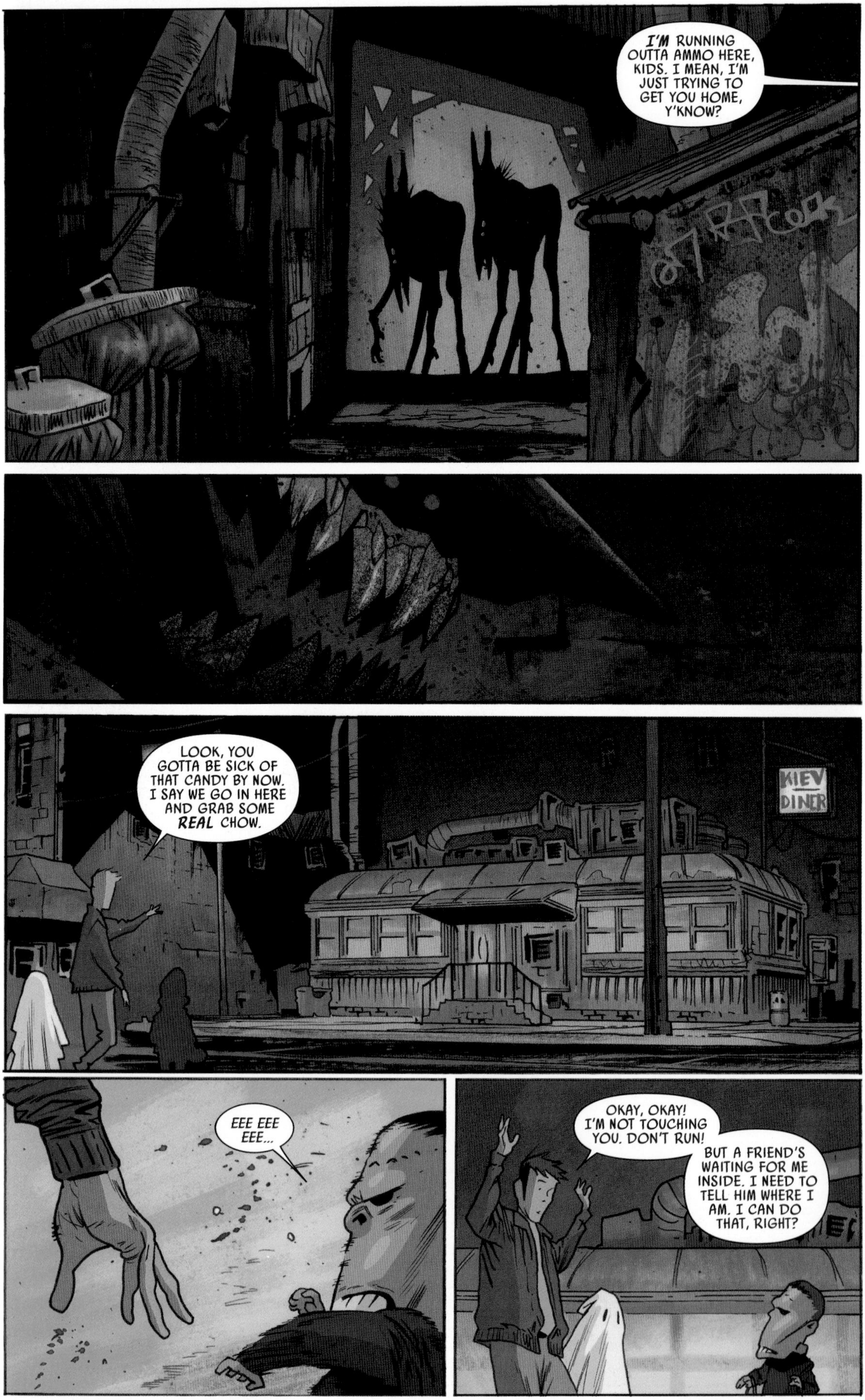
I'M RUNNING OUTTA AMMO HERE, KIDS. I MEAN, I'M JUST TRYING TO GET YOU HOME, Y'KNOW?
LOOK, YOU GOTTA BE SICK OF THAT CANDY BY NOW. I SAY WE GO IN HERE AND GRAB SOME REAL CHOW.
KIEV DINER
EEE EEE EEE...
OKAY, OKAY! I'M NOT TOUCHING YOU. DON'T RUN!
BUT A FRIEND'S WAITING FOR ME INSIDE. I NEED TO TELL HIM WHERE I AM. I CAN DO THAT, RIGHT?

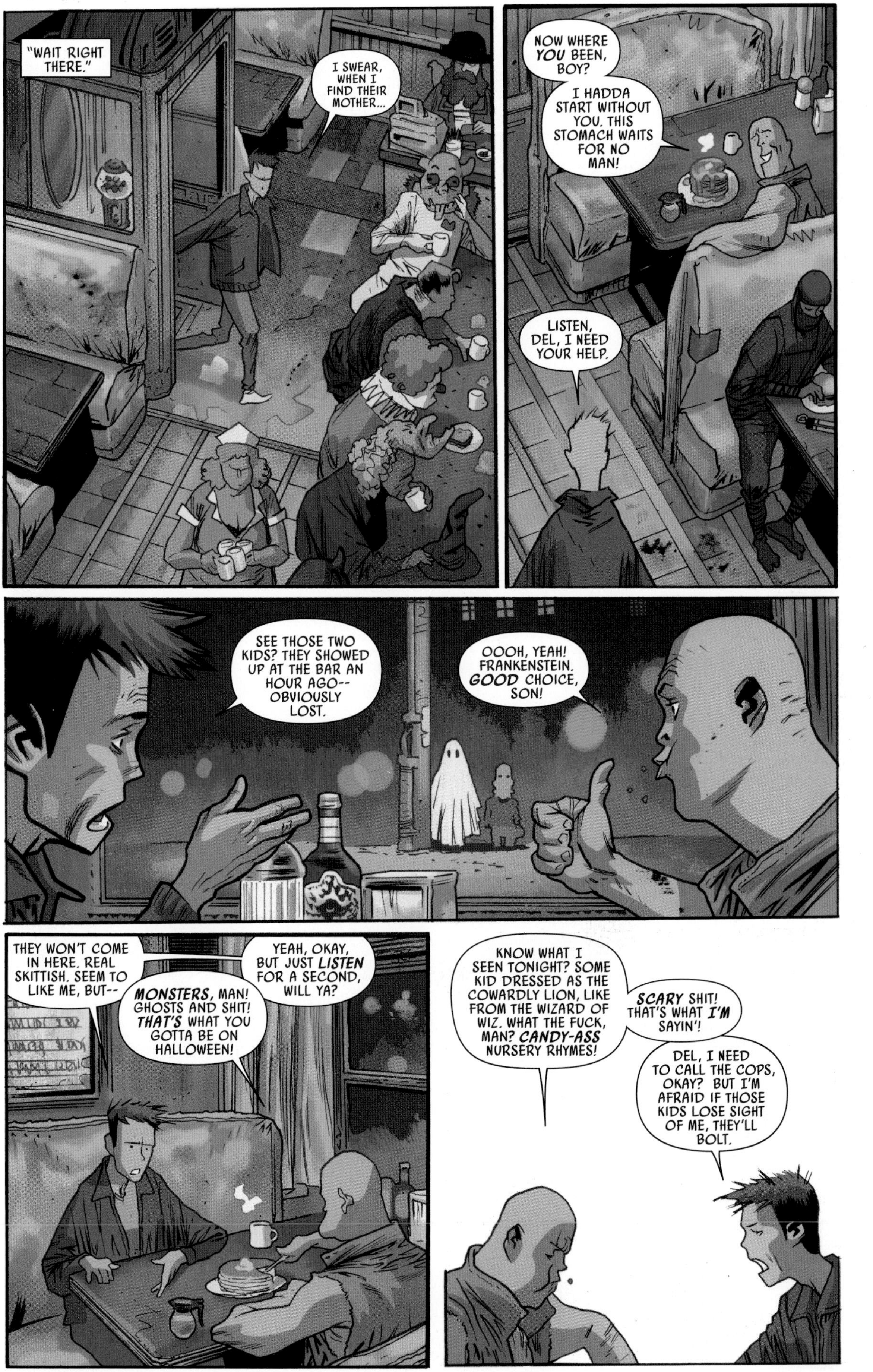
"WAIT RIGHT THERE."
I SWEAR, WHEN I FIND THEIR MOTHER...
NOW WHERE *YOU* BEEN, BOY?
I HADDA START WITHOUT YOU. THIS STOMACH WAITS FOR NO MAN!
LISTEN, DEL, I NEED YOUR HELP.
SEE THOSE TWO KIDS? THEY SHOWED UP AT THE BAR AN HOUR AGO-- OBVIOUSLY LOST.
OOOH, YEAH! FRANKENSTEIN. ***GOOD*** CHOICE, SON!
THEY WON'T COME IN HERE. REAL SKITTISH. SEEM TO LIKE ME, BUT--
***MONSTERS,*** MAN! GHOSTS AND SHIT! ***THAT'S*** WHAT YOU GOTTA BE ON HALLOWEEN!
YEAH, OKAY, BUT JUST ***LISTEN*** FOR A SECOND, WILL YA?
KNOW WHAT I SEEN TONIGHT? SOME KID DRESSED AS THE COWARDLY LION, LIKE FROM THE WIZARD OF WIZ. WHAT THE FUCK, MAN? ***CANDY-ASS*** NURSERY RHYMES!
***SCARY*** SHIT! THAT'S WHAT ***I'M*** SAYIN'!
DEL, I NEED TO CALL THE COPS, OKAY? BUT I'M AFRAID IF THOSE KIDS LOSE SIGHT OF ME, THEY'LL BOLT.

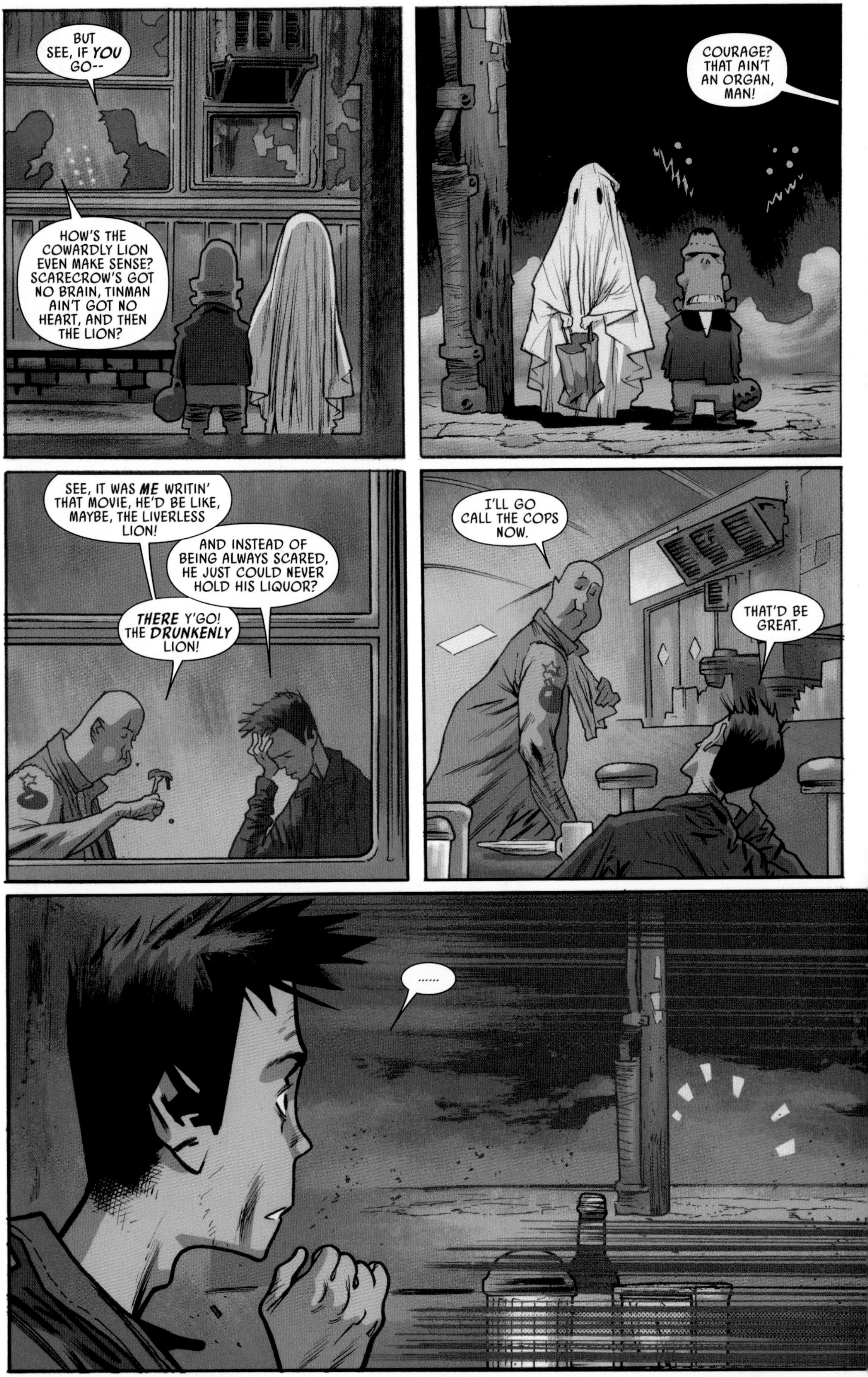
BUT SEE, IF YOU GO--
HOW'S THE COWARDLY LION EVEN MAKE SENSE? SCARECROW'S GOT NO BRAIN, TINMAN AIN'T GOT NO HEART, AND THEN THE LION?
COURAGE? THAT AIN'T AN ORGAN, MAN!
SEE, IT WAS ME WRITIN' THAT MOVIE, HE'D BE LIKE, MAYBE, THE LIVERLESS LION!
AND INSTEAD OF BEING ALWAYS SCARED, HE JUST COULD NEVER HOLD HIS LIQUOR?
THERE Y'GO! THE DRUNKENLY LION!
I'LL GO CALL THE COPS NOW.
THAT'D BE GREAT.
......

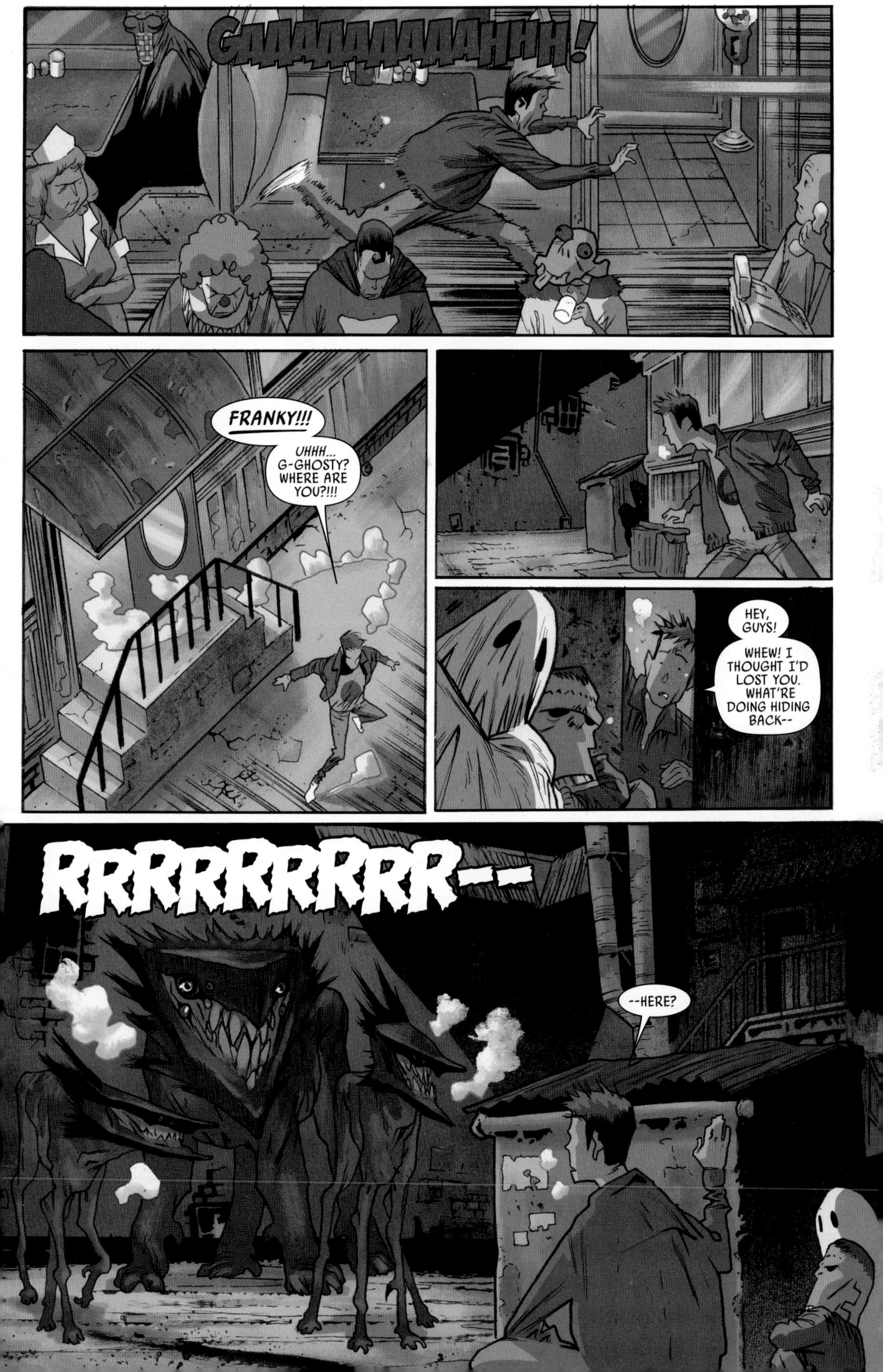
GAAAAAAAAAHHH!
FRANKY!!!
UHHH... G-GHOSTY? WHERE ARE YOU?!!!
HEY, GUYS!
WHEW! I THOUGHT I'D LOST YOU. WHAT'RE DOING HIDING BACK--
RRRRRRRRRR--
--HERE?

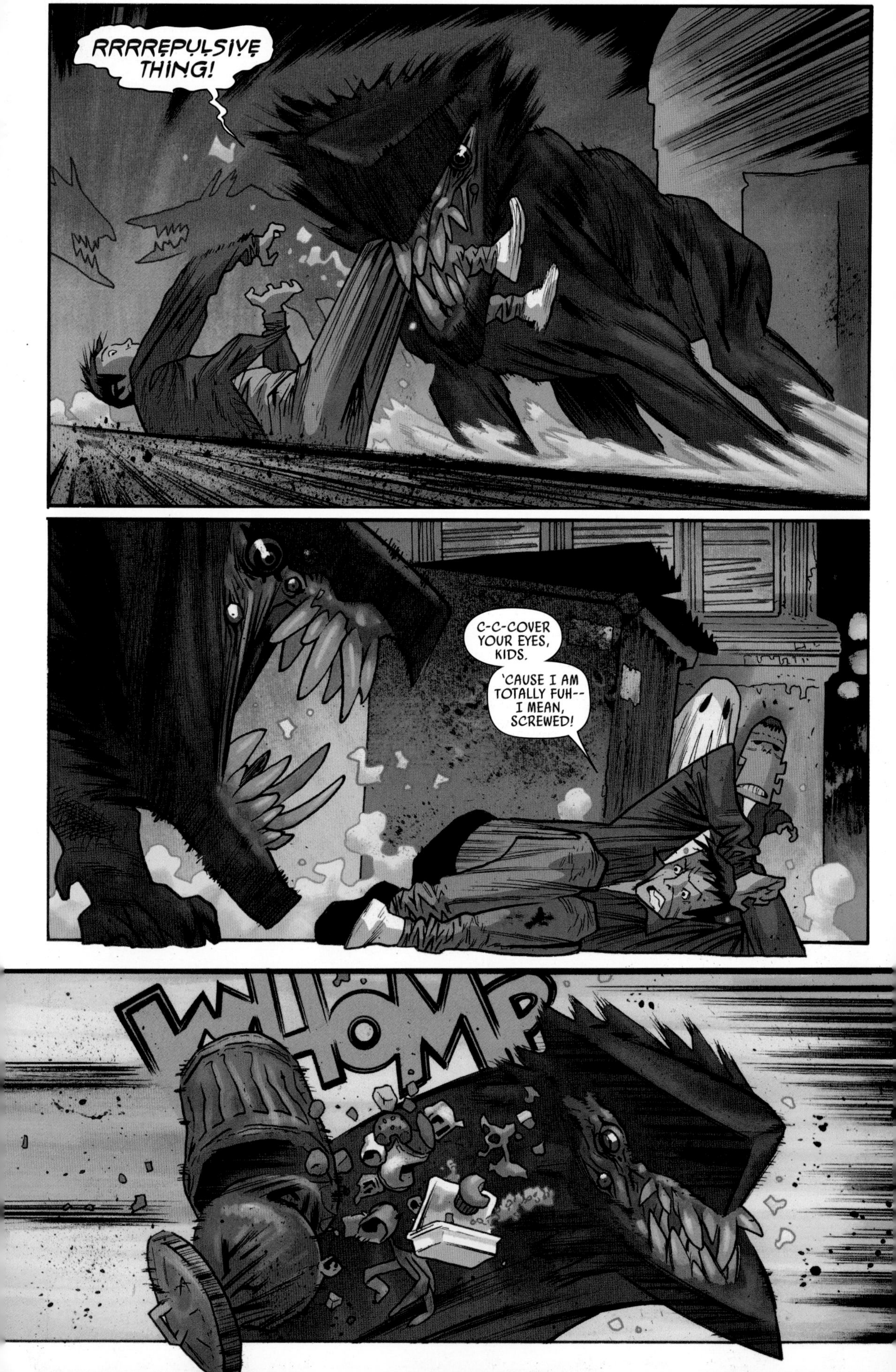
RRRREPULSIVE THING!
C-C-COVER YOUR EYES, KIDS.
'CAUSE I AM TOTALLY FUH-- I MEAN, SCREWED!
WHOMP!

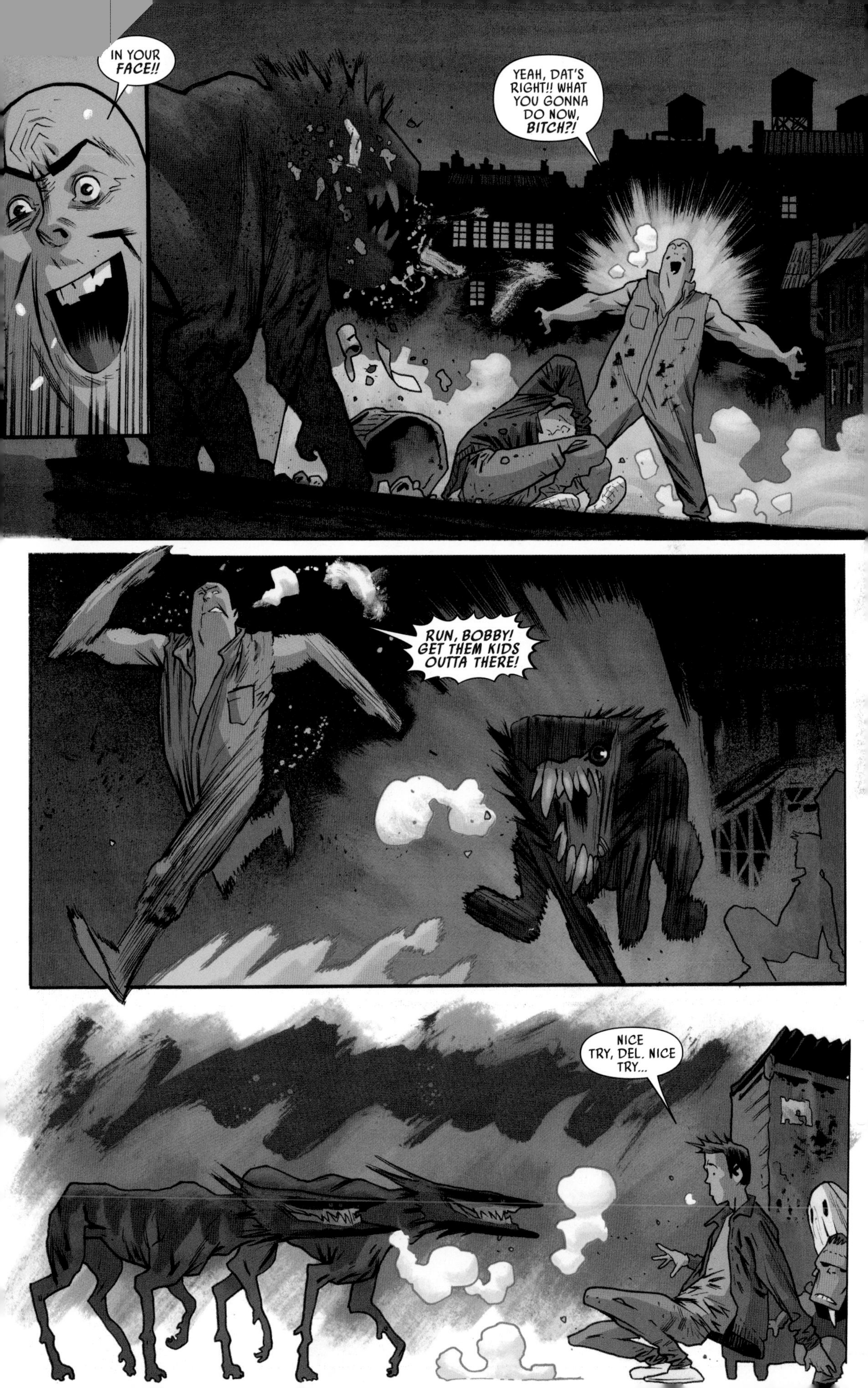

IN YOUR FACE!!
YEAH, DAT'S RIGHT!! WHAT YOU GONNA DO NOW, BITCH?!
RUN, BOBBY! GET THEM KIDS OUTTA THERE!
NICE TRY, DEL. NICE TRY...

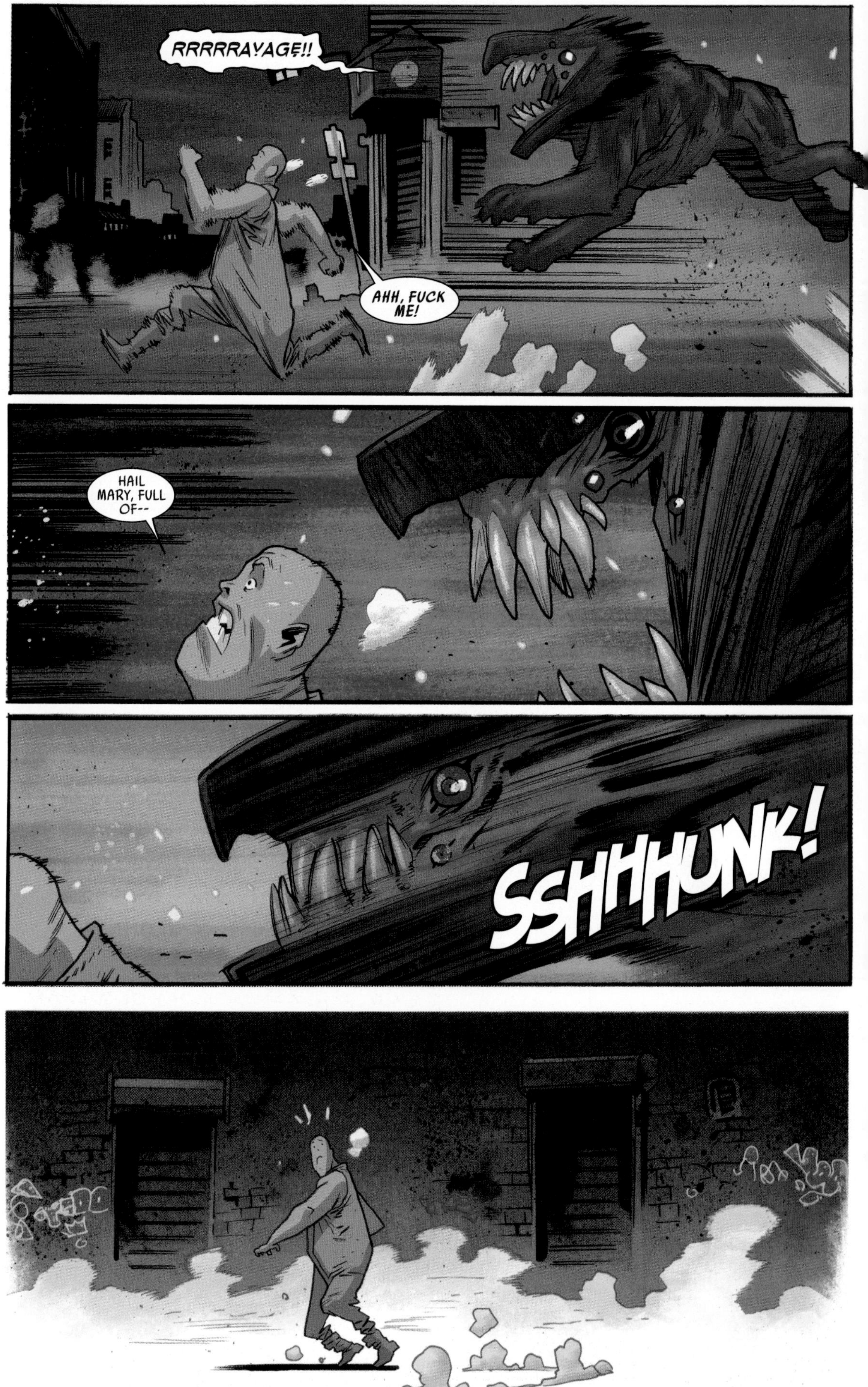
RRRRRAVAGE!!
AHH, FUCK ME!
HAIL MARY, FULL OF--
SSHHHUNK!

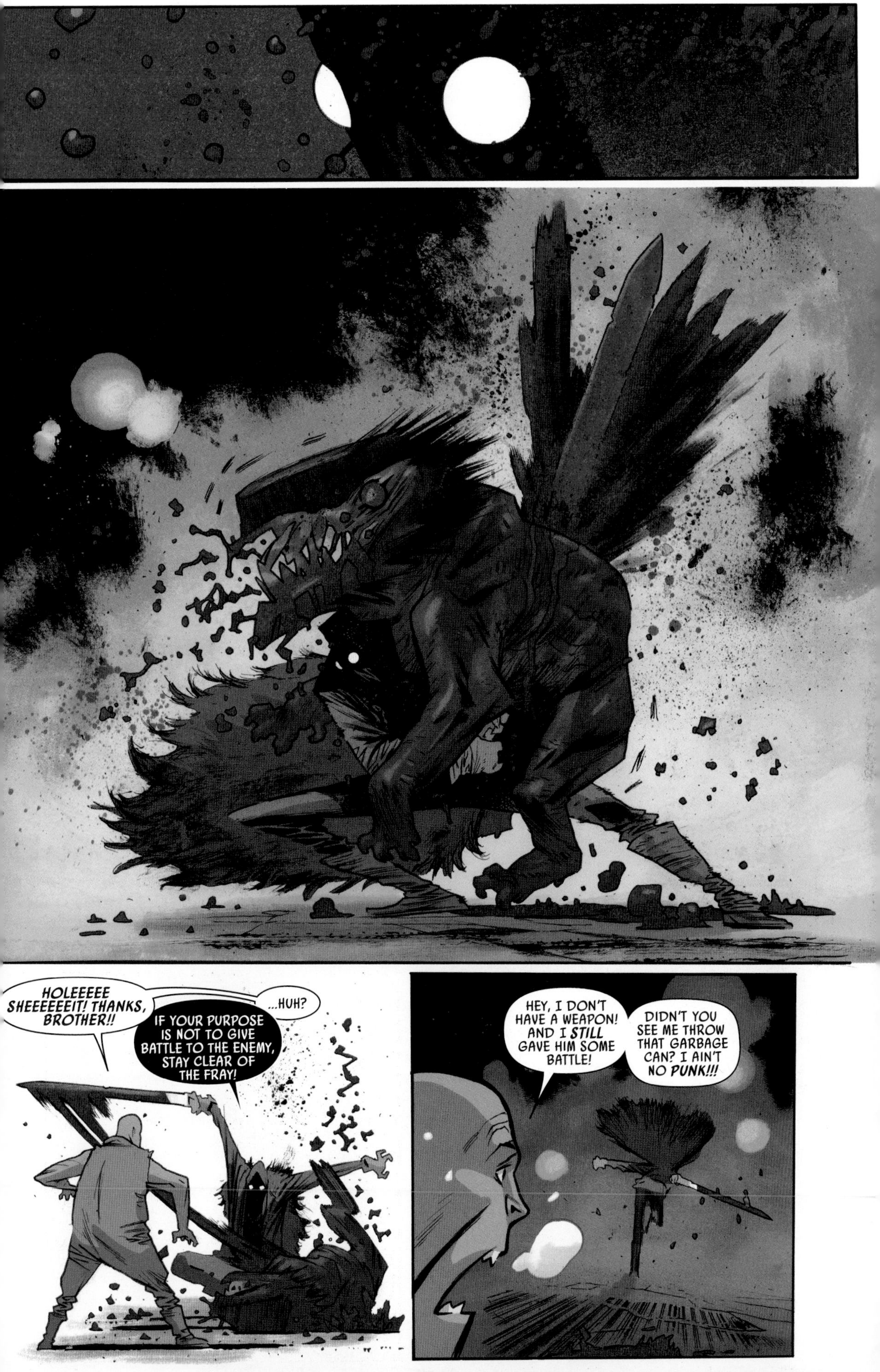
HOLEEEEE SHEEEEEEIT! THANKS, BROTHER!!
...HUH?
IF YOUR PURPOSE IS NOT TO GIVE BATTLE TO THE ENEMY, STAY CLEAR OF THE FRAY!
HEY, I DON'T HAVE A WEAPON! AND I STILL GAVE HIM SOME BATTLE!
DIDN'T YOU SEE ME THROW THAT GARBAGE CAN? I AIN'T NO PUNK!!!

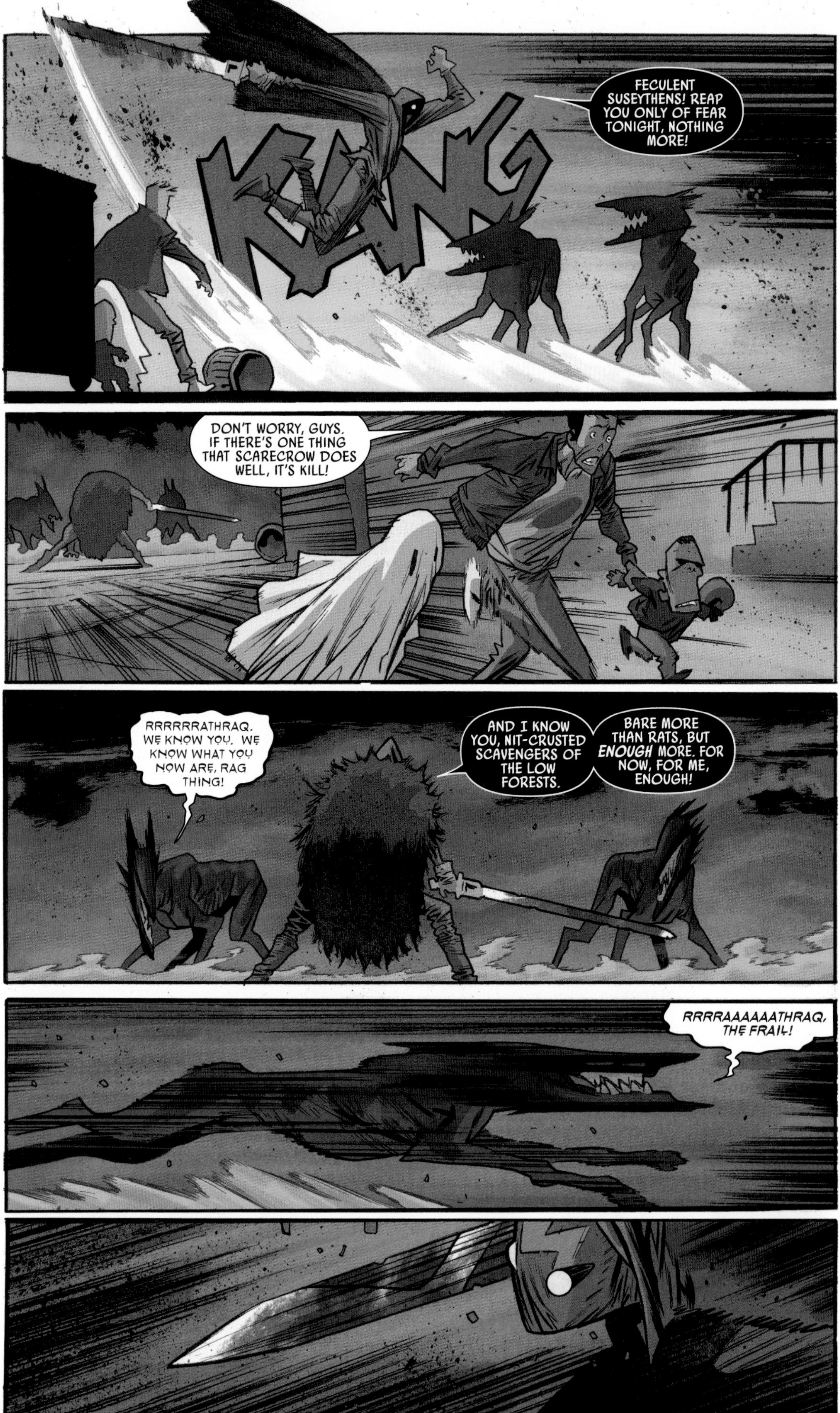
FECULENT SUSEYTHENS! REAP YOU ONLY OF FEAR TONIGHT, NOTHING MORE!
KLANG
DON'T WORRY, GUYS. IF THERE'S ONE THING THAT SCARECROW DOES WELL, IT'S KILL!
RRRRRRATHRAQ. WE KNOW YOU. WE KNOW WHAT YOU NOW ARE, RAG THING!
AND I KNOW YOU, NIT-CRUSTED SCAVENGERS OF THE LOW FORESTS.
BARE MORE THAN RATS, BUT ENOUGH MORE. FOR NOW, FOR ME, ENOUGH!
RRRRAAAAAAATHRAQ, THE FRAIL!

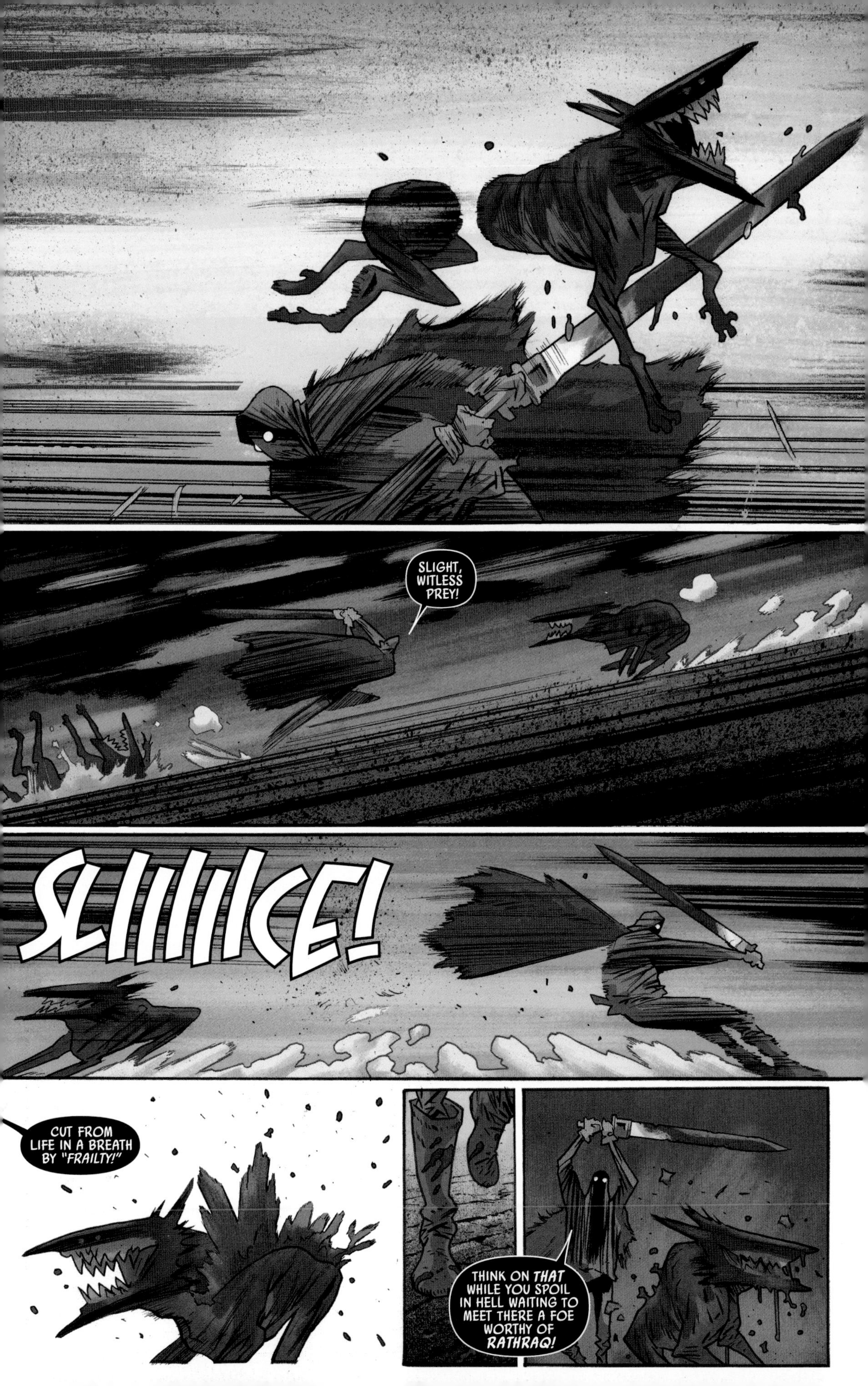
SLIGHT, WITLESS PREY!
SLIIIICE!
CUT FROM LIFE IN A BREATH BY "FRAILTY!"
THINK ON THAT WHILE YOU SPOIL IN HELL WAITING TO MEET THERE A FOE WORTHY OF RATHRAQ!

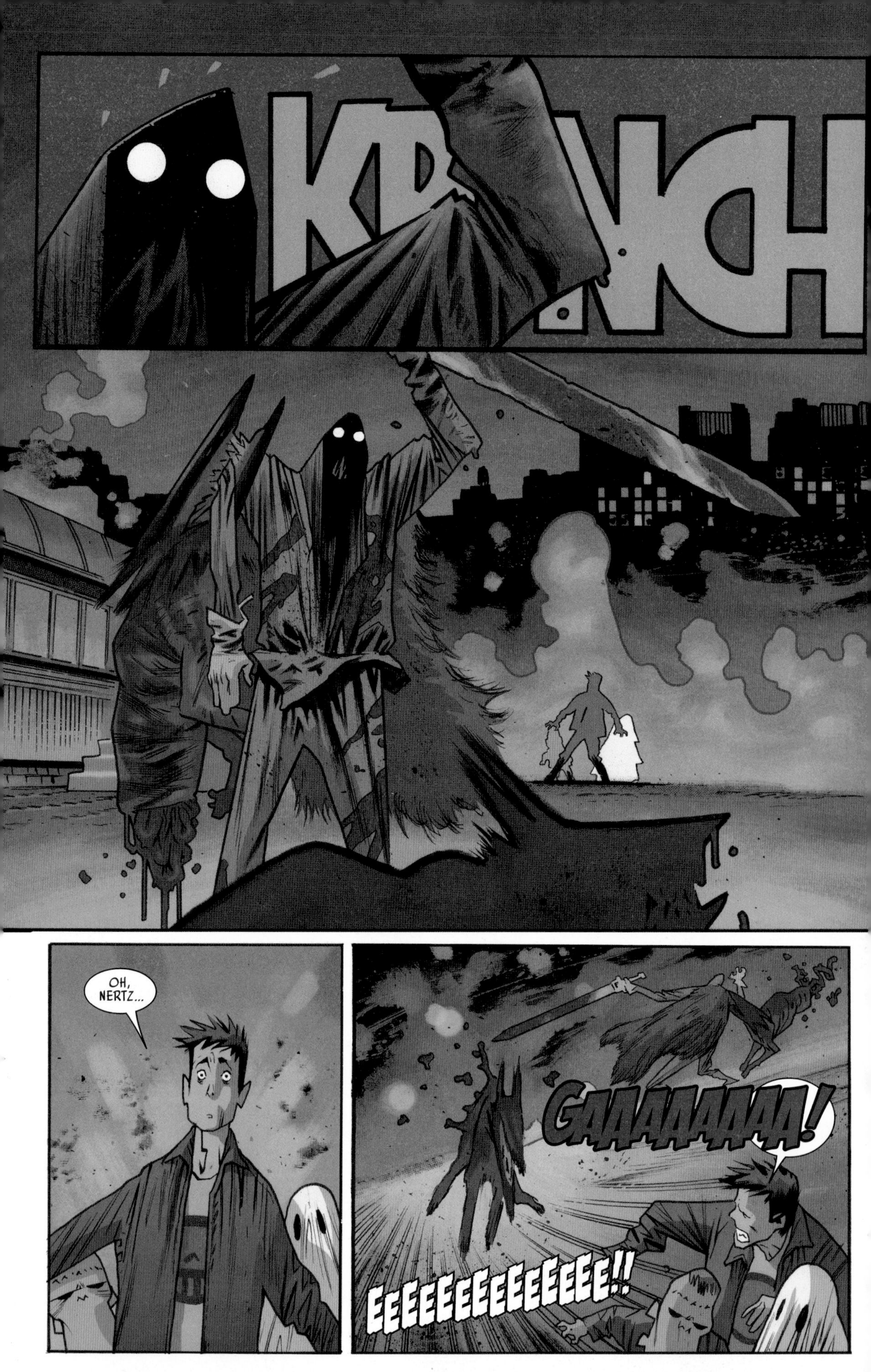
OH, NERTZ...
GAAAAAAAA!
EEEEEEEEEEEEEE!!

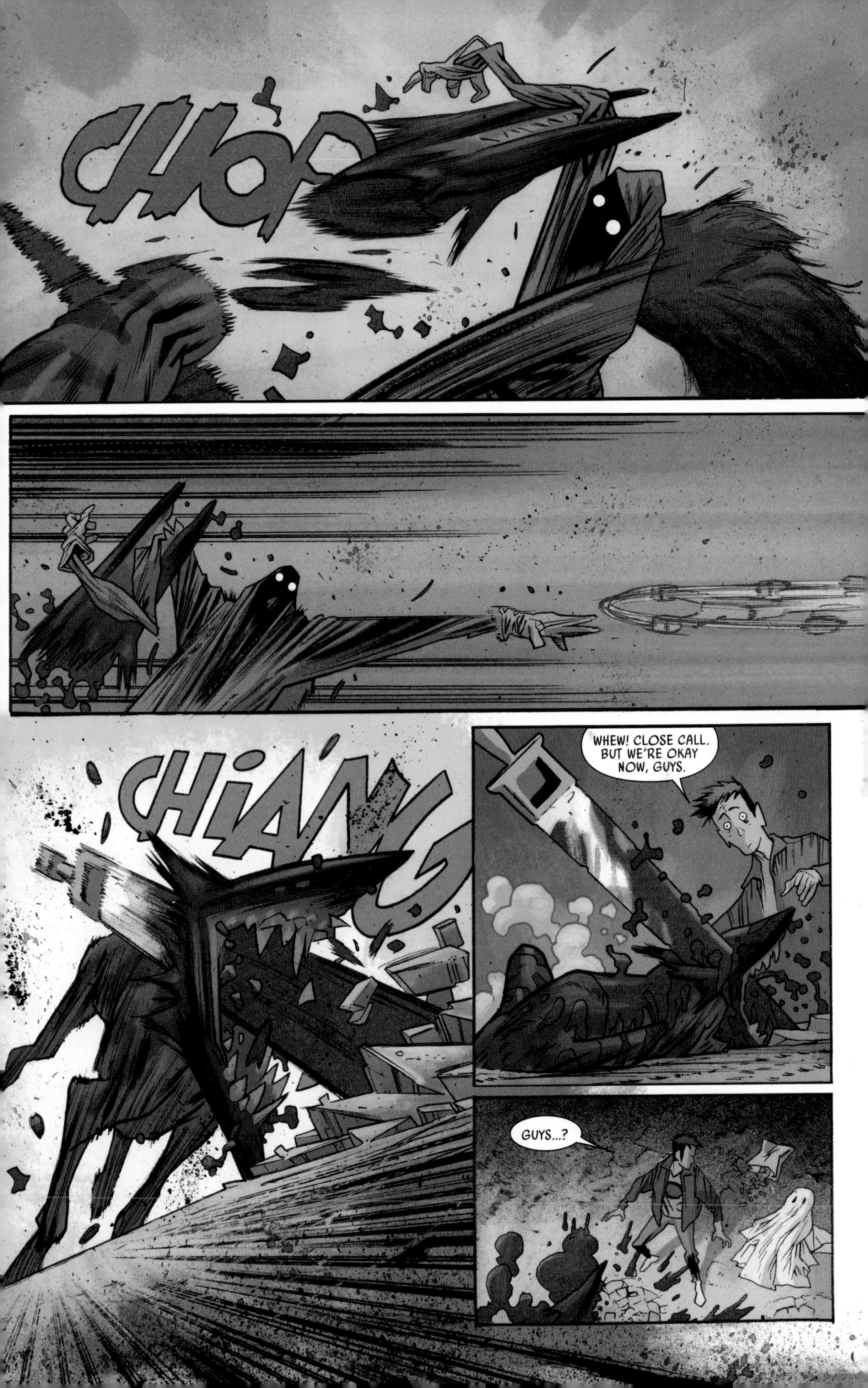
CHOP
CHIANG
WHEW! CLOSE CALL. BUT WE'RE OKAY NOW, GUYS.
GUYS...?

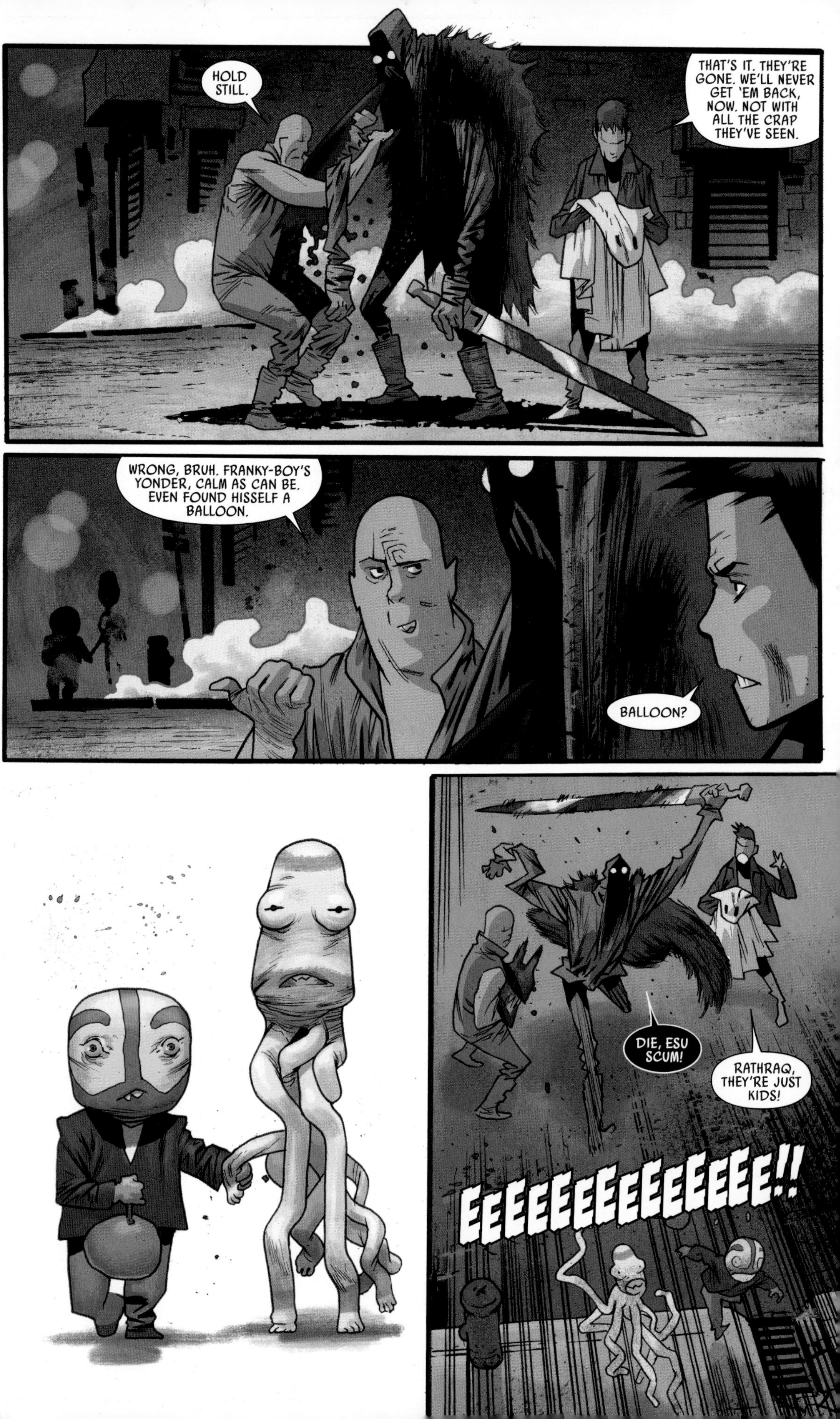
HOLD STILL.
THAT'S IT. THEY'RE GONE. WE'LL NEVER GET 'EM BACK, NOW. NOT WITH ALL THE CRAP THEY'VE SEEN.
WRONG, BRUH. FRANKY-BOY'S YONDER, CALM AS CAN BE. EVEN FOUND HISSELF A BALLOON.
BALLOON?
DIE, ESU SCUM!
RATHRAQ, THEY'RE JUST KIDS!
EEEEEEEEEEEEEE!!

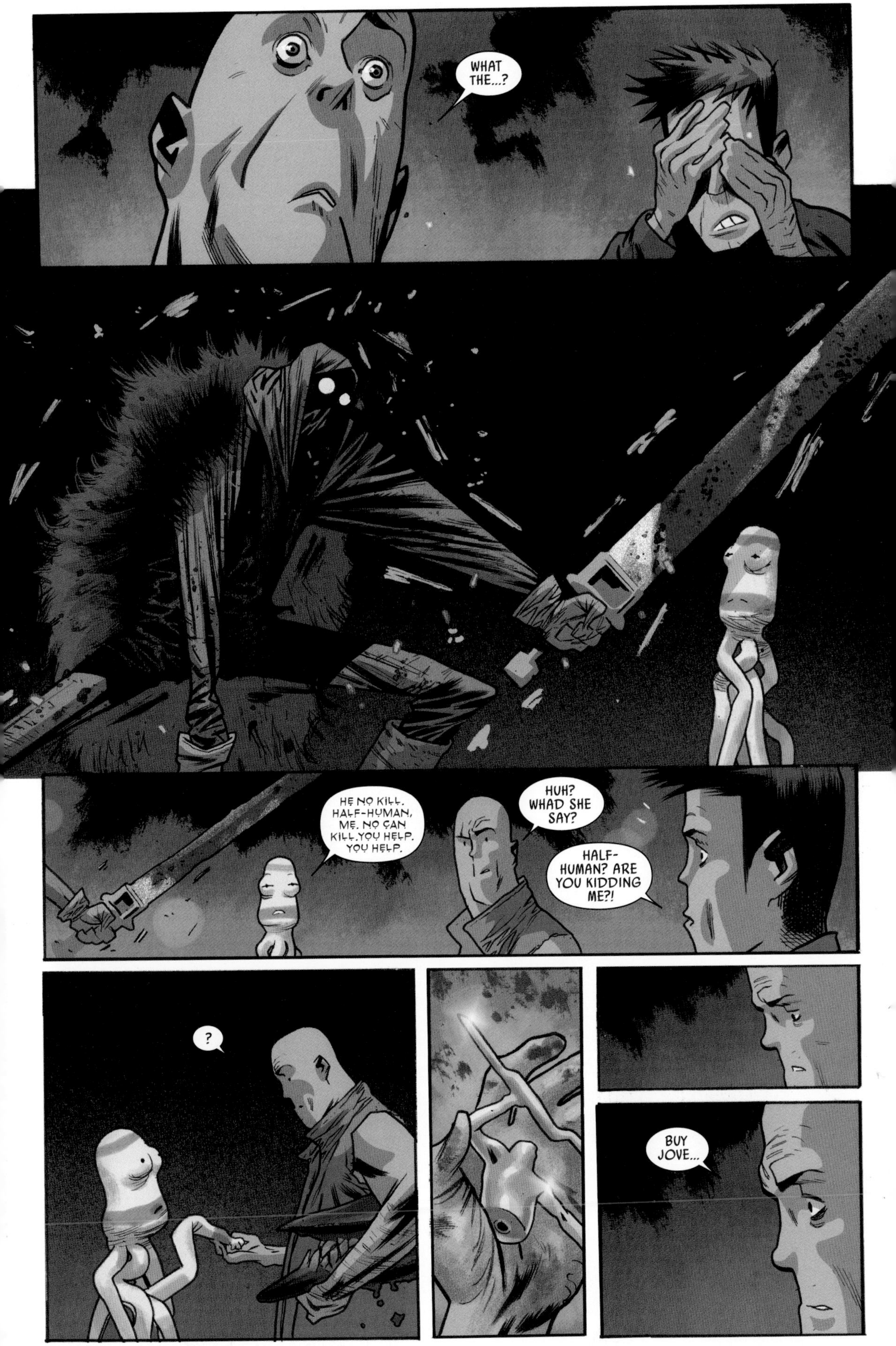
WHAT THE...?
HE NO KILL. HALF-HUMAN, ME. NO CAN KILL. YOU HELP. YOU HELP.
HUH? WHAD SHE SAY?
HALF-HUMAN? ARE YOU KIDDING ME?!
?
BUY JOVE...

# CHAPTER FOUR

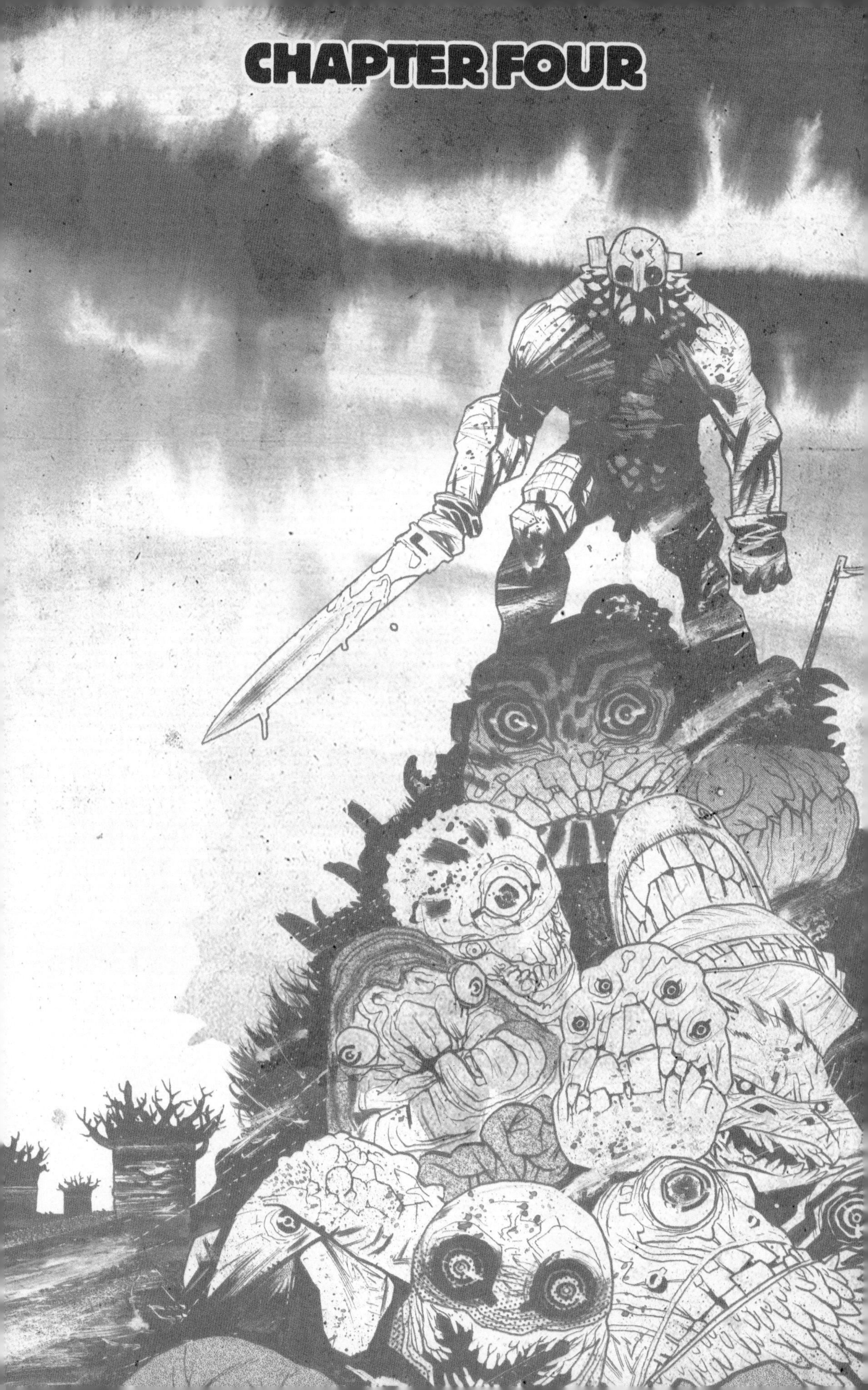

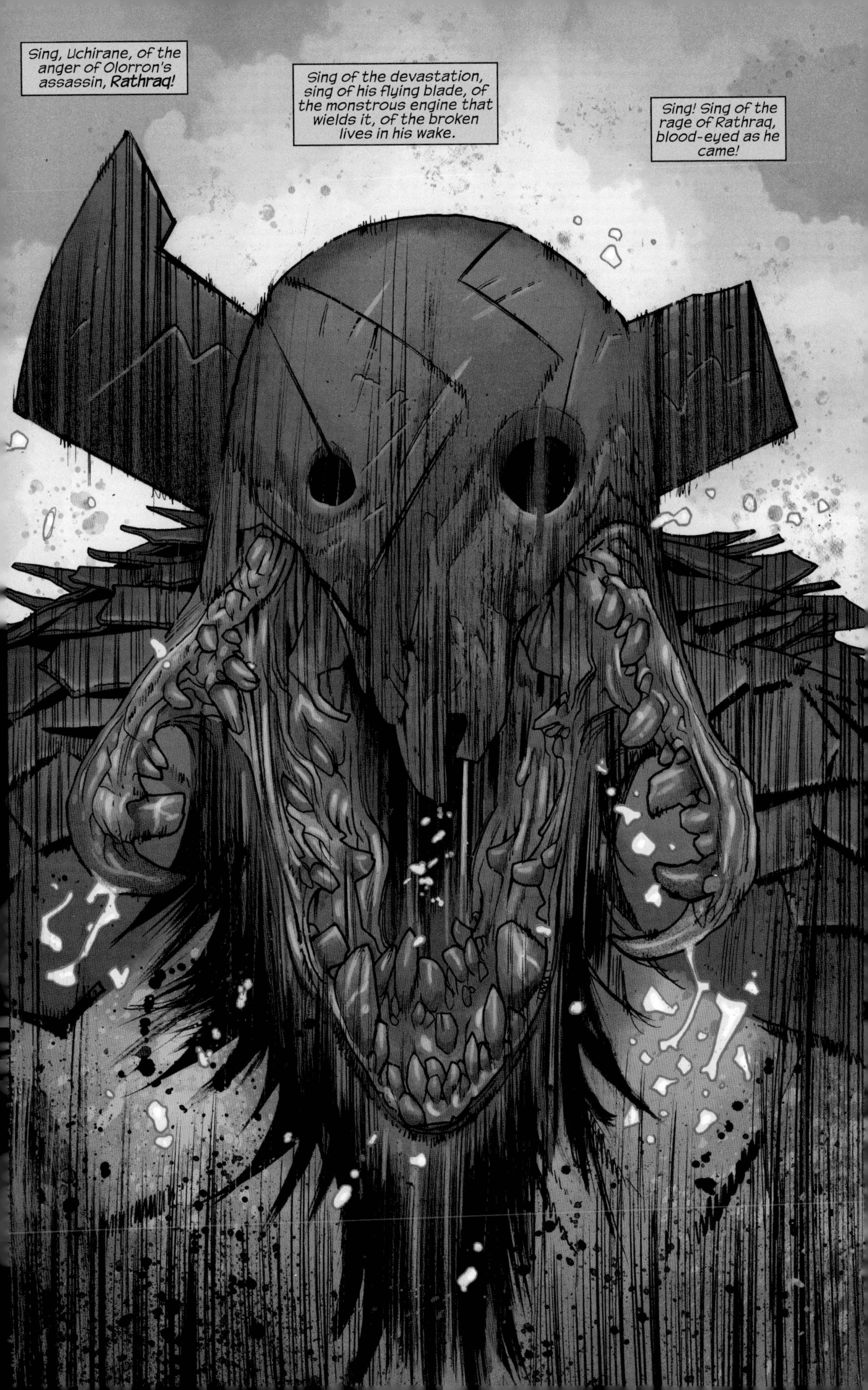
Sing, Uchirane, of the anger of Olorron's assassin, Rathraq!
Sing of the devastation, sing of his flying blade, of the monstrous engine that wields it, of the broken lives in his wake.
Sing! Sing of the rage of Rathraq, blood-eyed as he came!

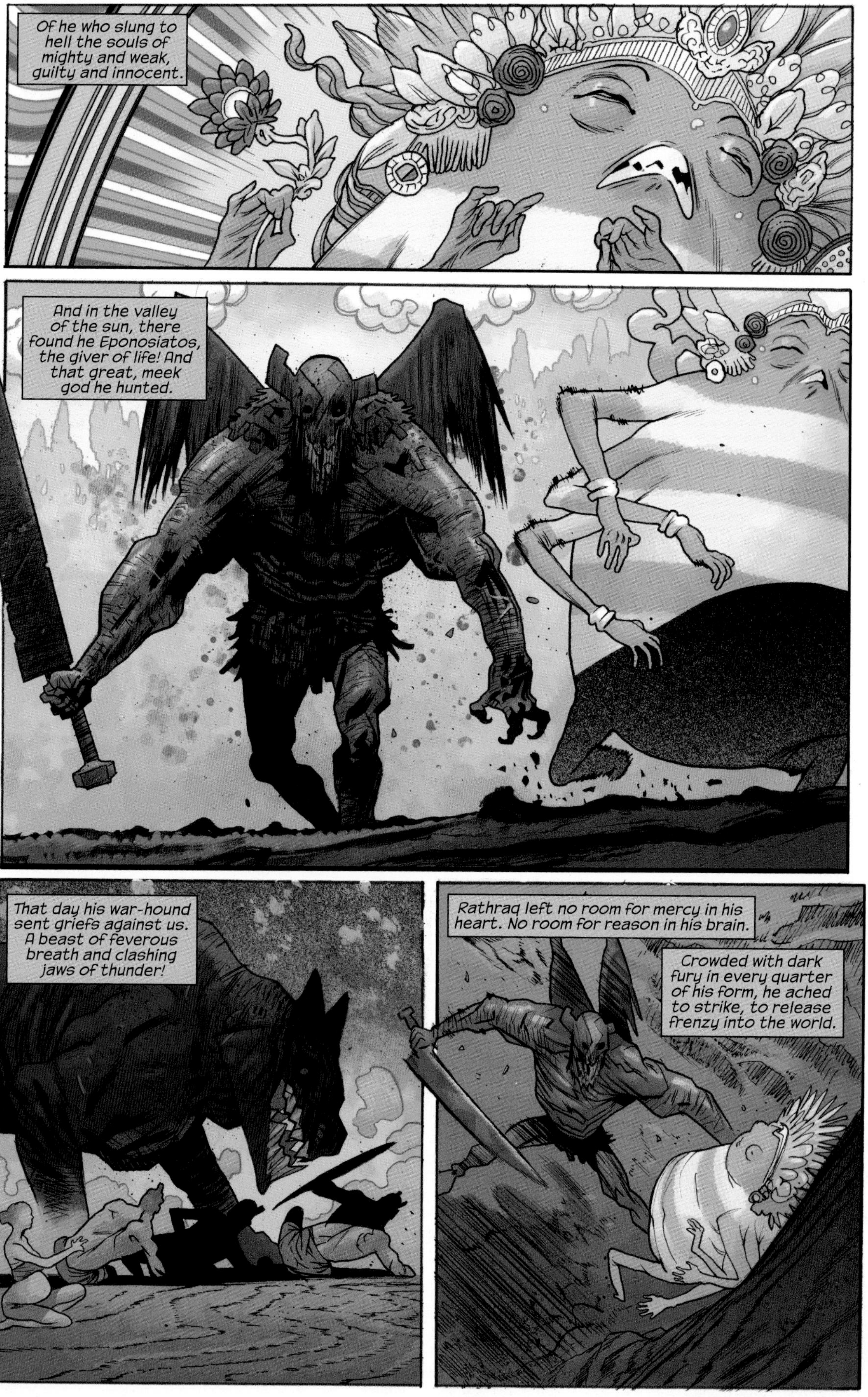
Of he who slung to hell the souls of mighty and weak, guilty and innocent.
And in the valley of the sun, there found he Eponosiatos, the giver of life! And that great, meek god he hunted.
That day his war-hound sent griefs against us. A beast of feverous breath and clashing jaws of thunder!
Rathraq left no room for mercy in his heart. No room for reason in his brain.
Crowded with dark fury in every quarter of his form, he ached to strike, to release frenzy into the world.

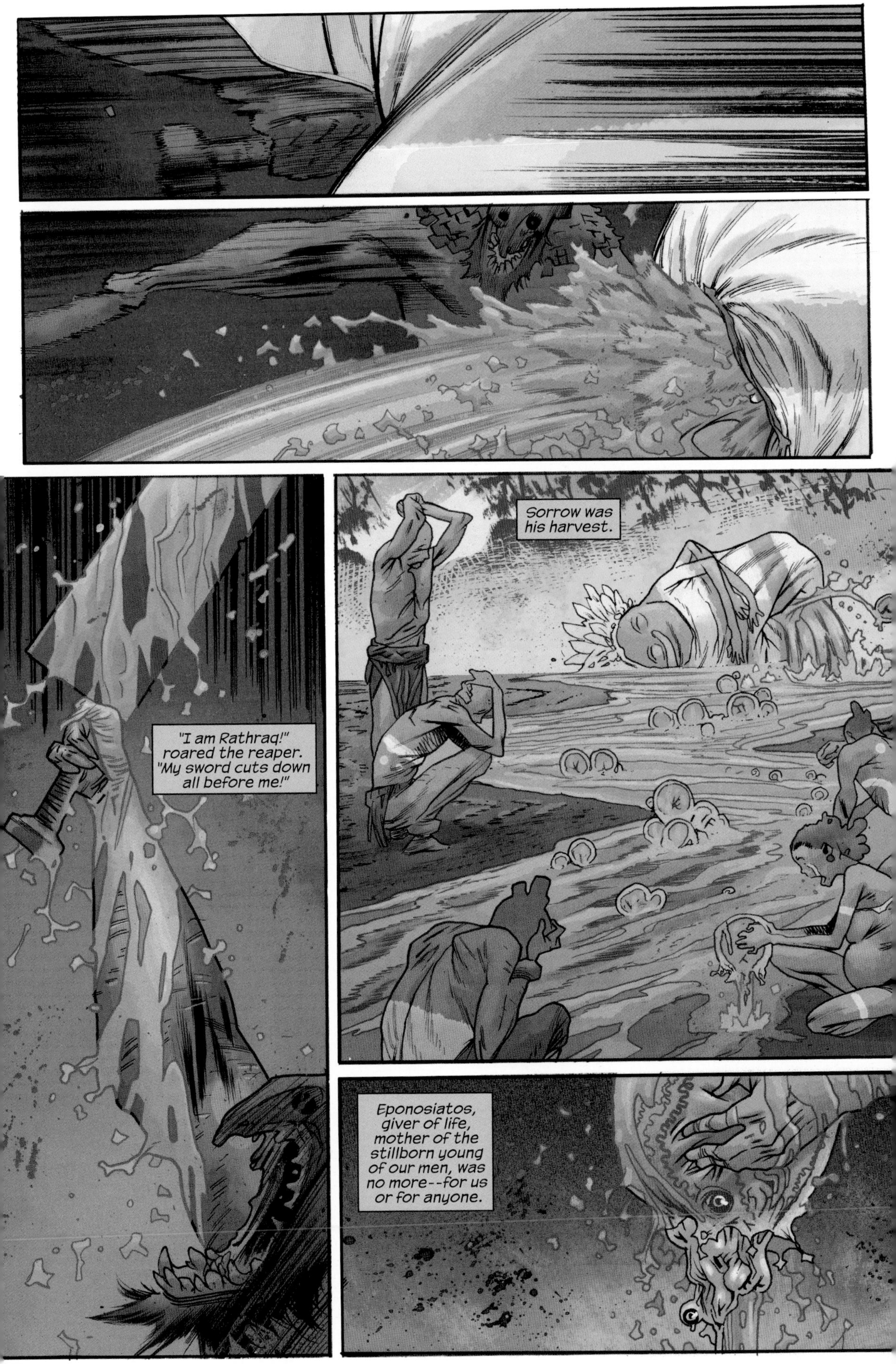
"I am Rathraq!" roared the reaper. "My sword cuts down all before me!"
Sorrow was his harvest.
Eponosiatos, giver of life, mother of the stillborn young of our men, was no more--for us or for anyone.

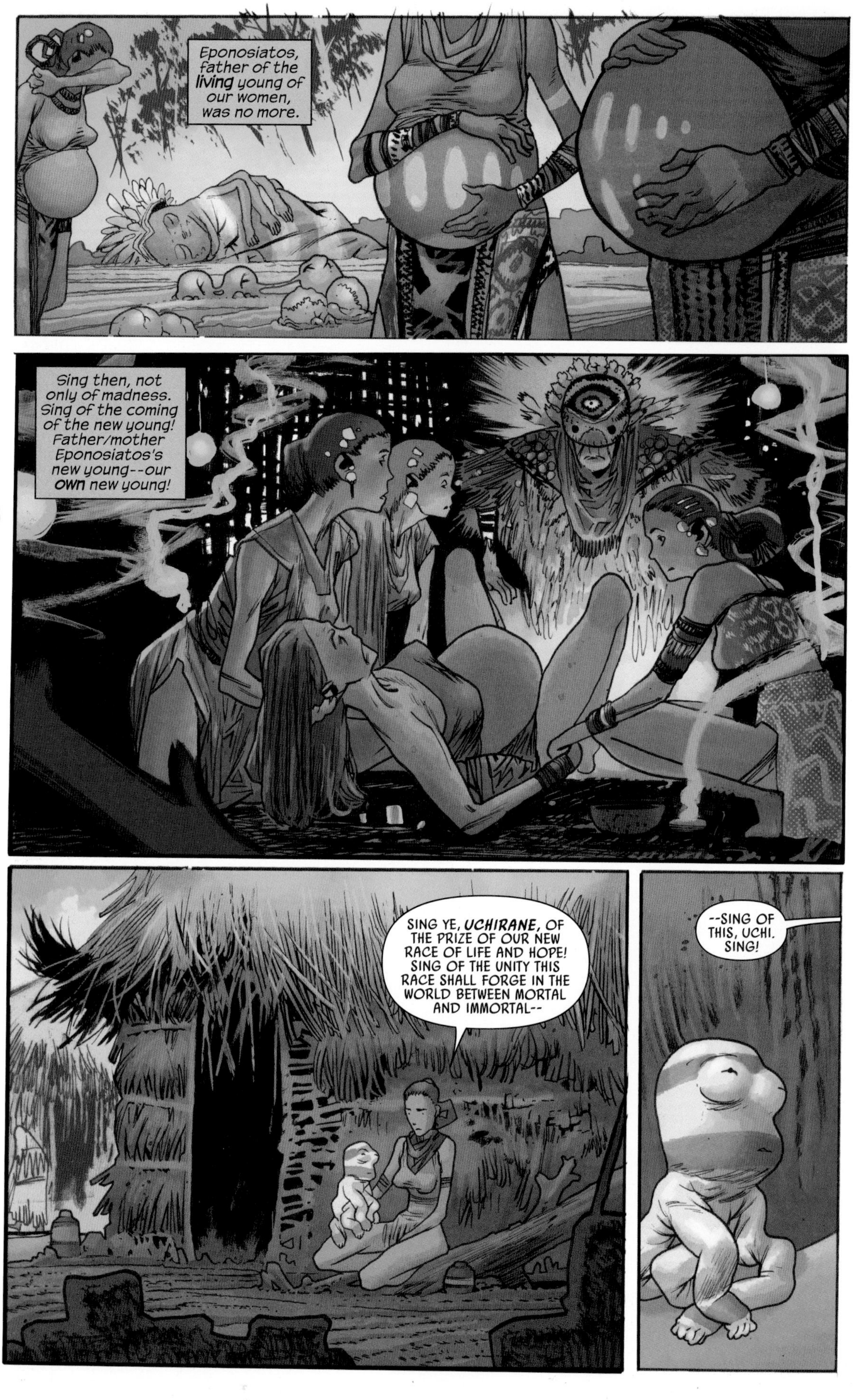
Eponosiatos, father of the **living** young of our women, was no more.
Sing then, not only of madness. Sing of the coming of the new young! Father/mother Eponosiatos's new young--our **own** new young!
SING YE, **UCHIRANE,** OF THE PRIZE OF OUR NEW RACE OF LIFE AND HOPE! SING OF THE UNITY THIS RACE SHALL FORGE IN THE WORLD BETWEEN MORTAL AND IMMORTAL--
--SING OF THIS, UCHI. SING!

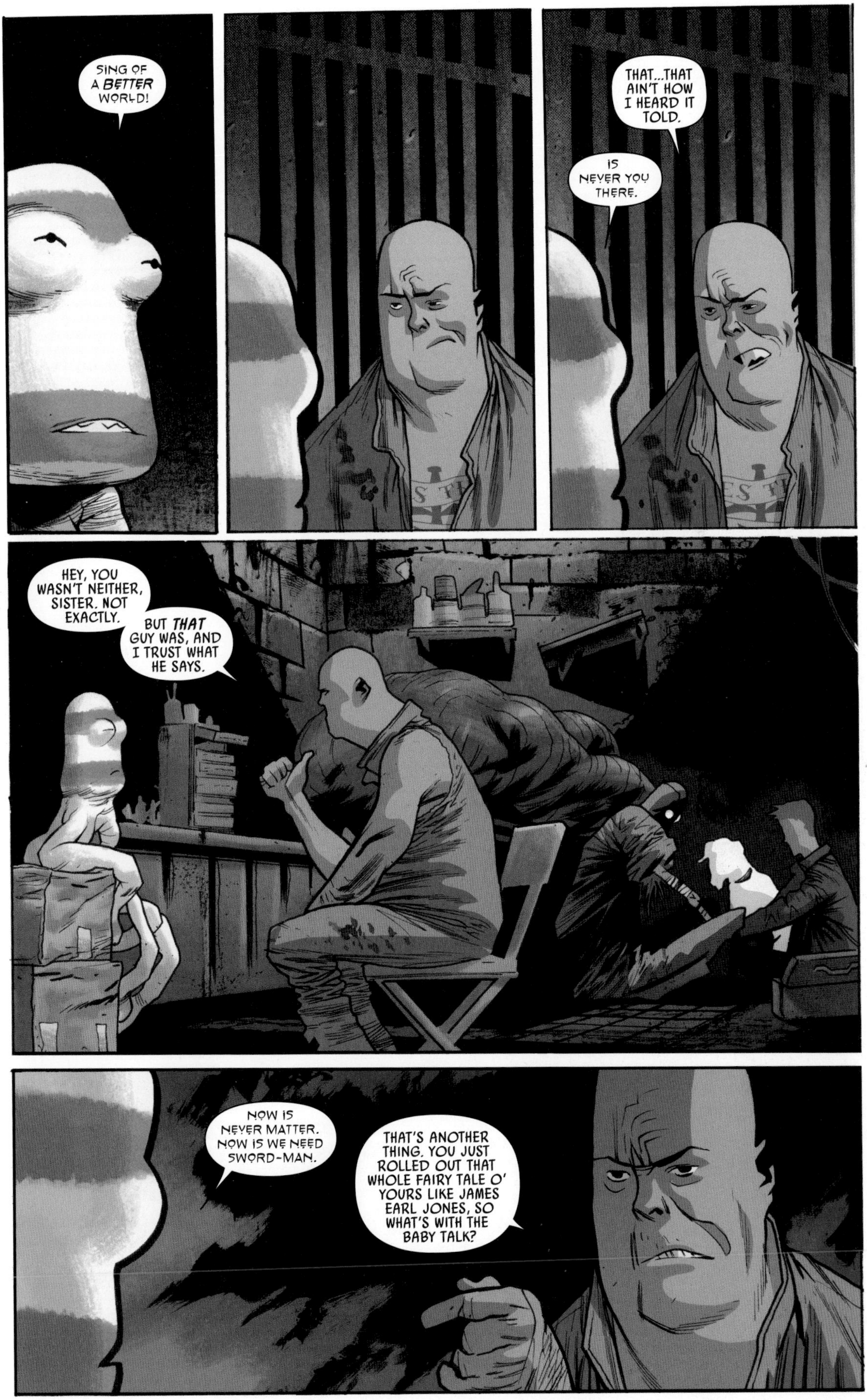
SING OF A BETTER WORLD!
THAT...THAT AIN'T HOW I HEARD IT TOLD.
IS NEVER YOU THERE.
HEY, YOU WASN'T NEITHER, SISTER. NOT EXACTLY.
BUT THAT GUY WAS, AND I TRUST WHAT HE SAYS.
NOW IS NEVER MATTER. NOW IS WE NEED SWORD-MAN.
THAT'S ANOTHER THING. YOU JUST ROLLED OUT THAT WHOLE FAIRY TALE O' YOURS LIKE JAMES EARL JONES, SO WHAT'S WITH THE BABY TALK?

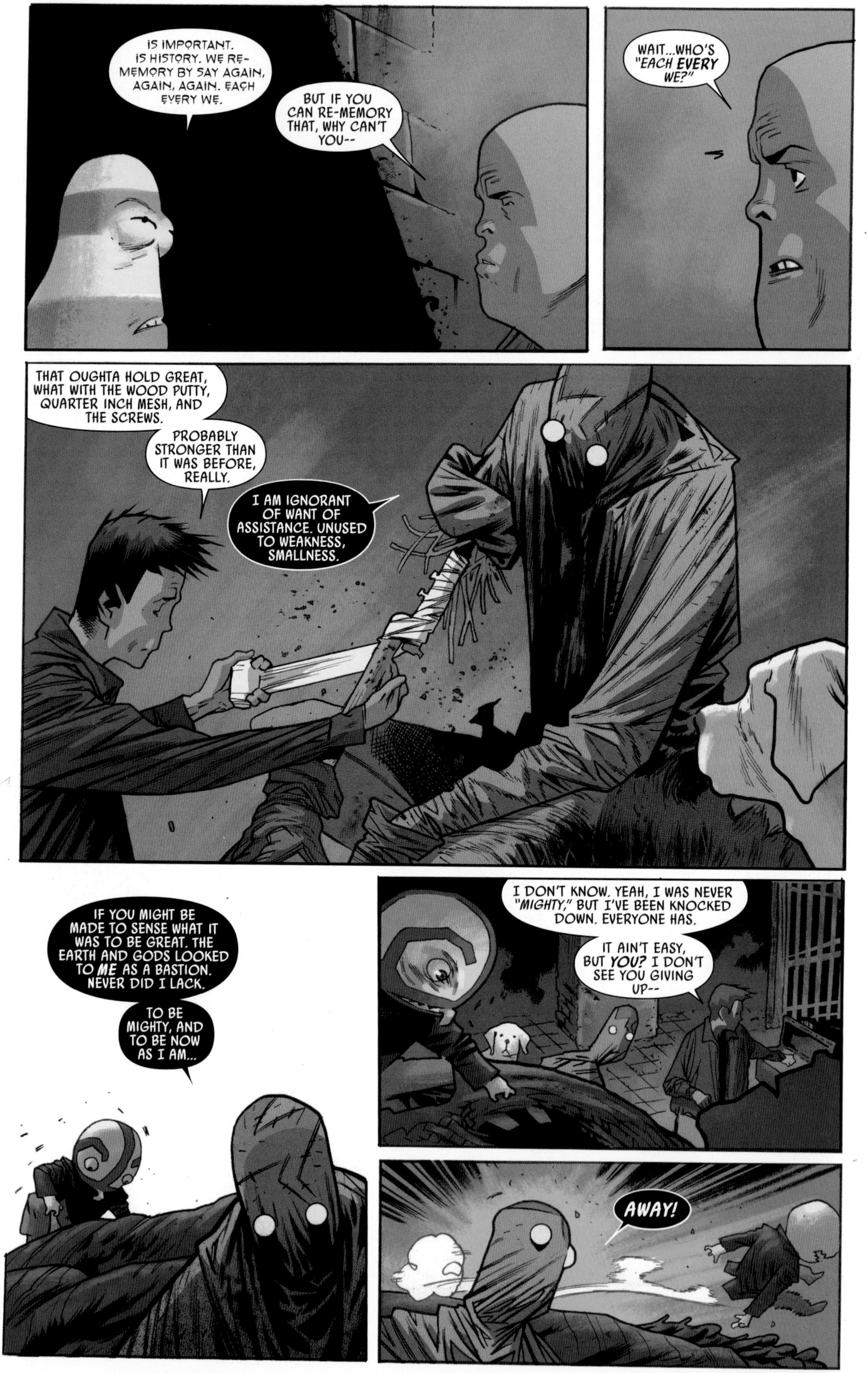
IS IMPORTANT. IS HISTORY. WE RE-MEMORY BY SAY AGAIN, AGAIN, AGAIN. EACH EVERY WE.
BUT IF YOU CAN RE-MEMORY THAT, WHY CAN'T YOU--
WAIT...WHO'S "EACH EVERY WE?"
THAT OUGHTA HOLD GREAT, WHAT WITH THE WOOD PUTTY, QUARTER INCH MESH, AND THE SCREWS.
PROBABLY STRONGER THAN IT WAS BEFORE, REALLY.
I AM IGNORANT OF WANT OF ASSISTANCE. UNUSED TO WEAKNESS, SMALLNESS.
IF YOU MIGHT BE MADE TO SENSE WHAT IT WAS TO BE GREAT. THE EARTH AND GODS LOOKED TO ME AS A BASTION. NEVER DID I LACK.
TO BE MIGHTY, AND TO BE NOW AS I AM...
I DON'T KNOW. YEAH, I WAS NEVER "MIGHTY," BUT I'VE BEEN KNOCKED DOWN. EVERYONE HAS.
IT AIN'T EASY, BUT YOU? I DON'T SEE YOU GIVING UP--
AWAY!

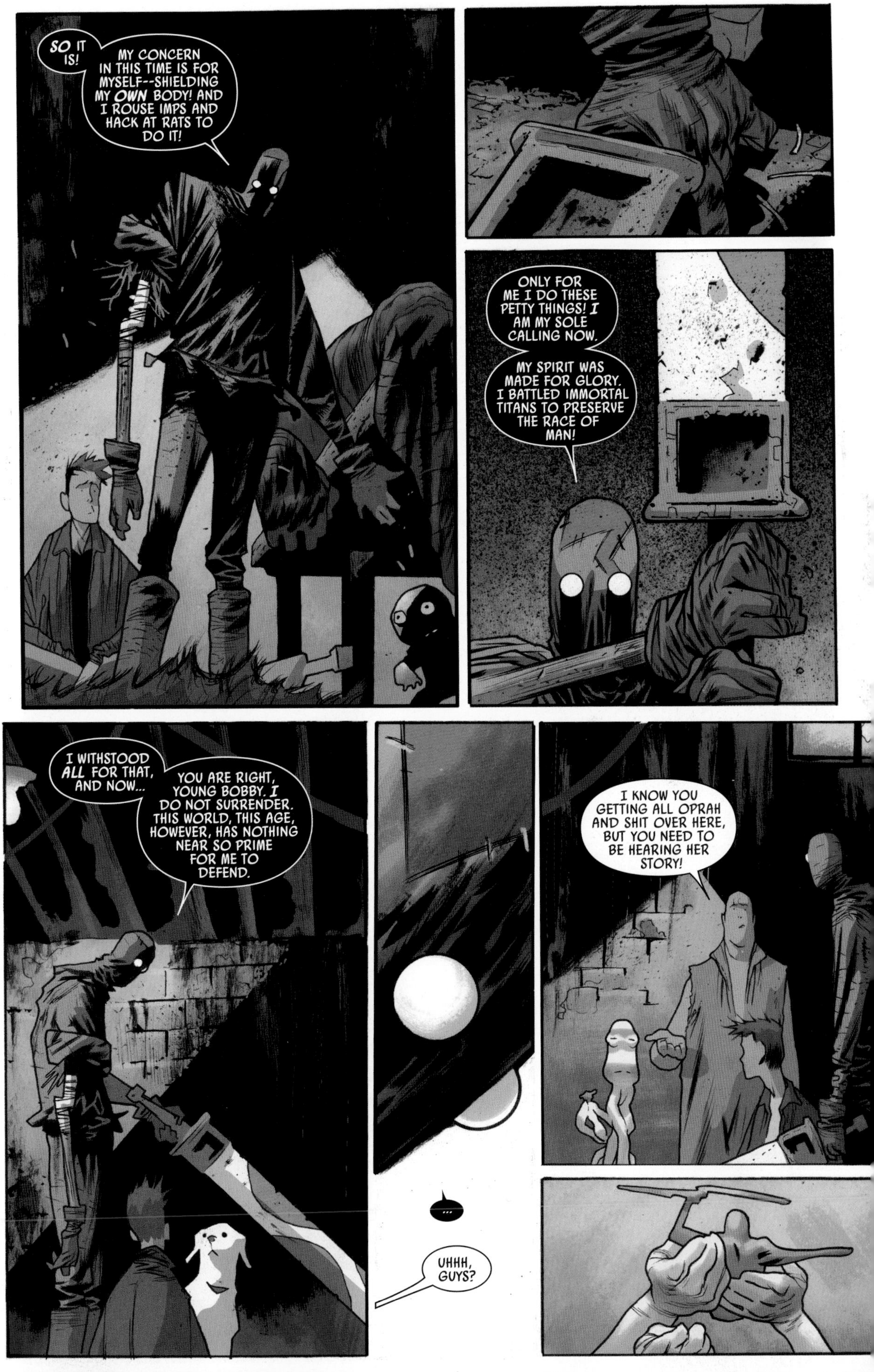
SO IT IS!
MY CONCERN IN THIS TIME IS FOR MYSELF--SHIELDING MY OWN BODY! AND I ROUSE IMPS AND HACK AT RATS TO DO IT!
ONLY FOR ME I DO THESE PETTY THINGS! I AM MY SOLE CALLING NOW.
MY SPIRIT WAS MADE FOR GLORY. I BATTLED IMMORTAL TITANS TO PRESERVE THE RACE OF MAN!
I WITHSTOOD ALL FOR THAT, AND NOW...
YOU ARE RIGHT, YOUNG BOBBY. I DO NOT SURRENDER. THIS WORLD, THIS AGE, HOWEVER, HAS NOTHING NEAR SO PRIME FOR ME TO DEFEND.
I KNOW YOU GETTING ALL OPRAH AND SHIT OVER HERE, BUT YOU NEED TO BE HEARING HER STORY!
...
UHHH, GUYS?

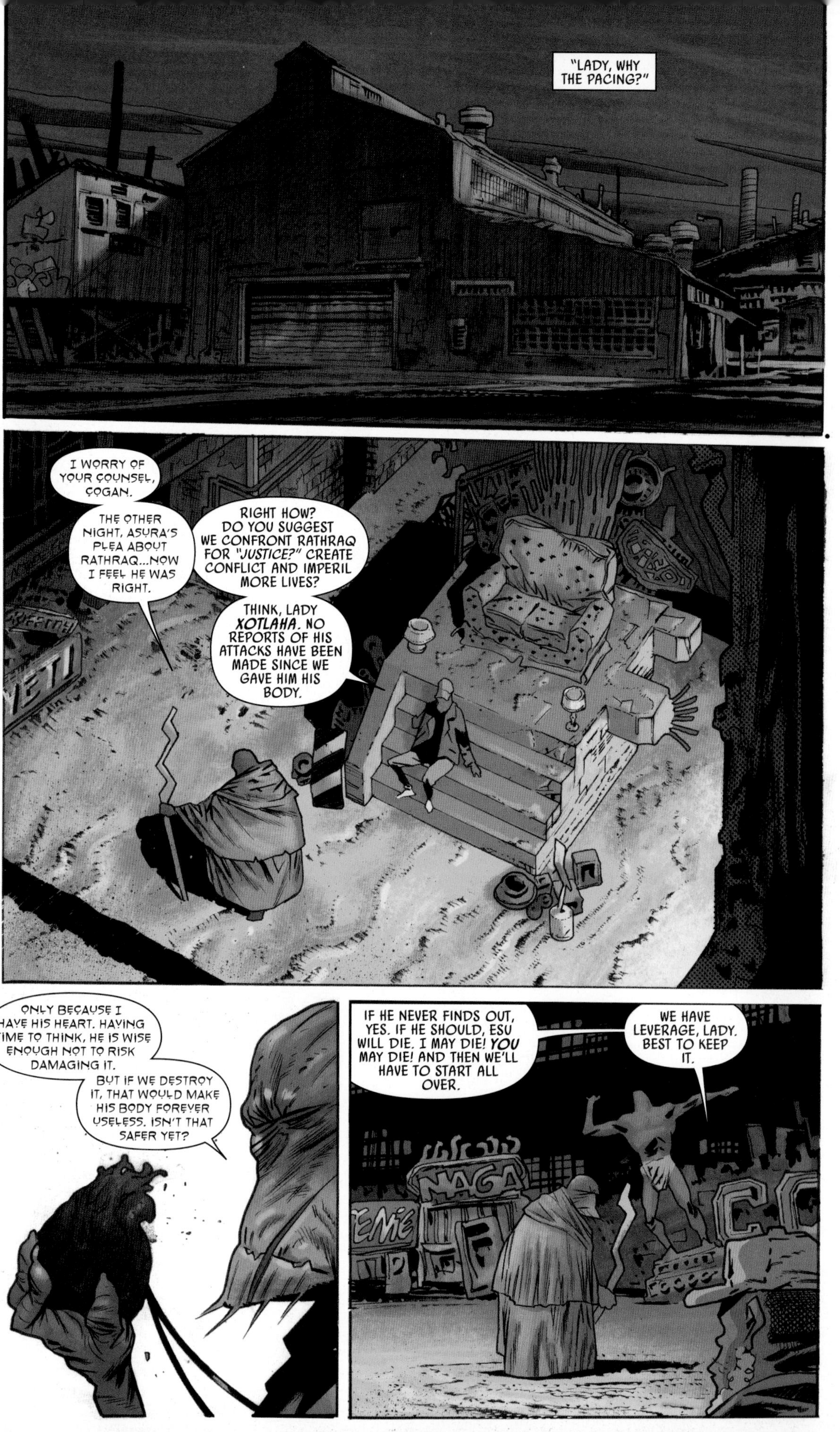
"LADY, WHY THE PACING?"
I WORRY OF YOUR COUNSEL, COGAN.
THE OTHER NIGHT, ASURA'S PLEA ABOUT RATHRAQ...NOW I FEEL HE WAS RIGHT.
RIGHT HOW? DO YOU SUGGEST WE CONFRONT RATHRAQ FOR "JUSTICE?" CREATE CONFLICT AND IMPERIL MORE LIVES?
THINK, LADY XOTLAHA. NO REPORTS OF HIS ATTACKS HAVE BEEN MADE SINCE WE GAVE HIM HIS BODY.
YETI
ONLY BECAUSE I HAVE HIS HEART. HAVING TIME TO THINK, HE IS WISE ENOUGH NOT TO RISK DAMAGING IT.
BUT IF WE DESTROY IT, THAT WOULD MAKE HIS BODY FOREVER USELESS. ISN'T THAT SAFER YET?
IF HE NEVER FINDS OUT, YES. IF HE SHOULD, ESU WILL DIE. I MAY DIE! YOU MAY DIE! AND THEN WE'LL HAVE TO START ALL OVER.
WE HAVE LEVERAGE, LADY. BEST TO KEEP IT.
NAGA

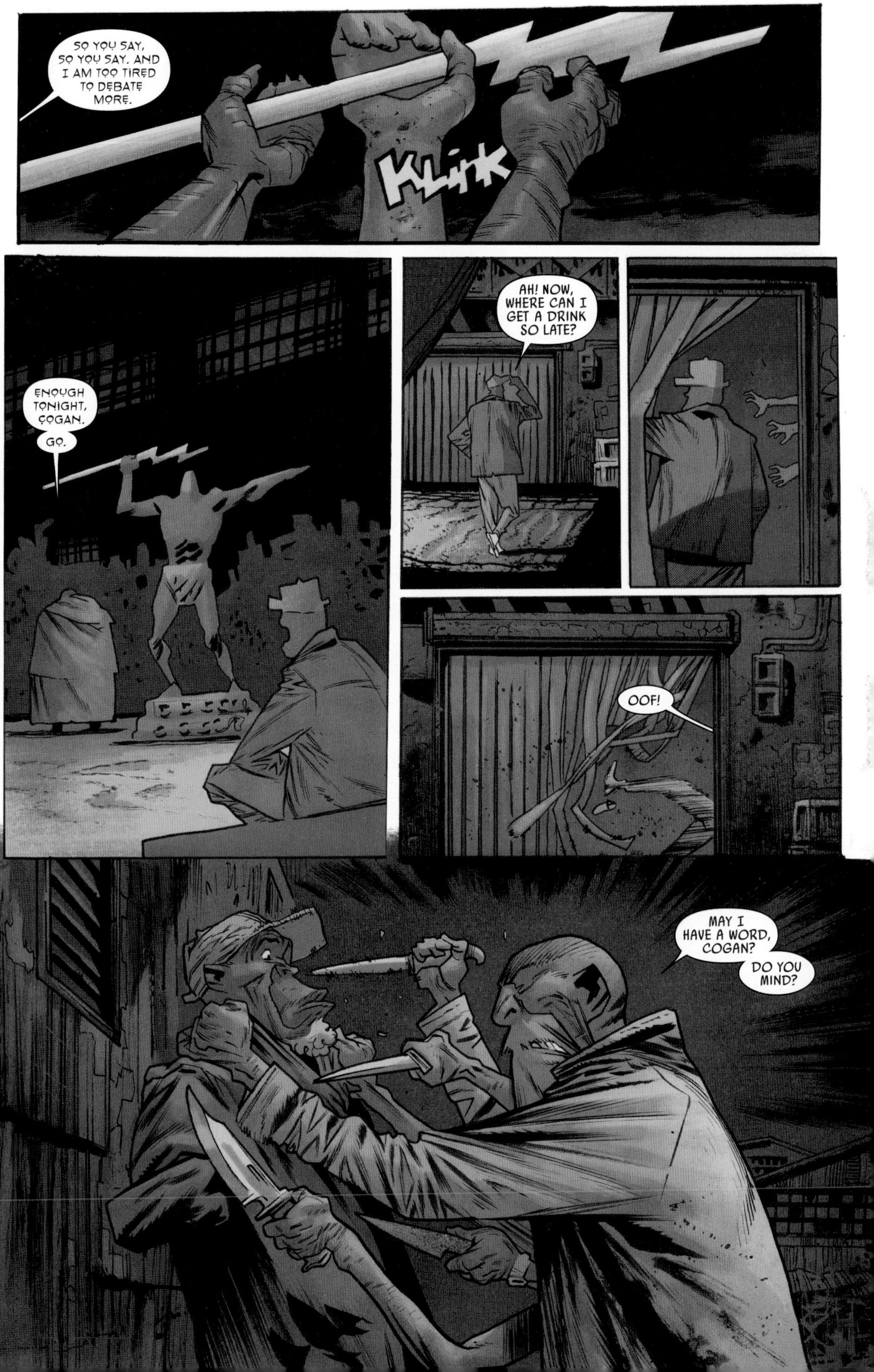
SO YOU SAY, SO YOU SAY. AND I AM TOO TIRED TO DEBATE MORE.
KLINK
ENOUGH TONIGHT, COGAN.
GO.
AH! NOW, WHERE CAN I GET A DRINK SO LATE?
OOF!
MAY I HAVE A WORD, COGAN?
DO YOU MIND?

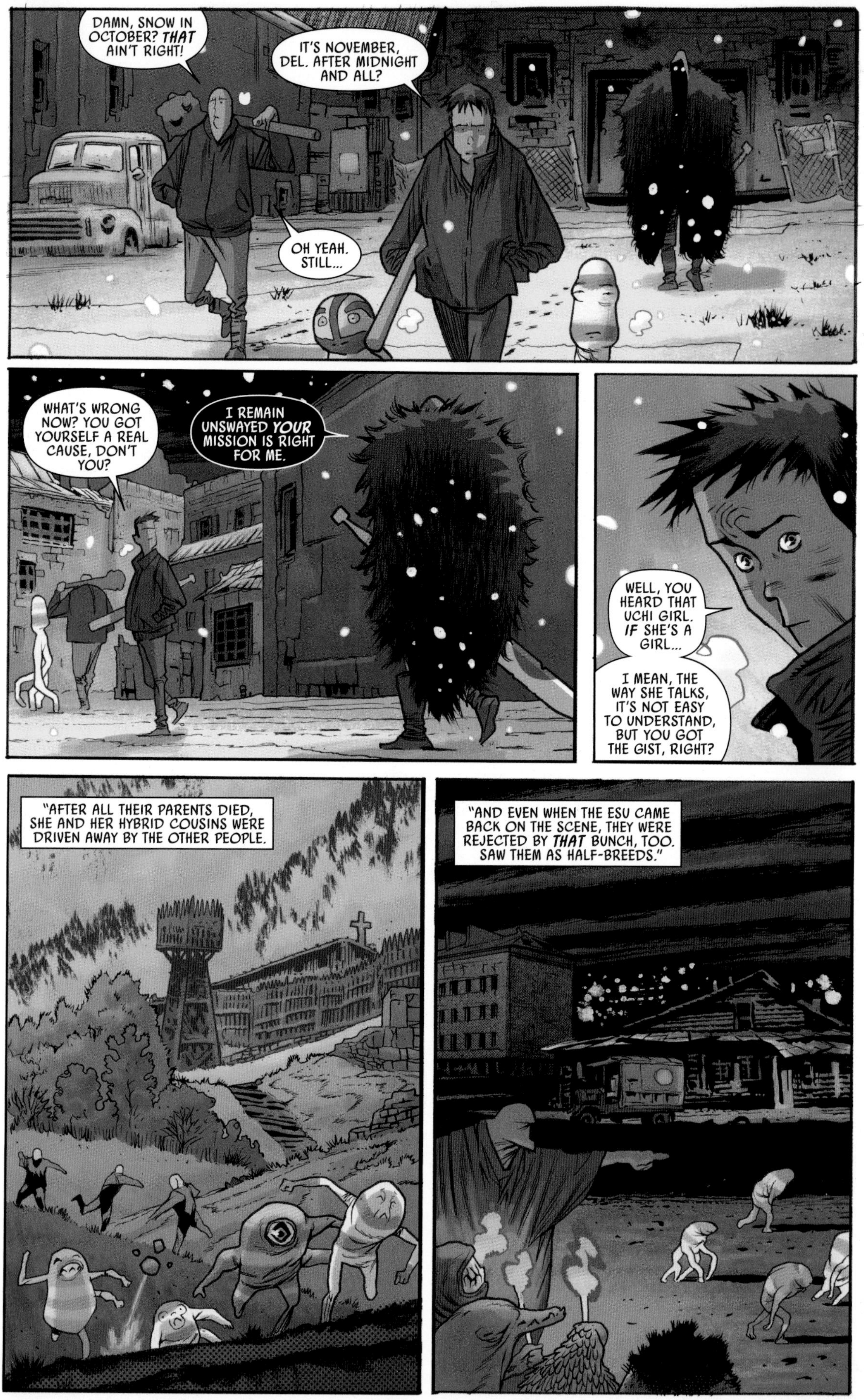
DAMN, SNOW IN OCTOBER? THAT AIN'T RIGHT!
IT'S NOVEMBER, DEL. AFTER MIDNIGHT AND ALL?
OH YEAH. STILL...
WHAT'S WRONG NOW? YOU GOT YOURSELF A REAL CAUSE, DON'T YOU?
I REMAIN UNSWAYED YOUR MISSION IS RIGHT FOR ME.
WELL, YOU HEARD THAT UCHI GIRL. IF SHE'S A GIRL...
I MEAN, THE WAY SHE TALKS, IT'S NOT EASY TO UNDERSTAND, BUT YOU GOT THE GIST, RIGHT?
"AFTER ALL THEIR PARENTS DIED, SHE AND HER HYBRID COUSINS WERE DRIVEN AWAY BY THE OTHER PEOPLE.
"AND EVEN WHEN THE ESU CAME BACK ON THE SCENE, THEY WERE REJECTED BY THAT BUNCH, TOO. SAW THEM AS HALF-BREEDS."

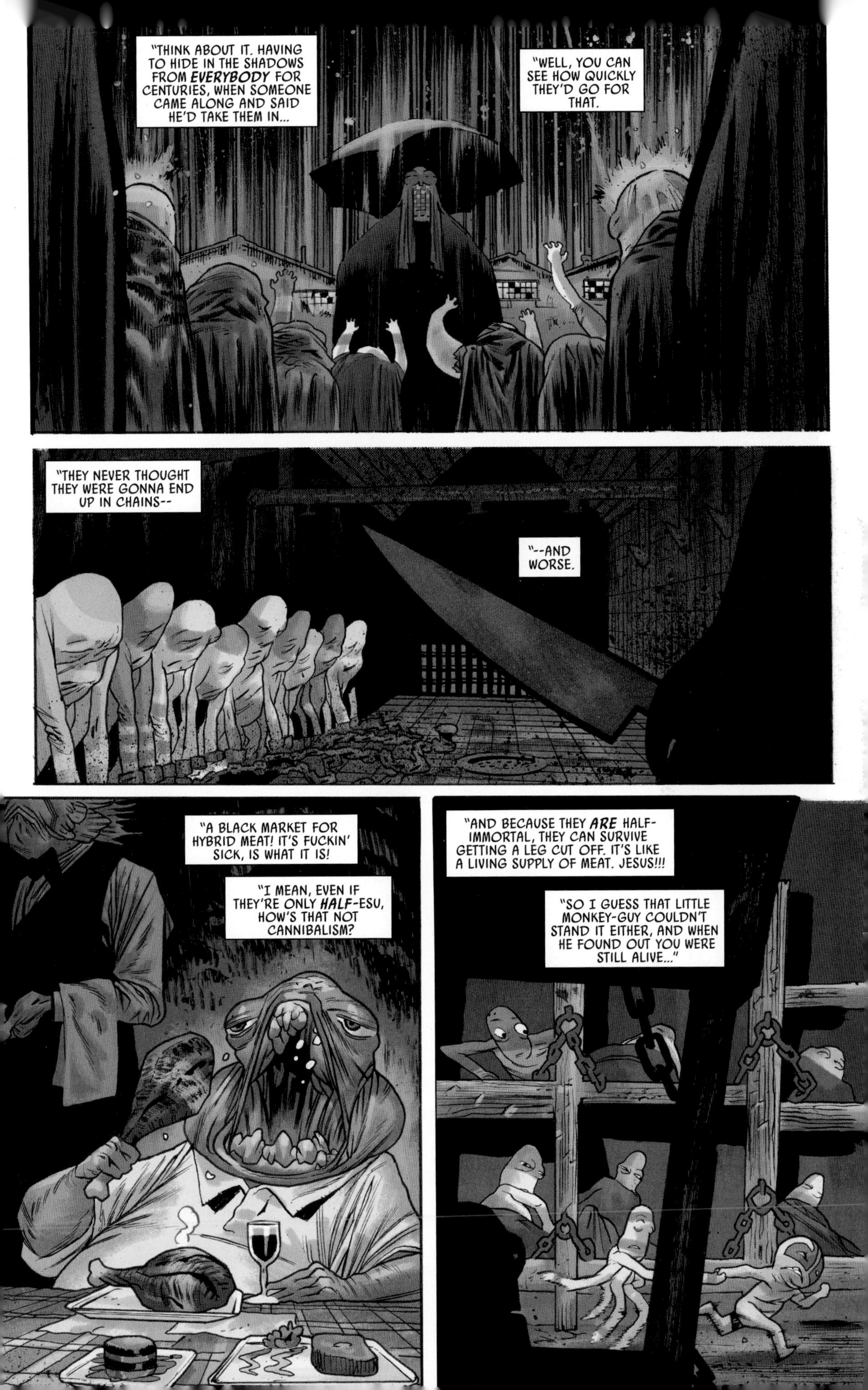
"THINK ABOUT IT. HAVING TO HIDE IN THE SHADOWS FROM EVERYBODY FOR CENTURIES, WHEN SOMEONE CAME ALONG AND SAID HE'D TAKE THEM IN...
"WELL, YOU CAN SEE HOW QUICKLY THEY'D GO FOR THAT.
"THEY NEVER THOUGHT THEY WERE GONNA END UP IN CHAINS--
"--AND WORSE.
"A BLACK MARKET FOR HYBRID MEAT! IT'S FUCKIN' SICK, IS WHAT IT IS!
"I MEAN, EVEN IF THEY'RE ONLY HALF-ESU, HOW'S THAT NOT CANNIBALISM?
"AND BECAUSE THEY ARE HALF-IMMORTAL, THEY CAN SURVIVE GETTING A LEG CUT OFF. IT'S LIKE A LIVING SUPPLY OF MEAT. JESUS!!!
"SO I GUESS THAT LITTLE MONKEY-GUY COULDN'T STAND IT EITHER, AND WHEN HE FOUND OUT YOU WERE STILL ALIVE..."

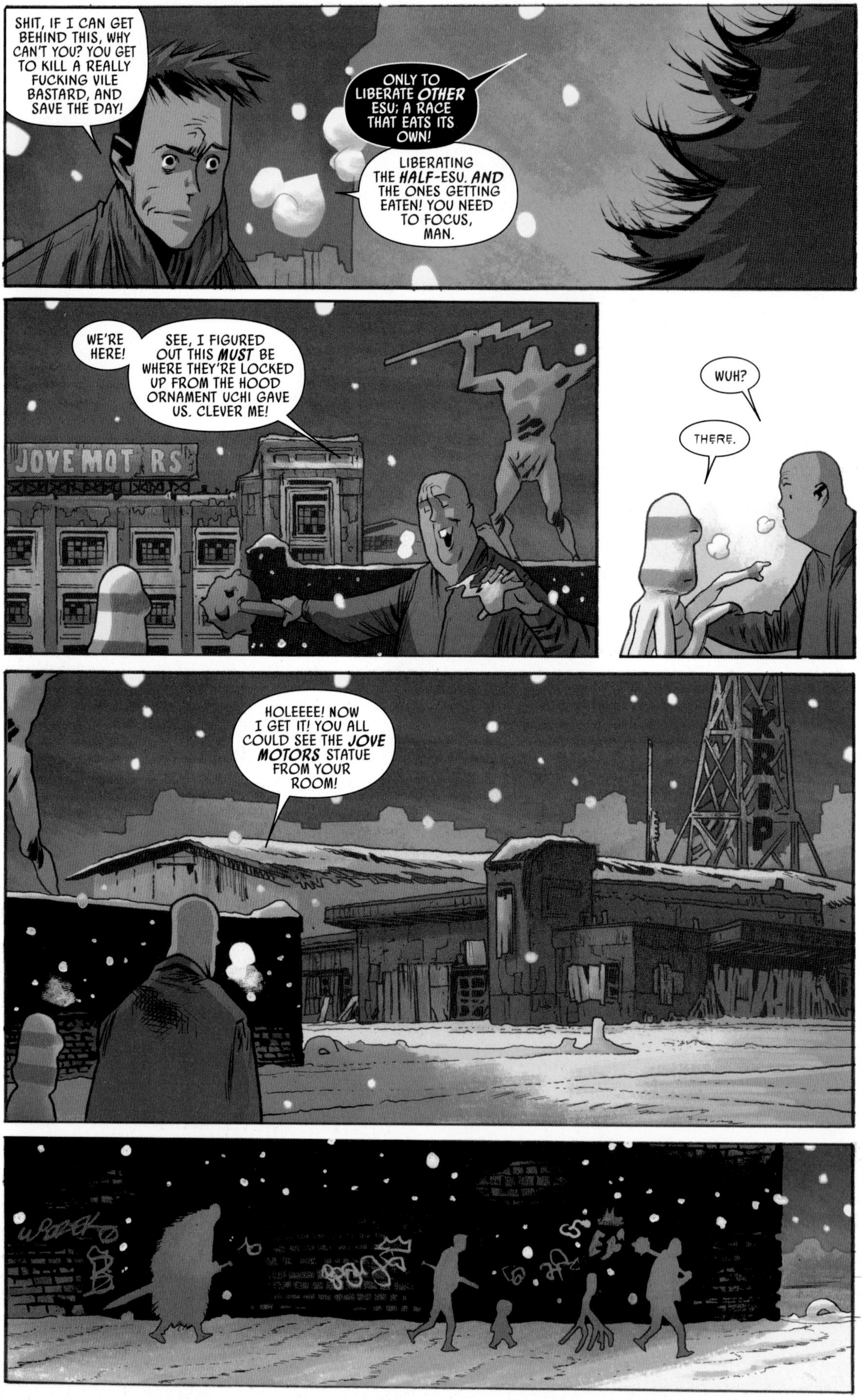
SHIT, IF I CAN GET BEHIND THIS, WHY CAN'T YOU? YOU GET TO KILL A REALLY FUCKING VILE BASTARD, AND SAVE THE DAY!
ONLY TO LIBERATE OTHER ESU; A RACE THAT EATS ITS OWN!
LIBERATING THE HALF-ESU. AND THE ONES GETTING EATEN! YOU NEED TO FOCUS, MAN.
WE'RE HERE!
SEE, I FIGURED OUT THIS MUST BE WHERE THEY'RE LOCKED UP FROM THE HOOD ORNAMENT UCHI GAVE US. CLEVER ME!
JOVE MOT RS
WUH?
THERE.
HOLEEEE! NOW I GET IT! YOU ALL COULD SEE THE JOVE MOTORS STATUE FROM YOUR ROOM!
KRIP

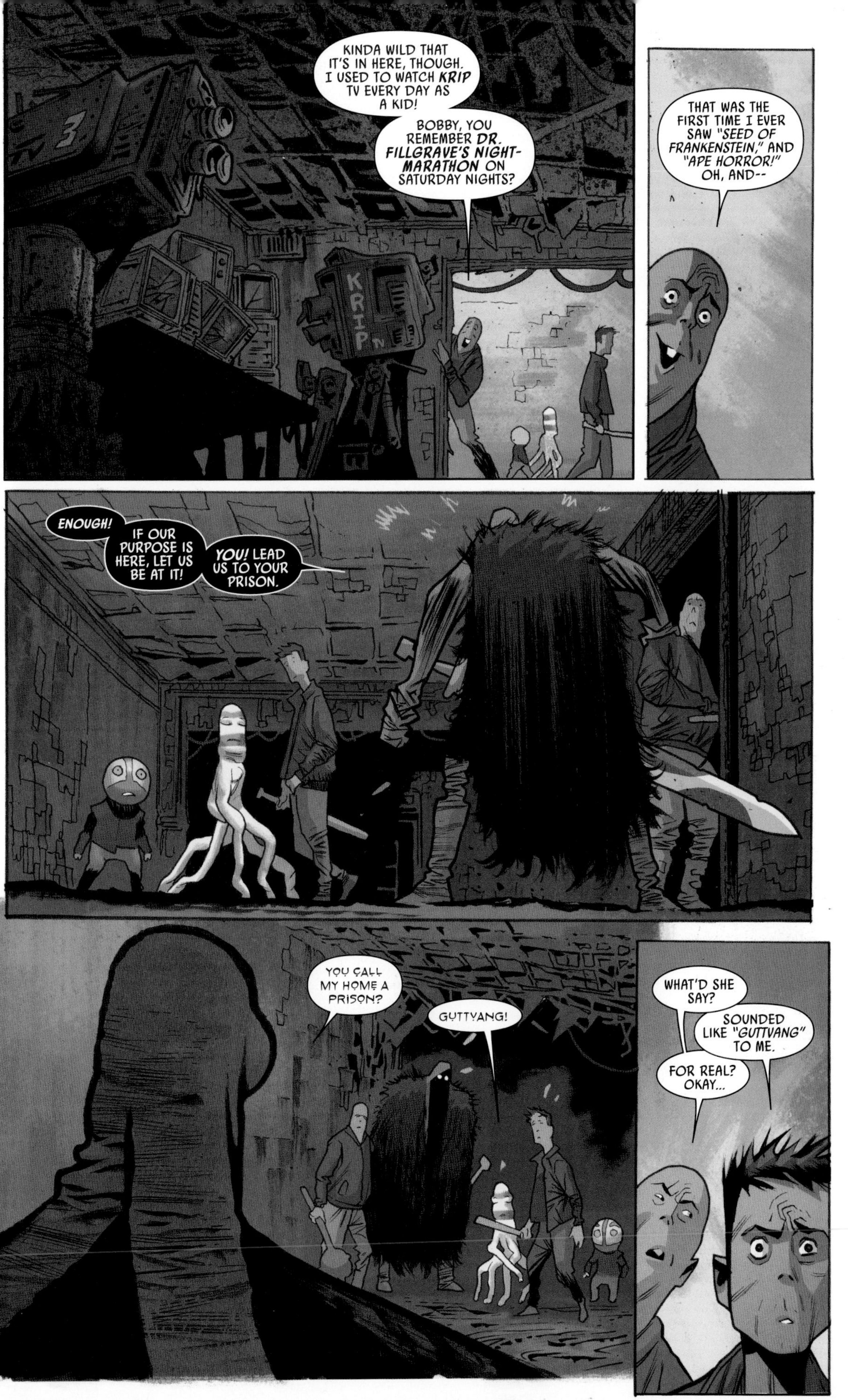
KINDA WILD THAT IT'S IN HERE, THOUGH. I USED TO WATCH KRIP TV EVERY DAY AS A KID!
BOBBY, YOU REMEMBER DR. FILLGRAVE'S NIGHT-MARATHON ON SATURDAY NIGHTS?
THAT WAS THE FIRST TIME I EVER SAW "SEED OF FRANKENSTEIN," AND "APE HORROR!" OH, AND--
ENOUGH!
IF OUR PURPOSE IS HERE, LET US BE AT IT!
YOU! LEAD US TO YOUR PRISON.
YOU CALL MY HOME A PRISON?
GUTTVANG!
WHAT'D SHE SAY?
SOUNDED LIKE "GUTTVANG" TO ME.
FOR REAL? OKAY...

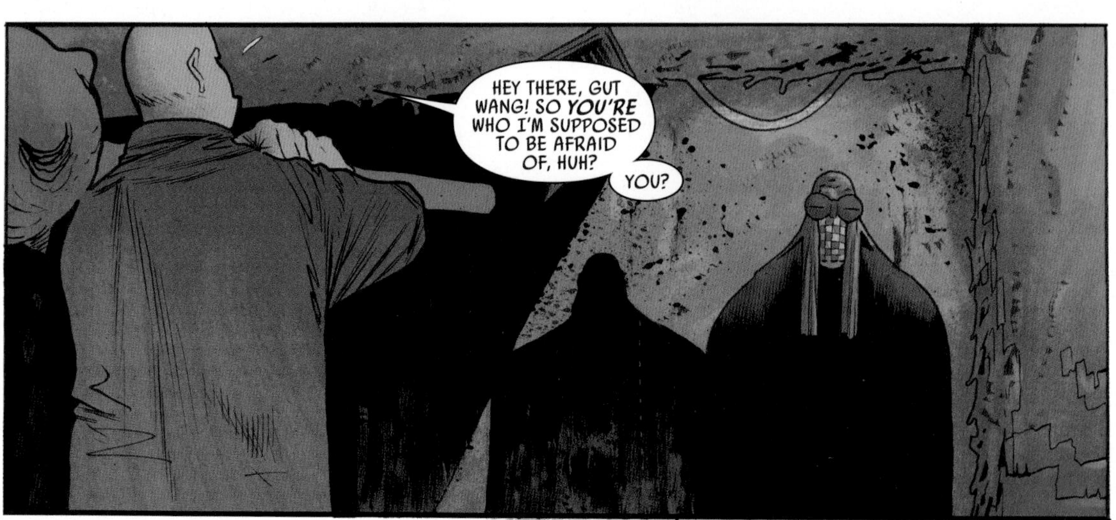
HEY THERE, GUT WANG! SO YOU'RE WHO I'M SUPPOSED TO BE AFRAID OF, HUH?
YOU?

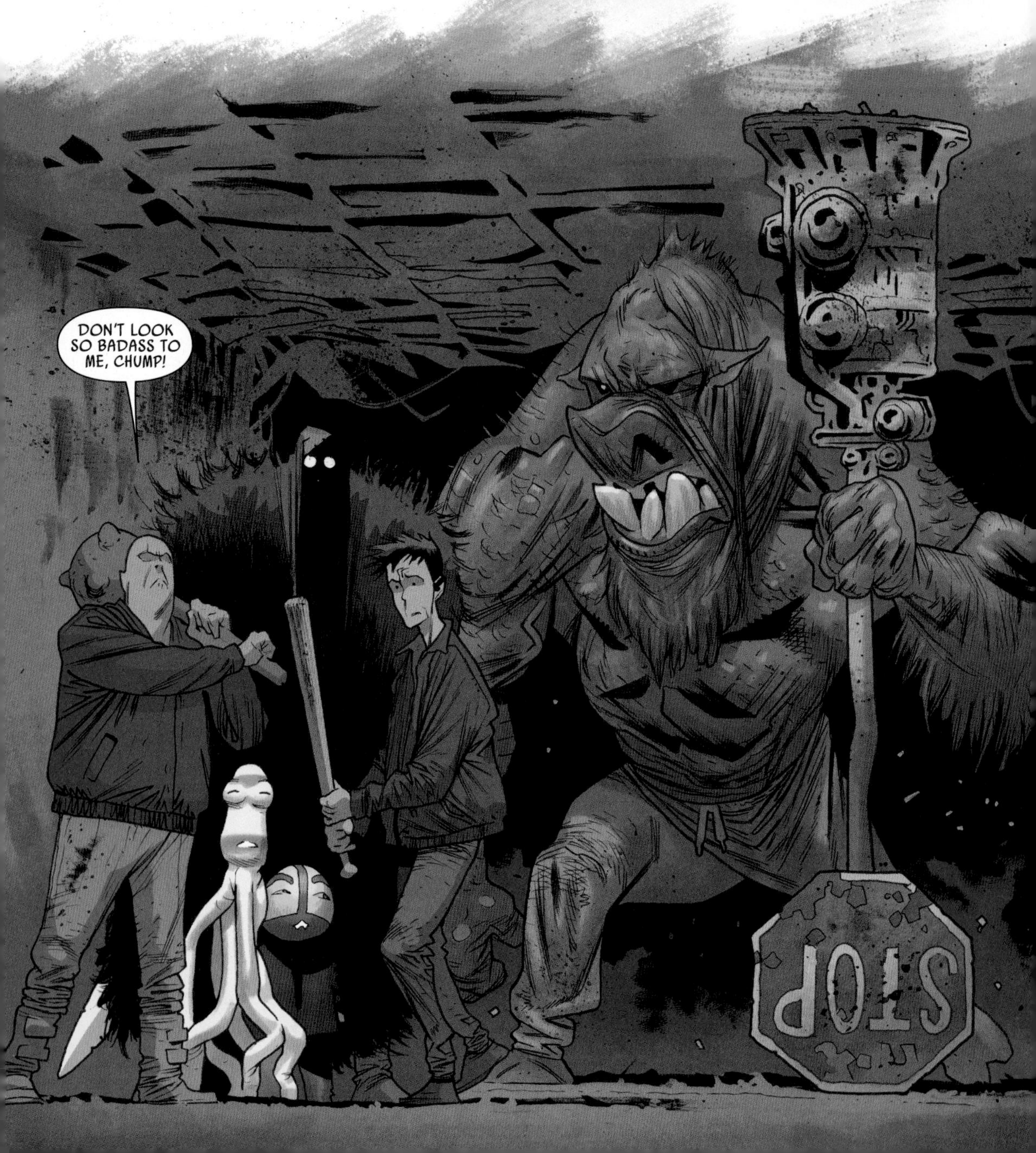
DON'T LOOK SO BADASS TO ME, CHUMP!
STOP

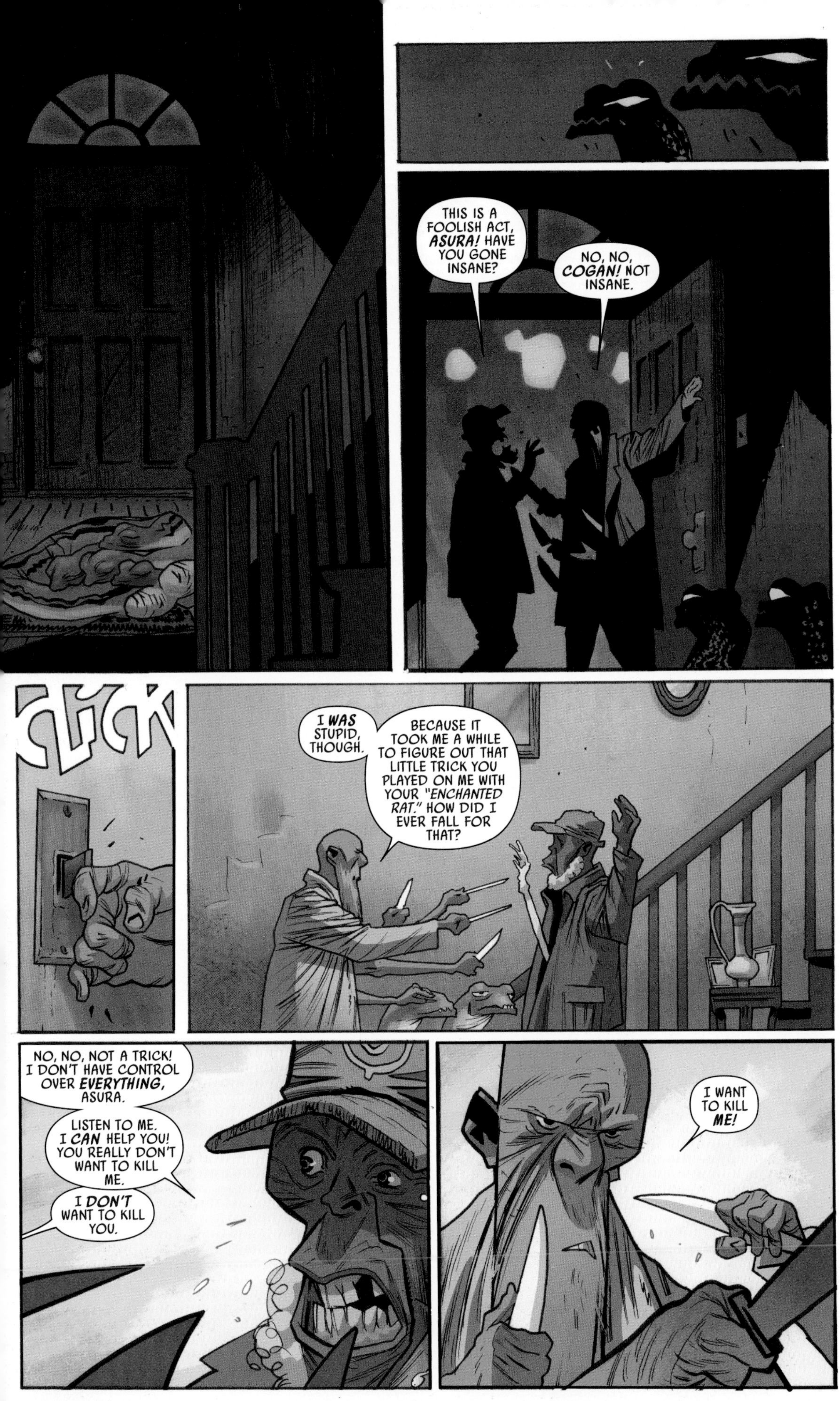
THIS IS A FOOLISH ACT, ASURA! HAVE YOU GONE INSANE?
NO, NO, COGAN! NOT INSANE.
CLICK
I WAS STUPID, THOUGH.
BECAUSE IT TOOK ME A WHILE TO FIGURE OUT THAT LITTLE TRICK YOU PLAYED ON ME WITH YOUR "ENCHANTED RAT." HOW DID I EVER FALL FOR THAT?
NO, NO, NOT A TRICK! I DON'T HAVE CONTROL OVER EVERYTHING, ASURA.
LISTEN TO ME. I CAN HELP YOU! YOU REALLY DON'T WANT TO KILL ME.
I DON'T WANT TO KILL YOU.
I WANT TO KILL ME!

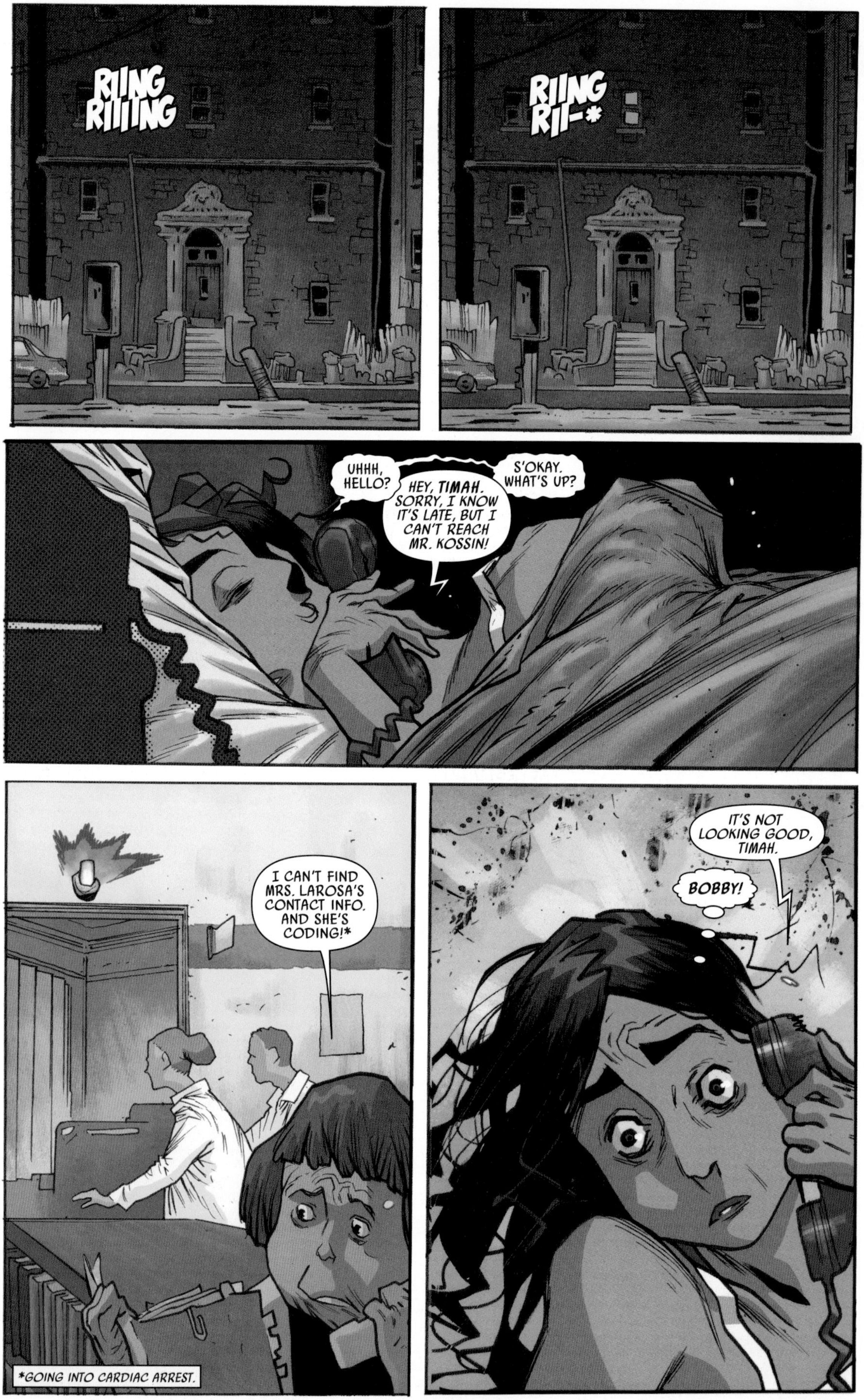
RIING RIIIING
RIING RII-*
UHHH, HELLO?
HEY, TIMAH. SORRY, I KNOW IT'S LATE, BUT I CAN'T REACH MR. KOSSIN!
S'OKAY. WHAT'S UP?
I CAN'T FIND MRS. LAROSA'S CONTACT INFO. AND SHE'S CODING!*
*GOING INTO CARDIAC ARREST.
IT'S NOT LOOKING GOOD, TIMAH.
BOBBY!

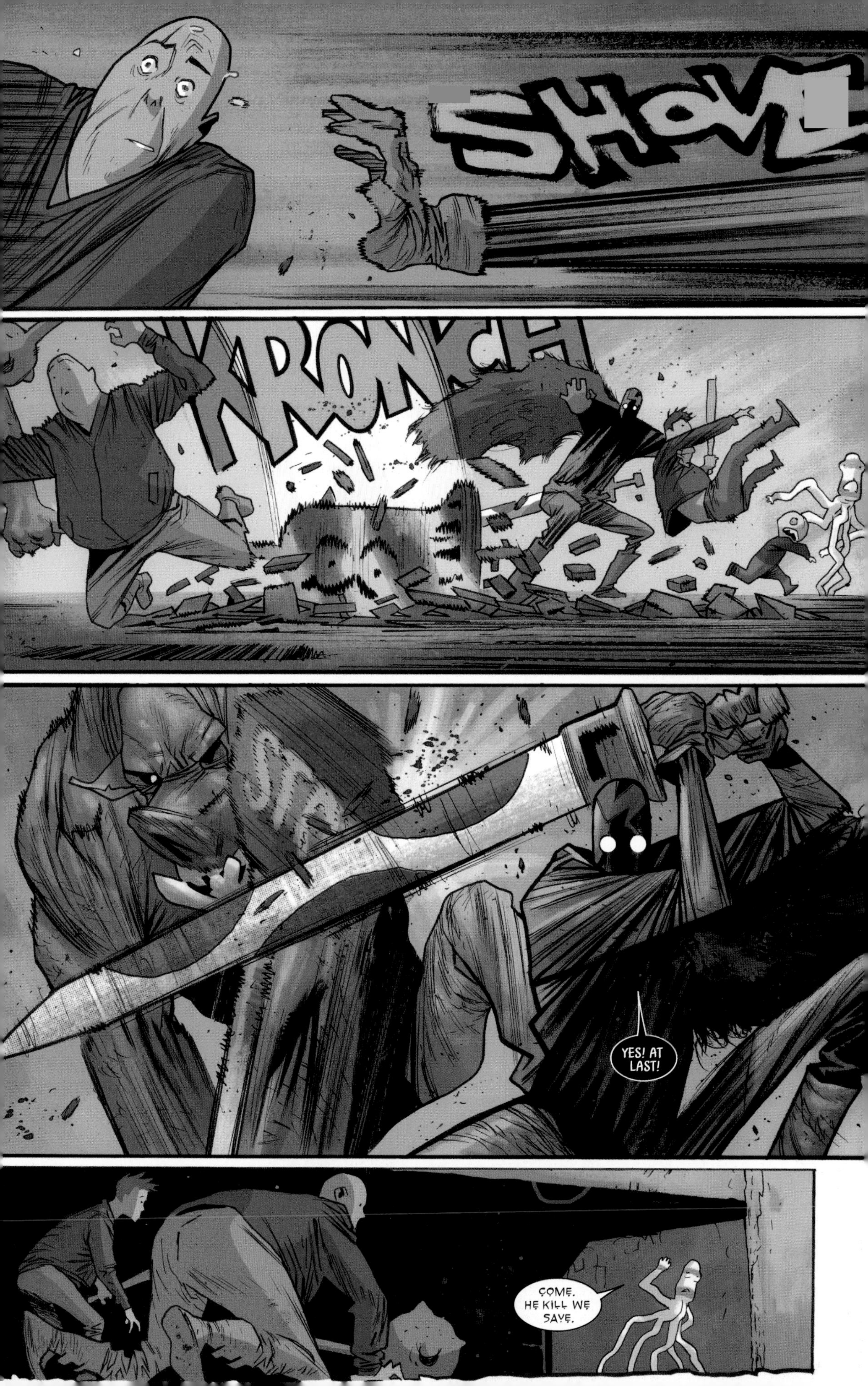
SHOV
KRONCH
YES! AT LAST!
COME. HE KILL WE SAVE.

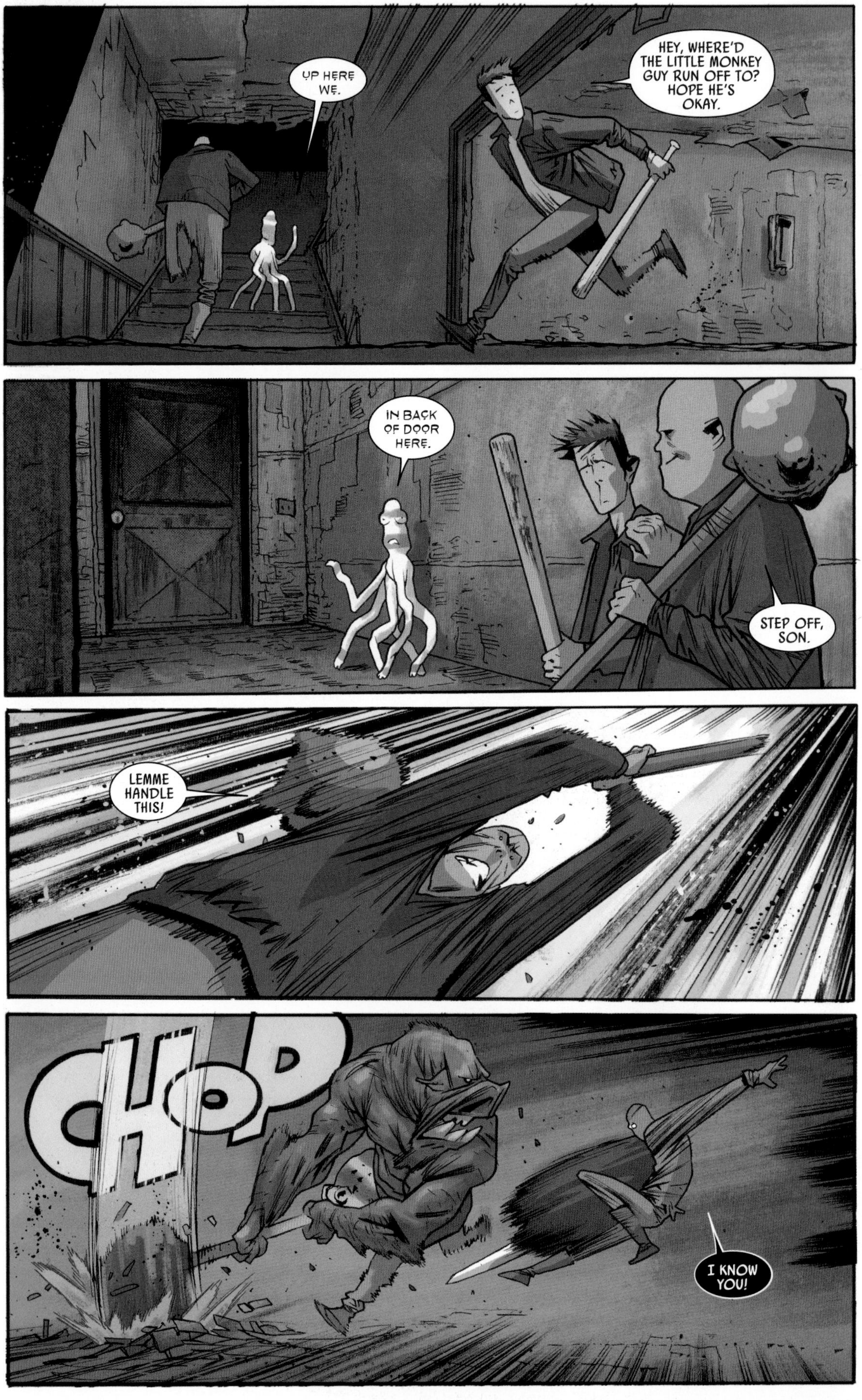
UP HERE WE.
HEY, WHERE'D THE LITTLE MONKEY GUY RUN OFF TO? HOPE HE'S OKAY.
IN BACK OF DOOR HERE.
STEP OFF, SON.
LEMME HANDLE THIS!
CHOP
I KNOW YOU!

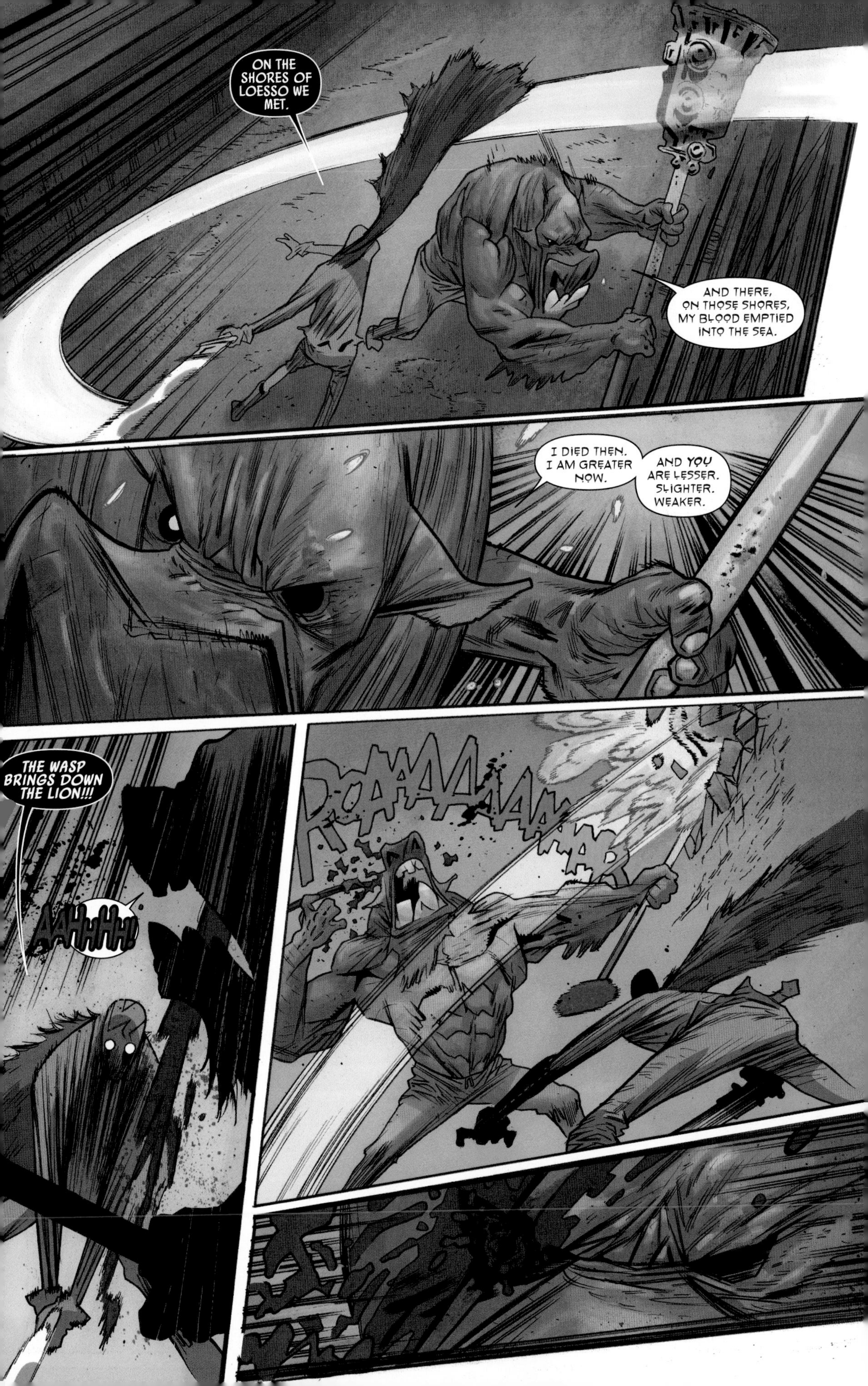
ON THE SHORES OF LOESSO WE MET.
AND THERE, ON THOSE SHORES, MY BLOOD EMPTIED INTO THE SEA.
I DIED THEN. I AM GREATER NOW.
AND YOU ARE LESSER. SLIGHTER. WEAKER.
THE WASP BRINGS DOWN THE LION!!!
AAHHHH!
ROAAAAAAAAAR

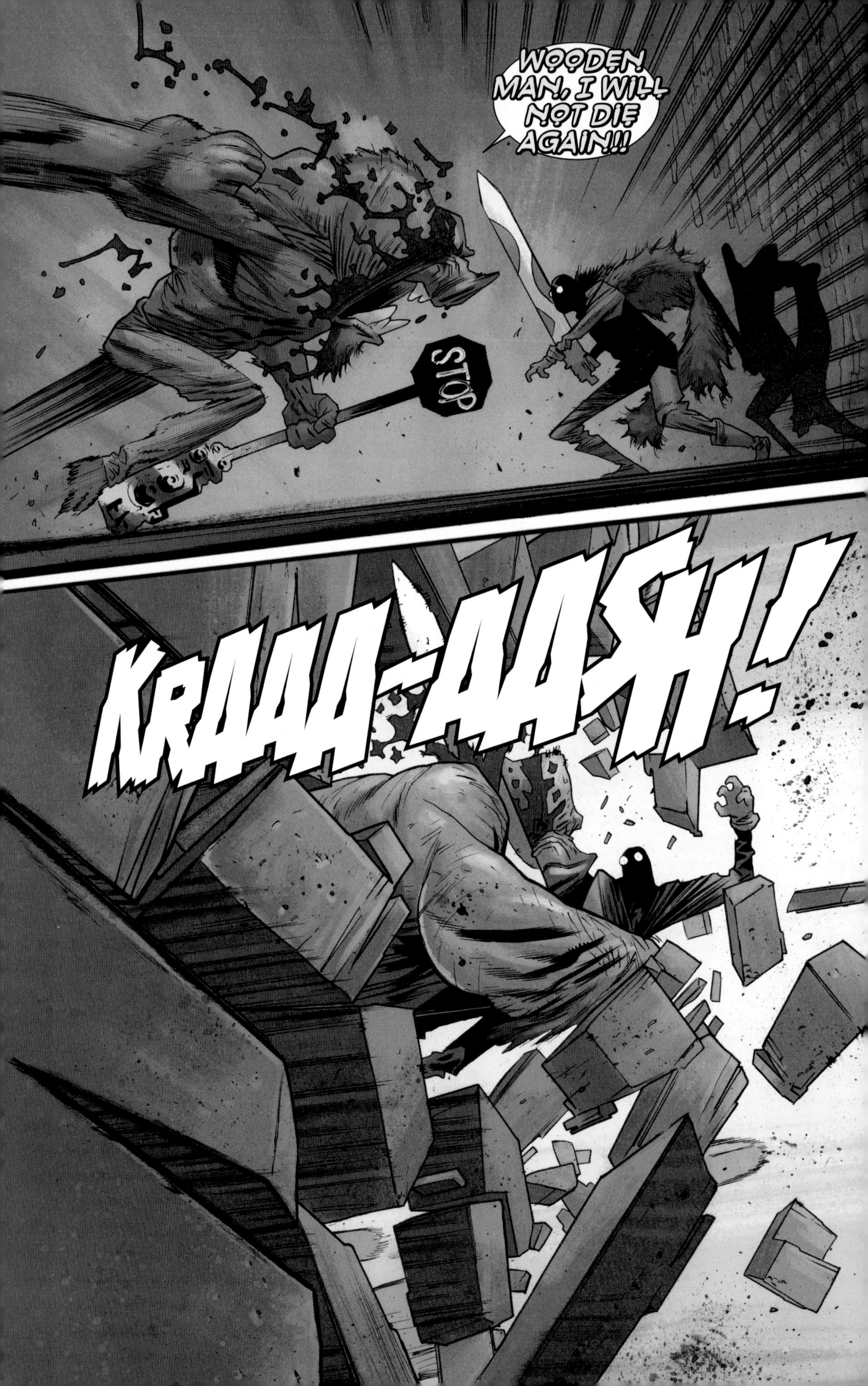
WOODEN MAN, I WILL NOT DIE AGAIN!!
STOP
KRAAA-AASH!

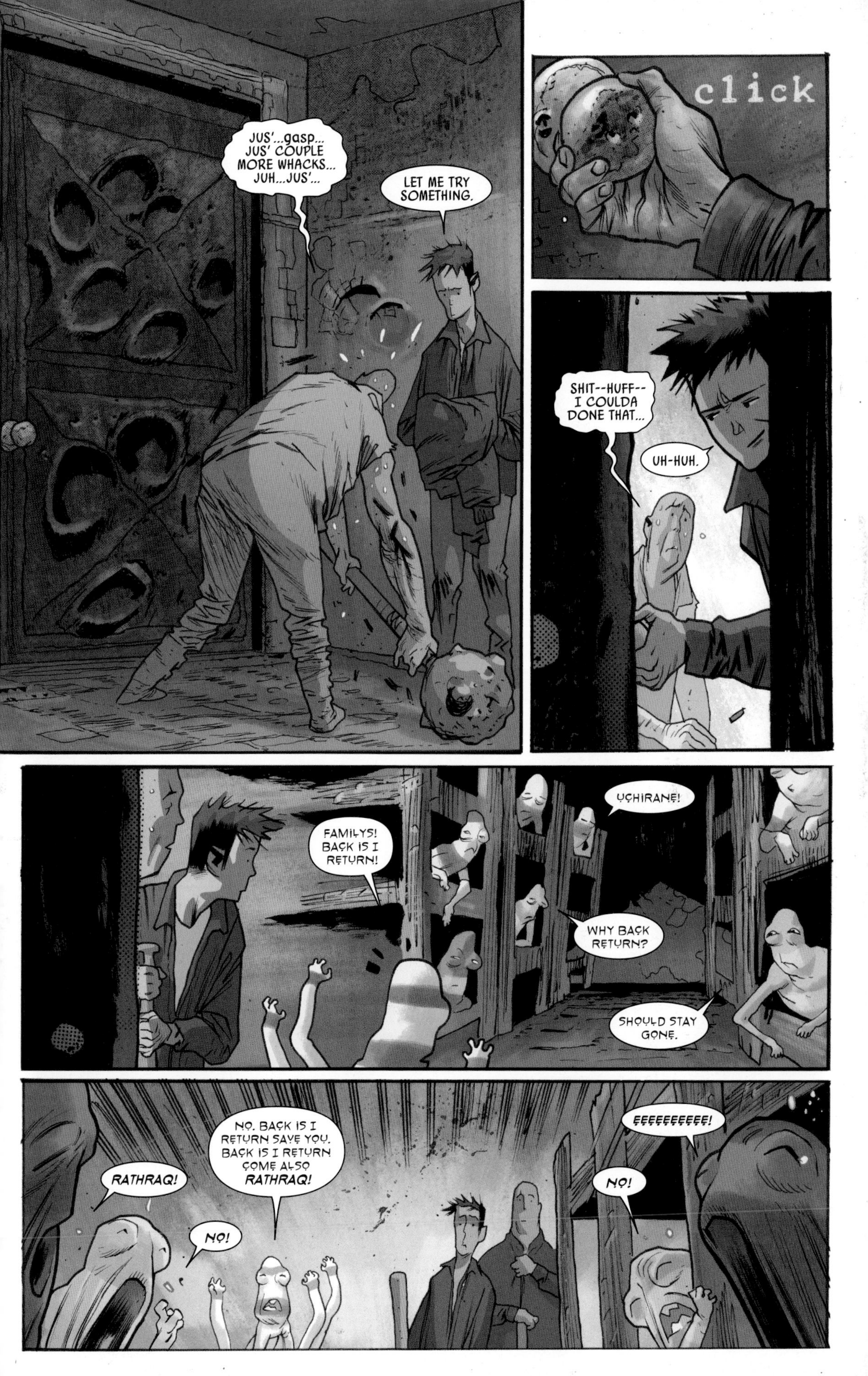
JUS'...gasp... JUS' COUPLE MORE WHACKS... JUH...JUS'...
LET ME TRY SOMETHING.
click
SHIT--HUFF-- I COULDA DONE THAT...
UH-HUH.
FAMILYS! BACK IS I RETURN!
UCHIRANE!
WHY BACK RETURN?
SHOULD STAY GONE.
RATHRAQ!
NO. BACK IS I RETURN SAVE YOU. BACK IS I RETURN COME ALSO RATHRAQ!
NO!
EEEEEEEEEE!
NO!

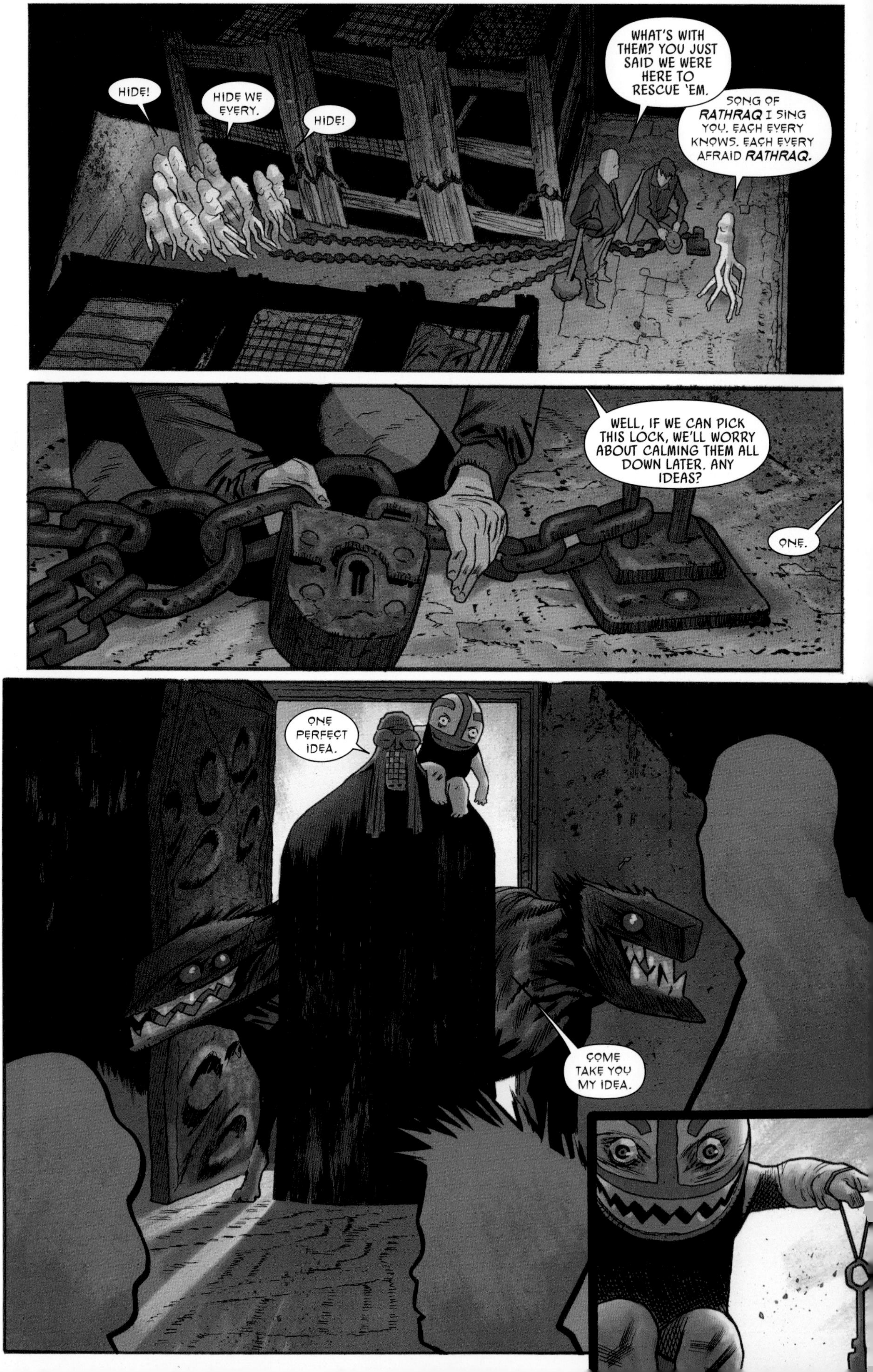
HIDE!
HIDE WE EVERY.
HIDE!
WHAT'S WITH THEM? YOU JUST SAID WE WERE HERE TO RESCUE 'EM.
SONG OF RATHRAQ I SING YOU. EACH EVERY KNOWS. EACH EVERY AFRAID RATHRAQ.
WELL, IF WE CAN PICK THIS LOCK, WE'LL WORRY ABOUT CALMING THEM ALL DOWN LATER. ANY IDEAS?
ONE.
ONE PERFECT IDEA.
COME TAKE YOU MY IDEA.

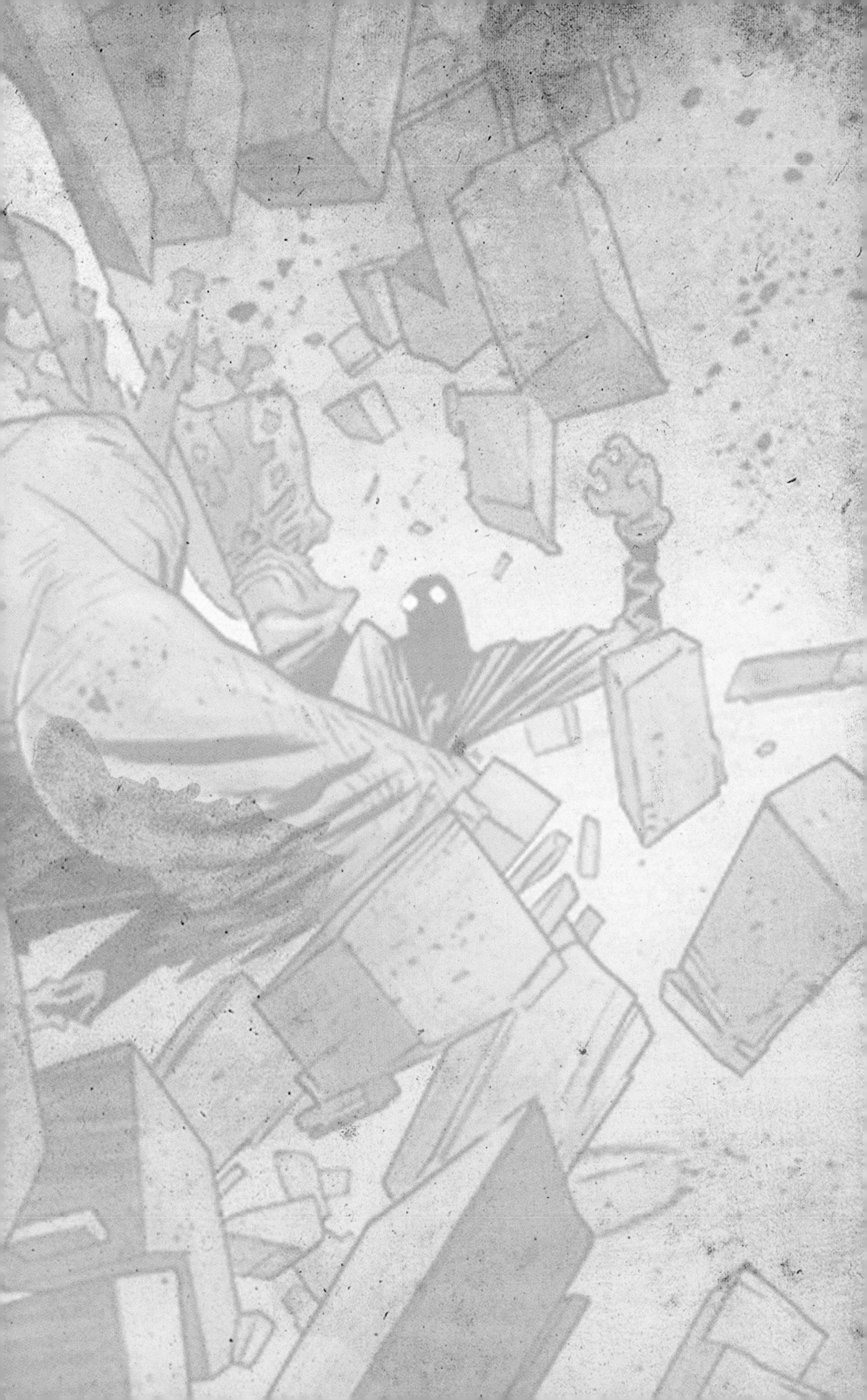

# CHAPTER FIVE

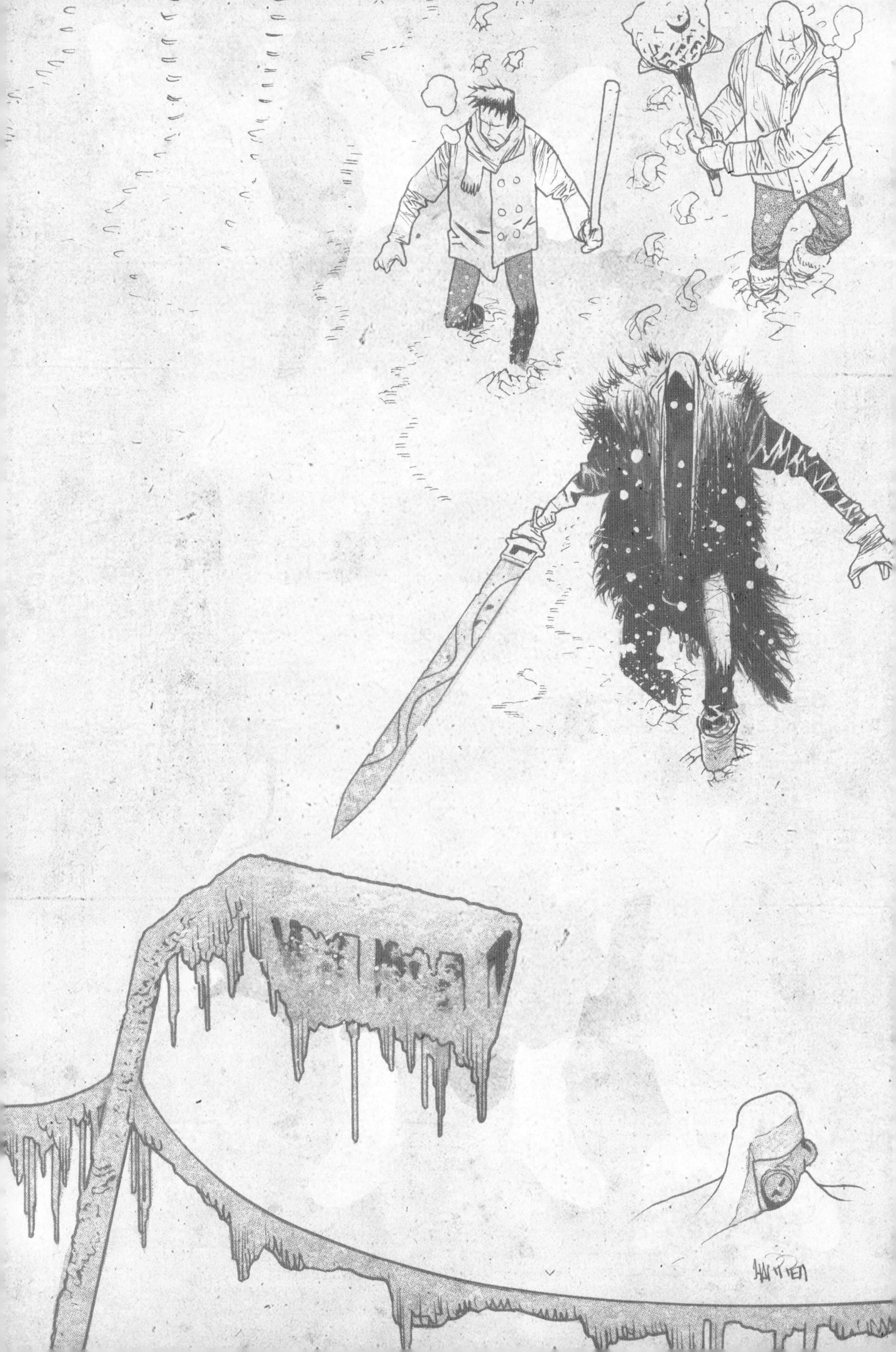

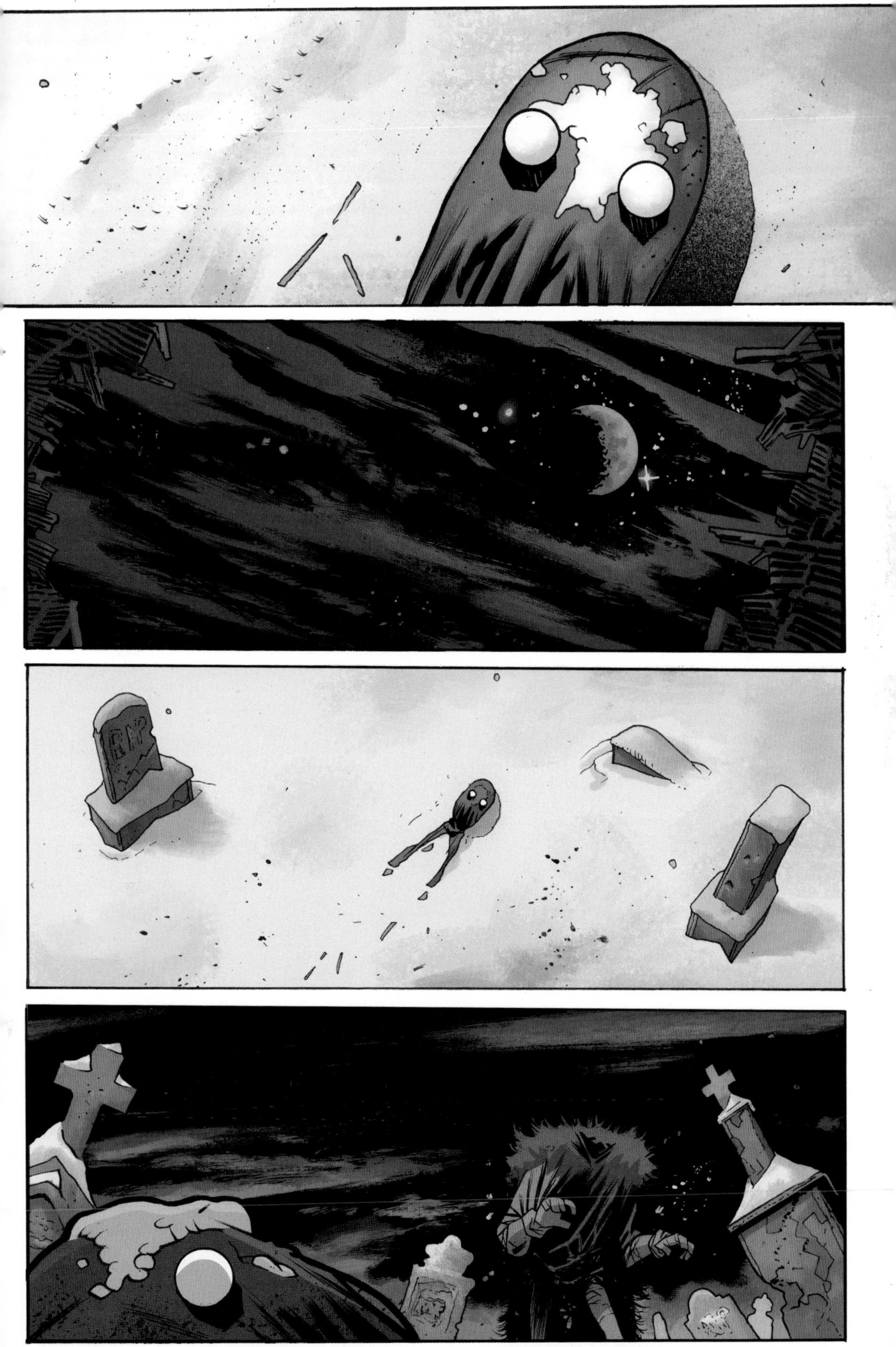
RIP

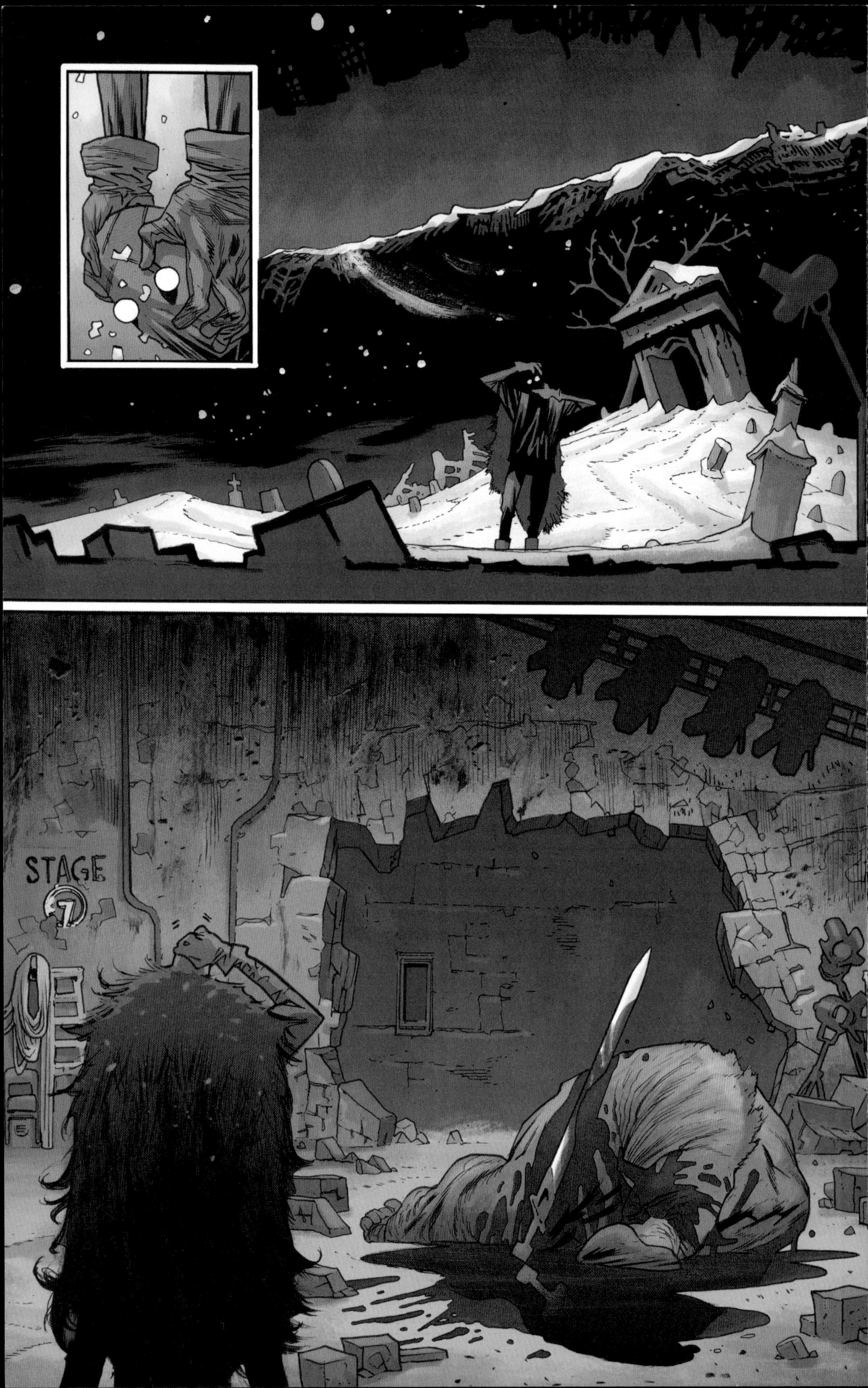
STAGE
7

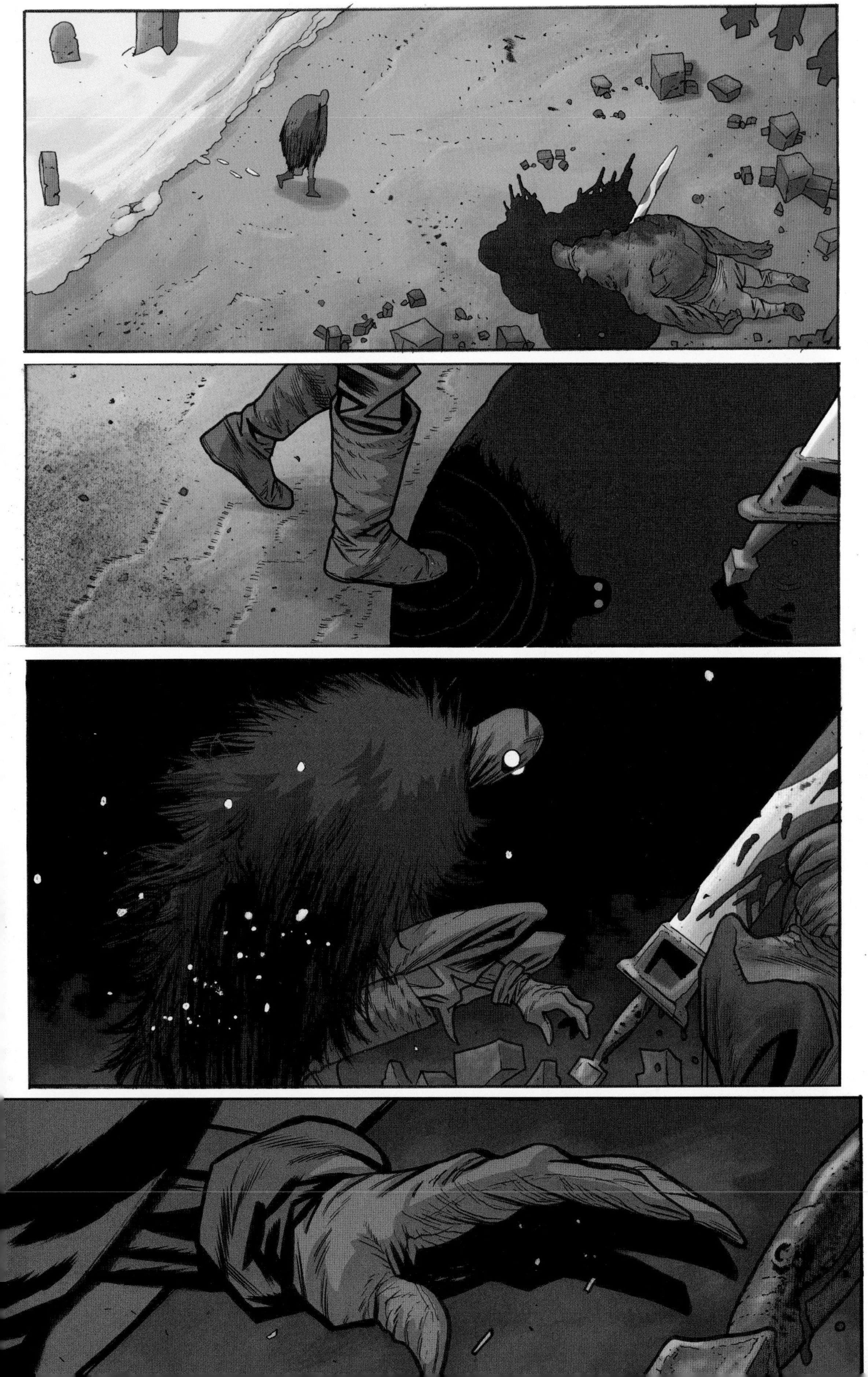

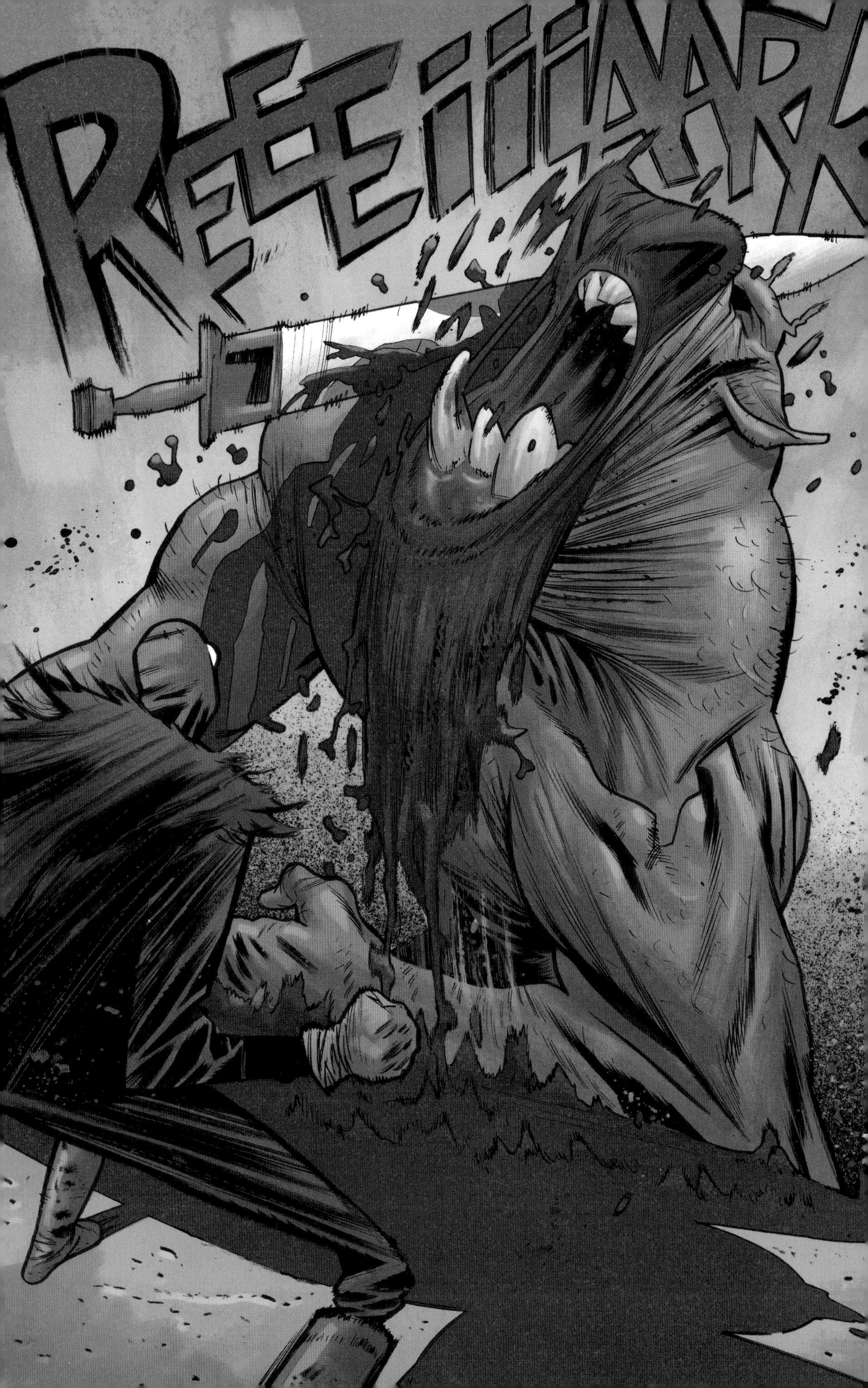

QUITE A MOMENT FOR US. FOR US ALL.

A MOMENT OF EXCITEMENT AND ANTICIPATION FOR ME--BUT FOR YOU--

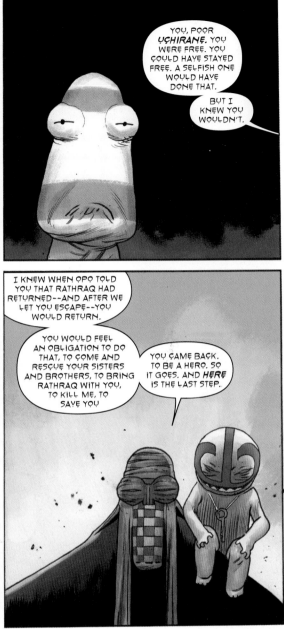

YOU, POOR *UCHIRANE.* YOU WERE FREE. YOU COULD HAVE STAYED FREE. A SELFISH ONE WOULD HAVE DONE THAT.

BUT I KNEW YOU WOULDN'T.

I KNEW WHEN OPO TOLD YOU THAT RATHRAQ HAD RETURNED--AND AFTER WE LET YOU ESCAPE--YOU WOULD RETURN.

YOU WOULD FEEL AN OBLIGATION TO DO THAT, TO COME AND RESCUE YOUR SISTERS AND BROTHERS, TO BRING RATHRAQ WITH YOU, TO KILL ME, TO SAVE YOU

YOU CAME BACK. TO BE A HERO. SO IT GOES. AND *HERE* IS THE LAST STEP.

AND *THERE* IS THE LOCK. WILL YOU COME FOR THE KEY?

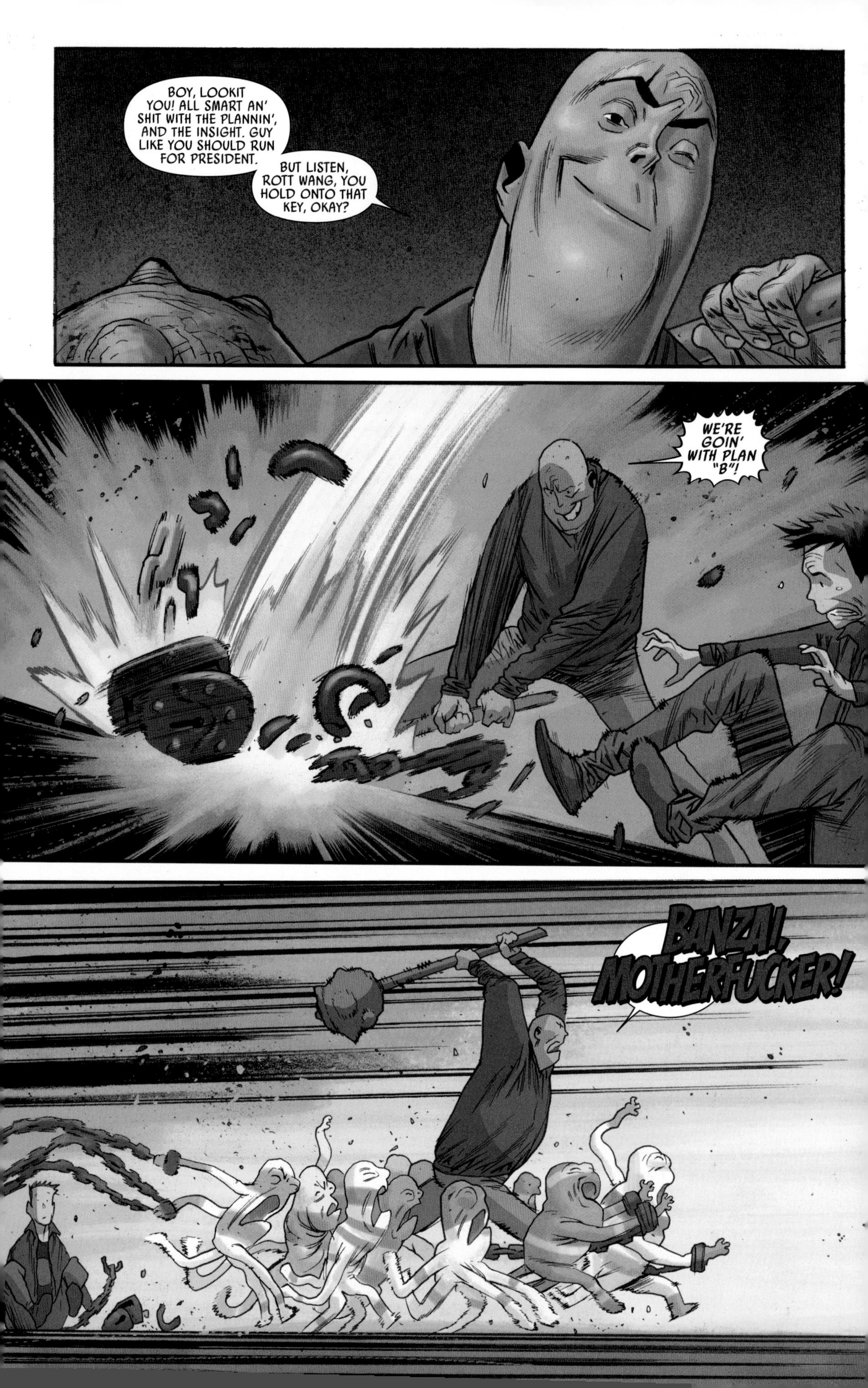
BOY, LOOKIT YOU! ALL SMART AN' SHIT WITH THE PLANNIN', AND THE INSIGHT. GUY LIKE YOU SHOULD RUN FOR PRESIDENT.
BUT LISTEN, ROTT WANG, YOU HOLD ONTO THAT KEY, OKAY?
WE'RE GOIN' WITH PLAN "B"!
BANZAI, MOTHERFUCKER!

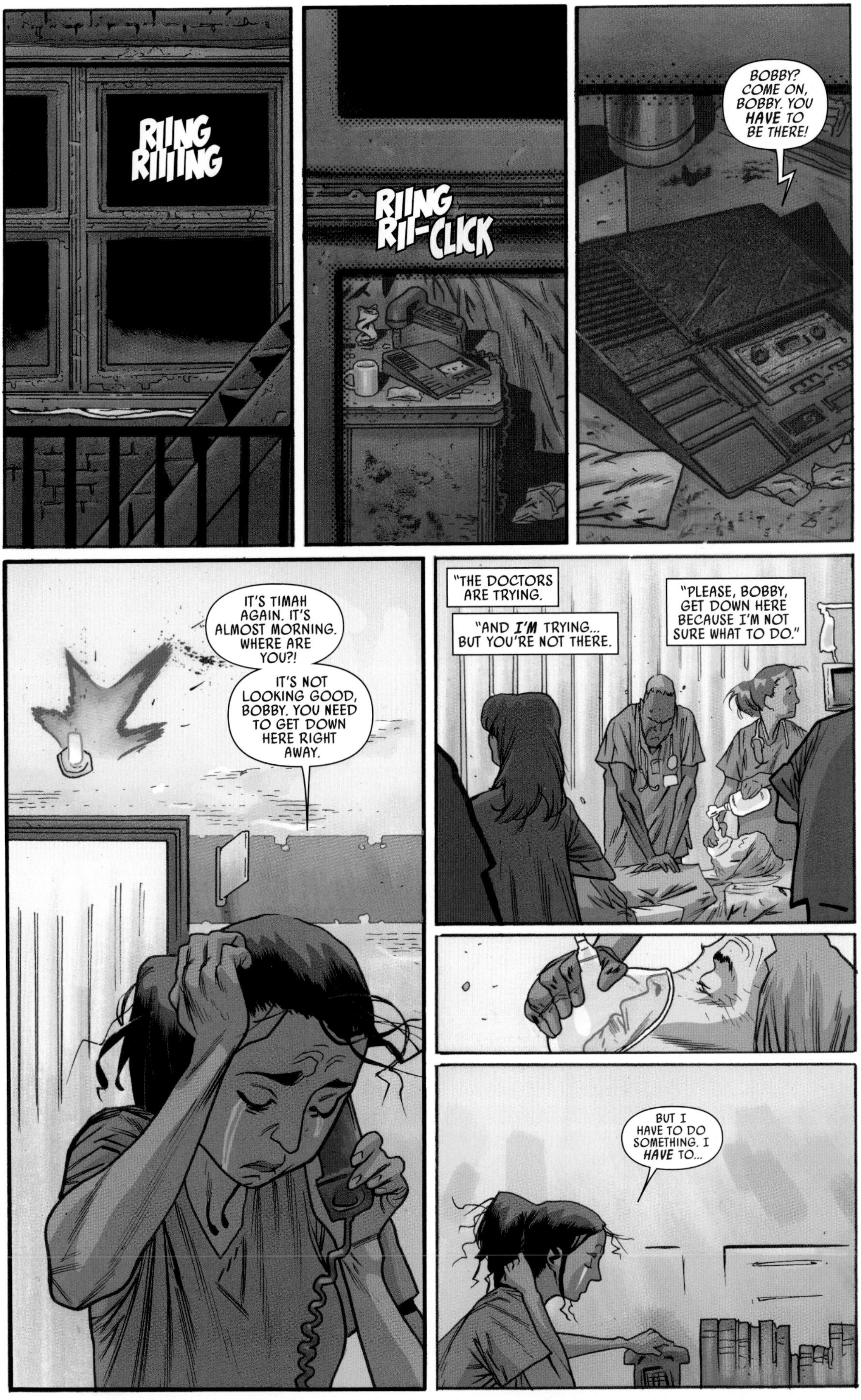
RIING RIIIING
RIING RII-CLICK
BOBBY? COME ON, BOBBY. YOU HAVE TO BE THERE!
IT'S TIMAH AGAIN. IT'S ALMOST MORNING. WHERE ARE YOU?!
IT'S NOT LOOKING GOOD, BOBBY. YOU NEED TO GET DOWN HERE RIGHT AWAY.
"THE DOCTORS ARE TRYING.
"AND I'M TRYING... BUT YOU'RE NOT THERE.
"PLEASE, BOBBY, GET DOWN HERE BECAUSE I'M NOT SURE WHAT TO DO."
BUT I HAVE TO DO SOMETHING. I HAVE TO...

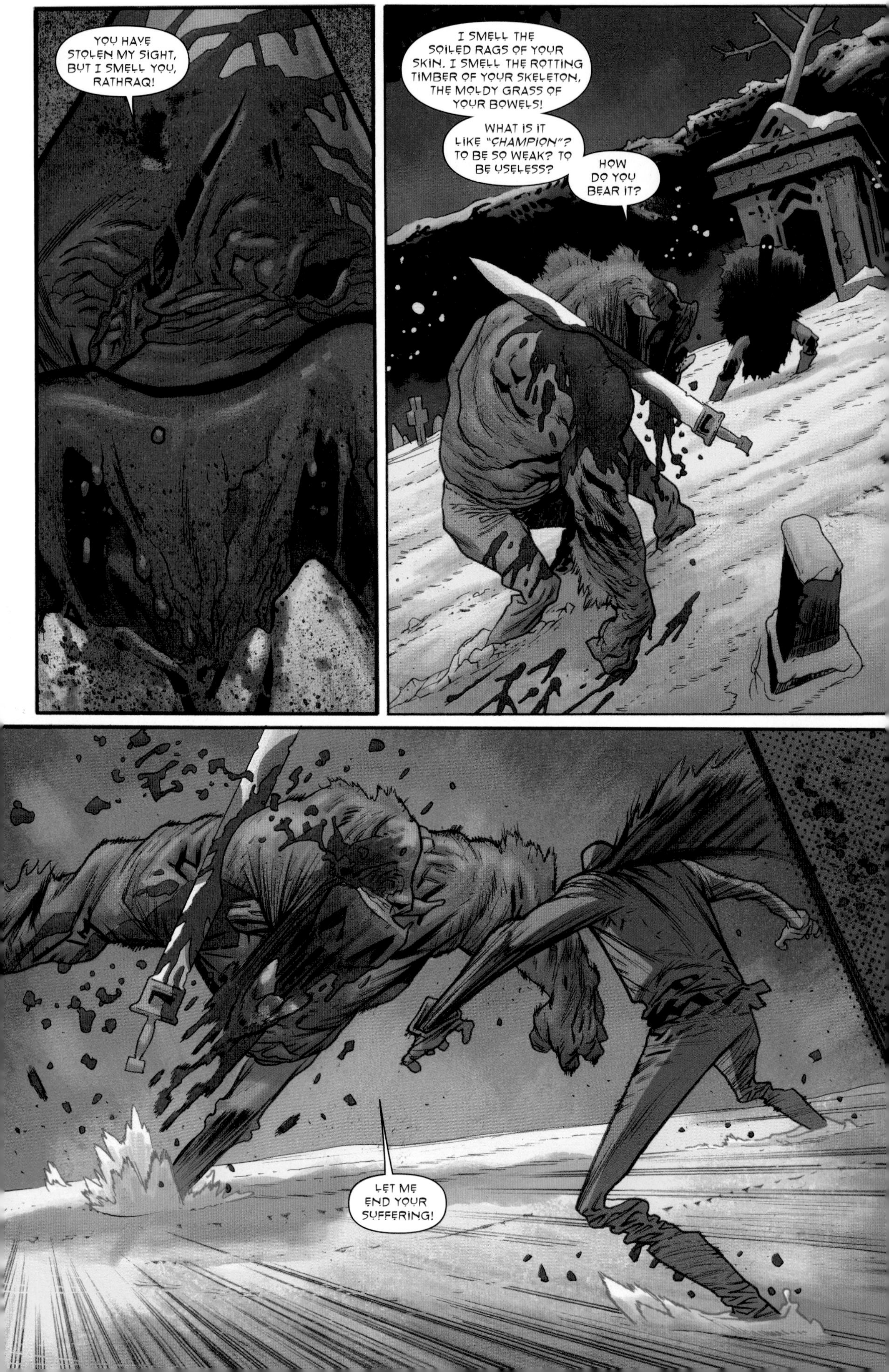
YOU HAVE STOLEN MY SIGHT, BUT I SMELL YOU, RATHRAQ!
I SMELL THE SOILED RAGS OF YOUR SKIN. I SMELL THE ROTTING TIMBER OF YOUR SKELETON, THE MOLDY GRASS OF YOUR BOWELS!
WHAT IS IT LIKE "CHAMPION"? TO BE SO WEAK? TO BE USELESS?
HOW DO YOU BEAR IT?
LET ME END YOUR SUFFERING!

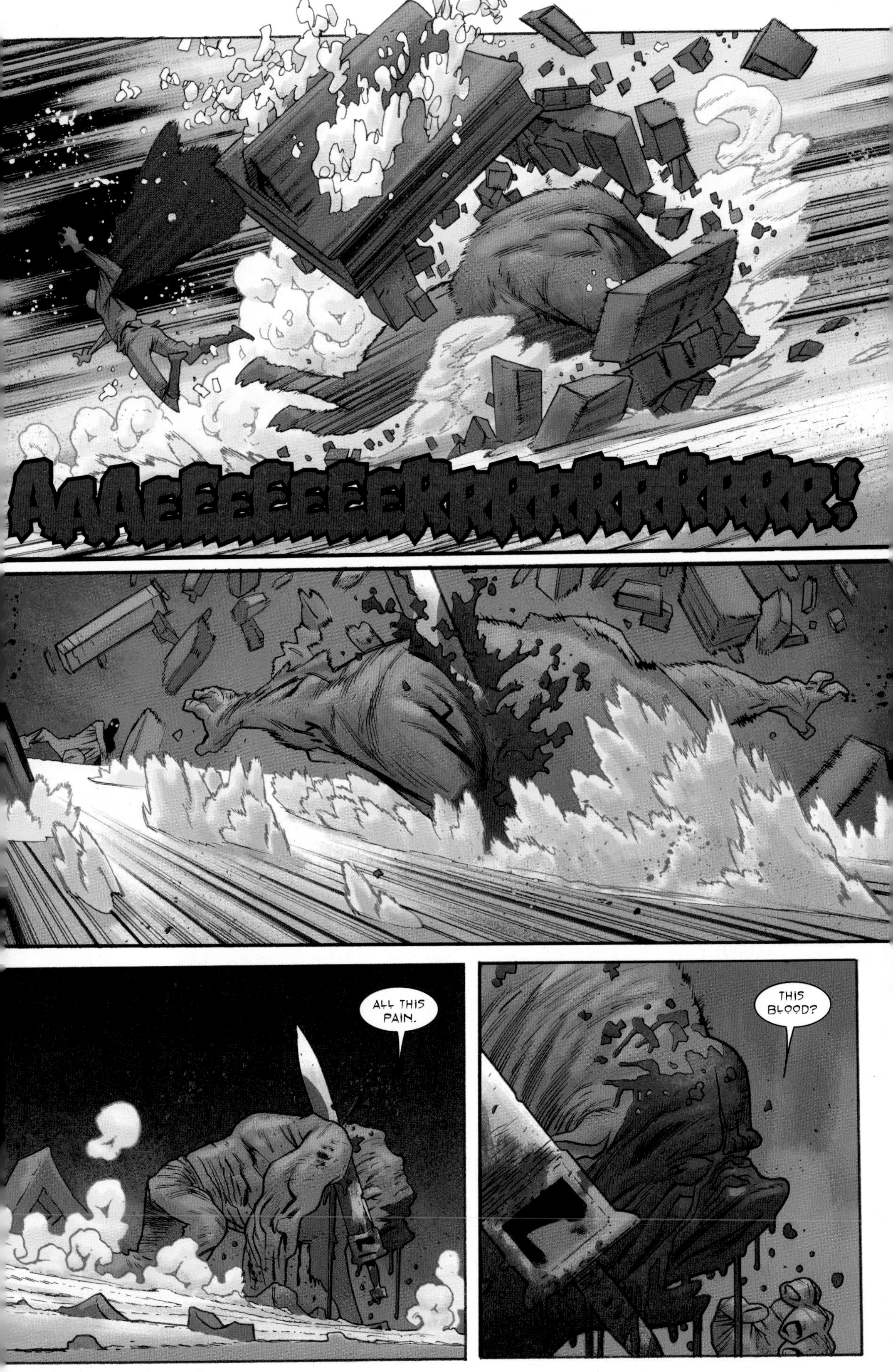
AAAEEEEEEEERRRRRRRRRRRR!
ALL THIS PAIN.
THIS BLOOD?

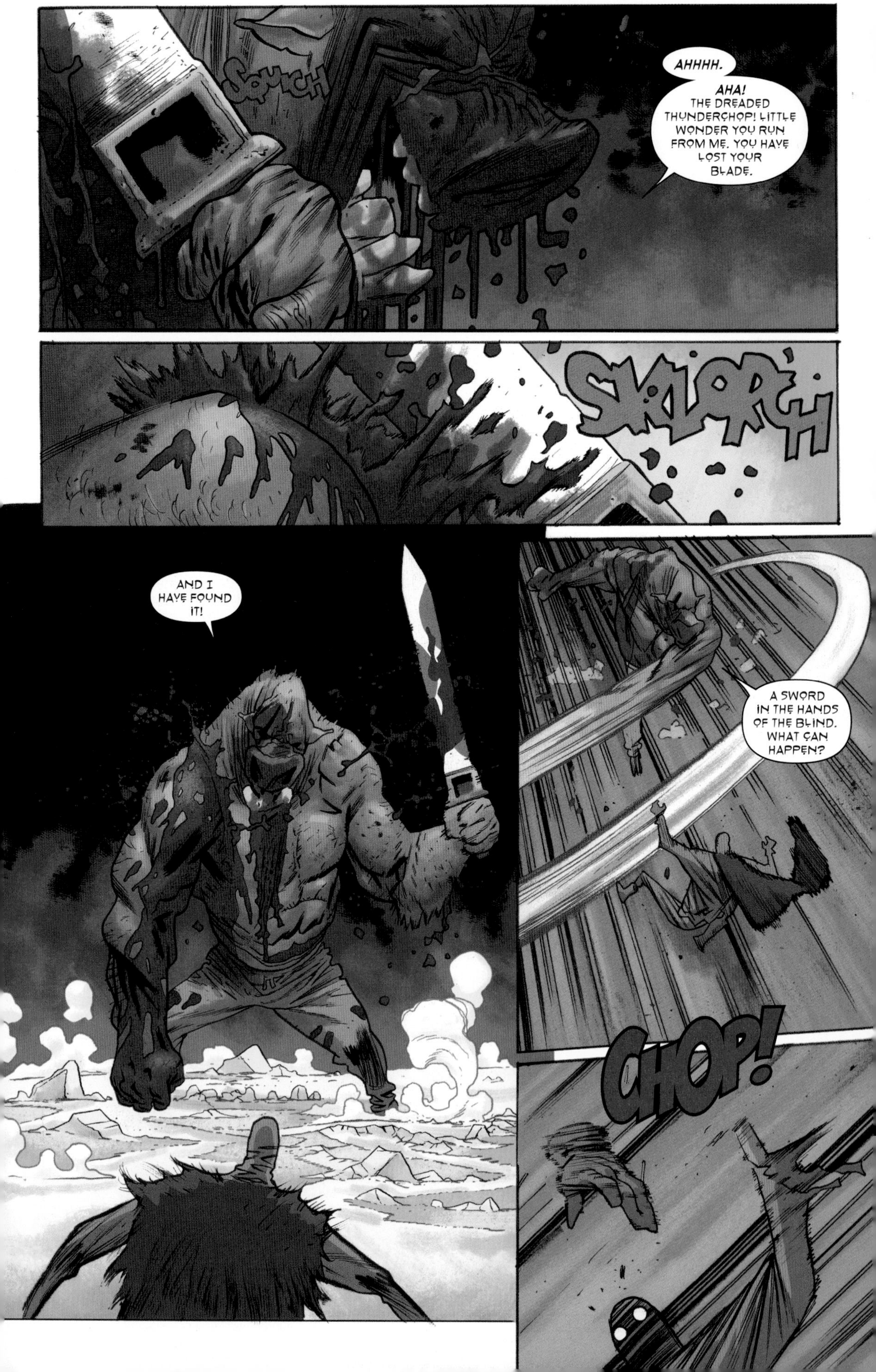
SQUICH
AHHHH.
AHA! THE DREADED THUNDERCHOP! LITTLE WONDER YOU RUN FROM ME. YOU HAVE LOST YOUR BLADE.
SKLORCH
AND I HAVE FOUND IT!
A SWORD IN THE HANDS OF THE BLIND. WHAT CAN HAPPEN?
CHOP!

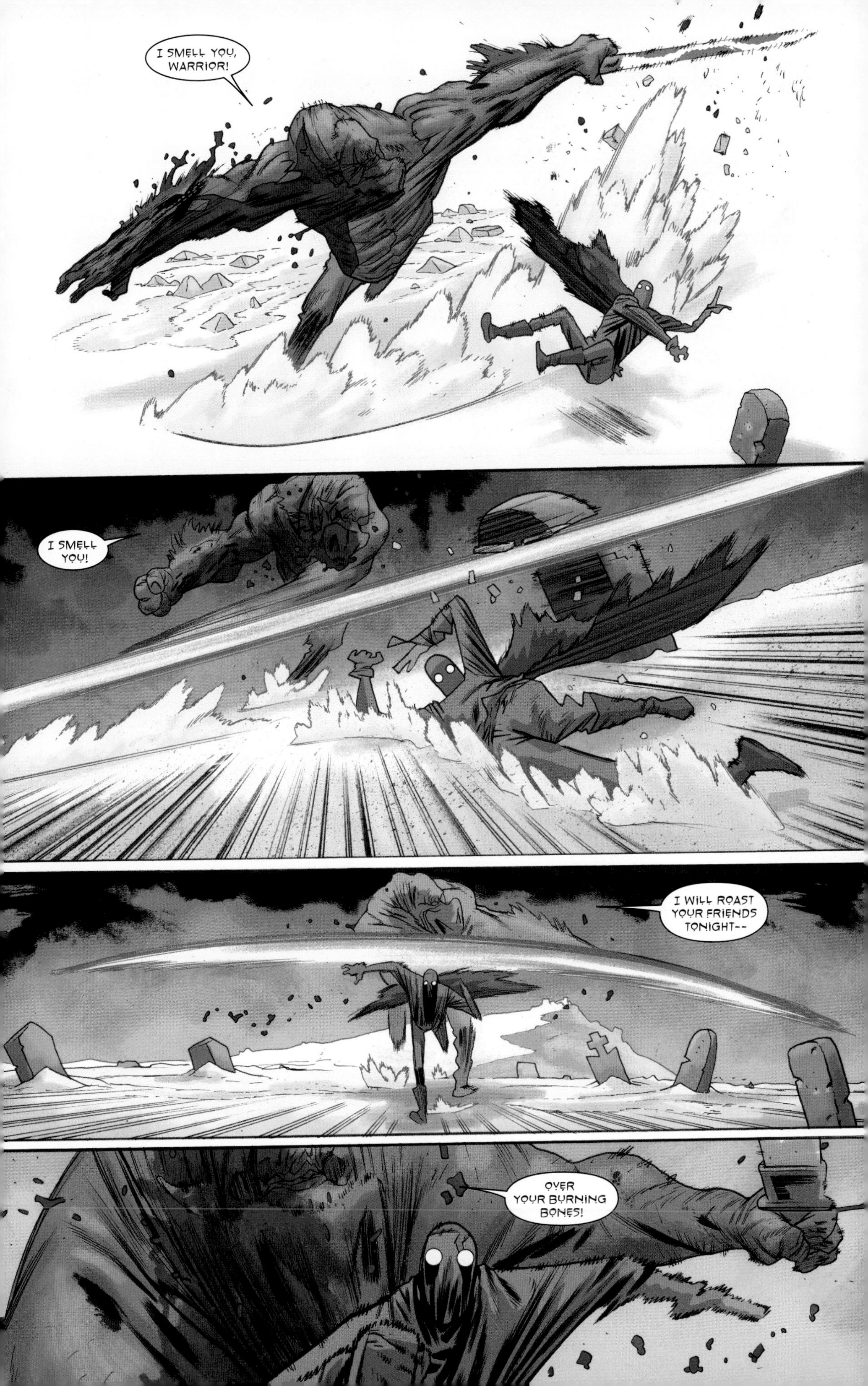
I SMELL YOU, WARRIOR!
I SMELL YOU!
I WILL ROAST YOUR FRIENDS TONIGHT--
OVER YOUR BURNING BONES!

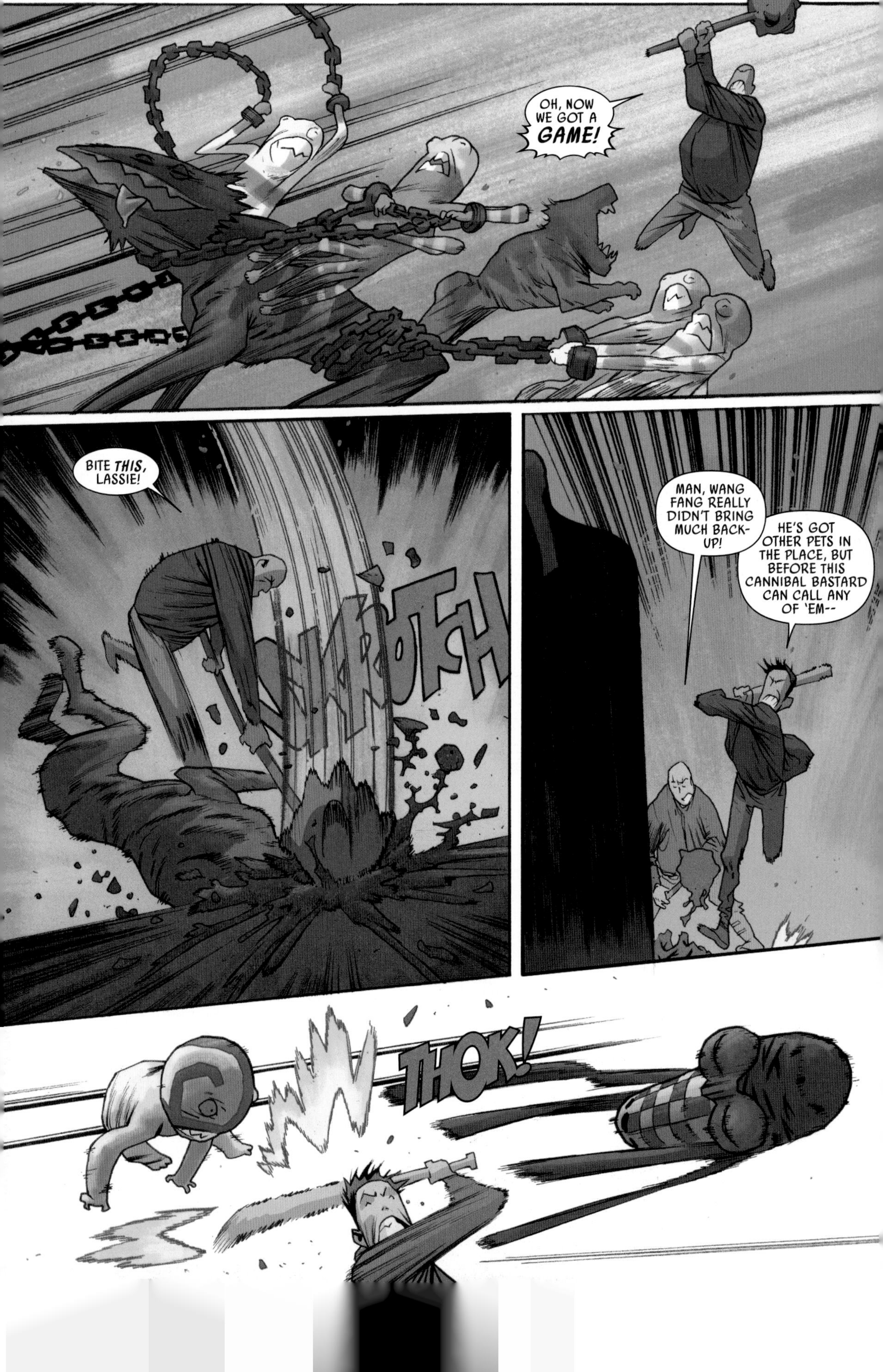
OH, NOW WE GOT A GAME!
BITE THIS, LASSIE!
MAN, WANG FANG REALLY DIDN'T BRING MUCH BACK-UP!
HE'S GOT OTHER PETS IN THE PLACE, BUT BEFORE THIS CANNIBAL BASTARD CAN CALL ANY OF 'EM--
THOK!

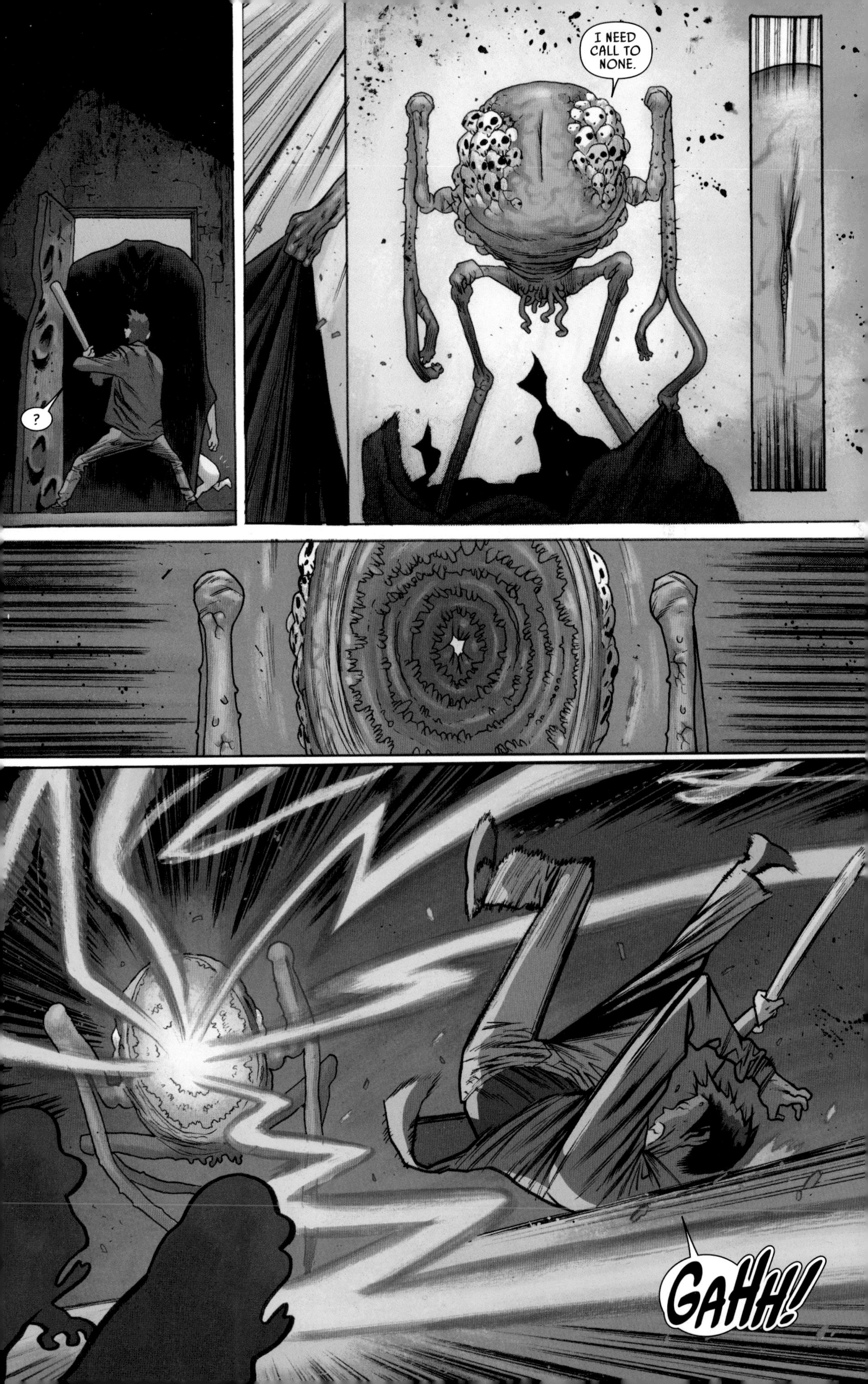
?
I NEED CALL TO NONE.
GAHH!

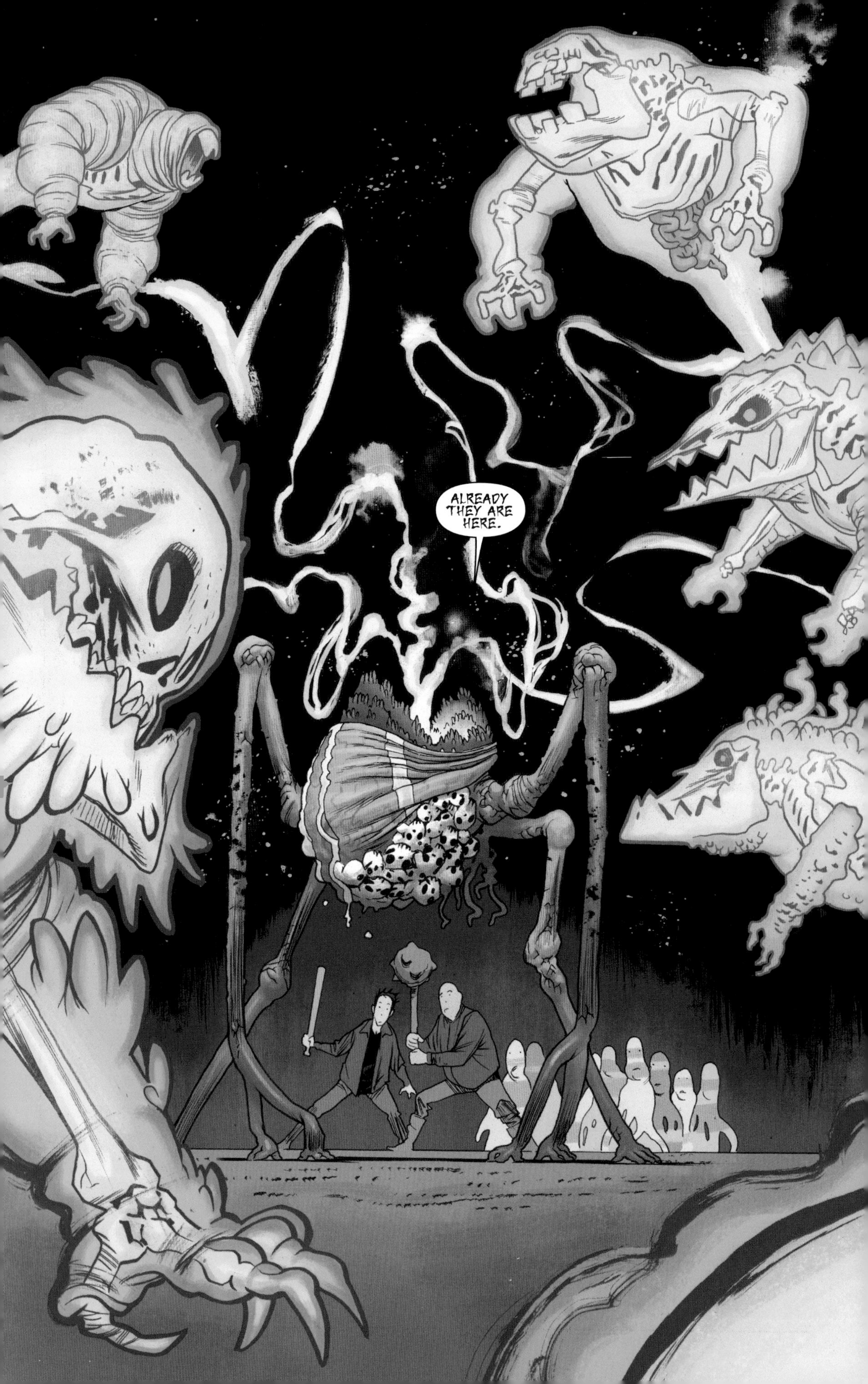
ALREADY THEY ARE HERE.

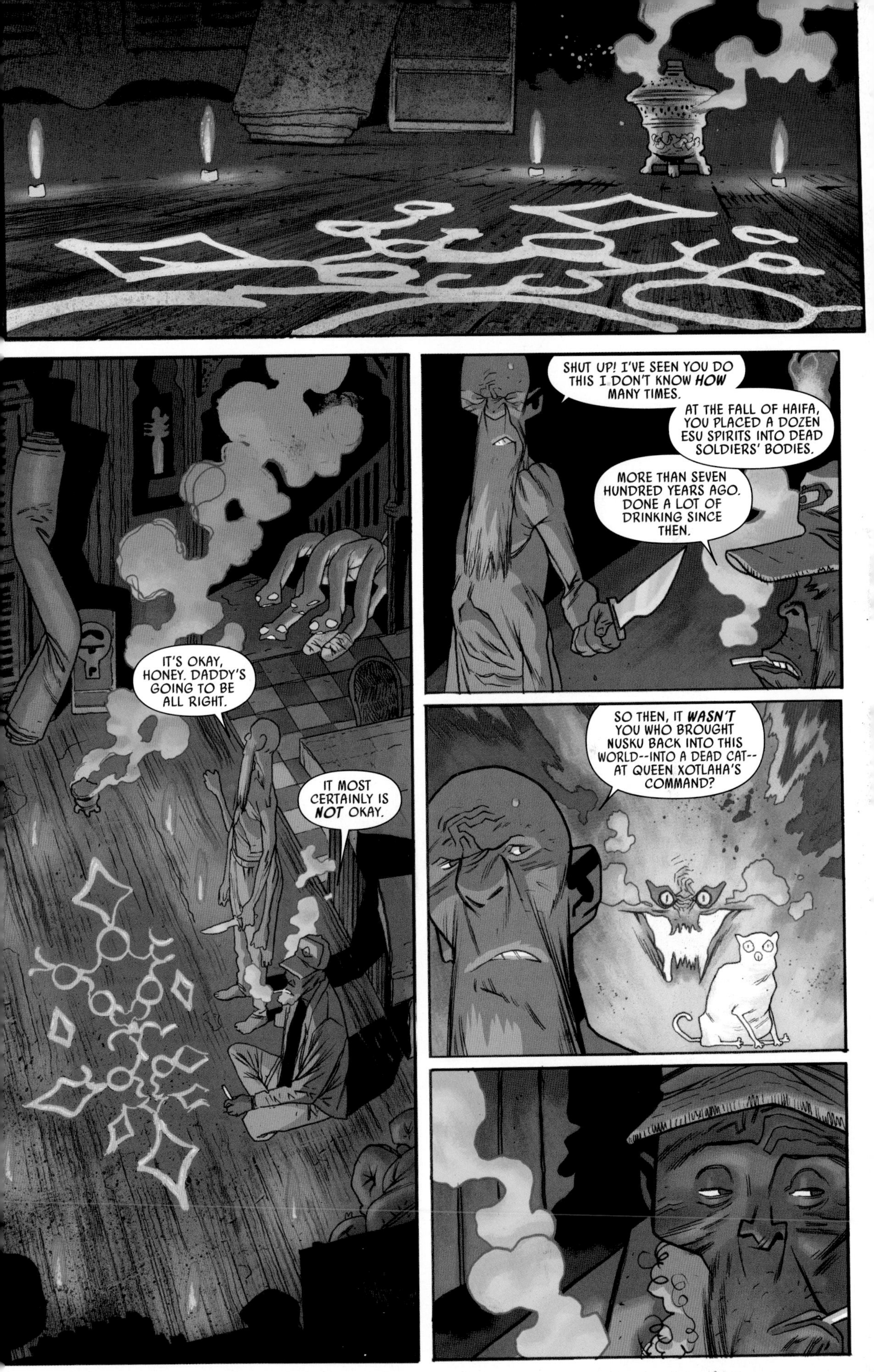
IT'S OKAY, HONEY. DADDY'S GOING TO BE ALL RIGHT.
IT MOST CERTAINLY IS NOT OKAY.
SHUT UP! I'VE SEEN YOU DO THIS I DON'T KNOW HOW MANY TIMES.
AT THE FALL OF HAIFA, YOU PLACED A DOZEN ESU SPIRITS INTO DEAD SOLDIERS' BODIES.
MORE THAN SEVEN HUNDRED YEARS AGO. DONE A LOT OF DRINKING SINCE THEN.
SO THEN, IT WASN'T YOU WHO BROUGHT NUSKU BACK INTO THIS WORLD--INTO A DEAD CAT--AT QUEEN XOTLAHA'S COMMAND?

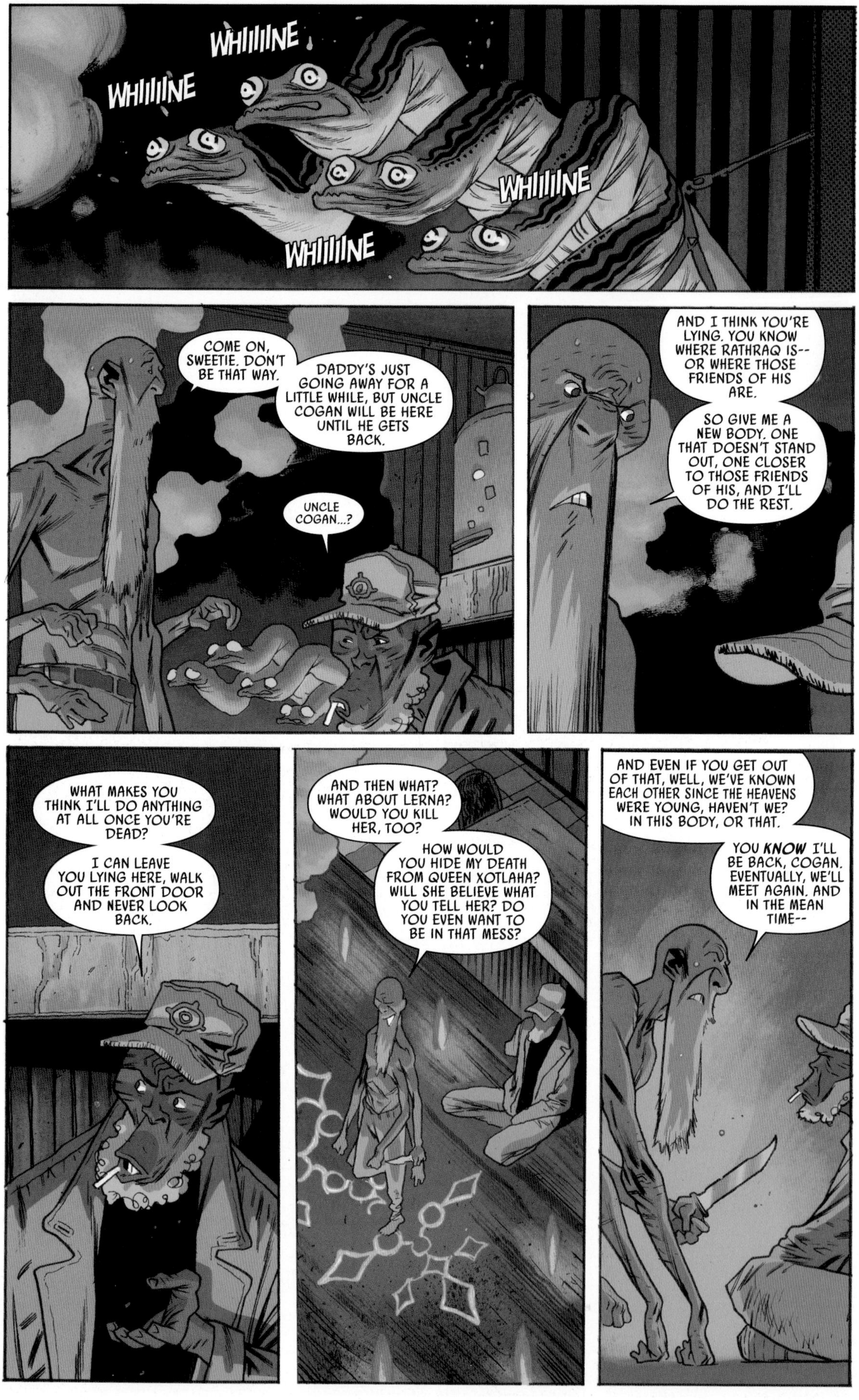
WHIIIIINE
WHIIIIINE
WHIIIIINE
WHIIIIINE
COME ON, SWEETIE. DON'T BE THAT WAY.
DADDY'S JUST GOING AWAY FOR A LITTLE WHILE, BUT UNCLE COGAN WILL BE HERE UNTIL HE GETS BACK.
UNCLE COGAN...?
AND I THINK YOU'RE LYING. YOU KNOW WHERE RATHRAQ IS-- OR WHERE THOSE FRIENDS OF HIS ARE.
SO GIVE ME A NEW BODY. ONE THAT DOESN'T STAND OUT, ONE CLOSER TO THOSE FRIENDS OF HIS, AND I'LL DO THE REST.
WHAT MAKES YOU THINK I'LL DO ANYTHING AT ALL ONCE YOU'RE DEAD?
I CAN LEAVE YOU LYING HERE, WALK OUT THE FRONT DOOR AND NEVER LOOK BACK.
AND THEN WHAT? WHAT ABOUT LERNA? WOULD YOU KILL HER, TOO?
HOW WOULD YOU HIDE MY DEATH FROM QUEEN XOTLAHA? WILL SHE BELIEVE WHAT YOU TELL HER? DO YOU EVEN WANT TO BE IN THAT MESS?
AND EVEN IF YOU GET OUT OF THAT, WELL, WE'VE KNOWN EACH OTHER SINCE THE HEAVENS WERE YOUNG, HAVEN'T WE? IN THIS BODY, OR THAT.
YOU KNOW I'LL BE BACK, COGAN. EVENTUALLY, WE'LL MEET AGAIN. AND IN THE MEAN TIME--

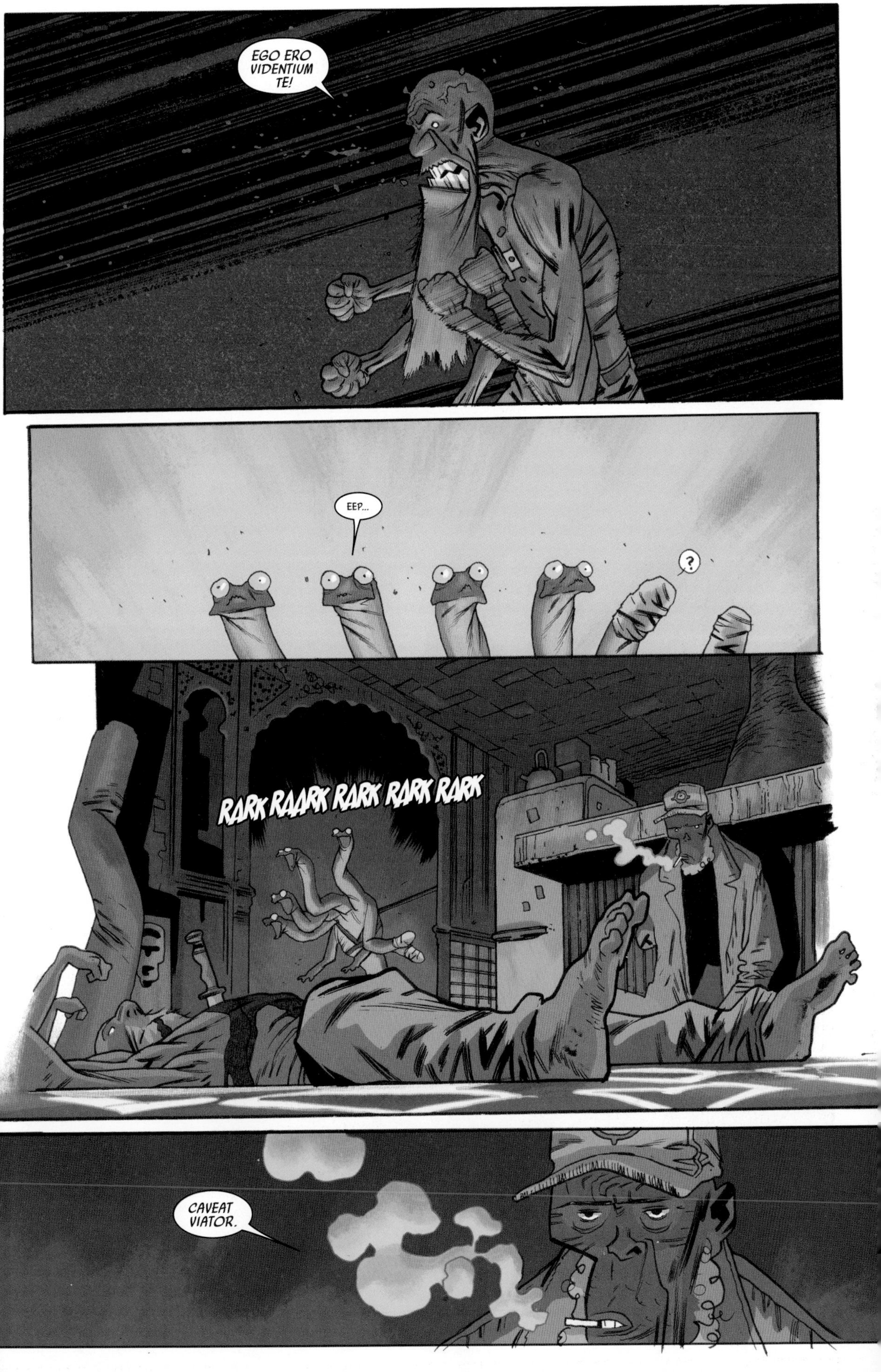
EGO ERO VIDENTIUM TE!
EEP...
?
RARK RAARK RARK RARK RARK
CAVEAT VIATOR.

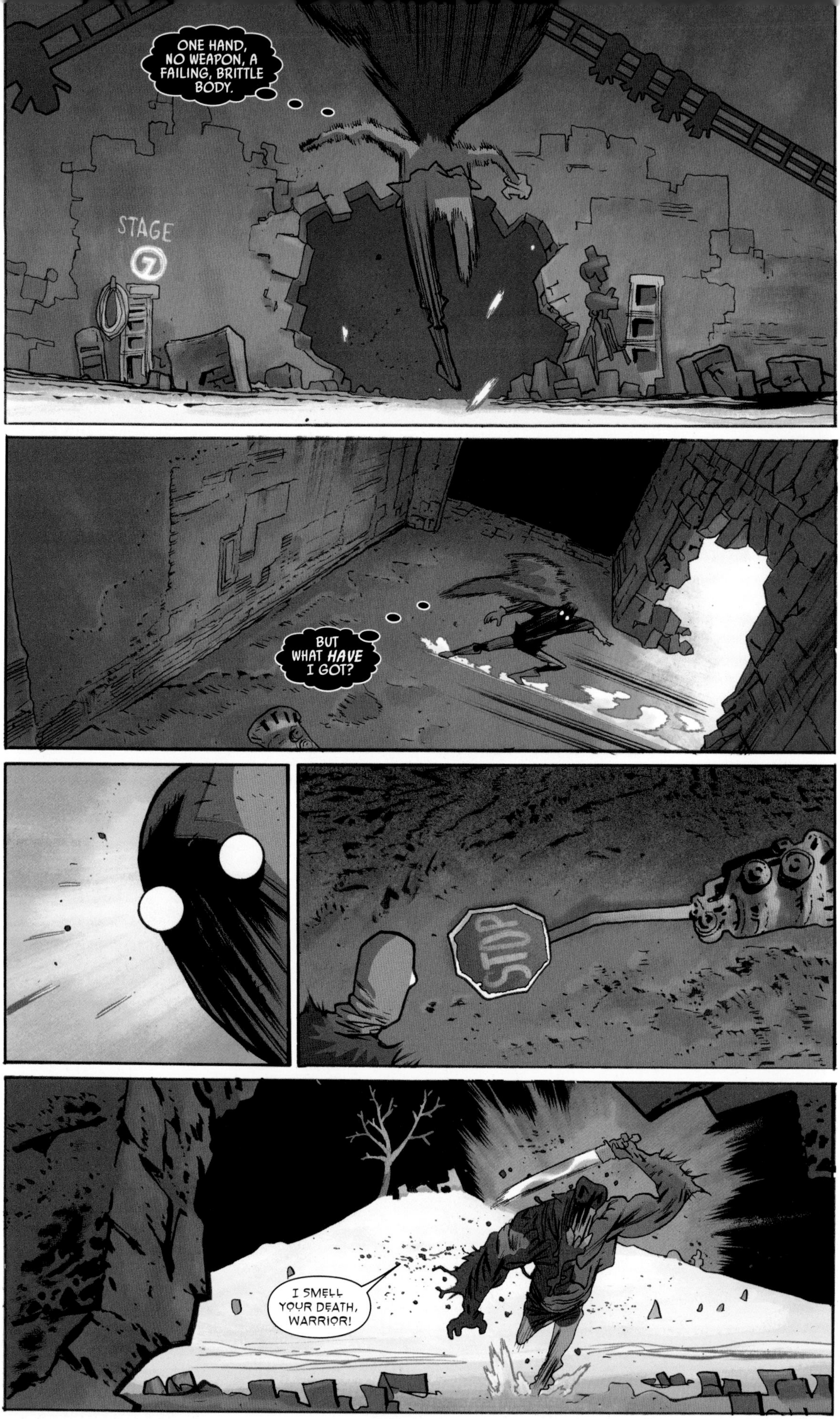
ONE HAND, NO WEAPON, A FAILING, BRITTLE BODY.
STAGE 7
BUT WHAT HAVE I GOT?
STOP
I SMELL YOUR DEATH, WARRIOR!

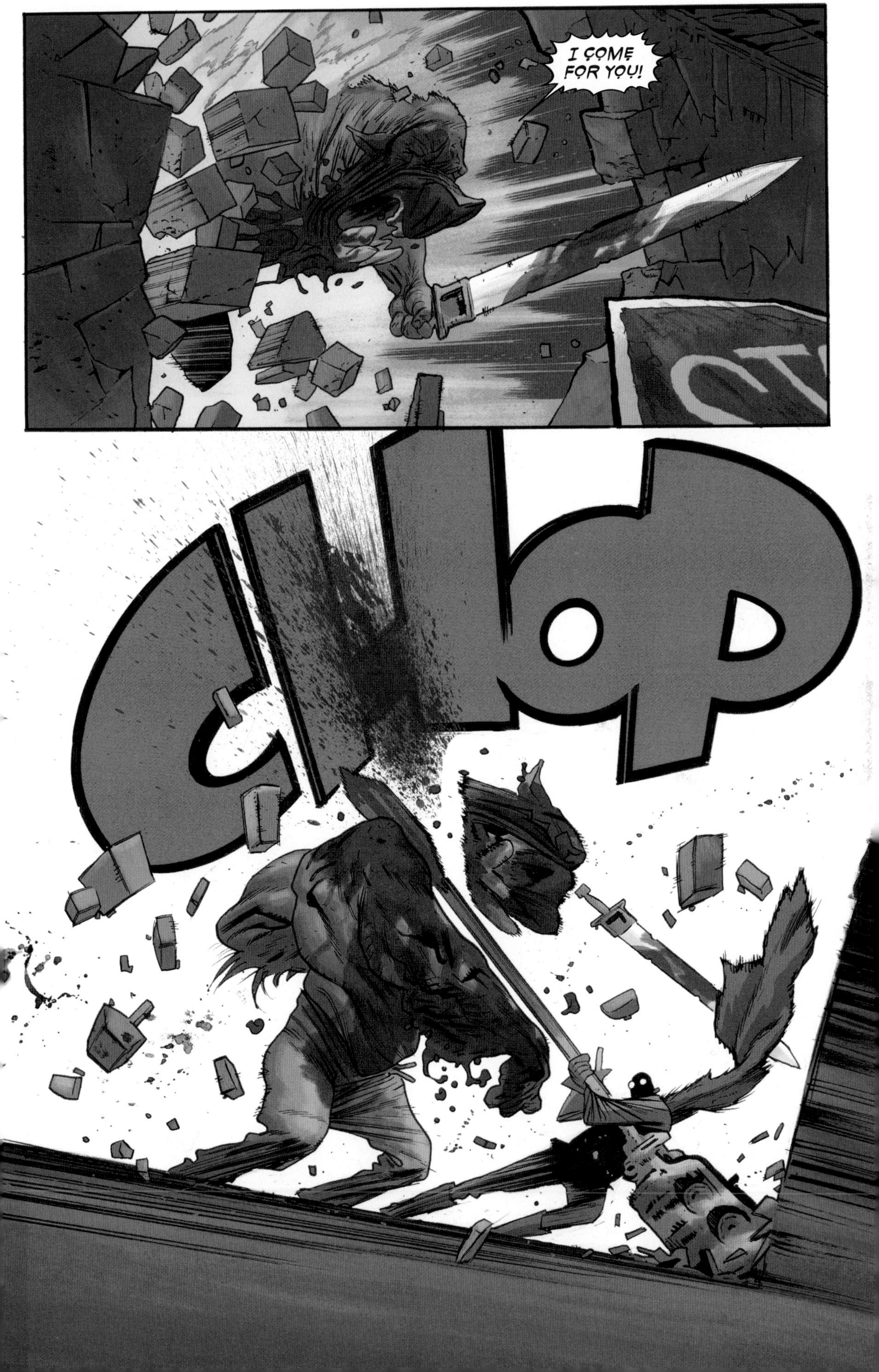
I COME FOR YOU!
CHOP

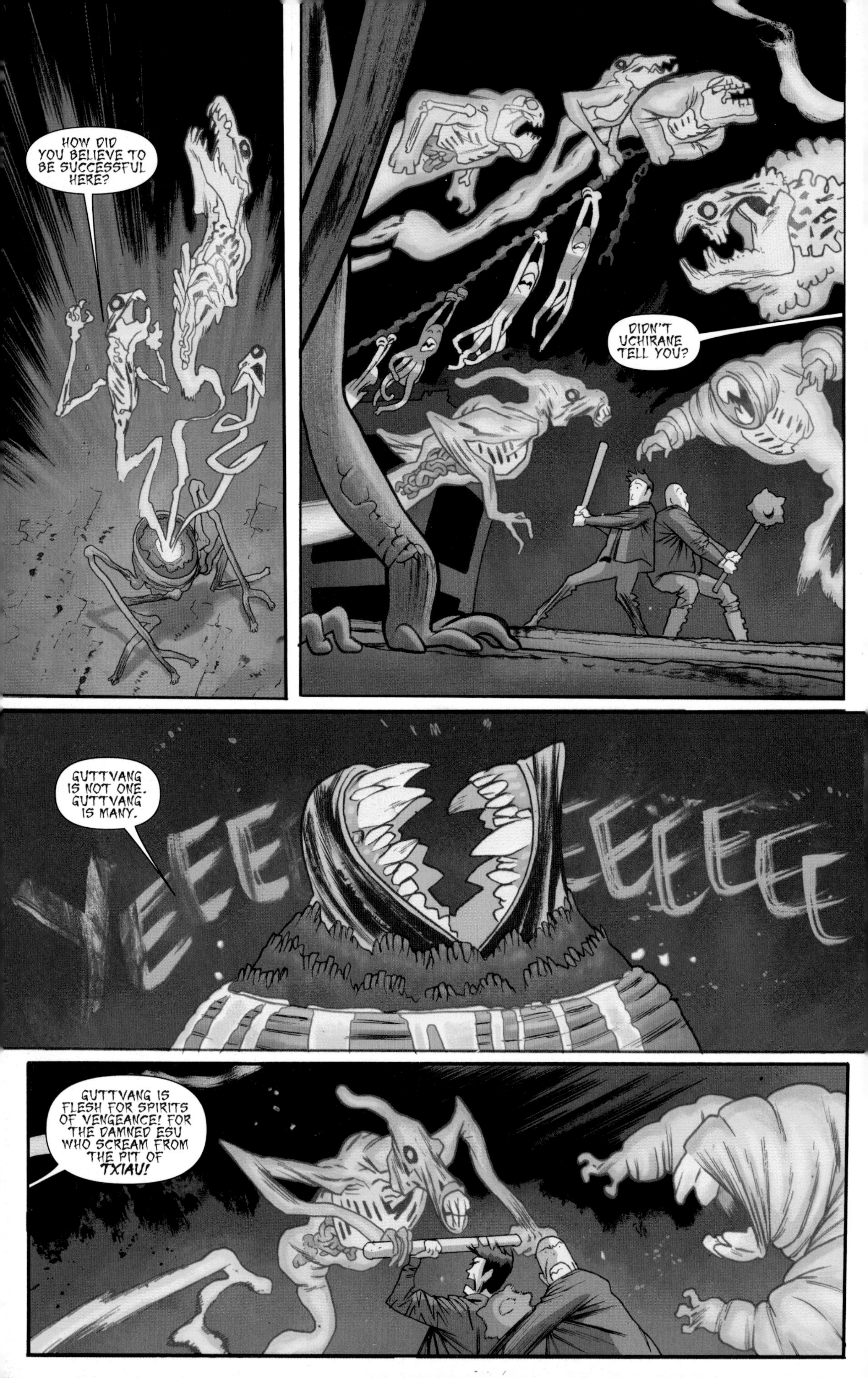
HOW DID YOU BELIEVE TO BE SUCCESSFUL HERE?
DIDN'T UCHIRANE TELL YOU?
GUTTVANG IS NOT ONE. GUTTVANG IS MANY.
YEEEEEEEEEEE
GUTTVANG IS FLESH FOR SPIRITS OF VENGEANCE! FOR THE DAMNED ESU WHO SCREAM FROM THE PIT OF TXIAU!

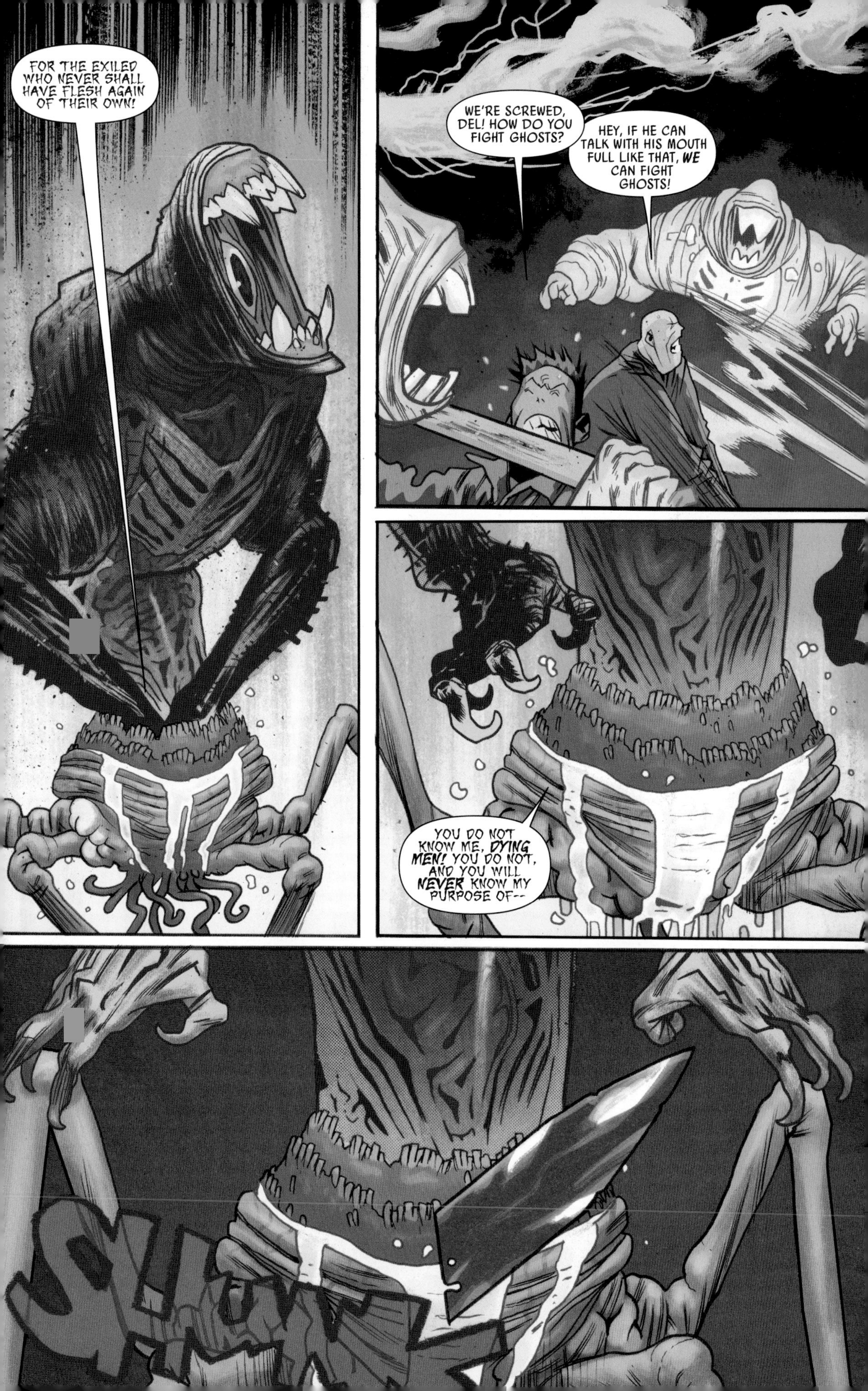
FOR THE EXILED WHO NEVER SHALL HAVE FLESH AGAIN OF THEIR OWN!
WE'RE SCREWED, DEL! HOW DO YOU FIGHT GHOSTS?
HEY, IF HE CAN TALK WITH HIS MOUTH FULL LIKE THAT, WE CAN FIGHT GHOSTS!
YOU DO NOT KNOW ME, DYING MEN! YOU DO NOT, AND YOU WILL NEVER KNOW MY PURPOSE OF--

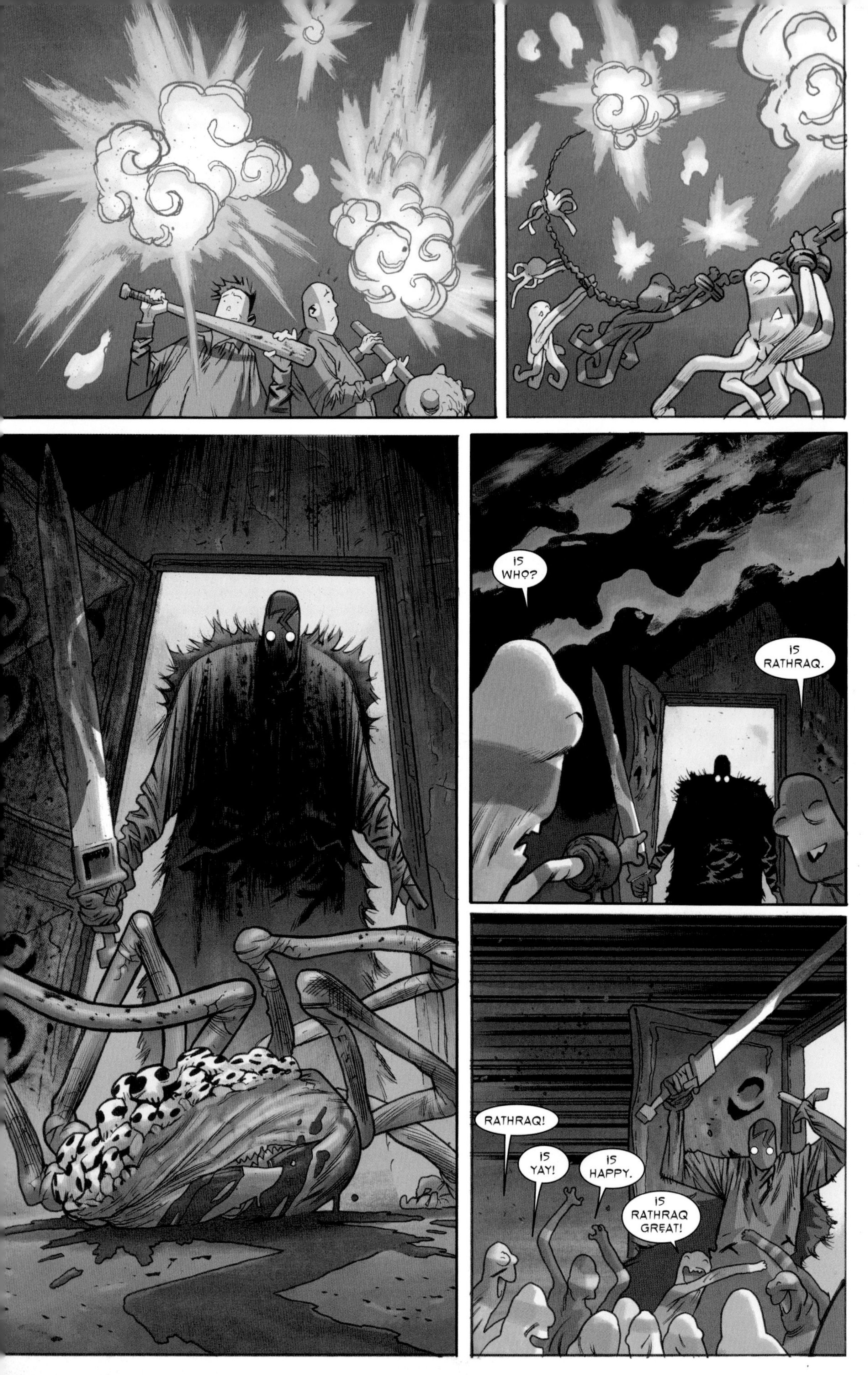
IS WHO?
IS RATHRAQ.
RATHRAQ!
IS YAY!
IS HAPPY.
IS RATHRAQ GREAT!

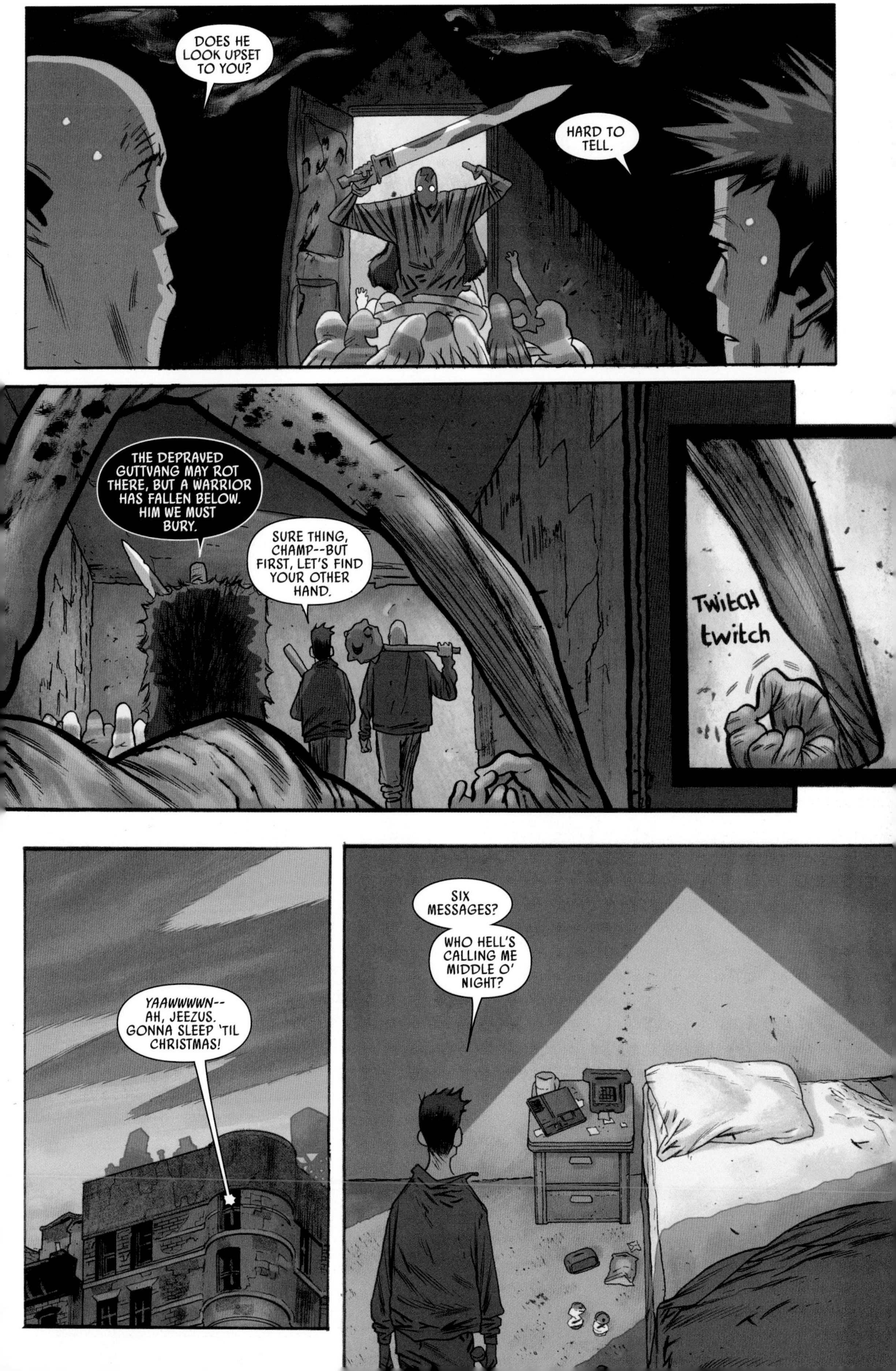
DOES HE LOOK UPSET TO YOU?
HARD TO TELL.
THE DEPRAVED GUTTVANG MAY ROT THERE, BUT A WARRIOR HAS FALLEN BELOW. HIM WE MUST BURY.
SURE THING, CHAMP--BUT FIRST, LET'S FIND YOUR OTHER HAND.
TWITCH twitch
YAAWWWWN--AH, JEEZUS. GONNA SLEEP 'TIL CHRISTMAS!
SIX MESSAGES?
WHO HELL'S CALLING ME MIDDLE O' NIGHT?

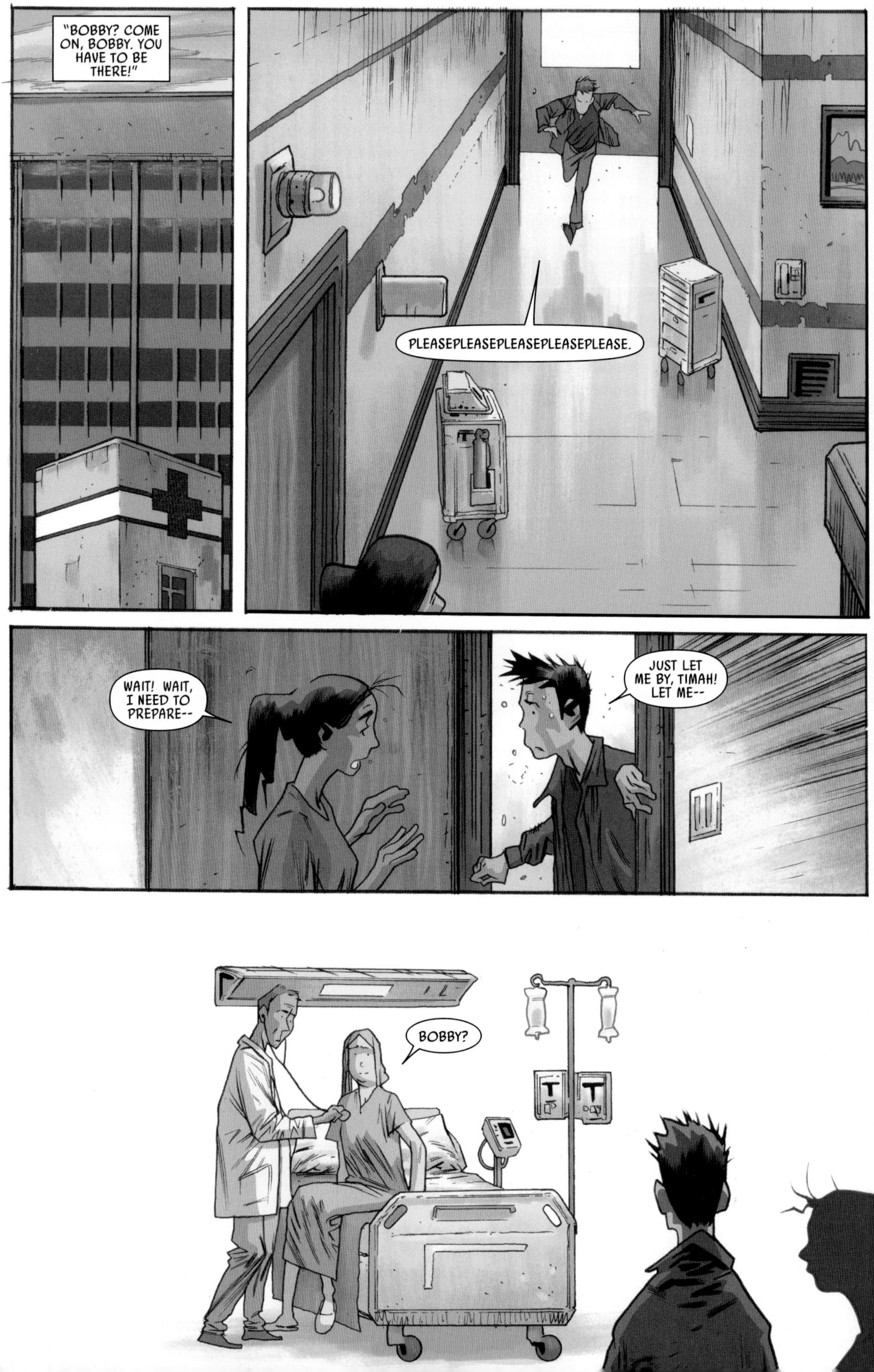
"BOBBY? COME ON, BOBBY. YOU HAVE TO BE THERE!"
PLEASEPLEASEPLEASEPLEASEPLEASE.
WAIT! WAIT, I NEED TO PREPARE--
JUST LET ME BY, TIMAH! LET ME--
BOBBY?

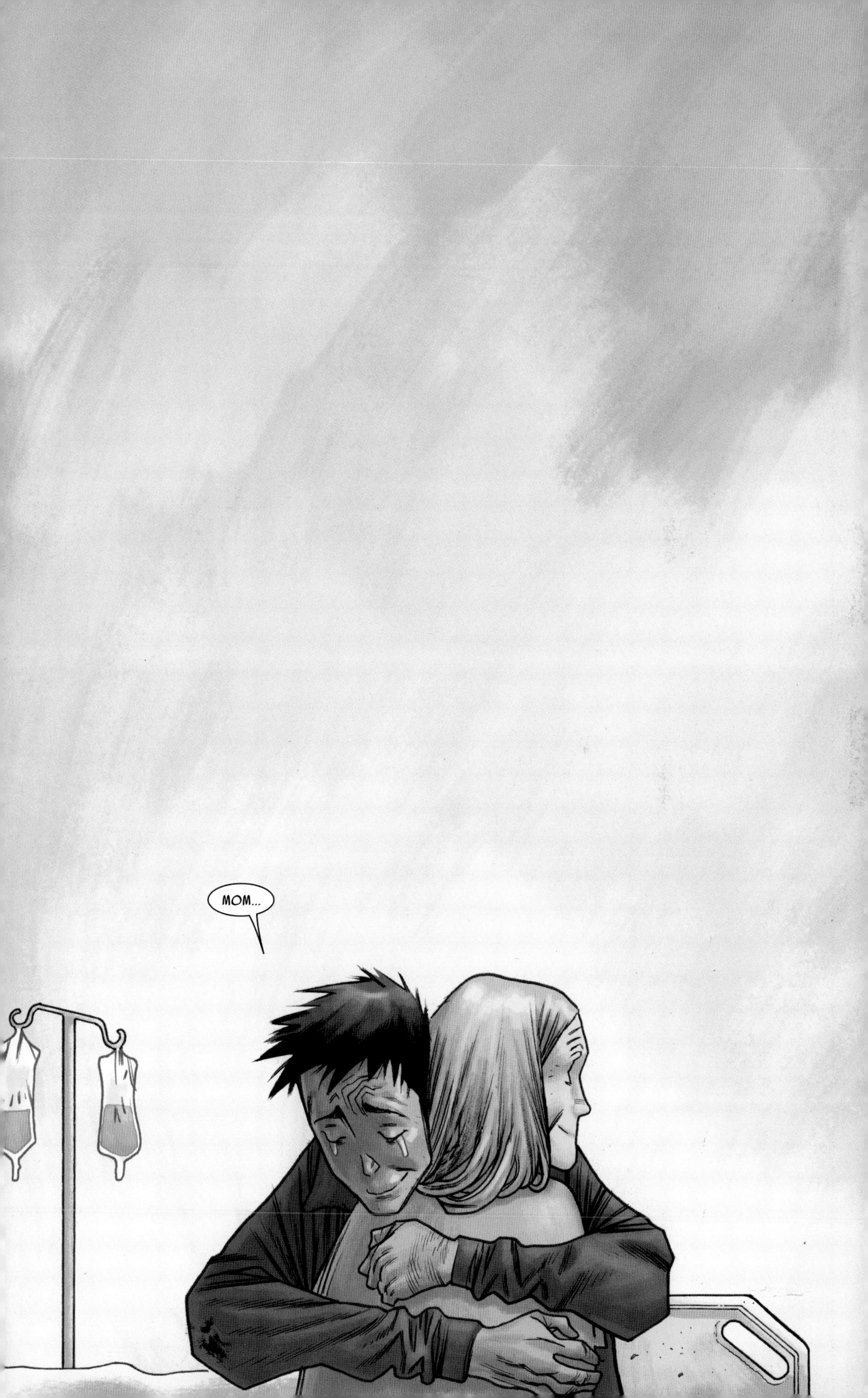
MOM...

# VARIANTS

## 1

**2ND PRINTING COVER FOR RUMBLE #2**
art by **JAMES HARREN**

@JamesHarren1

## 2

**2ND PRINTING COVER FOR RUMBLE #3**
art by **JAMES HARREN**

@JamesHarren1

## 3

**VARIANT COVER FOR RUMBLE #6**
art by **LEE BERMEJO**

@ljbermejo

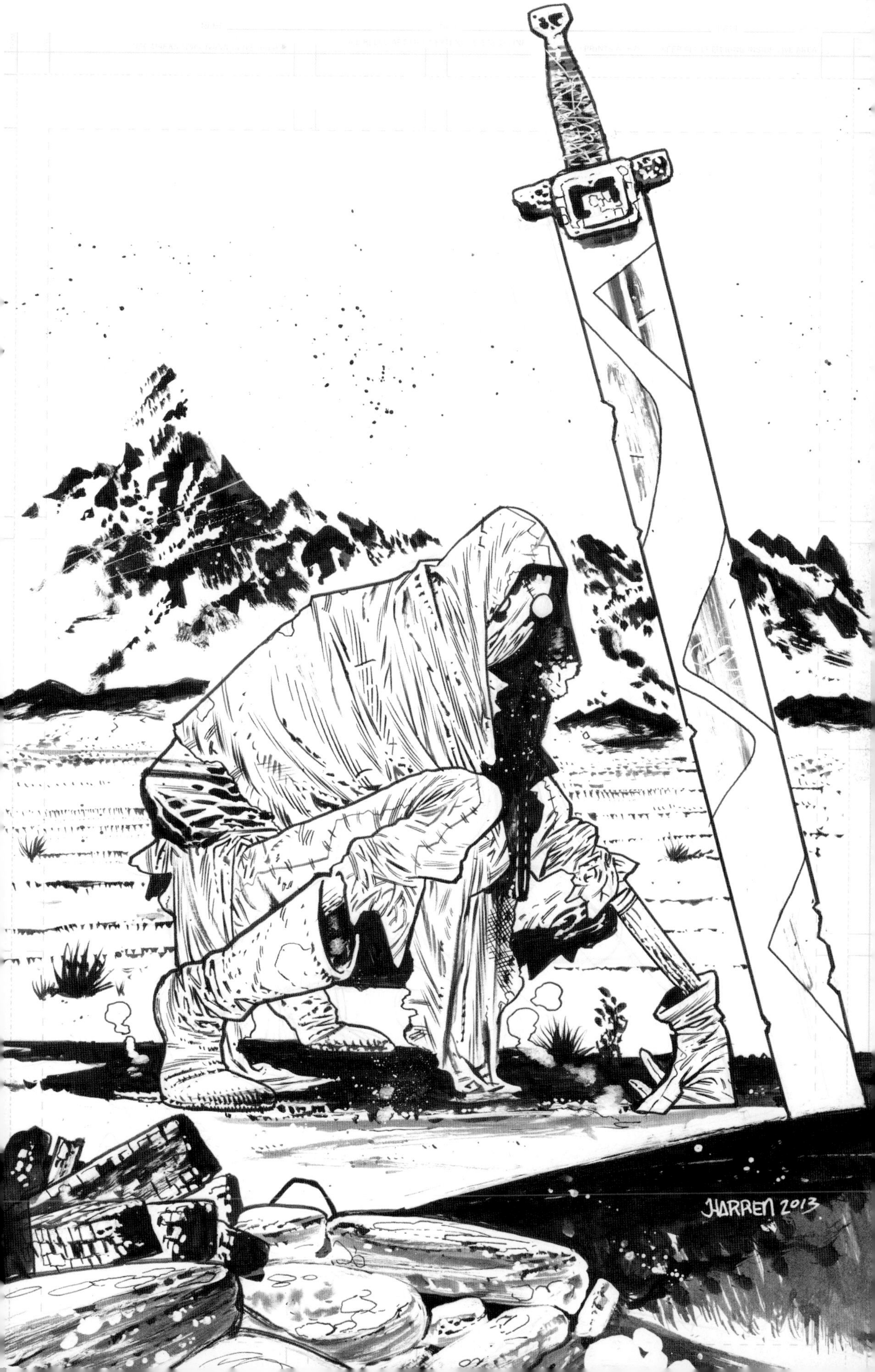
JHARREN 2013

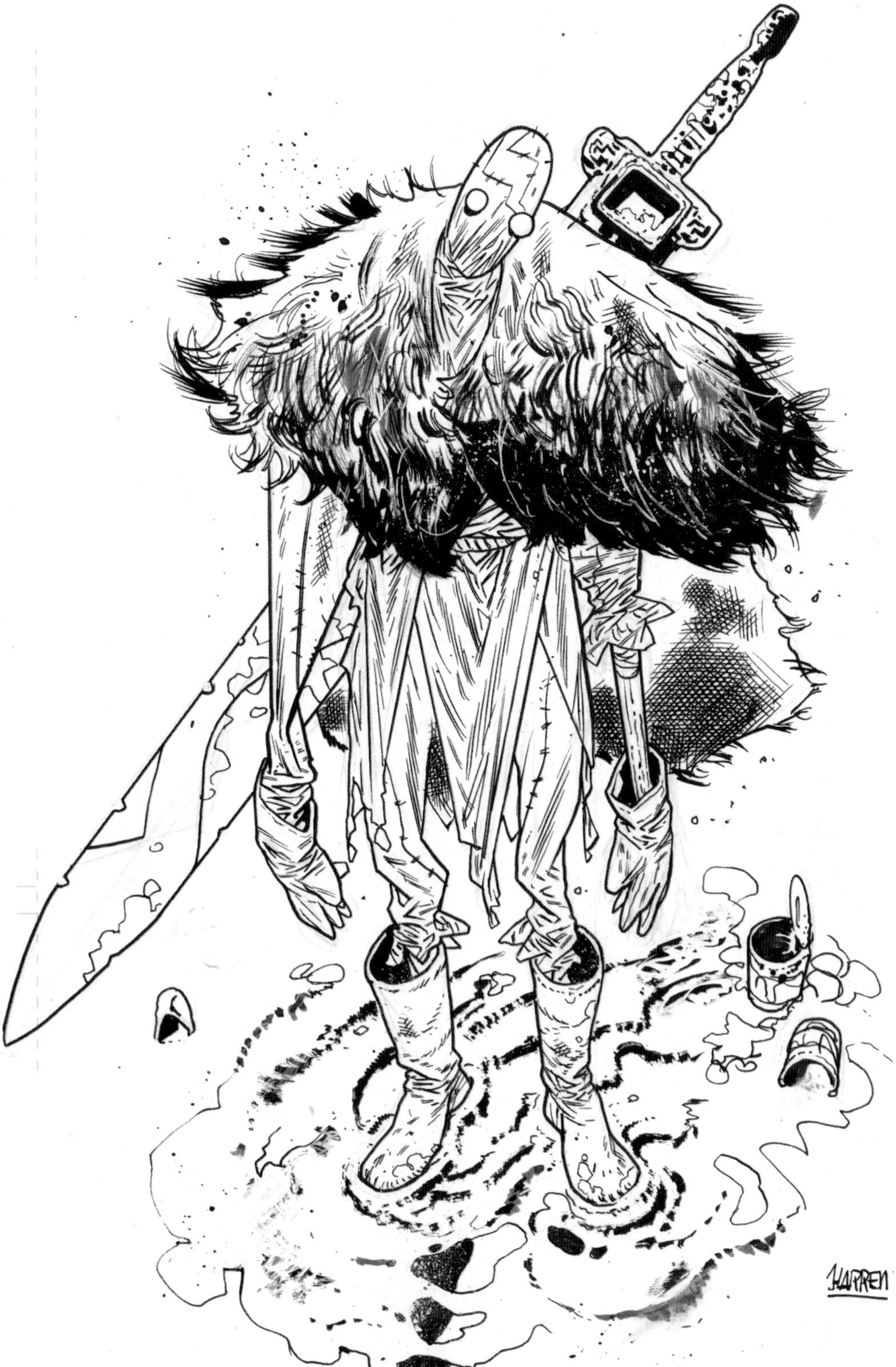
JHARREN

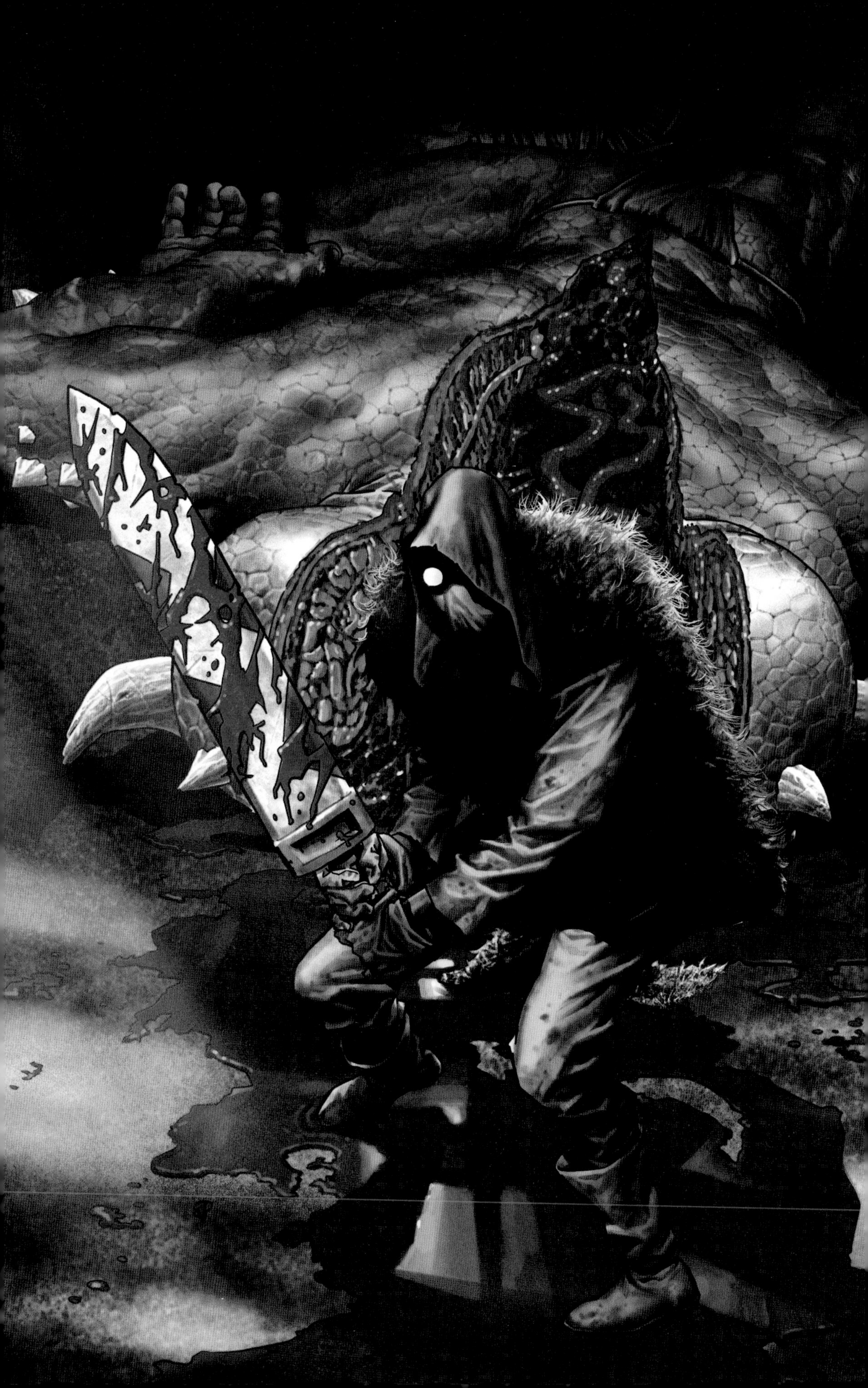

# PIN-UPS

## 1
art by **SUMEYYE KESGIN**
@SumeyyeKesgin1
colors by **DAVE STEWART**
@Dragonmnky

## 2
art by **LUCAS VARELA**
@LucVarela

## 3
art by **AARON CONLEY**
@AaronConley77
colors by **DAVE STEWART**
@Dragonmnky

## 4
art by **TROY NIXEY**
troynixey.bigcartel.com
colors by **MIKE SPICER**
@SpicerColor

## 5
art by **FALYNN KOCH**
@FalynnK

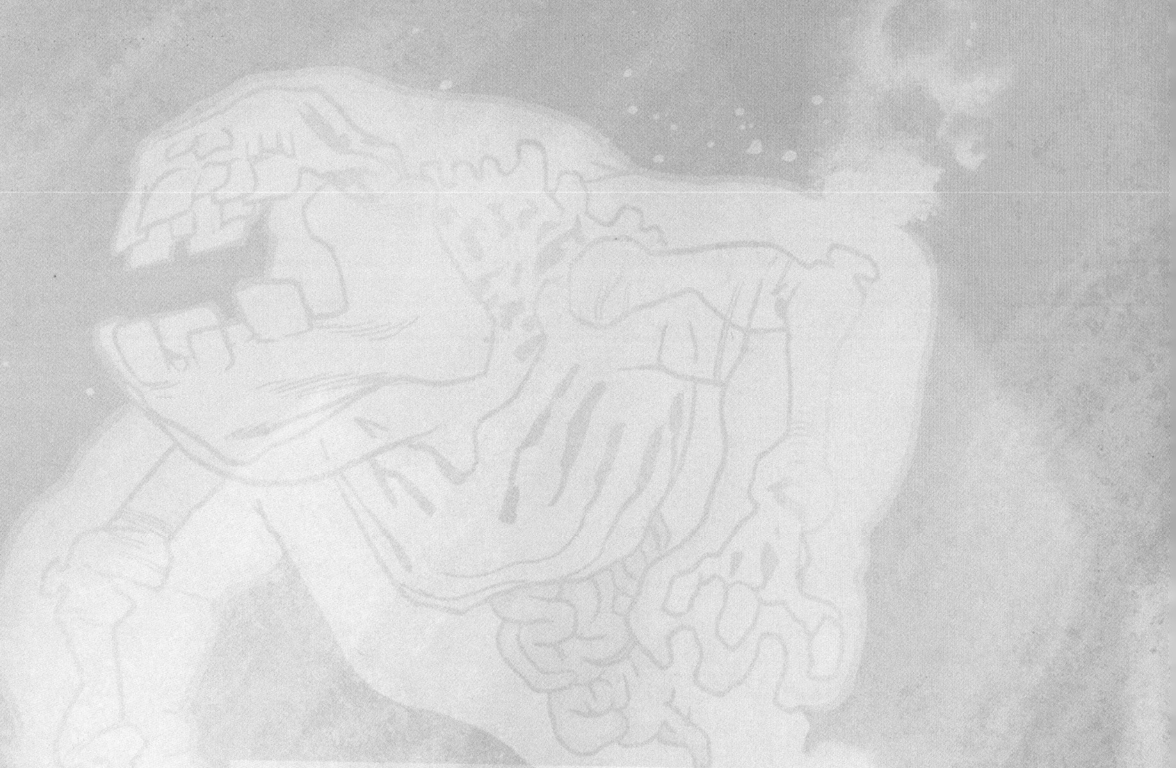

**6**

art by **REBECCA KIRBY**

reweki.tumblr.com

colors by **JOSEPH BERGIN III**

@sayunclecomics

**7**

art by **JULIAN TOTINO TEDESCO**

@totinotedesco

**8**

art by **DEVMALYA PRAMANIK**

@TheWarblazer

colors by **DAVE STEWART**

@Dragonmnky

**9**

art by **CORIN HOWELL**

@Rin237

colors by **RUSSELL BADGETT**

@RussTheBadger

**10**

art by **STEPHEN GREEN**

@WorldClassNinja

colors by **DAVE STEWART**

@Dragonmnky

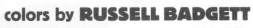

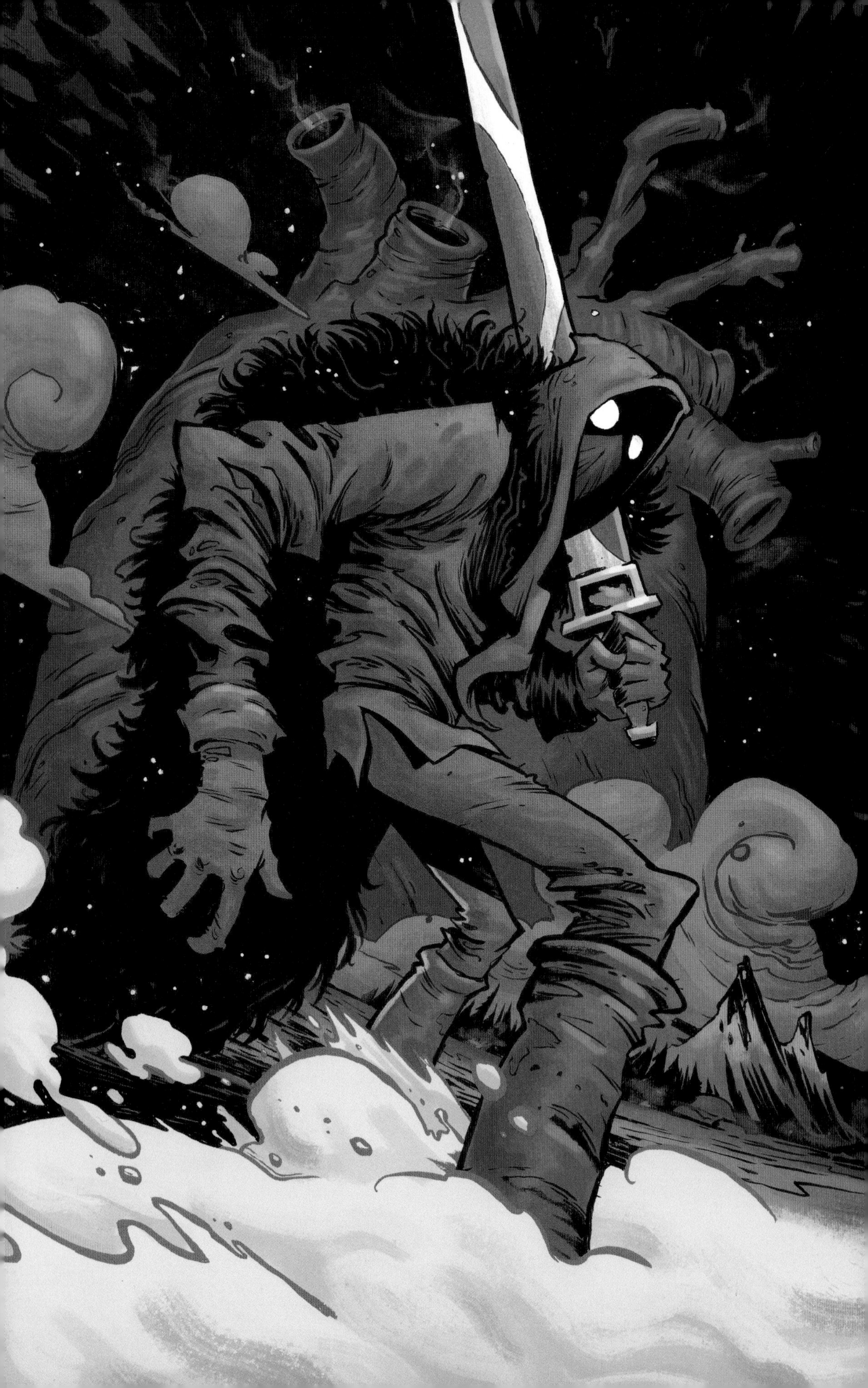

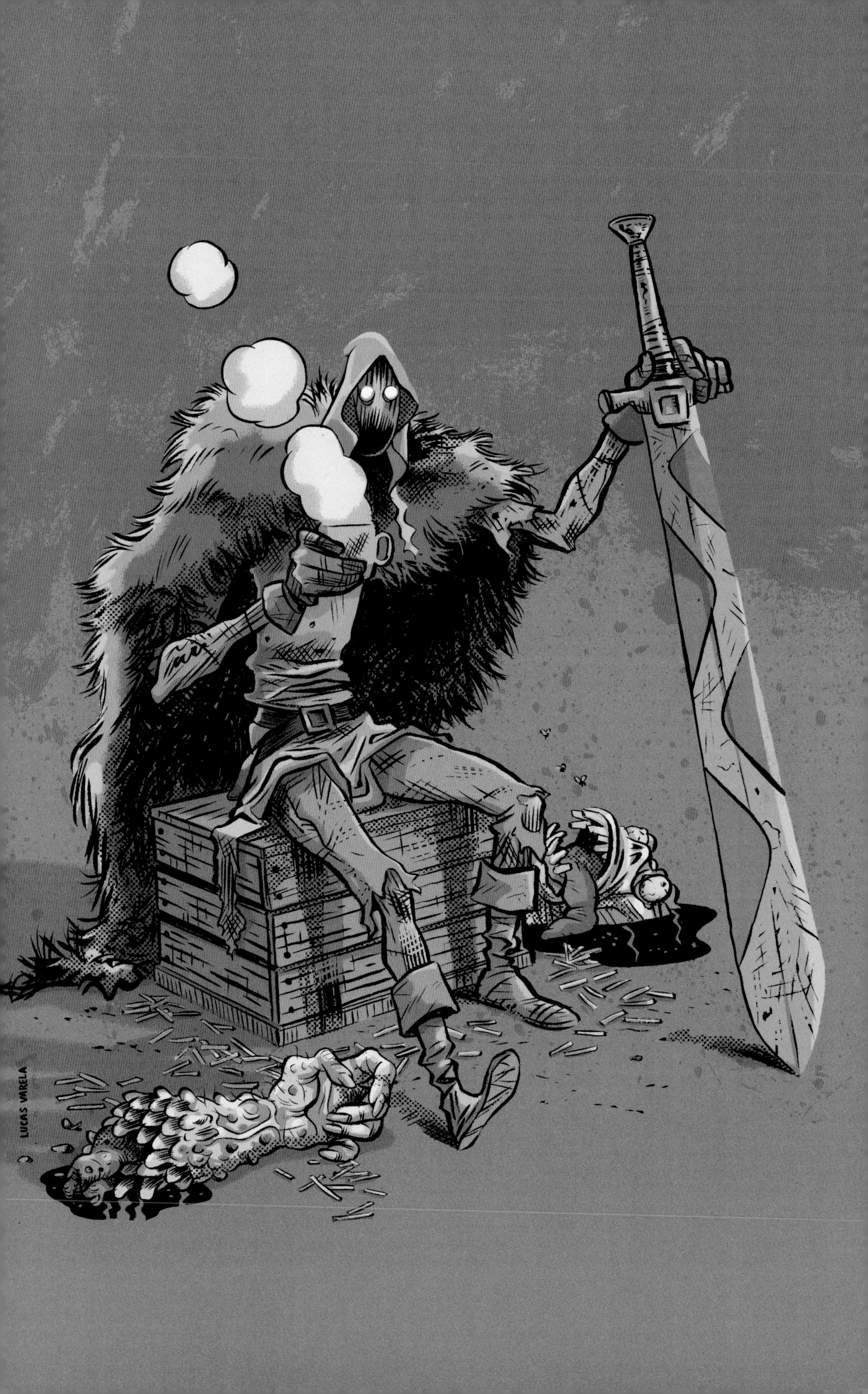
LUCAS VARELA

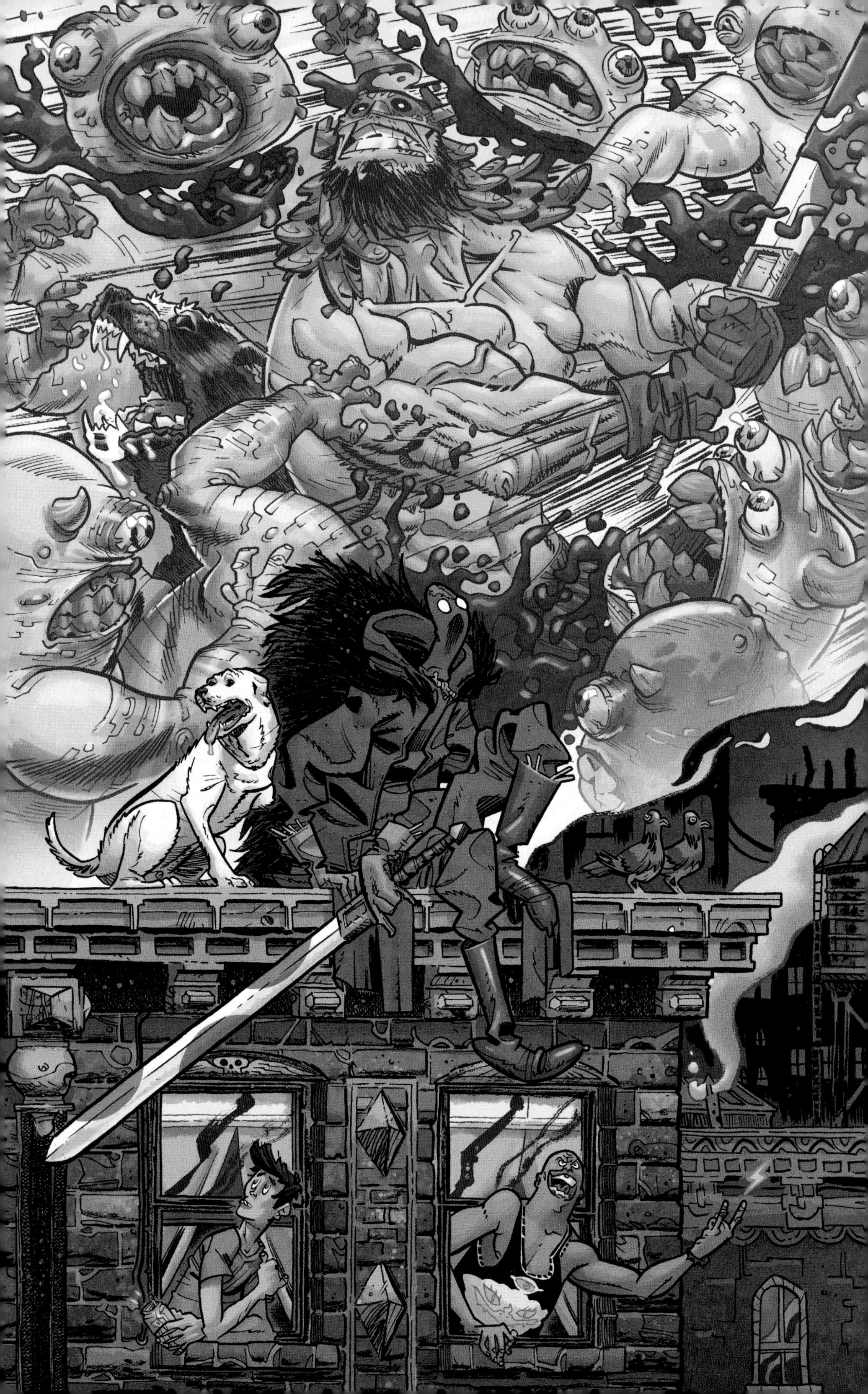

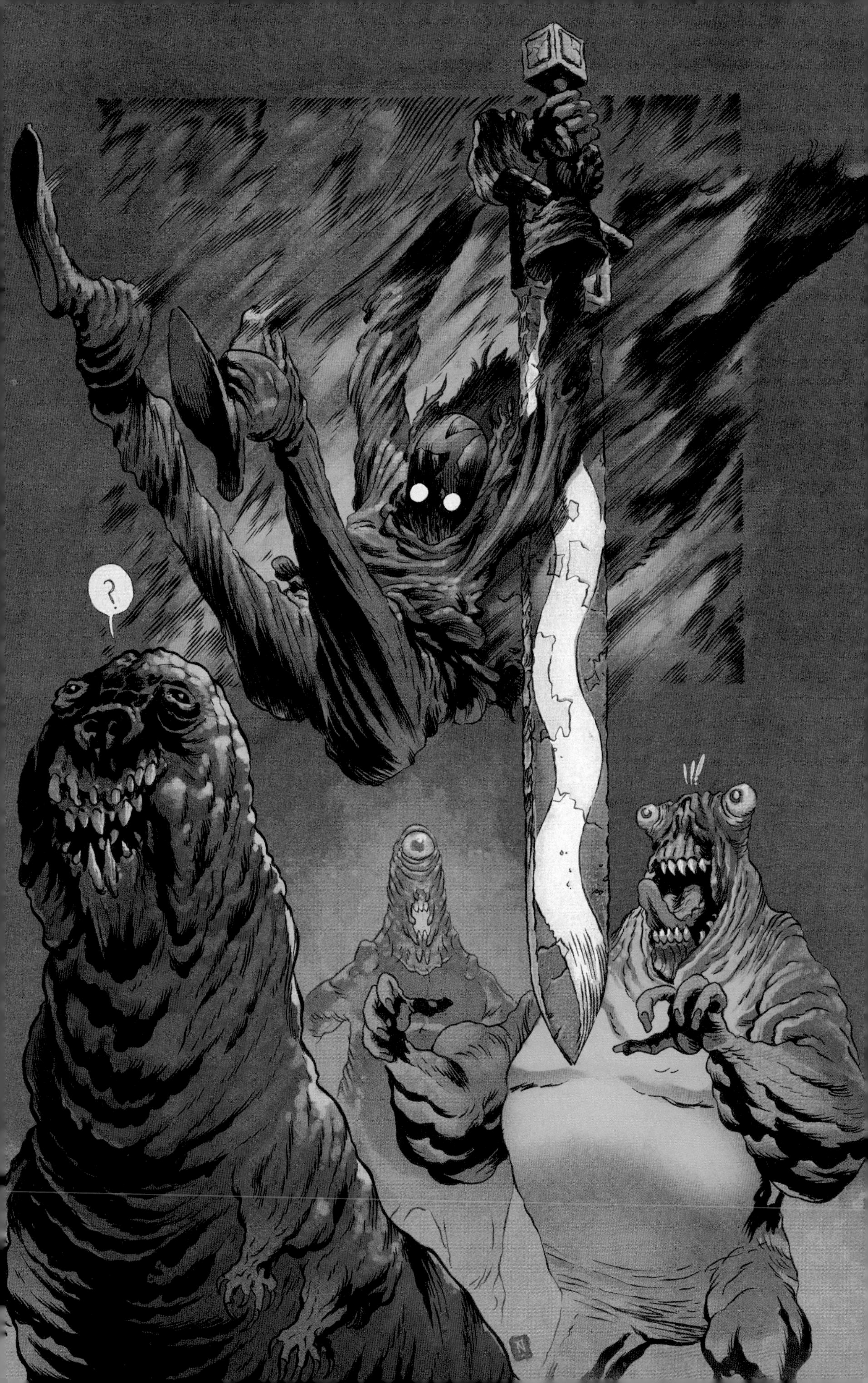
?
!!

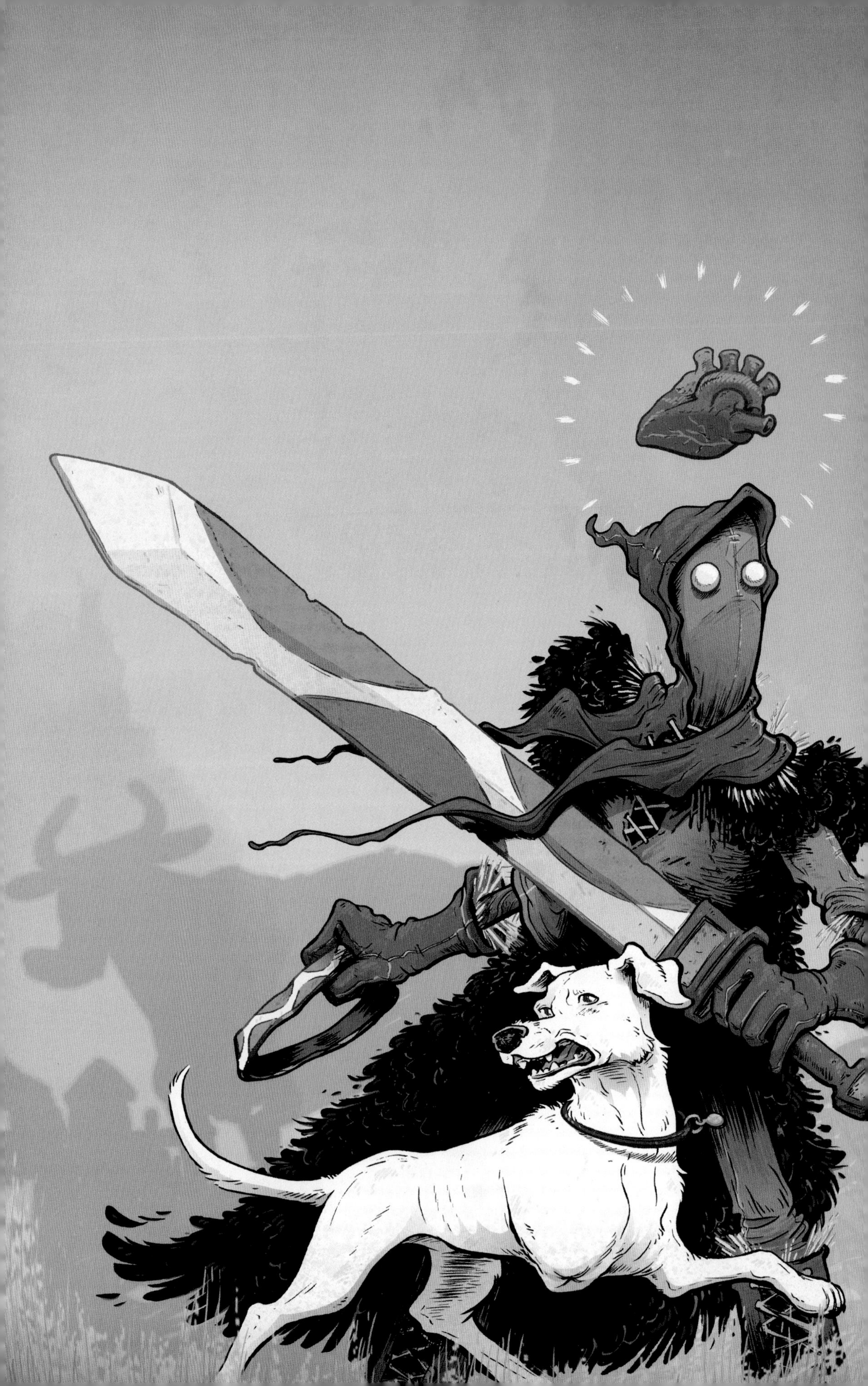

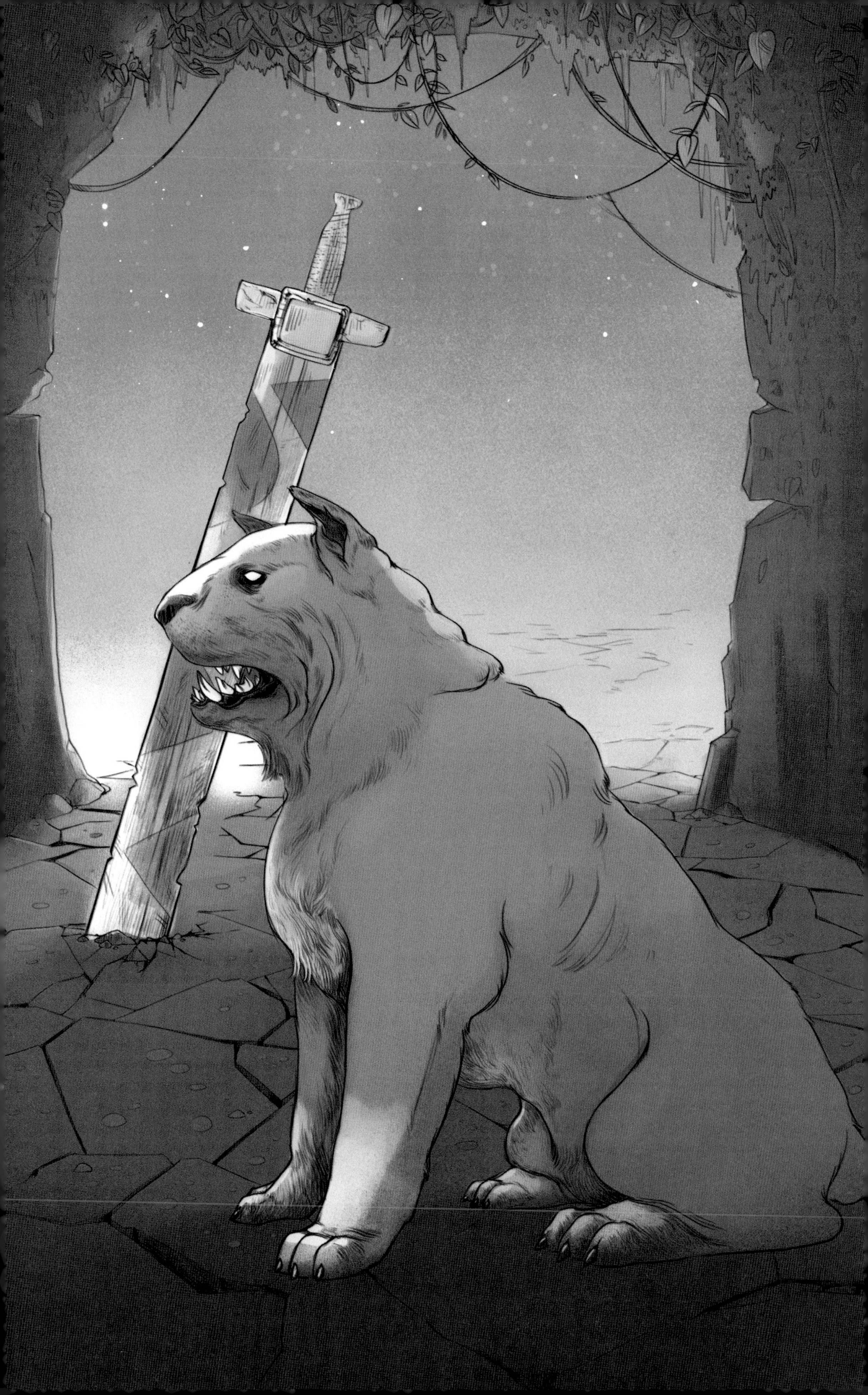

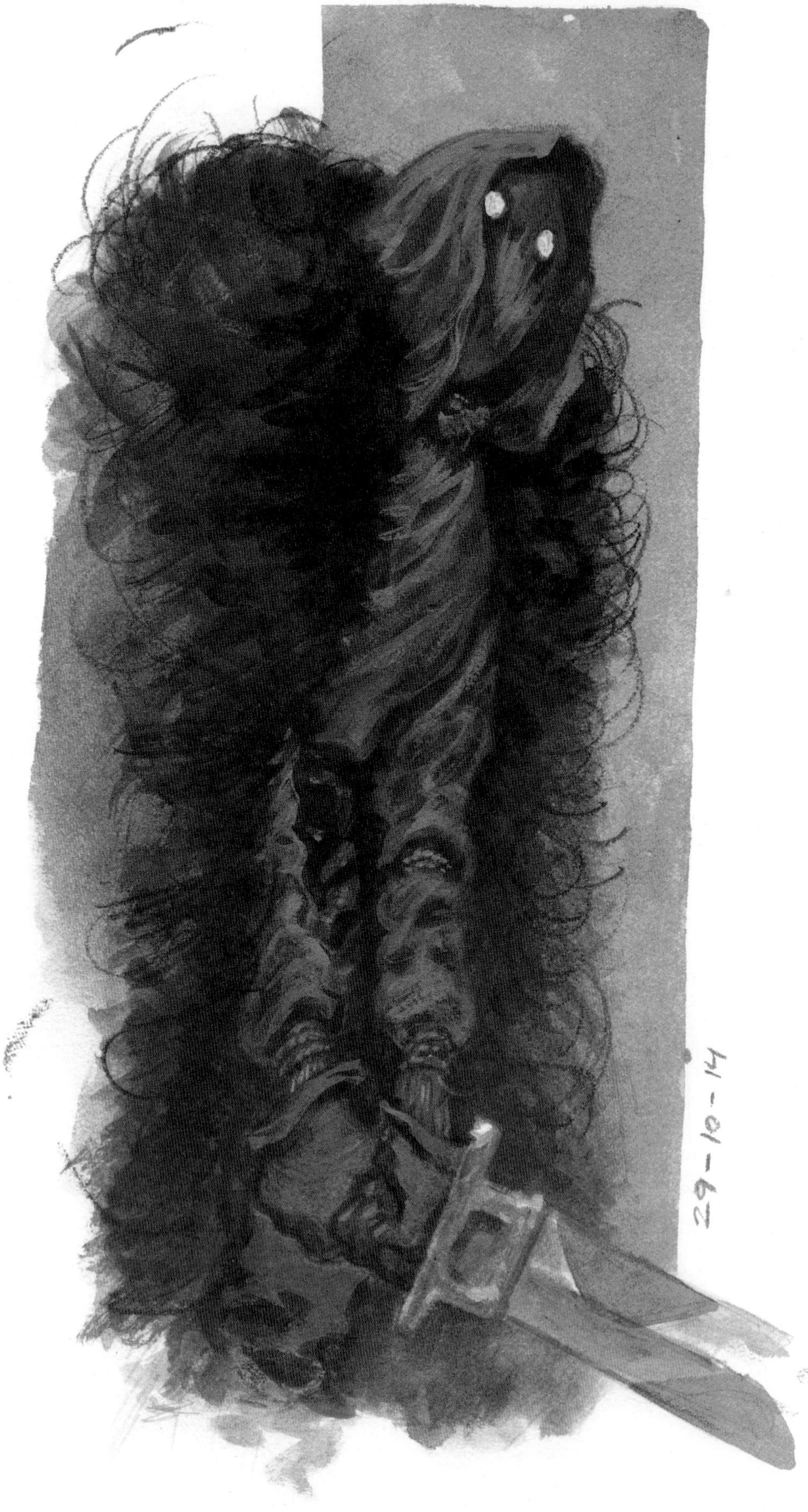
29-10-14

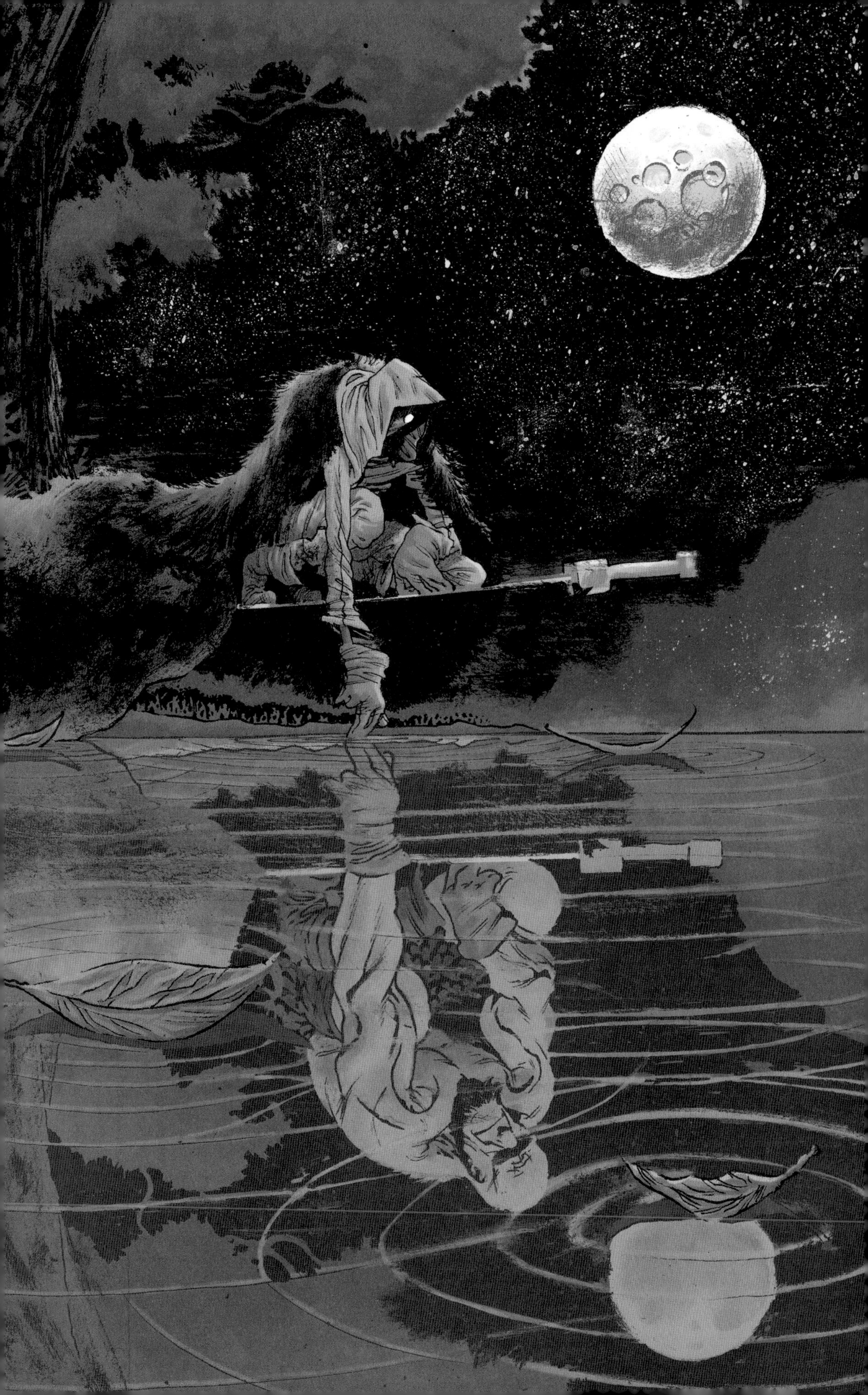

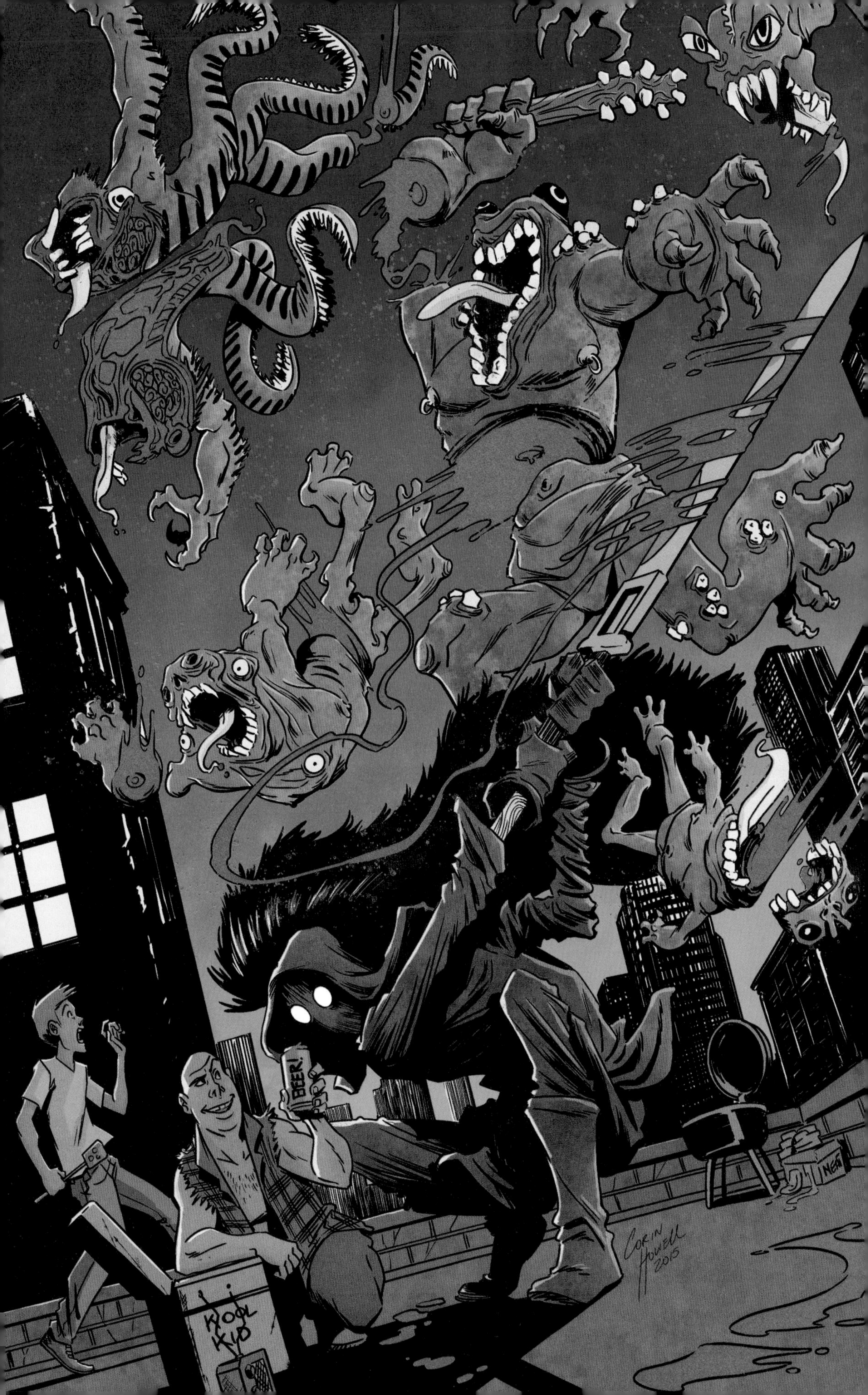
BEER!
KOOL KID
CORIN HOWELL 2015

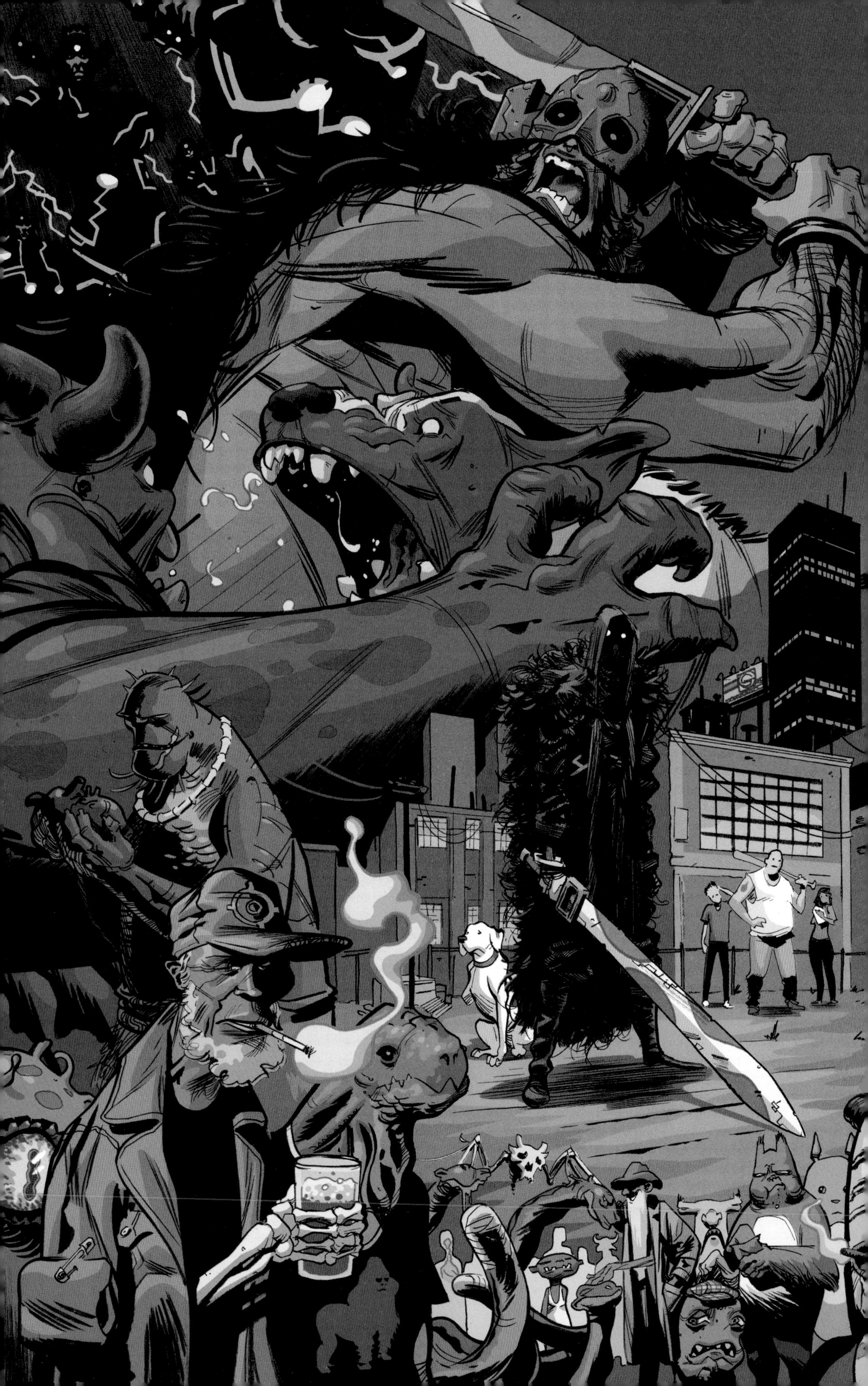

# SKETCHBOOK

## with additional notes by artist, JAMES HARREN

These are some design ideas for the tribespeople of Pangea. I believe I looked at aboriginal body paint. This would've been a good design if I really committed. They wound up a pretty indistinct blob in the background. I blame deadlines. And the economy.

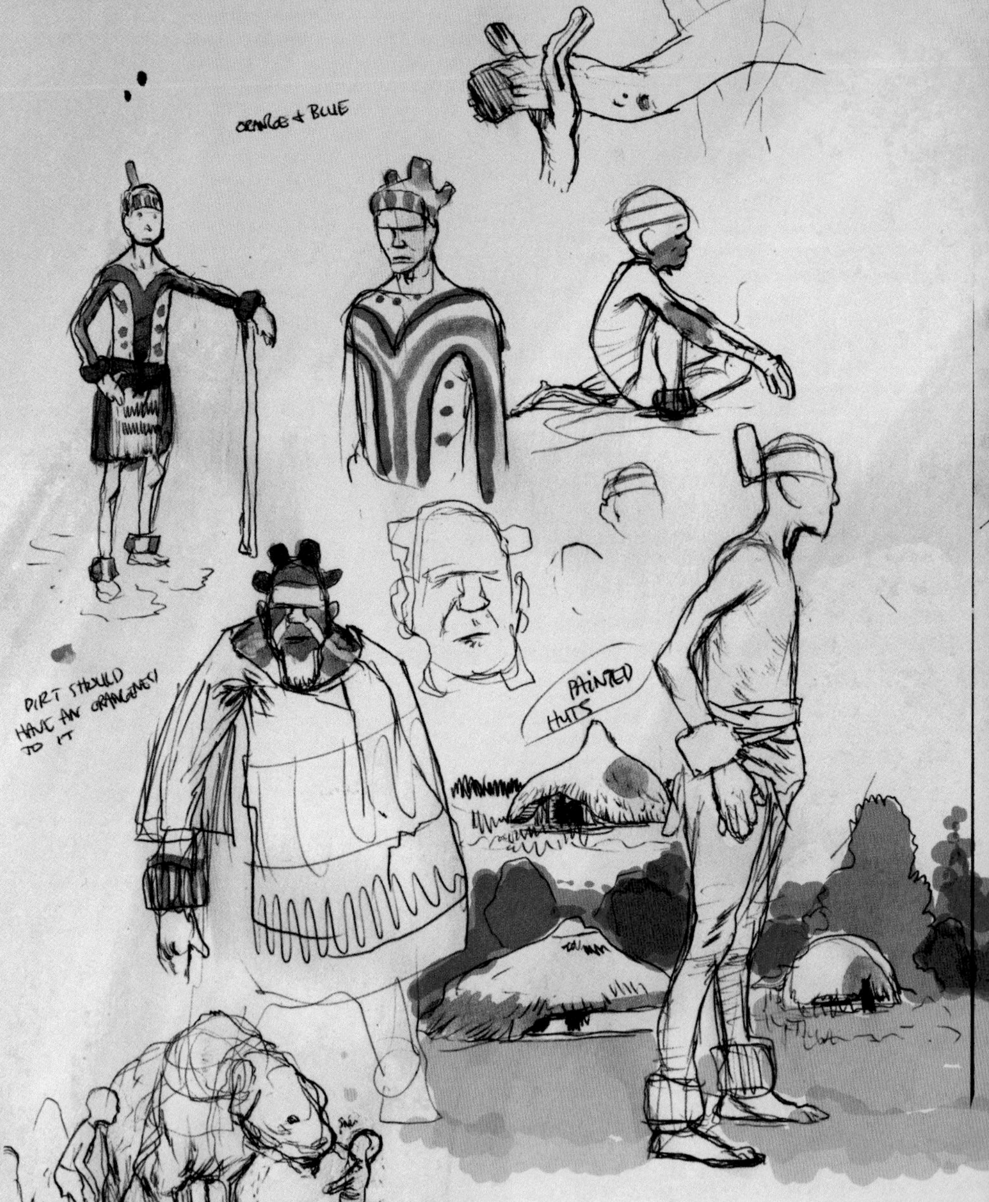
ORANGE & BLUE
DIRT SHOULD HAVE AN ORANGENESS TO IT
PAINTED HUTS

PA

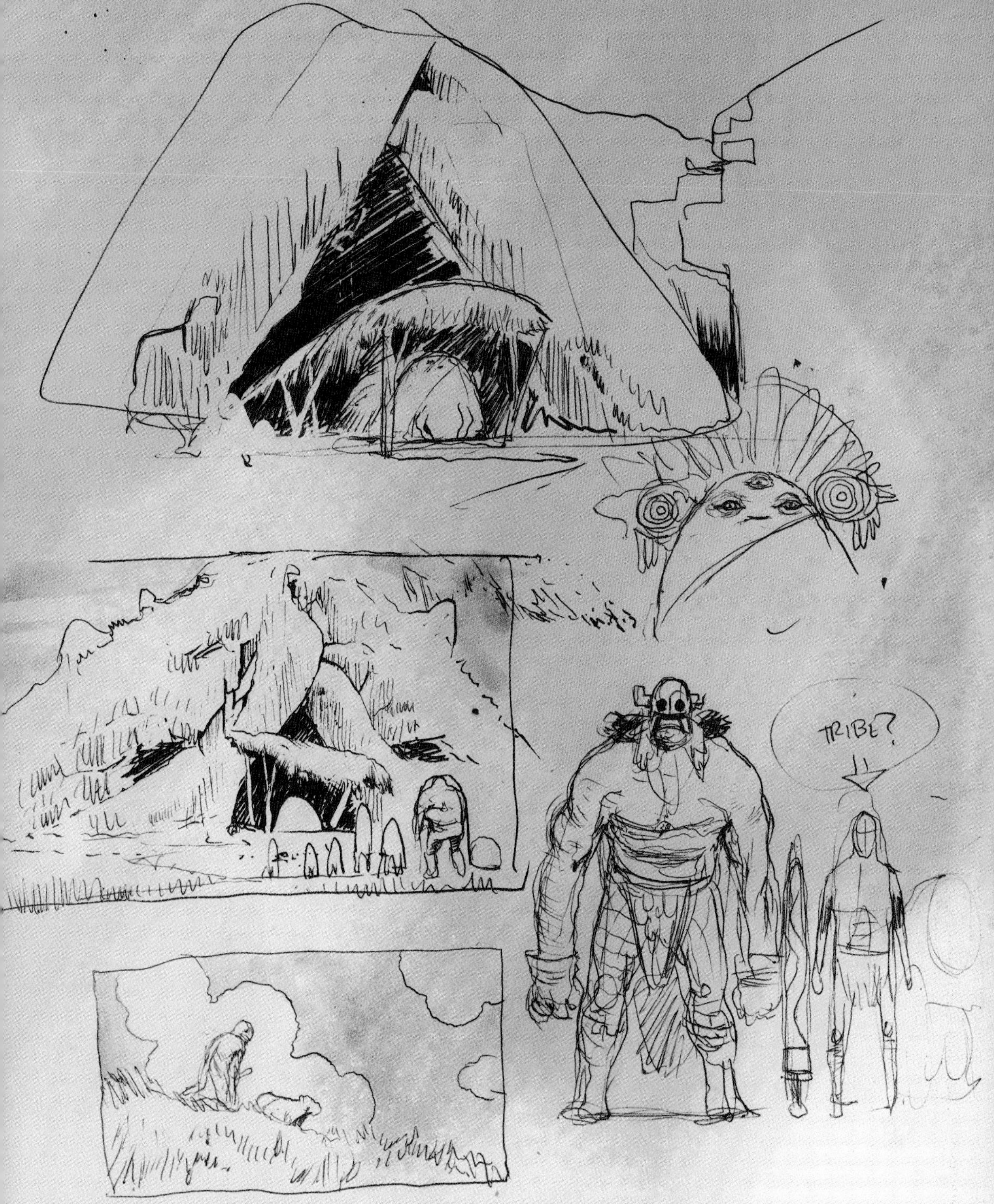
TRIBE?

**Some Pangea studies for issue 6. Also, some scale sketches for Godraq's presence among the early human tribesemen.**

NGEA

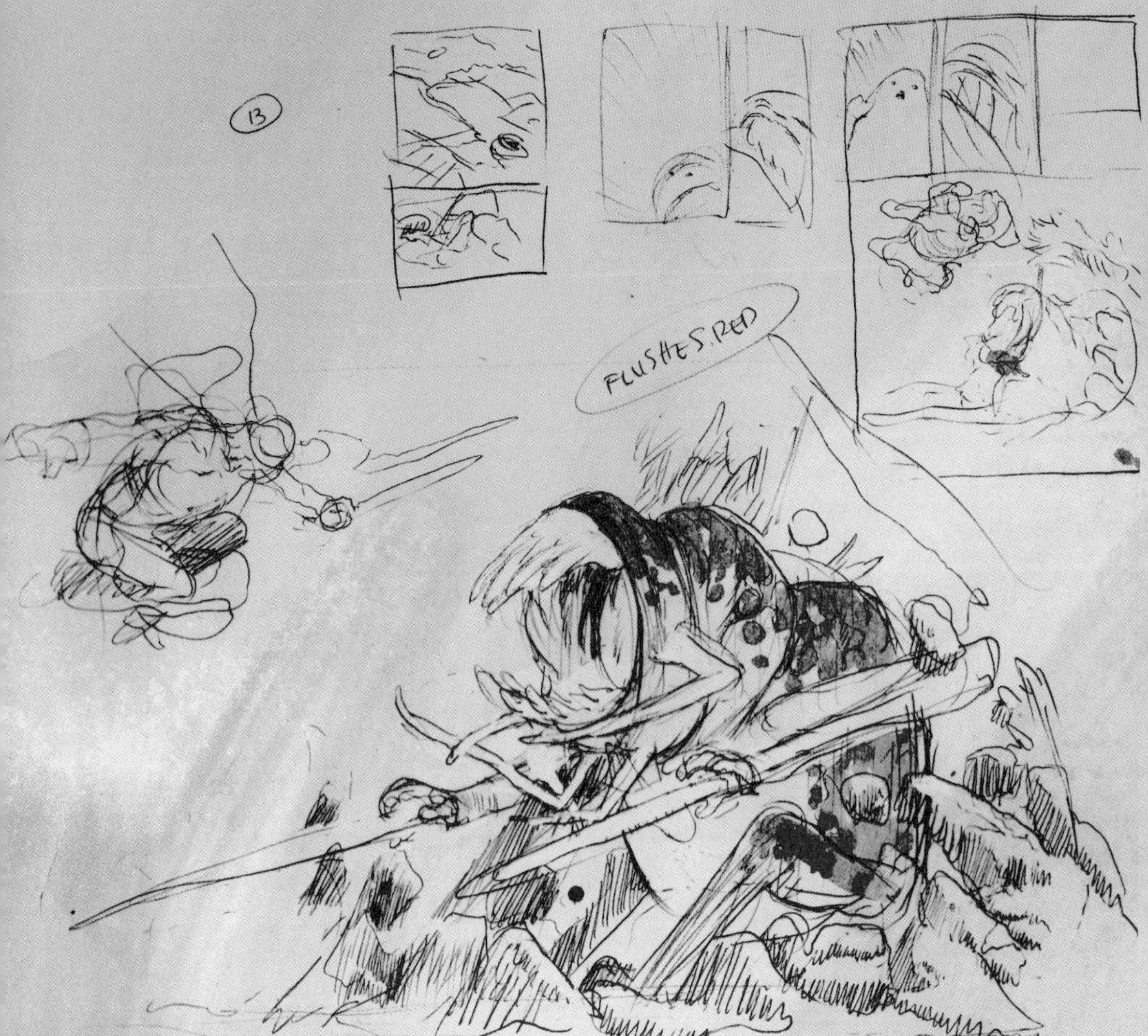

13
FLUSHES RED


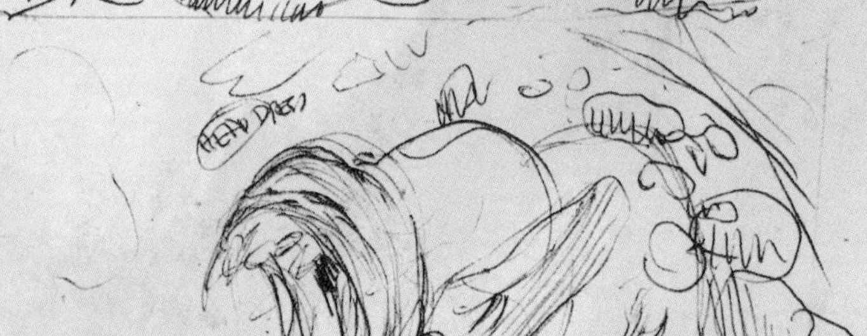

Some passes at the Pangea monster from issue 6. The adorable pudgy part that he presents to the tribe would wind up only being his head and the big pointy monster grub part would be burrowed underground.

# THE GRUB DEITY

Here are some more passes at our Pangea monster. A lot of these sketches wound up more successful than the execution on the page. But that's pretty much how it always goddamn fucking cockshit goes.

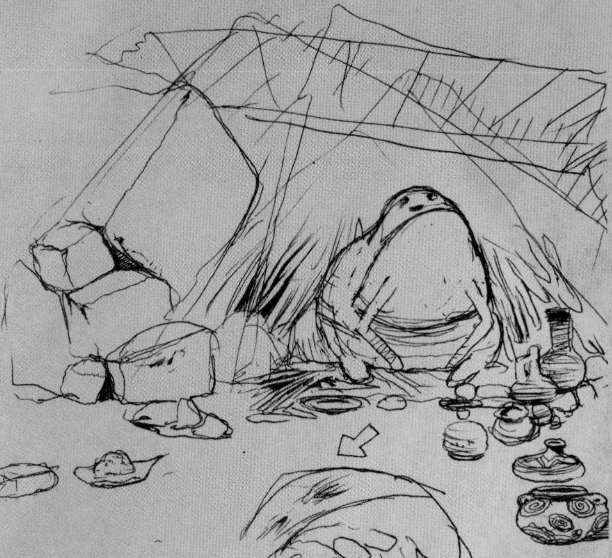

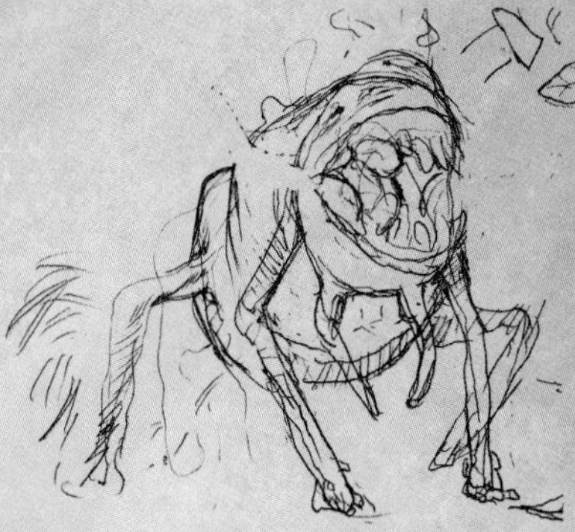

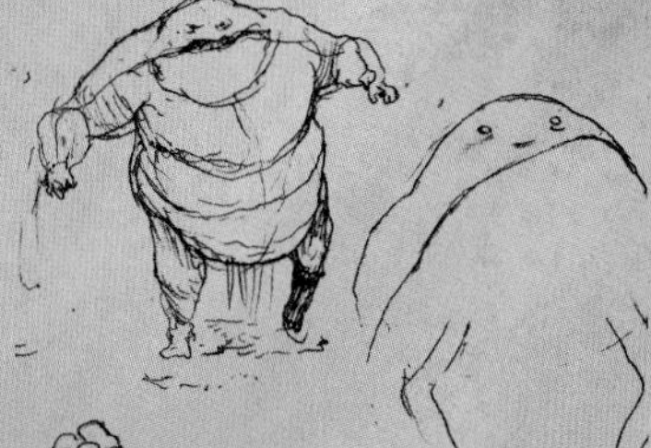

I think when I introduced color here I had the idea that we could tie the natural coloring of his grubby skin to how the tribe would paint themselves and their children and homes.

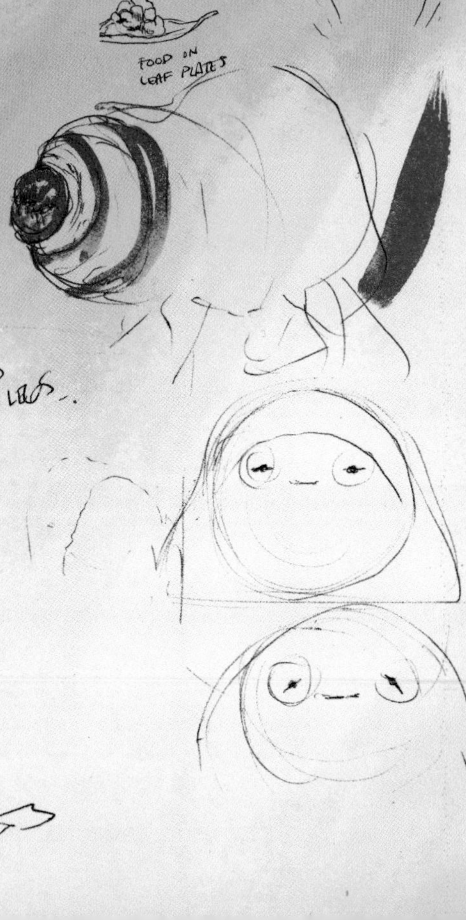
FOOD ON LEAF PLATES

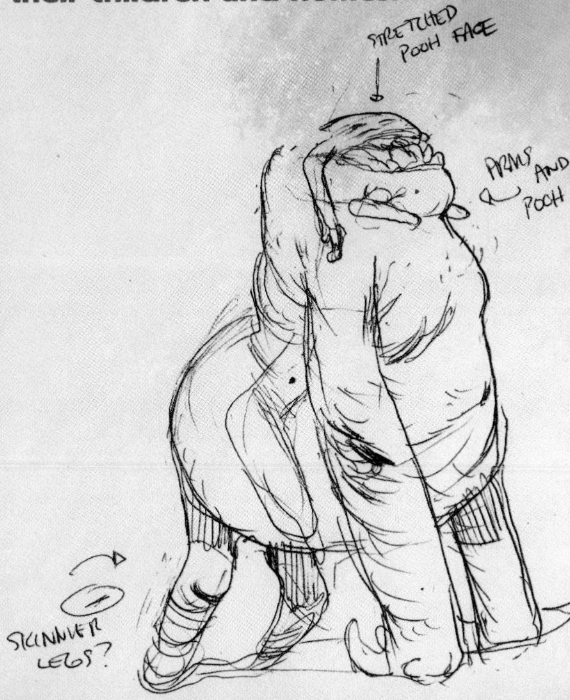
STRETCHED POOH FACE
ARMS AND POOH LEGS
SKINNIER LEGS?

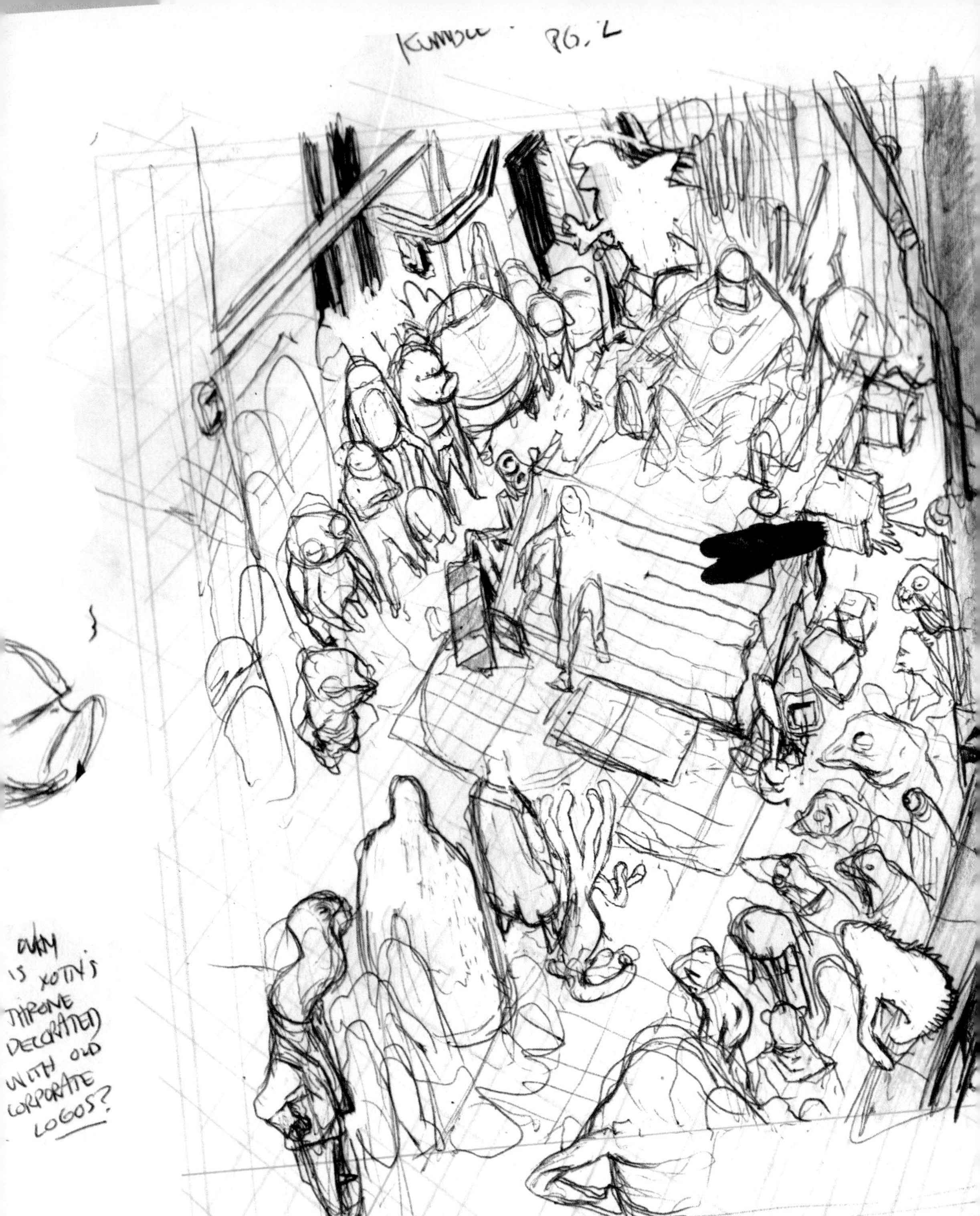
RUMBLE · PG. 2
OKAY IS XOTIY'S THRONE DECORATED WITH OLD CORPORATE LOGOS?

**Here's the preliminary thumbnail to page 2 of issue 7. This was a good opportunity to tease the scope and variety of the world. I hope we can do backstories for each and every weirdo in here.**

**This is the preliminary thumbnail to one of my favorite pages. I LOVE drawing Cogan! For all you process people, I do these at reduced size on 8"x11" computer paper with ballpoint pen and blue pencil. Then, I scan it in and print it out in blue line so I can finally go in and ink overtop. For speed, and to maintain spontaneity, I prefer to skip any actual pencilling stage.**

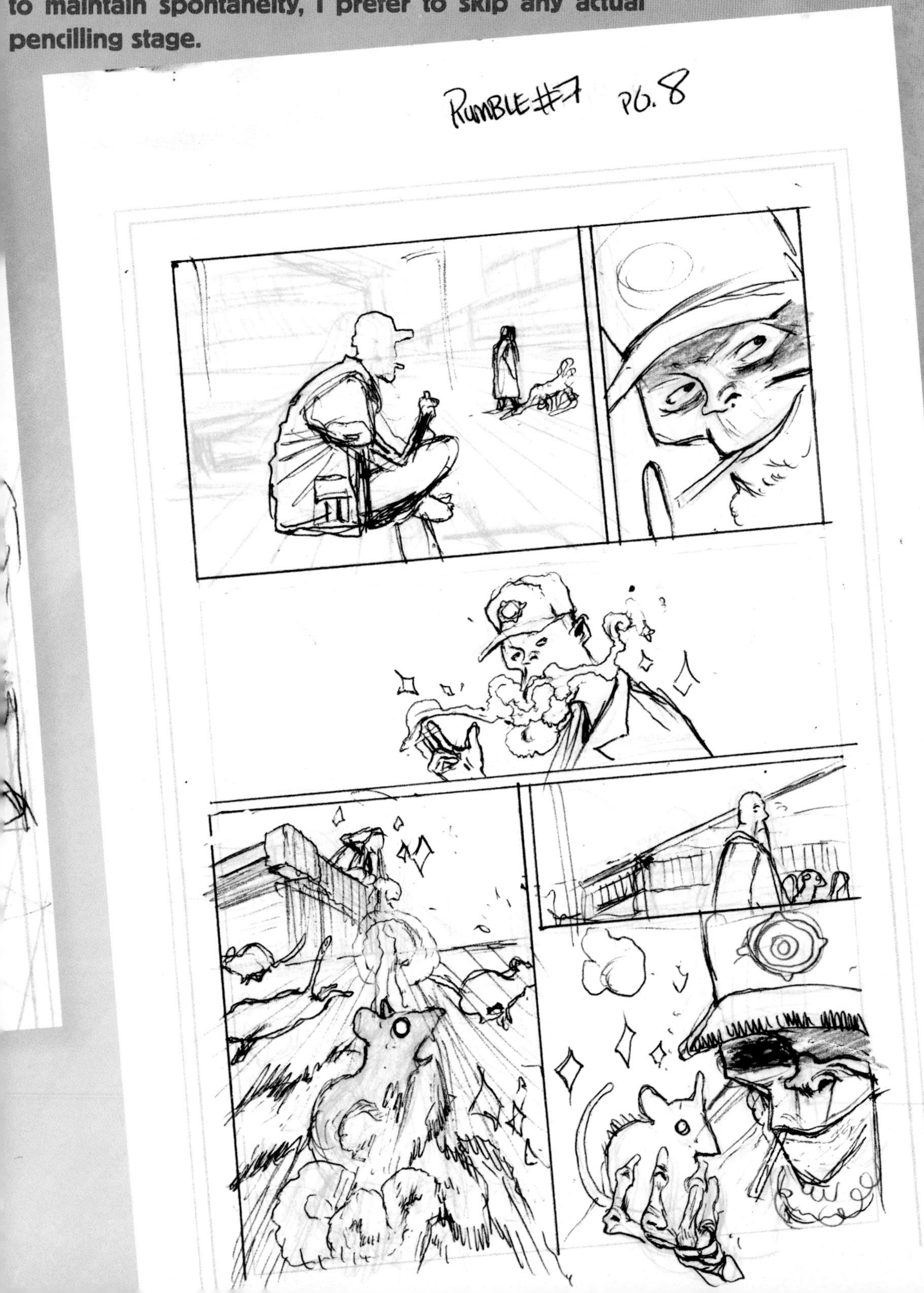
RUMBLE #7 PG. 8

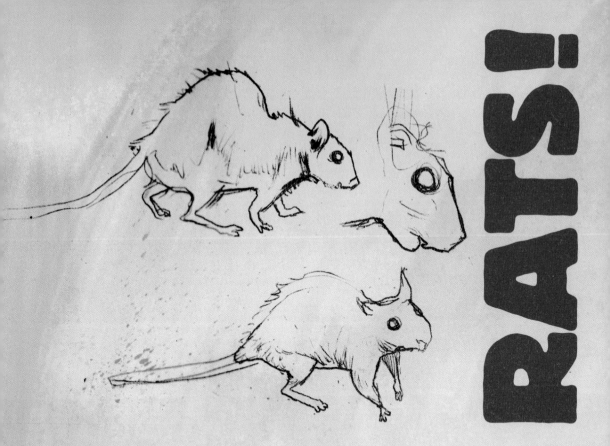

# RATS!

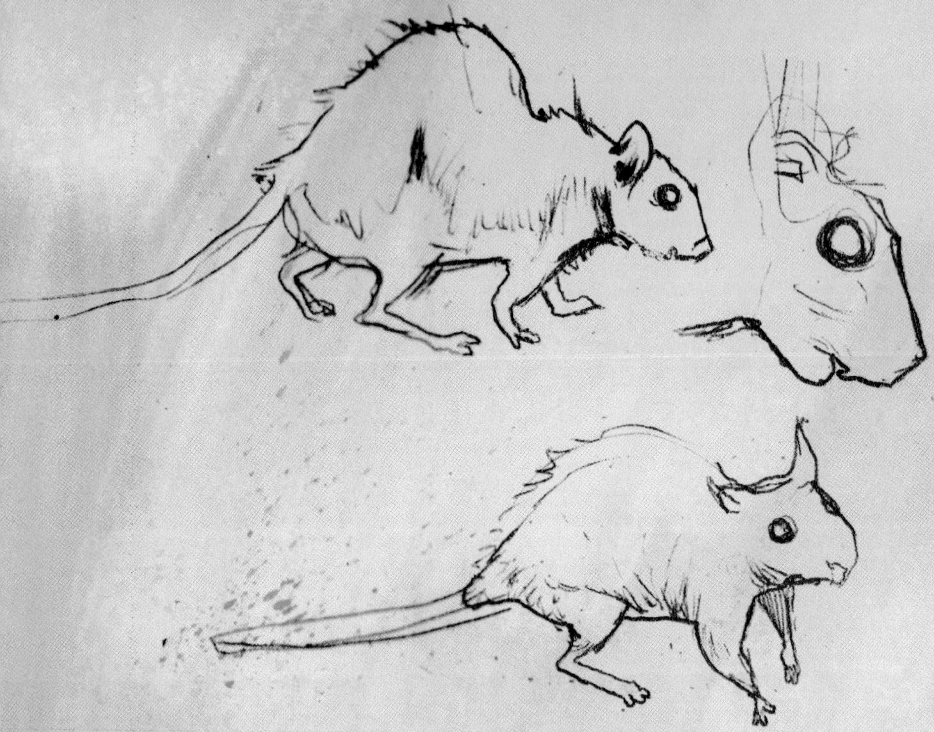

Those blurry things that scurry passed my feet in Brooklyn. While doing layouts for this issue it became apparent that I can't draw rats. At all. They were always just amorphous grey blurs on the subway tracks to me. I didn't realize how distinct their silhouette is compared to other rodents. So these were some (very quick) studies to try and nail a look down.

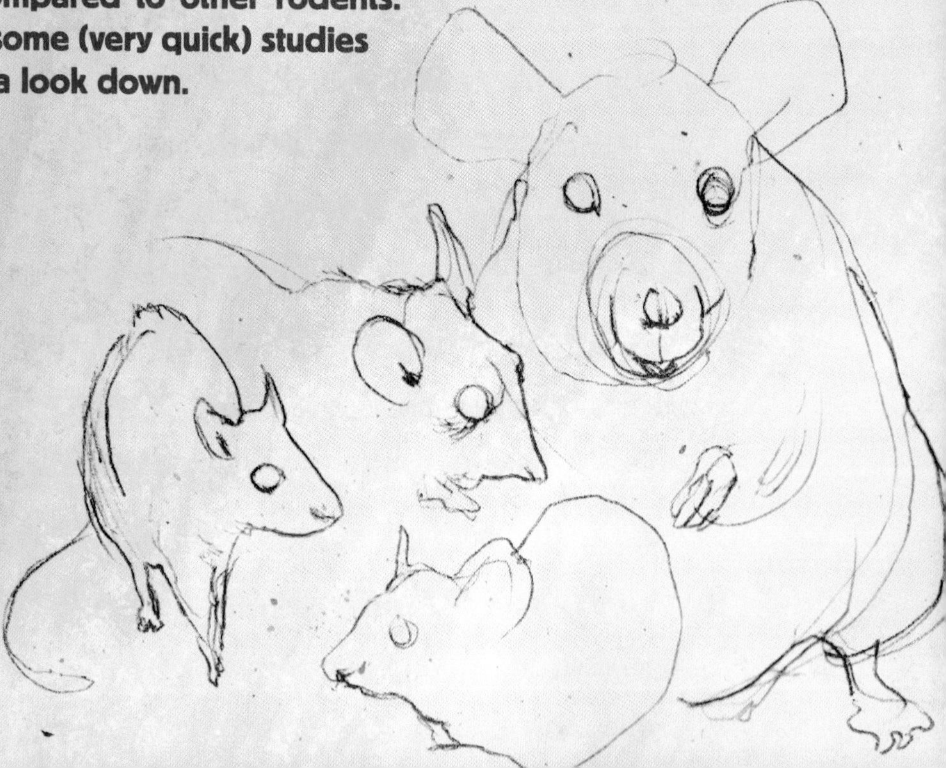

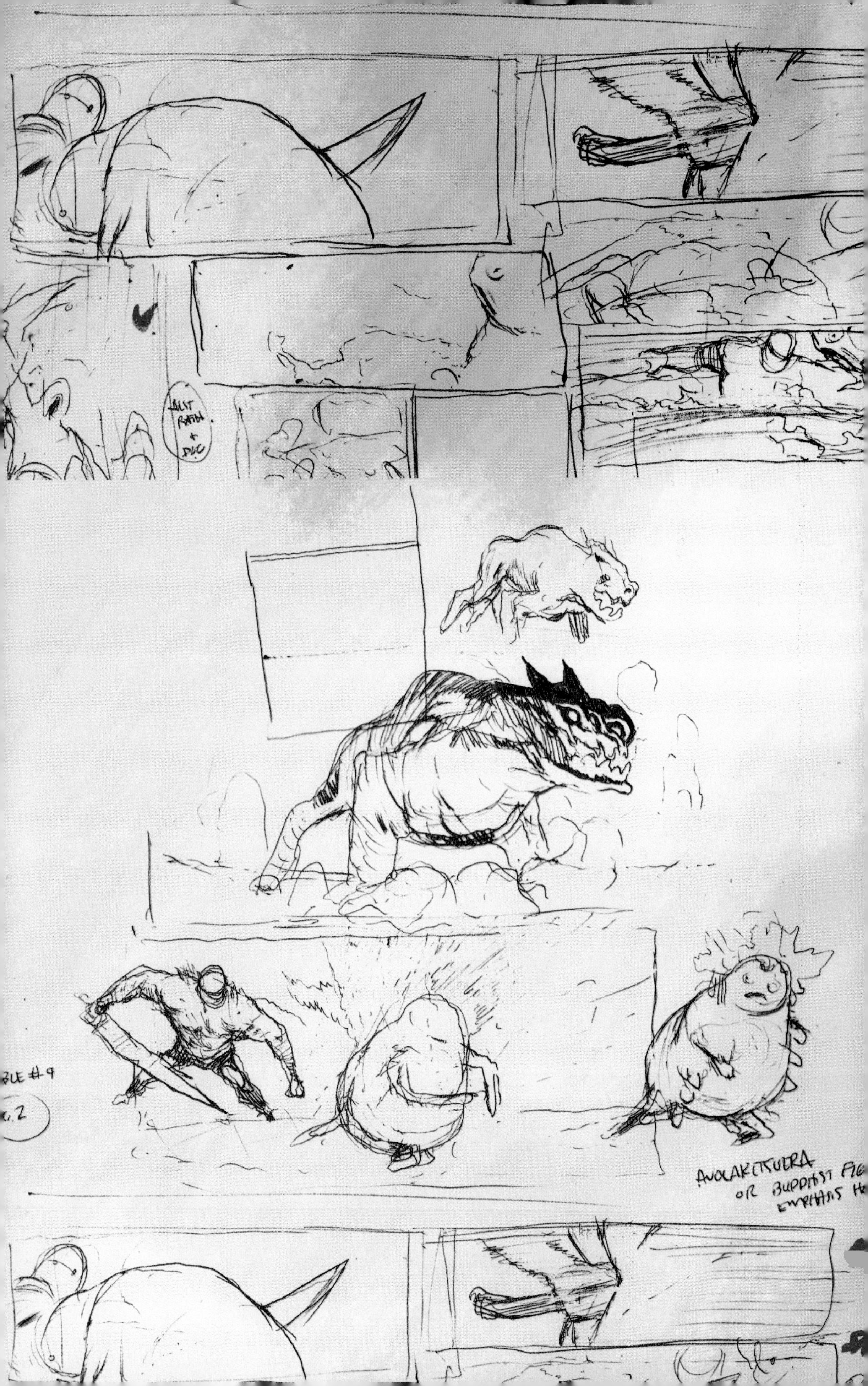
AVOLAKITSVERA
OR BUDDHIST FIG
EMPHASIS

# ISSUE EIGHT

**Just a couple page layouts for the special Halloween issue.**

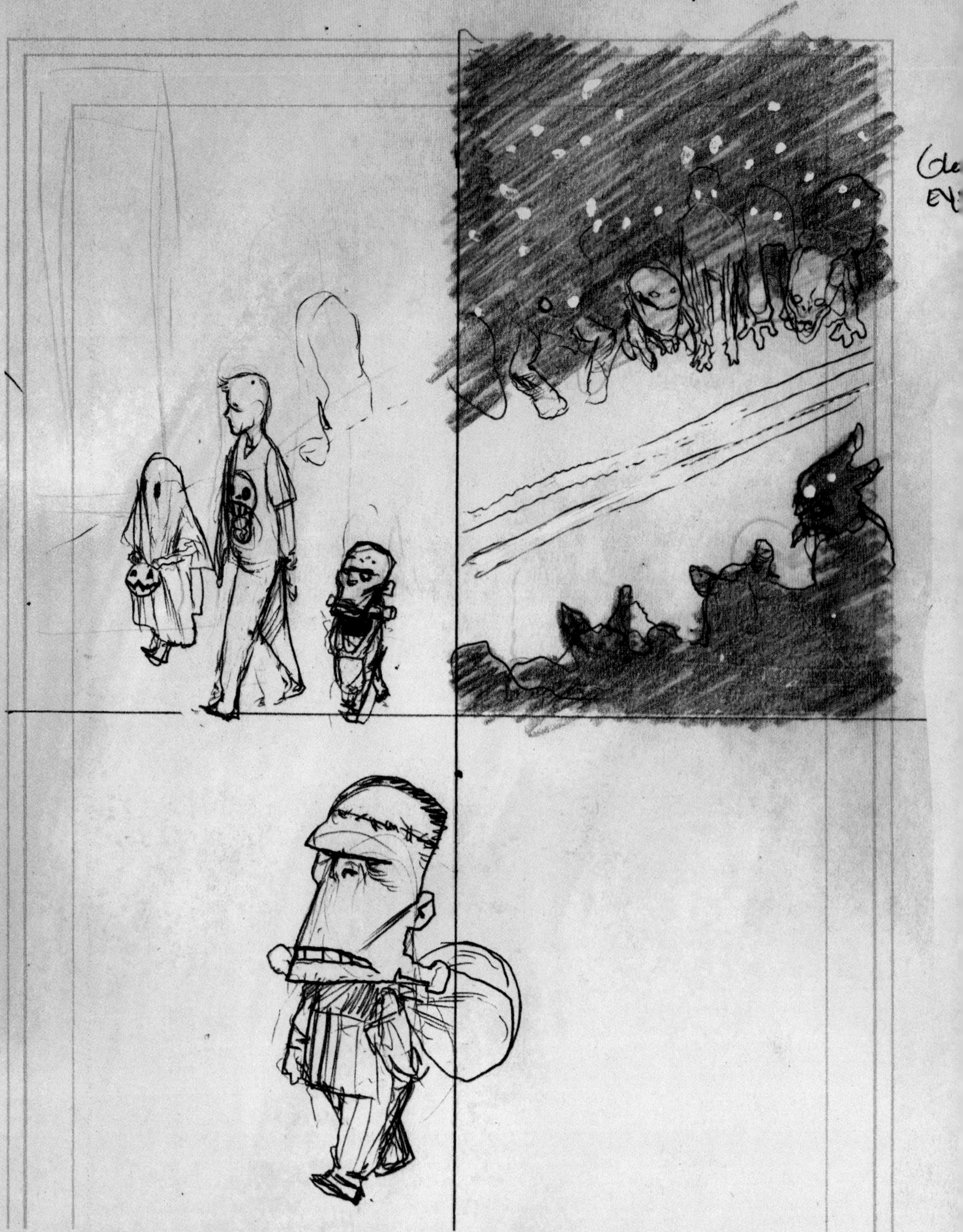

2

RUMBLE #8 CVR

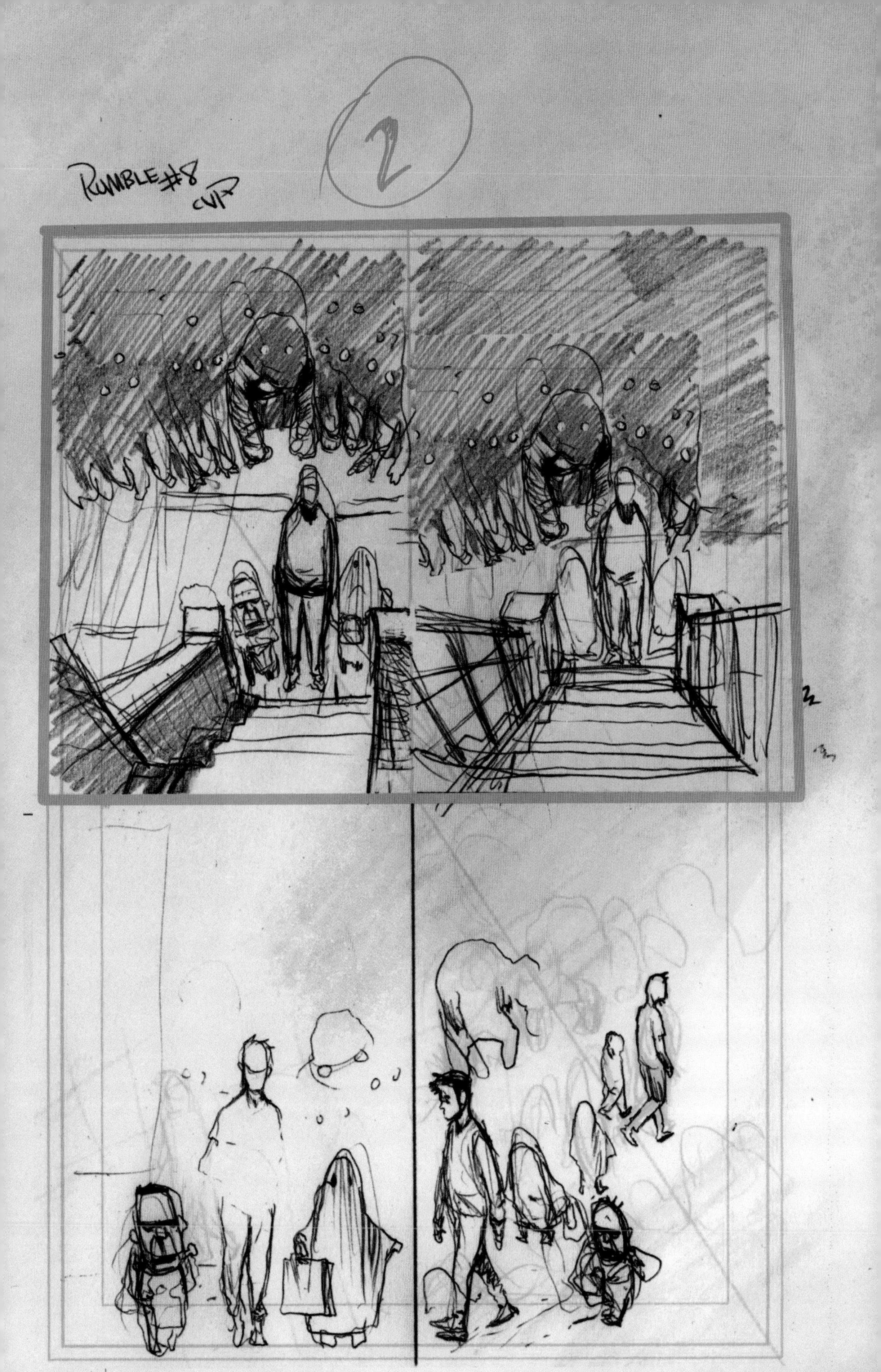

# EIGHT

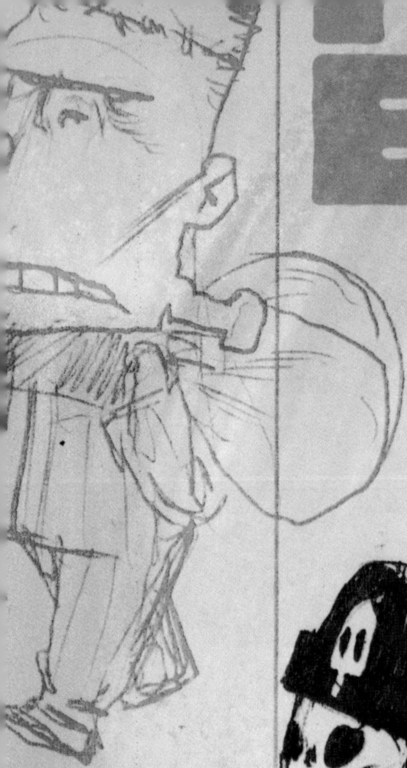

Some tiny trick-or-treaters for issue #8.
Loved drawing these guys!

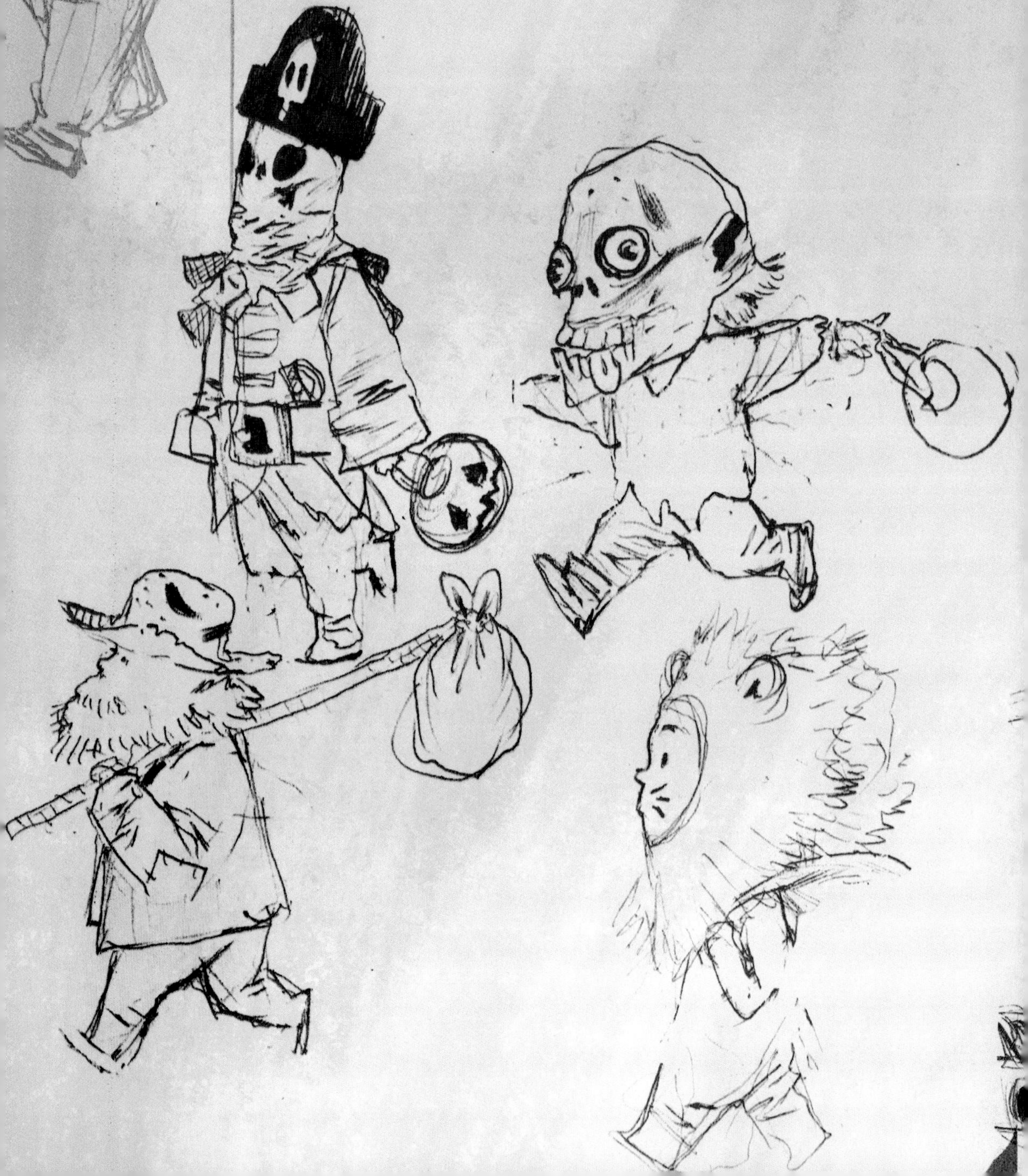

Here are a few diner studies.

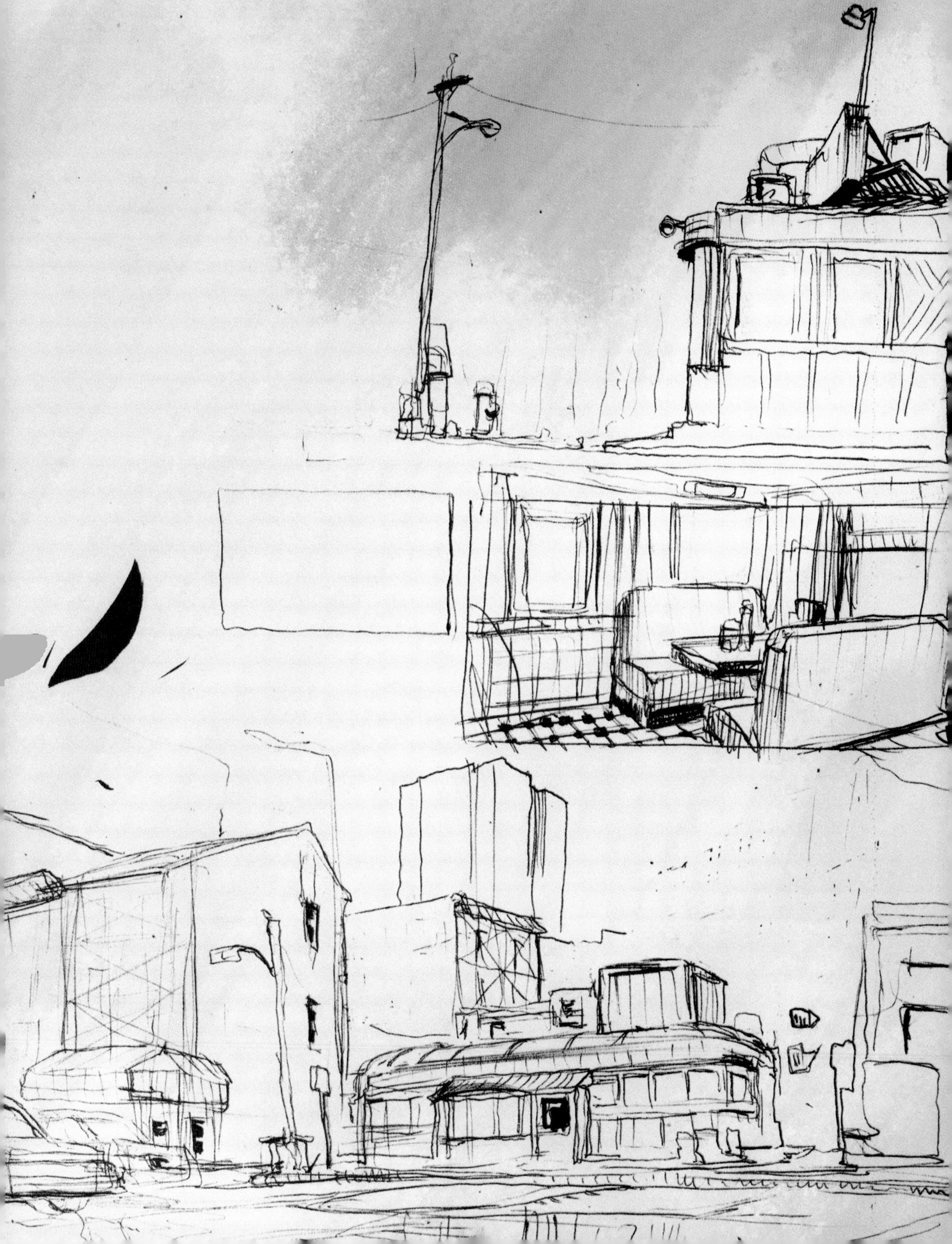

# WOLF WASPS

Some passes at the monsters from issue 8. In the script John described them as wolf wasps, but I didn't want to introduce any insectoid designs into our world because I knew I would just wind up biting old BPRD designs. So they wound up looking more wolf (and lion) than wasp.

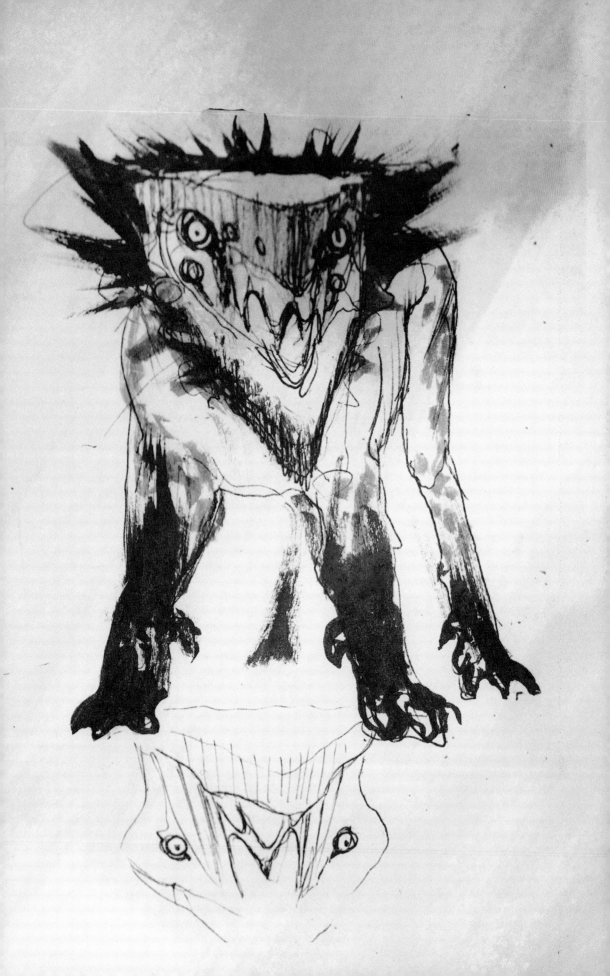

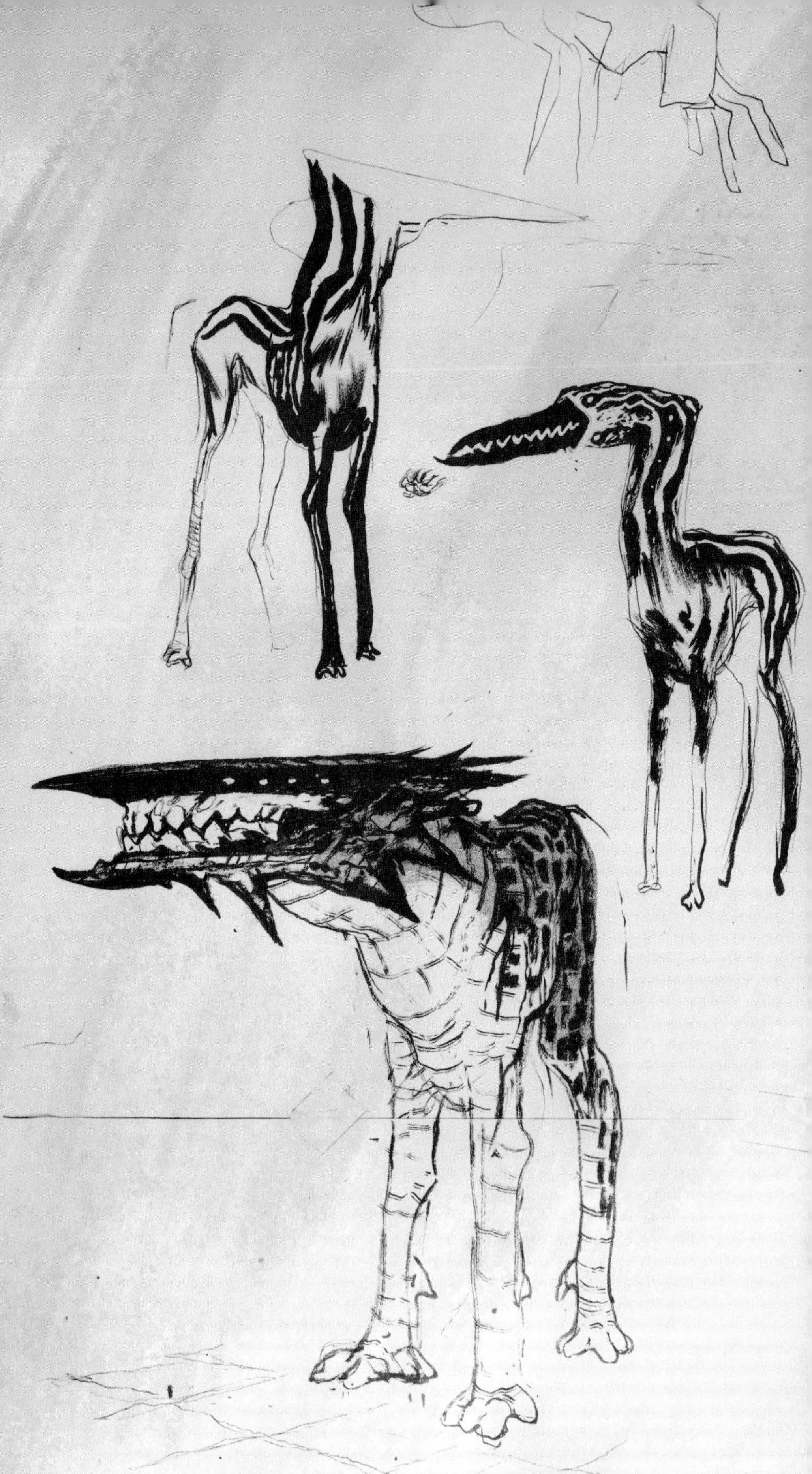

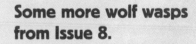

**Some more wolf wasps from Issue 8.**

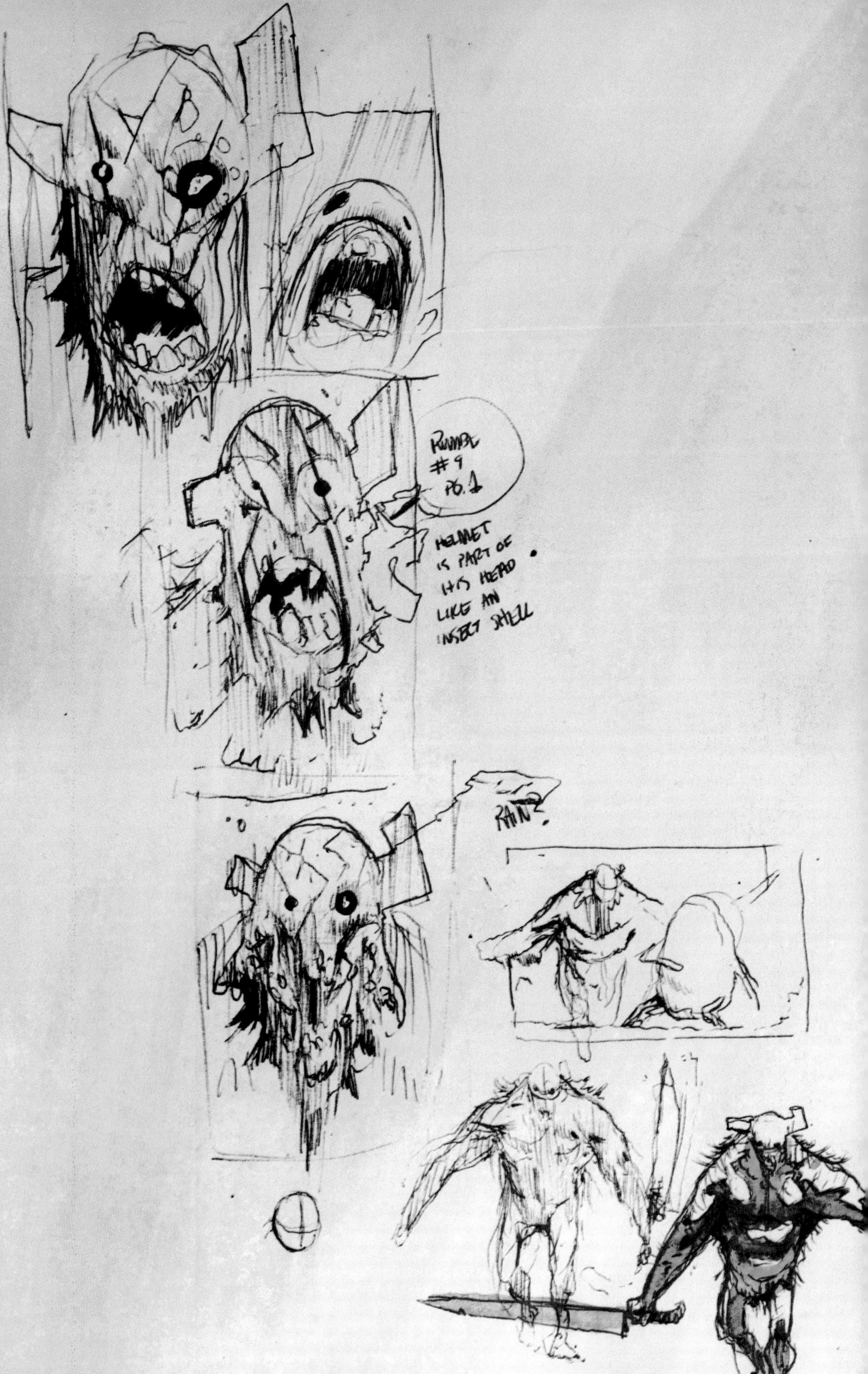
RUMBLE
#9
PG.1
HELMET IS PART OF HIS HEAD LIKE AN INSECT SHELL
RAIN?